A Woman Is No Man

Palestine, 1990. Seventeen-year-old Isra prefers reading books
to entertaining the suitors her father has chosen for her. Over
the course of a week, the naive and dreamy girl finds herself
quickly betrothed and married, and is soon living in Brooklyn.
There Isra struggles to adapt to the expectations of her oppressive mother-in-law, Fareeda, and strange new husband, Adam,
a pressure that intensifies as she begins to have children—four
daughters instead of the sons Fareeda tells Isra she must bear.

Brooklyn, 2008. Eighteen-year-old Deya, Isra's oldest daughter, must meet with potential husbands at her grandmother Fareeda's insistence, though her only desire is to go to college. Deya
can't help but wonder if her options would have been different
had her parents survived the car crash that killed them when
Deya was only eight. But her grandmother is firm on the matter:
the only way to secure a worthy future for Deya is through marriage to the right man.

But fate has a will of its own, and soon Deya will find herself
on an unexpected path that leads her to shocking truths about
her family—knowledge that will force her to question everything she thought she knew about her parents, the past, and her
own future.

HARPER PERENNIAL OLIVE EDITIONS

This book is part of a special series from Harper Perennial called
Olive Editions—exclusive small-format editions of some of our
bestselling and celebrated titles, featuring beautiful and unique
hand-drawn cover illustrations. All Olive Editions are available
for a limited time only.

A
Woman
Is No
Man

A
Woman
Is No
Man

A Novel

Etaf Rum

A hardcover edition of this book was published in 2019 by HarperCollins Publishers.

HarperCollins books may be purchased for educational, business, or sales promotional use. For information, please email the Special Markets Department at SPsales@harpercollins.com.

FIRST HARPER PERENNIAL OLIVE EDITION PUBLISHED 2021.

Library of Congress Cataloging-in-Publication Data has been applied for.

ISBN 978-0-06-313902-2 (Olive Edition)

21 22 23 24 25   LSC   10 9 8 7 6 5 4 3 2 1

To Reyann and Isah,
nur hayati

There is no greater agony than bearing an untold story inside you.

—*Maya Angelou*

I write for those women who do not speak, for those who do not have a voice because they were so terrified, because we are taught to respect fear more than ourselves. We've been taught that silence would save us, but it won't.

—*Audre Lorde*

I was born without a voice, one cold, overcast day in Brooklyn, New York. No one ever spoke of my condition. I did not know I was mute until years later, when I opened my mouth to ask for what I wanted and realized no one could hear me. Where I come from, voicelessness is the condition of my gender, as normal as the bosoms on a woman's chest, as necessary as the next generation growing inside her belly. But we will never tell you this, of course. Where I come from, we've learned to conceal our condition. We've been taught to silence ourselves, that our silence will save us. It is only now, many years later, that I know this to be false. Only now, as I write this story, do I feel my voice coming.

You've never heard this story before. No matter how many books you've read, how many tales you know, believe me: no one has ever told you a story like this one. Where I come from, we keep these stories to ourselves. To tell them to the outside world is unheard of, dangerous, the ultimate shame.

But you have seen us. Take a walk in New York City on a sunny afternoon. Walk down the length of Manhattan until the streets become curved and tangled as they are in the Old World. Go east, over the Brooklyn Bridge, Manhattan's skyline thinning behind you. There will be a heavy traffic jam on the other side. Hail a yellow cab and ride it down Flatbush Avenue, that central artery of south Brooklyn. You'll go south on Third Avenue, where the buildings are smaller—only three, four stories high, with old faces. The Verrazano-Narrows Bridge hovers on the horizon like a giant gull, wings spread, the sweeping view of the Manhattan skyline a distant mirage. Head south for a while, past the warehouses refurbished into chic cafés and trendy oyster bars, and the small family-owned hardware stores that have been there for generations. When the American cafés start to thin, replaced by signs in foreign tongues, you'll know you're getting close. Cross east two blocks to Fifth Avenue. There you will find Bay Ridge. Our three-square-mile neighborhood is the melting pot of Brooklyn. On our streets you'll find Latinos, Middle Easterners, Italians, Russians, Greeks, and Asians, all speaking their native tongues, keeping their traditions and cultures alive. Murals and graffiti cover the buildings. Colorful flags hang from windows and balconies. The sweet smell of churros, shish kebabs, and potpourri fills the air—a stew of humanity converging. Get out at the corner of Seventy-Second and Fifth Avenue, where you'll find yourself surrounded by bakeries, hookah bars, and halal meat markets. Walk down the tree-lined sidewalk of Seventy-Second Street until you reach an old row house no different from the others—faded red brick, a dusty brown door, number 545. This is where our family lives.

But our story does not begin in Bay Ridge, not really. To get there, first we must turn back the pages to before I found my voice, before I was even born. We are not yet in the house on Seventy-Second Street, not yet in Brooklyn, not yet in America. We have yet to board the plane that will carry us from the Middle East to this new world, have yet to soar over the Atlantic, have yet to even know that one day we will. The year is 1990, and we are in Palestine. This is the beginning.

Isra

For most of her seventeen years Isra Hadid cooked dinner with her mother daily, rolling grape leaves on warm afternoons, or stuffing spaghetti squash, or simmering pots of lentil soup when the air became crisp and the vineyards outside their home went empty. In the kitchen she and Mama would huddle against the stove as if sharing a secret, steam swirling around them, until the sunset cast a sliver of orange through the window. Looking out, the Hadids had a mountaintop view of the countryside—hillsides covered with red-tiled rooftops and olive trees, bright and thick and wild. Isra always cracked the window open because she loved the smell of figs and almonds in the morning, and at night, the rustling sounds of the cemeteries down the hill.

It was late, and the call for *maghrib* prayer would soon come, bringing an end to the cooking. Isra and Mama would withdraw to the bathroom, rolling up the sleeves of their house gowns, washing the dull red sauce off their fingertips. Isra had been praying since she was seven years old, kneeling beside Mama five times a day between sunrise and sunset. Lately she had begun to look forward to prayer, standing together with Mama, shoulders joined, feet slightly grazing, the only time Isra ever felt human touch. She heard the thick sound of the *adhan* calling them for prayer.

"*Maghrib* prayer will have to wait today," Mama said in Arabic, looking out the kitchen window. "Our guests are here."

There was a knock at the front door and Mama hurried to the sink, where she gave her hands a quick rinse and dried them with a clean rag. Leaving the kitchen, she wrapped a black *thobe* around her small frame and a matching hijab over her long, dark hair. Though Mama was only thirty-five years old, Isra thought she looked much older, the lines of labor dug deeply into her face.

She met Isra's eyes. "Don't forget to wash the garlic smell off your hands before greeting our guests."

Isra washed her hands, trying not to dirty the rose-colored kaftan that Mama had chosen for the occasion. "Do I look okay?"

"You look fine," Mama said, turning to leave. "Be sure to pin your hijab properly so your hair doesn't show. We don't want our guests to get the wrong impression."

Isra did as she was told. In the hall, she could hear her father, Yacob, recite his usual *salaam* as he led the guests to the *sala*. Soon he would hurry to the kitchen and ask for water, so she grabbed three glass cups from the cupboard and prepared them for him. Their guests would often complain about the steep hillside pathway to their home, especially on days like this when the air grew hot and it felt as though their house sat only a few inches from the sun. Isra lived on one of the steepest hills in Palestine, on a piece of land Yacob claimed to have purchased for the mountain view, which made him feel powerful, like a king. Isra would listen quietly to her father's remarks. She never dared tell Yacob how far from powerful they were. The truth was, Yacob's family had been evacuated from their seaside home in the Lydd when he was only ten years old, during Israel's invasion of Palestine. This was the real reason they lived on the outskirts of Birzeit, on a steep hill overlooking two graveyards—a Christian cemetery on the left and a Muslim one on the right. It was a piece of land no one else wanted, and all they could afford.

Still, Isra loved the hilltop view of Birzeit. Past the graveyards, she could see her all-girls school, a four-story cement building laced with grapevines, and across from it, separated by a field of almond trees, the blue-domed mosque where Yacob and her three brothers prayed while she and Mama prayed at home. Looking out the kitchen window, Isra always felt a mixture of longing and fear. What lay beyond the edges of her village? Yet as much as she wanted to go out there and venture into the world, there was also a comfort and safety in the known. And Mama's voice in her ear, reminding her: *A woman belongs at home.* Even if Isra left, she wouldn't know where to go.

"Brew a kettle of chai," Yacob said as he entered the kitchen and Isra handed him the glasses of water. "And add a few extra mint leaves."

Isra needed no telling: she knew the customs by heart. Ever since she could remember, she had watched her mother serve and entertain. Mama always set a box of Mackintosh's chocolates on the coffee table in the *sala* when they had guests, and she always served roasted watermelon seeds before bringing out the baklava. The drinks, too, had an order: mint chai first and Turkish coffee last. Mama said it was an insult to invert the order, and it was true. Isra had once overheard a woman tell of a time she'd been greeted with a cup of Turkish coffee at a neighbor's house. "I left immediately," the woman had said. "They might as well have kicked me out."

Isra reached for a set of red-and-gold porcelain cups, listening for Mama in the *sala*. She could hear Yacob chuckle over something now, and then the sound of other men laughing. Isra wondered what was so funny.

A few months before, the week she turned seventeen, Isra had returned from school to find Yacob sitting in the *sala* with a young man and his parents. Each time she thought of that day, the first time she'd been proposed to, what stood out most was Yacob, yelling at Mama after the guests left, furious that she hadn't served the chai in the antique set of teacups they saved for special occasions. "Now they will know we are poor!" Yacob had shouted, his open palm twitching. Mama had said nothing, quietly retreating to the kitchen. Their poverty was one of the reasons Yacob was so eager to marry off Isra. His sons were the ones who helped him plow the fields and earn a living, and who would one day carry on the family name. A daughter was only a temporary guest, quietly awaiting another man to scoop her away, along with all her financial burden.

Two men had proposed to Isra since—a bread baker from Ramallah and a cabdriver from Nablus—but Yacob had declined both. He couldn't stop talking about a family who was visiting from America in search of a bride, and now Isra understood why: he had been waiting for this suitor.

Isra was unsure how she felt about moving to America, a place she'd only seen in the news, or read about briefly in her school library. From them she'd gathered that Western culture was not as rigid as their own. This filled her with both excitement and dread. What would become of her life if she moved away to America? How could a conservative girl like her adapt to such a liberal place?

She had often stayed up all night thinking about the future, eager to know how her life would turn out when she left Yacob's house. Would a man ever love her? How many children would she have? What would she name them? Some nights she had dreamed she'd marry the love of her life and that they'd live together in a small hilltop house with wide windows and a red-tiled roof. Other nights she could see the faces of her children—two boys and two girls—looking up at her and her husband, a loving family like the kind she'd read about in books. But none of that hope came to her now. She had never imagined a life in America. She didn't even know where to begin. And this realization terrified her.

She wished she could open her mouth and tell her parents, *No! This isn't the life I want.* But Isra had learned from a very young age that obedience was the single path to love. So she only defied in secret, mostly with her books. Every evening after returning from school, after she'd soaked a pot of rice and hung her brothers' clothes and set the *sufra* and washed the dishes following dinner, Isra would retreat quietly to her room and read under the open window, the pale moonlight illuminating the pages. Reading was one of the many things Mama had forbidden, but Isra had never listened.

She remembered once telling Mama that she couldn't find any fruit on the mulberry trees when in fact she had spent the afternoon reading in the graveyard. Yacob had beaten her twice that night, punishment for her defiance. He'd called her a *sharmouta*, a whore. He'd said he'd show her what happened to disobedient girls, then he'd shoved her against the wall and whipped her with his belt. The room had gone white. Everything had looked flat. She'd closed her eyes until she'd gone numb, until she couldn't move. But as fear rose up in Isra, thinking of those moments, so did something else. A strange sort of courage.

Isra arranged the steaming cups on the serving tray and entered the *sala*. Mama said the trick to maintaining balance was to never look directly at the steam, so she looked at the ground instead. For a moment, Isra paused. From the corner of her eye, she could see the men and women sitting on opposite sides of the room. She peeked at Mama, who sat in her usual way: head bowed, eyes studying the red Turkish rug in front of her. Isra glanced at the pattern. Spirals and swirls, each curling up in the exact same way, picking up where the last one ended. She looked away. She had the urge to steal a glimpse of the young man, but could feel Yacob eyeing her, could almost hear him in her ear: *A proper girl never lays her gaze on a man!*

Isra kept her eyes toward the ground but allowed herself a glance across the floor. She noticed the younger man's socks, gray and pink plaid with white stitching across the top. They were unlike anything she had ever seen on the streets of Birzeit. She felt her skin prickle.

Clouds of steam rose from the serving tray, covering Isra's face, and quickly she circled around the room until she had served all the men. She walked over to serve the suitor's mother next. Isra noticed how the woman's navy-blue hijab was tossed around her head as if by accident, barely covering her henna-stained hair. Isra had never seen a Muslim woman wear her hijab this way in real life. Maybe on television, in the black-and-white Egyptian movies Isra and Mama watched together, or in Lebanese music videos, where women danced around in revealing clothing, or even in one of the illustrations of Isra's favorite book, *A Thousand and One Nights*, a collection of Middle Eastern folk tales set in medieval times. But never in Birzeit.

As Isra leaned in, she could see the suitor's mother studying her. She was a plump, stooping woman with a crooked smile and dark almond eyes that squinted at the corners. From her expression, Isra decided the woman must be displeased with her appearance. After all, Mama had often said that Isra was a plain

girl—her face as dull as wheat, her eyes as black as charcoal. Isra's most striking feature was her hair, long and dark like the
Nile. Only no one could see it now beneath her hijab. Not that it
would've made a difference, Isra thought. She was nothing special.

It was this last thought that stung Isra. As she stood before
the suitor's mother, she could feel her upper lip trembling. She
walked closer to the woman, clutching the serving tray in her
hands. She could feel Yacob glaring at her, could hear him clear
his throat, could see Mama dig her fingers into her thighs, but
Isra leaned toward the woman anyway, the porcelain cup trembling, and asked: "Would you like some Turkish coffee?"

But it hadn't worked. The Americans hadn't even seemed to
notice that she'd served the coffee first. In fact, the suitor had
proposed soon after, and Yacob had agreed at once, smiling
wider than Isra had ever seen.

"What were you thinking, serving them coffee first?" Mama
yelled when the guests had left and she and Isra returned to the
kitchen to finish cooking. "You're not young anymore—almost
eighteen! Do you want to sit in my house forever?"

"I was nervous," Isra muttered, hoping Yacob wouldn't punish her. "It was an accident."

"Sure it was." Mama unwrapped the *thobe* from around her
thin frame. "Like the time you put salt in Umm Ali's chai because she said you were as thin as a lamppost."

"That was an accident, too."

"You should be thankful their family isn't as traditional as
we are," Mama said, "or you might've blown your chance of going to America."

Isra looked at her mother with wet eyes. "What will happen
to me in America?"

Mama didn't look up. She stood hunched over the cutting

board dicing onions, garlic, and tomatoes, the main components of all their meals. As Isra inhaled the familiar scents, she wished Mama would hold her, whisper in her ear that everything would be okay, maybe even offer to sew her a few hijabs in case they didn't make them in America. But Mama was silent.

"Be thankful," Mama eventually said, tossing a handful of onions into a skillet. "God has presented you with a good opportunity. A good future in America. Better than this." She waved her hands over the rusted countertops, the old barrel they used to heat water for bathing, the peeling vinyl floors. "Is this how you want to spend your life? Living with no heat in the winters, sleeping on a paper-thin mattress, barely enough food?"

When Isra said nothing, staring at the sizzling skillet, Mama reached out and lifted her chin. "Do you know how many girls would kill to be in your shoes, to leave Palestine and move to America?"

Isra dropped her gaze. She knew Mama was right, but she couldn't picture a life in America. The trouble was, Isra didn't feel she belonged in Palestine either, where people lived carefully, following tradition so they wouldn't be shunned. Isra dreamed of bigger things—of not being forced to conform to conventions, of adventure, and most of all, of love. At night, after she had finished reading and tucked her book beneath her mattress, Isra would lay in bed and wonder what it would be like to fall in love, to be loved in return. She could imagine the man, even if she couldn't see his face. He would build her a library with all her favorite stories and poetry. They would read by the window every night—Rumi, Hafez, and Gibran. She would tell him about her dreams, and he would listen. She would brew mint chai for him in the mornings and simmer homemade soups in the evenings. They would take walks in the mountains, hand in hand, and she would feel, for the first time in her life, worthy of another person's love. *Look at Isra and her husband*, people would say. *A love you only see in fairy tales.*

Isra cleared her throat. "But Mama, what about love?"

Mama glared at her through the steam. "What about it?"

"I've always wanted to fall in love."

"Fall in love? What are you saying? Did I raise a *sharmouta*?"

"No . . . no . . ." Isra hesitated. "But what if the suitor and I don't love each other?"

"Love each other? What does love have to do with marriage? You think your father and I love each other?"

Isra's eyes shifted to the ground. "I thought you must, a little."

Mama sighed. "Soon you'll learn that there's no room for love in a woman's life. There's only one thing you'll need, and that's *sabr*, patience."

Isra tried to curb her disappointment. She chose her next words carefully. "Maybe life in America will be different for women."

Mama stared at her, flat and unblinking. "Different how?"

"I don't know," Isra said, softening her voice so as not to upset her mother. "But maybe American culture isn't as strict as ours. Maybe women are treated better."

"Better?" Mama mocked, shaking her head as she sautéed the vegetables. "You mean like in those fairy tales you read?"

She could feel her face redden. "No, not like that."

"Like what, then?"

Isra wanted to ask Mama if marriage in America was like her parents' marriage, where the man determined everything in the family and beat his wife if she displeased him. Isra had been five years old the first time she'd witnessed Yacob hit Mama. It was over an undercooked piece of lamb. Isra could still remember the pleading look in Mama's eyes, begging him to stop, Yacob's sullen face as he struck her. A darkness had rumbled through Isra then, a new awareness of the world unfolding. A world where not only children were beaten but mothers, too. Looking in Mama's eyes that night, watching her weep violently, Isra had felt an unforgettable rage.

She considered her words again. "Do you think maybe women have more respect in America?"

Mama fixed her with a glare. "Respect?"

"Or maybe worth? I don't know."

Mama set the stirring spoon down. "Listen to me, daughter. No matter how far away from Palestine you go, a woman will always be a woman. Here or there. Location will not change her *naseeb*, her destiny."

"But that's not fair."

"You are too young to understand this now," Mama said, "but you must always remember." She lifted Isra's chin. "There is nothing out there for a woman but her *bayt wa dar*, her house and home. Marriage, motherhood—*that* is a woman's only worth."

Isra nodded, but inside she refused to accept. She pressed her palms against her thighs and shook her tears away. Mama was wrong, she told herself. Just because she had failed to find happiness with Yacob, that didn't mean Isra would fail, too. She would love her husband in a way Mama hadn't loved Yacob— she would strive to understand him, to please him—and surely in this way she would earn his love.

Looking up, Isra realized that Mama's hands were trembling. A few tears fell down her cheeks.

"Are you crying, Mama?"

"No, no." She looked away. "These onions are strong."

It wasn't until the Islamic marriage ceremony, one week later, that Isra saw the suitor again. His name was Adam Ra'ad.

Adam's eyes met hers only briefly as the cleric read from the Holy Qur'an, then again as they each uttered the word *qubul*, "I accept," three times. The signing of the marriage contract was quick and simple, unlike the elaborate wedding party, which would be held after Isra received her immigrant visa. Isra overheard Yacob say it would only take a couple of weeks, since Adam was an American citizen.

From the kitchen window, Isra could see Adam outside, smoking a cigarette. She studied her new husband as he paced up and down the pathway in front of their house, a half smile set across his face, his eyes squinting. From a slight distance, he looked to be about thirty, maybe a little older, the lines on his face beginning to set. A finely trimmed black mustache covered his upper lip. Isra imagined what it would be like to kiss him and could feel her cheeks flush. Adam, she thought. Adam and *Isra*. It had a nice ring to it.

Adam wore a navy-blue shirt with buttons lined up the front and tan khakis, cuffed at his ankles. His shoes were shiny brown leather with tiny holes pricked in them and a solid black heel of good quality. His feet caressed the dirt with ease. She pictured a younger version of him, barefoot, kicking a soccer ball in the streets of Birzeit. It wasn't hard to imagine. His feet balanced on the uneven dirt path as if he had been raised on land like this. How old had he been when he left Palestine? A child? A teenager? A man?

"Why don't you and Adam go sit in the balcony?" Yacob told Isra when Adam came back inside. Adam met her eyes and smiled, revealing a row of stained teeth. She looked away. "Go on now," Yacob said. "You two need to get to know one another."

Isra flushed as she led the way to the balcony. Adam followed her, looking uneasily at the ground, both hands in his pockets. She wondered if he was nervous but dismissed the thought. He was a man. What could he possibly be nervous of?

Outside, it was a beautiful March morning. Ideal weather for fruit picking. Isra had recently pruned the fig tree that leaned against the house in preparation for the summer bloom. Beside it grew two slanted almond trees, beginning to flower. Isra watched Adam's eyes widen as he admired the scenery. Grapevines covered the balcony, and he traced his fingers across a cluster of buds that would swell into grapes by summer. From the look on his face, she wondered if he had ever seen a grapevine before. Perhaps not since he was a child. She wanted to ask him so many things. Why had they left Palestine, and when? How had they made it to America? She opened her mouth and searched for the words, but none came.

There was a wrought-iron swing at the center of the balcony. Adam sat on it and waited for her to join him. She took a deep breath as she settled beside him. They could see the graveyards from their seat, both dilapidated, and Isra blushed at the sight. She hoped Adam wouldn't think less of her. She tried to take strength in what Yacob always said, "It doesn't matter where you live as long as your home is yours. Free of occupation and blood."

It was a quiet morning. For a while they just sat there, lost in the view. Isra felt a shiver down her spine. She couldn't help but think of the jinn who lived in cemeteries and ruins. Growing up, Isra had heard countless stories of the supernatural creatures, who were said to possess humans. Many of the neighborhood women swore they had witnessed an evil presence near the two cemeteries. Isra muttered a quick prayer under her breath. She wondered if it was a bad omen, facing a graveyard as she sat with her husband for the first time.

Beside her Adam stared absently into the distance. What was he thinking? Why wouldn't he say something? Was he waiting for her to speak first? Surely he should speak first! She thought about the interactions between men and women she'd read about in books. Small introductions first, personal tales next, then affection grew. That was how two people fell in love. Or at least how Sinbad the Sailor fell in love with Princess Shera in *A Thousand and One Nights*. Except Shera was a bird for most of the story. Isra decided to be more realistic.

Adam turned to look at her. She swallowed, tugging on the edges of her hijab. His eyes lingered on the loose strands of black hair poking out from underneath. It occurred to her that he had not yet seen her hair. She waited for him to say something, but he only stared. His gaze moved up and down, his lips slowly parted. There was something in his eyes that troubled her. An intensity. What was it? In the glassy tint of his gaze, she could see the days of the rest of her life stacked together like pages. If only she could flip through them, so she knew what was to come.

Isra broke his gaze and returned her eyes to the graveyards. Perhaps he was only nervous, she told herself. Or perhaps he didn't like her. It was reasonable. After all, she had never been called beautiful. Her eyes were small and dark, her jaw angular. More than once, Mama had mocked her sharp features, saying her nose was long and pointed, her forehead too large. She was certain Adam was looking at her forehead now. She pulled on her hijab. Perhaps she should bring out the box of Mackintosh's chocolates Mama saved for special occasions. Or maybe she should brew some chai. She started to offer him some grapes but remembered they were not yet ripe.

As she turned to face Adam once more, she noticed his knees shaking. Then, in a flash, he zoomed closer and planted a kiss on her cheek.

Isra slapped him.

Shocked, she waited for him to apologize, to muster up something about how he hadn't meant to kiss her, how his body acted of its own accord. But he only looked away, face flushed, and buried his eyes between the graves.

With great effort, she forced herself to look at the cemeteries. She thought perhaps there was something between the graves she could not see, some secret to make sense of what was happening. She thought about *A Thousand and One Nights*, how Princess Shera had wanted to become human so she could marry Sindbad. Isra didn't understand. Why would anyone want to be a woman when she could be a bird?

"He tried to kiss me," Isra told Mama after Adam and his family left, whispering so Yacob wouldn't hear.

"What do you mean, he tried to kiss you?"

"He tried to kiss me, and I slapped him! I'm sorry, Mama. Everything happened so fast, and I didn't know what else to do." Isra's hands were shaking, and she placed them between her thighs.

"Good," Mama said after a long pause. "Make sure you don't let him touch you until *after* the wedding ceremony. We don't want this American family to go around saying we raised a *sharmouta*. That's what men do, you know. Always put the blame on the woman." Mama stuck out the tip of her pinkie. "Don't even give him a finger."

"No. Of course not!"

"Reputation is everything. Make sure he doesn't touch you again."

"Don't worry, Mama. I won't."

The next day, Adam and Isra took a bus to Jerusalem, to a place called the US Consulate General, where people applied for immigrant visas. Isra was nervous about being alone with Adam again, but there was nothing she could do. Yacob couldn't join them because his Palestinian *hawiya*, issued by the Israeli military authorities, prevented him from traveling to Jerusalem with ease. Isra had a *hawiya* too, but now that she was married to an American citizen, she would have less difficulty crossing the checkpoints.

The checkpoints were the reason Isra had never been to Jerusalem, which, along with most Palestinian cities, was under Israeli control and couldn't be entered without a permit. The permits were required at each of the hundreds of checkpoints and roadblocks Israel had constructed on Palestinian land, restricting travel between, and sometimes within, their own cities and towns. Some checkpoints were manned by heavily armed Israeli soldiers and guarded with tanks; others were made up of gates, which were locked when soldiers were not on duty. Adam cursed every time they stopped at one of these roadblocks, irritated at the tight controls and heavy traffic. At each one he waved his American passport at the Israeli soldiers, speaking to them in English. Isra could understand a little from having studied English in school, and she was impressed at how well he spoke the language.

When they finally arrived at the consulate, they waited in line for hours. Isra stood behind Adam, head bowed, only speaking when spoken to. But Adam barely said a word, and Isra wondered if he was angry at her for slapping him on the balcony. She contemplated apologizing, but secretly she thought she had nothing to apologize for. Even though they had signed the Islamic marriage contract, he had no right to kiss her like that, not until the night of the wedding ceremony. Yet the word *sorry* brewed on her tongue. She forced herself to swallow it down.

At the main window, they were told it would take only ten

days for Isra to receive her visa. Now Yacob could plan the wedding, she thought as they strolled around Jerusalem afterward.
Walking the narrow roads of the old city, Isra was overwhelmed
by sensations. She smelled chamomile, sage, mint, and lentils
from the open burlap sacks lined up in front of a spice shop, and
the sweet aroma of freshly baked *knafa* from a nearby *dukan*.
She spotted wire cages holding chickens and rabbits in front of a
butcher shop, and several boutiques displaying myriads of gold-
plated jewelry. Old men in *hattas* sold colorful scarves on street
corners. Women in full black attire hurried through the streets.
Some wore embroidered hijabs, tight-fitted pants, and round
sunglasses. Others wore no hijab at all, and Isra knew they were
Israeli. Their heels click-clacked on the uneven sidewalk. Boys
whistled. Cars weaved through the narrow roads, honking, leaving a trail of diesel fumes behind. Israeli soldiers monitored the
streets, long rifles slung across their slender bodies. The air was
filled with dirt and noise.

For lunch, Adam ordered falafel sandwiches from a food cart
near Al-Aqsa Mosque. Isra stared at the gold-topped dome in awe
as they ate.

"Isn't it beautiful?" Adam said between mouthfuls.

"It is," Isra said. "I've never seen it before."

Adam turned to face her. "Really?"

She nodded.

"Why not?"

"It's hard getting here."

"I've been gone for so long, I'd forgotten what it was like. We
must've been stopped by half a dozen roadblocks. It's absurd!"

"When did you leave Palestine?"

Adam chewed on his food. "We moved to New York in 1976,
when I was sixteen. My parents have visited a couple of times
since, but I've had to stay behind and take care of my father's deli."

"Have you ever been inside the mosque?"

"Of course. Many, many times. I wanted to be an imam growing up, you know. A priest. I spent Ramadan sleeping here one summer. I memorized the entire Qur'an."

"Really?"

"Yeah."

"So is that what you do in America? You're a priest?"

"Oh, no."

"Then what do you do?"

"I own a deli."

"But why aren't you an imam?" Isra asked, emboldened by their first conversation.

"I couldn't do that in America."

"What do you mean?"

"My father needed me to help him run the family business. I had to give that up."

"Oh." Isra paused. "I didn't expect that."

"Why not?"

"I just always thought . . ." She stopped, thinking better of it. "What?"

"I just assumed you'd be free." He gave her a curious expression. "You know, because you're a man."

Adam said nothing, continuing to stare. Finally he said, "I am free," and looked away.

Isra studied Adam for a long time as they finished their sandwiches. She couldn't help but think of the way his face had stiffened at the mention of his childhood dream. His tight smile. She pictured him in the mosque during Ramadan, leading the *maghrib* prayer, reciting the Qur'an in a strong, musical voice. It softened her to picture him working behind a cash register, counting money, and stocking shelves when he wanted to be leading prayer in a mosque. And Isra thought for the first time, sitting there beside him, that perhaps it would not be so hard to love him after all.

Isra spent her last night in Birzeit propped in a gold metal chair, lips painted the color of mulberries, skin draped in layers of white mesh, hair wound up and sprayed with glitter. Around her, the walls spun. She watched them grow bigger and bigger until she was almost invisible, then get smaller and smaller as if they were crushing her. Women in an assortment of colors danced around her. Children huddled in corners eating baklava and drinking Pepsi. Loud music struck the air like fireworks. Everyone was cheering, clapping to the beat of her quivering heart. She nodded and smiled to their congratulations, yet inside she wasn't sure how long she could stave off tears. She wondered if the guests understood what was happening, if they realized she was only a few hours away from boarding a plane with a man she barely knew and landing in a country whose culture was not her own.

Adam sat beside her, his black suit crisp against his white button-down shirt. He was the only man in the wedding hall. The others had a room of their own, away from the sight of the dancing women. Even Adam's younger brothers, Omar and Ali, whom Isra had only met minutes before the wedding, were forbidden. She couldn't tell how old they were, but they must've been in their twenties. Every now and then, one would poke his head in to watch the women on the dance floor, and a woman would remind him to stay in the men's section. Isra scanned the room for her own brothers. They were all too young to sit in the men's section, and she spotted them running around the far corner of the hall. She wondered if she would ever see them again.

If happiness were measured in sound, Adam's mother was

the happiest person in the room. Fareeda was a large, broad woman, and Isra felt the dance floor shrink in her presence. She wore a red-and-black *thobe*, with oriental patterns embroidered on the sleeves, and a wide belt of gold coins around her thick waist. Black kohl was smeared around her small eyes. She sang along to every song in a confident voice, twirling a long white stick in the air. Every minute or so, she brought her hand to her mouth and let out a *zughreta*, a loud, piercing sound. Her only daughter, Sarah, who looked about eleven or so, threw rose petals at the stage. She was a younger, slimmer version of her mother: dark almond eyes, black curls flowing wildly, skin as golden as wheat. Isra could almost see a grown version of Sarah sitting as she sat now, her tiny frame buried beneath a white bridal dress. She winced at the thought.

She looked around for her mother. Mama sat in the corner of the wedding hall, fidgeting with her fingers. So far she had not left her seat throughout the entire wedding, and Isra wondered if she wanted to dance. Perhaps she was too sad to dance, Isra thought. Or perhaps she was afraid to send the wrong message. Growing up, Isra had often heard women criticize the mother of the bride for celebrating too boisterously at the wedding, too excited to be rid of her daughter. She wondered if Mama was secretly excited to be rid of her.

Adam pounded on a *darbuka* drum. Startled, Isra looked away from Mama. She could see Fareeda handing Adam the white stick and pulling him down to the dance floor. He danced with the stick in one hand and the *darbuka* in the other. The music was deafening. Women around them clapped, glancing at Isra enviously as if she had won something that was rightfully theirs. She could almost hear them thinking, *How did a plain girl like her get so lucky? It should be my daughter going to America.*

Then Adam and Isra were dancing together. She didn't quite

know what to do. Even though Mama had always nagged her about dancing at events, saying it was good for her image, that mothers would be more likely to notice her if she was onstage, Isra had never listened. It felt unnatural to dance so freely, to display herself so openly. But Adam seemed perfectly comfortable. He was jumping on one foot, one hand behind his back, the other waving the stick in the air. With the Palestinian flag wrapped around his neck and a red velvet *tarboosh* on his head, Isra thought he looked like a sultan.

"Use your hands," he mouthed.

She lifted both arms above her waist, dangling her wrists. She could see Fareeda nodding in approval. A group of women encircled them, moving their hands to the rhythm of the *darbuka*. They wore patterned red *thobes* with gold coins attached at their hips. Some held up round, flaming candles. Others placed a lit candlestick over each finger, waving their shimmering hands in the air. One woman even wore a tiered crown made of candles, so that it looked as though her head were on fire. The dance floor glistened like a chandelier.

The music stopped. Adam grabbed Isra by the elbow and led her off the dance floor. Fareeda followed, carrying a white basket. Isra hoped she could return to her seat, but Adam stopped in the center of the stage. "Face the crowd," he told her.

Fareeda opened the basket to display a wealth of gold jewelry within. There were oohs and aahs from the crowd. She handed Adam one piece of gold at a time, and he secured each item on Isra's skin. Isra stared at his hands. His fingers were long and thick, and she tried to keep from flinching. Soon heavy necklaces hung from her neck, their thick coins cold against her skin. Bracelets laced her wrists like ropes, their ends shaped like snakes. Coin-shaped earrings pricked her ears; rings covered her fingers. After twenty-seven pieces of gold, Fareeda threw the empty basket in the air and let out another *zughreta*. The crowd cheered, and Isra stood before them, wrapped in gold, unable to move, a mannequin on display.

She had no idea what life had in store for her and could do nothing to alter this fact. She shivered in horror at the realization. But these feelings were only temporary, Isra reminded herself. Surely she would have more control over her life in the future. Soon she would be in America, the land of the free, where perhaps she could have the love she had always dreamed of, could lead a better life than her mother's. Isra smiled at the possibility. Perhaps someday, if Allah were to ever grant her daughters, they would lead a better life than hers, too.

Part 1

Deya

BROOKLYN
Winter 2008

Deya Ra'ad stood by her bedroom window and pressed her fingers against the glass. It was December, and a dust of snow covered the row of old brick houses and faded lawns, the bare plane trees lining the sidewalk, the cars parallel-parked down Seventy-Second Street. Inside her room, alongside the spines of her books, a crimson kaftan provided the only other color. Her grandmother, Fareeda, had sewn this dress, with heavy gold embroidery around the chest and sleeves, specifically for today's occasion: there was a marriage suitor in the *sala* waiting to see Deya. He was the fourth man to propose to her this year. The first had barely spoken English. The second had been divorced. The third had needed a green card. Deya was eighteen, not yet finished with high school, but her grandparents said there was no point prolonging her duty: marriage, children, family.

She walked past the kaftan, slipping on a gray sweater and blue jeans instead. Her three younger sisters wished her luck, and she smiled reassuringly as she left the room and headed upstairs. The first time she'd been proposed to, Deya had begged to keep her sisters with her. "It's not right for a man to see four sisters at once," Fareeda had replied. "And it's the eldest who must marry first."

"But what if I don't want to get married?" Deya had asked. "Why does my entire life have to revolve around a man?"

Fareeda had barely looked up from her coffee cup. "Because that's how you'll become a mother and have children of your own. Complain all you want, but what will you do with your life without marriage? Without a family?"

"This isn't Palestine, Teta. We live in America. There are other options for women here."

"Nonsense." Fareeda had squinted at the Turkish coffee grounds staining the bottom of her cup. "It doesn't matter where we live. Preserving our culture is what's most important. All you need to worry about is finding a good man to provide for you."

"But there are other ways here, Teta. Besides, I wouldn't need a man to provide for me if you let me go to college. I could take care of myself."

At this, Fareeda had lifted her head sharply to glare at her. "*Majnoona*? Are you crazy? No, no, no." She shook her head with distaste.

"But I know plenty of girls who get an education first. Why can't I?"

"College is out of the question. Besides, no one wants to marry a college girl."

"And why not? Because men only want a fool to boss around?"

Fareeda sighed deeply. "Because that's how things are. How they've always been done. You ask anyone, and they'll tell you. Marriage is what's most important for women."

Every time Deya replayed this conversation in her head, she

imagined her life was just another story, with plot and rising tension and conflict, all building to a happy resolution, one she just couldn't yet see. She did this often. It was much more bearable to pretend her life was fiction than to accept her reality for what it was: limited. In fiction, the possibilities of her life were endless. In fiction, she was in control.

For a long time Deya stared hesitantly into the darkness of the staircase, before climbing, very slowly, up to the first floor, where her grandparents lived. In the kitchen, she brewed an *ibrik* of chai. She poured the mint tea into five glass cups and arranged them on a silver serving tray. As she walked down the hall, she could hear Fareeda in the *sala* saying, in Arabic, "She cooks and cleans better than I do!" There was a rush of approving sounds in the air. Her grandmother had said the same thing to the other suitors, only it hadn't worked. They'd all withdrawn their marriage proposals after meeting Deya. Each time Fareeda had realized that no marriage would follow, that there was no *naseeb*, no destiny, she had smacked her own face with open palms and wept violently, the sort of dramatic performance she often used to pressure Deya and her sisters to obey her.

Deya carried the serving tray down the hall, avoiding her reflection in the mirrors that lined it. Pale-faced with charcoal eyes and fig-colored lips, a long swoop of dark hair against her shoulders. These days it seemed as though the more she looked at her face, the less of herself she saw reflected back. It hadn't always been this way. When Fareeda had first spoken to her of marriage as a child, Deya had believed it was an ordinary matter. Just another part of growing up and becoming a woman. She had not yet understood what it meant to become a woman. She hadn't realized it meant marrying a man she barely knew, nor that marriage was the beginning and end of her life's purpose. It was only as she grew older that Deya had truly understood her place in her community. She had learned that there was a certain way she had to live, certain rules she had to follow, and that, as a woman, she would never have a legitimate claim over her own life.

She put on a smile and entered the *sala*. The room was dim, every window covered with thick, red curtains, which Fareeda had woven to match the burgundy sofa set. Her grandparents sat on one sofa, the guests on the other, and Deya set a bowl of sugar on the coffee table between them. Her eyes fell to the ground, to the red Turkish rug her grandparents had owned since they emigrated to America. There was a pattern embossed across the edges: gold coils with no beginnings or ends, all woven together in ceaseless loops. Deya wasn't sure if the pattern had gotten bigger or if she had gotten smaller. She followed it with her eyes, and her head spun.

The suitor looked up when she neared him, peering at her through the peppermint steam. She served the chai without looking his way, all the while aware of his lingering gaze. His parents and her grandparents stared at her, too. Five sets of eyes digging into her. What did they see? The shadow of a person circling the room? Maybe not even that. Maybe they saw nothing at all, a serving tray floating on its own, drifting from one person to the next until the teakettle was empty.

She thought of her parents. How would they feel if they were here with her now? Would they smile at the thought of her in a white veil? Would they urge her, as her grandparents did, to follow their path? She closed her eyes and searched for them, but she found nothing.

Her grandfather turned to her sharply and cleared his throat. "Why don't you two go sit in the kitchen?" Khaled said. "That way you can get to know each other." Beside him, Fareeda eyed Deya anxiously, her face revealing its own message: *Smile. Act normal. Don't scare this man away, too.*

Deya recalled the last suitor who had withdrawn his marriage proposal. He had told her grandparents that she was too insolent, too questioning. That she wasn't Arab enough. But what had her grandparents expected when they came to this country? That their children and grandchildren would be fully Arab, too? That their culture would remain untouched? It wasn't her fault she wasn't Arab enough. She had lived her entire life straddled between two cultures. She was neither Arab nor American. She belonged nowhere. She didn't know who she was.

Deya sighed and met the suitor's eyes. "Follow me."

She observed him as they settled across from each other at the kitchen table. He was tall and slightly plump, with a closely shaved beard. His pecan hair was parted to one side and brushed back from his face. Better-looking than the other ones, Deya thought. He opened his mouth as if to speak but proceeded to say nothing. Then, after a few moments of silence, he cleared his throat and said, "I'm Nasser."

She tucked her fingers between her thighs, tried to act normal. "I'm Deya."

There was a pause. "I, um . . ." He hesitated. "I'm twenty-four. I work in a convenience store with my father while I finish school. I'm studying to be a doctor."

She gave a slow, reluctant smile. From the eager look on his face, she could tell he was waiting for her to do as he did, recite a vague representation of herself, sum up her essence in one line. When she didn't say anything, he spoke again. "So, what do you do?"

It was easy for her to recognize that he was just being nice. They both knew a teenage Arab girl didn't *do* anything. Well, except cook, clean, and catch up on the latest Turkish soap operas. Maybe her grandmother would have allowed her and her sisters to do more had they lived back home, in Palestine, surrounded by people like them. But here, in Brooklyn, all Fareeda could do was shelter them at home and pray they remained good. Pure. Arab.

"I don't do much," Deya said.

"You must do something. You don't have any hobbies?"

"I like to read."

"What do you read?"

"Anything. It doesn't matter what it is, I'll read it. Trust me, I have the time."

"And why is that?" he asked, knotting his brows.

"My grandmother doesn't let us do much. She doesn't even like it when I read."

"Why not?"

"She thinks books are a bad influence."

"Oh." He flushed, as though finally understanding. After a moment he asked, "My mother said you go to an all-girls Islamic school. What grade are you in?"

"I'm a senior."

Another pause. He shifted in his seat. Something about his nervousness eased her, and she let her shoulders relax.

"Do you want to go to college?" Nasser asked.

Deya studied his face. She had never been asked that particular question the way he asked it. Usually it sounded like a threat, as though if she answered yes, a weight would shift in the scale of nature. Like it was the worst possible thing for a girl to want.

"I do," she said. "I like school."

He smiled. "I'm jealous. I've never been a good student."

She fixed her eyes on him. "Do you mind?"

"Mind what?"

"That I want to go to college."

"No. Why would I mind?"

Deya studied him carefully, unsure whether to believe him.

He could be pretending not to mind in order to trick her into thinking he was different than the previous suitors, more progressive. He could be telling her exactly what he thought she wanted to hear.

She straightened in her seat, avoiding his question. Instead she asked, "Why aren't you a good student?"

"I've never really liked school," he said. "But my parents insisted I apply to med school after college. They want me to be a doctor."

"And do you want to be a doctor?"

Nasser laughed. "Hardly. I'd rather run the family business, maybe even open my own business one day."

"Did you tell them that?"

"I did. But they said I had to go to college, and if not for medicine, then engineering or law."

Deya looked at him. She had never known herself to feel anything besides anger and annoyance during these arrangements. One man had spent their entire conversation telling her how much money he earned at his gas station; another man had interrogated her about school, whether she intended to stay home and raise children, whether she would be willing to wear the hijab permanently and not only as part of her school uniform.

Still, Deya had questions of her own. *What would you do to me if we married? Would you let me pursue my dreams? Would you leave me at home to raise the children while you worked? Would you love me? Would you own me? Would you beat me?* She could have asked those questions aloud, but she knew people only told you what you wanted to hear. That to understand someone, you had to listen to the words they didn't say, had to watch them closely.

"Why are you looking at me like that?" Nasser asked.

"Nothing, it's just that . . ." She looked at her fingers. "I'm surprised your parents forced you to go to college. I'd assumed they'd let you make your own choices."

"What makes you say that?"

"You know." She met his eyes. "Because you're a man."

Nasser looked at her curiously. "Is that what you think? That I can do anything I want because I'm a man?"

"That's the world we live in."

He leaned forward, resting his hands on the table. It was the closest Deya had ever sat to a man, and she leaned back in her seat, pressing her hands between her thighs.

"You're strange," Nasser said.

She could feel her face flush, and she looked away. "Don't let my grandmother hear you say that."

"Why not? I meant it as a compliment."

"She won't see it that way."

There was a pause, and Nasser reached for his teacup. "So," he said after taking a sip. "How do you imagine your life in the future?"

"What do you mean?"

"What do you want, Deya Ra'ad?"

She couldn't help but laugh. As if it mattered what she wanted. As if it were up to her. If it were up to her, she'd postpone marriage for another decade. She'd enroll in a study-abroad program, pick up and move to Europe, perhaps Oxford, spending her days in cafés and libraries with a book in one hand and a pen in the other. She'd be a writer, helping people understand the world through stories. But it wasn't up to her. Her grandparents had forbidden her to attend college before marriage, and she didn't want to ruin her reputation in the community by defying them. Or worse, be disowned, banned from seeing her sisters, the only home and family she had ever known. She was already abandoned and alone in so many ways;

to lose her remaining roots would be too much to bear. She was afraid of the life her grandparents had planned for her, but even more afraid of the unknown. So she tucked her dreams away, did as she was told.

"I just want to be happy," she told Nasser. "That's all."

"Well, that's simple enough."

"Is it?" She met his eyes. "If so, then why haven't I seen it?"

"I'm sure you have. Your grandparents must be happy."

Deya tried to keep from rolling her eyes. "Teta spends her days complaining about her life, how her children abandoned her, and Seedo barely comes home. Trust me. They're miserable."

Nasser shook his head. "Maybe you're judging them too harshly."

"Why? Are your parents happy?"

"Of course they are."

"Do they love each other?"

"Of course they love each other! They've been married for over thirty years."

"That doesn't mean anything," Deya scoffed. "My grandparents have been married for over fifty years, and they can't stand the sight of each other."

Nasser said nothing. From the expression on his face, Deya knew he found her pessimism unpleasant. But what should she have said to him instead? Should she have lied? It was already enough she was forced to live a life she didn't want to live. Should she really begin a marriage with lies? When would it end?

Eventually Nasser cleared his throat. "You know," he said. "Just because you can't see the happiness in your grandparents' life, that doesn't mean they're not happy. What makes one person happy doesn't always work for someone else. Take my mother— she values family over everything. As long as she has my father and her children, she's happy. But not everyone needs family, of course. Some people need money, others need companionship. Everyone is different."

"And what do you need?" Deya asked.

"What?"

"What do you need to be happy?"

Nasser bit the inside of his lip. "Financial security."

"Money?"

"No, not money." He paused. "I want to have a stable career and live comfortably, maybe even retire young."

She rolled her eyes. "Work, money, same thing."

"Maybe so," he said, blushing. "Why, what's your answer?"

"Nothing."

"That's not fair. You have to answer the question. What would make you happy?"

"Nothing. Nothing would make me happy."

He blinked at her. "What do you mean, nothing? Surely something must make you happy."

She turned to look out the window, feeling his eyes follow her face. "I don't believe in happiness."

"That's not true. Maybe you just haven't found it yet."

"It is true."

"Is it because—" He stopped. "Do you think it's because of your parents?"

She could tell he was trying to meet her eyes, but she kept them fixed on the window. "No," she lied. "Not because of them."

"Then why don't you believe in happiness?"

He would never understand, even if she tried to explain. She turned to face him. "I just don't believe in it, that's all."

He looked back at her with a glum expression. She wondered what he saw, whether he knew that if he opened her up, he would find, right behind her ribs, only a fist of rot and mud.

"I don't think you really mean that," he eventually said, smiling at her. "You know what I think?"

"What?"

"I think you're just pretending to see how I'd react. You wanted to see if I'd make a run for it."

"Interesting theory."

"I think it's true. In fact, I bet you do it often."

"Do what?"

"Push people away so they won't hurt you." She looked away. "It's okay. You don't have to admit it."

"There's nothing to admit."

"Fine. But can I tell you something?" She turned back toward him. "I won't hurt you. I promise."

She forced a smile, wishing she could trust him. But she didn't think she knew how.

Fareeda hurried into the kitchen as soon as Nasser left, her almond brown eyes wide and questioning: Did Deya like him? Did she think he'd liked her? Would she agree to the marriage proposal? Deya had said no to a few proposals, her answer ripe on the tip of her tongue. But mostly the suitor was first to withdraw his offer. On these occasions, after the parents had politely informed them that a match had not been made and Fareeda had cried and slapped her face, her grandmother had only become more persistent. A few phone calls, and she had found a new suitor by the end of the week.

But this time was different. "Looks like you didn't scare this one away," Fareeda said with a grin from the kitchen doorway. She was wearing the red-and-gold dress she wore when suitors visited, with a cream scarf draped loosely around her head. She moved closer. "His parents said they'd like to visit again soon.

What do you think? Did you like Nasser? Should I tell them yes?"

"I don't know," Deya said, shoving a wet rag across the kitchen table. "I need some time to think about it."

"Think about it? What's there to think about? You should be thankful you even have a choice in the matter. Some girls aren't that lucky—*I* certainly never was."

"This isn't a choice," Deya mumbled.

"Why, of course it is!" Fareeda ran her fingers against the kitchen table to make sure it was clean. "My parents never asked me if I wanted to marry your grandfather. They just told me what to do, and I did it."

"Well, I don't have parents," Deya said. "Or uncles or aunts, or anyone besides my sisters for that matter!"

"Nonsense. You have us," Fareeda said, though she didn't meet her eyes.

Deya's grandparents had raised Deya and her three sisters since she was seven years old. For years it had just been the six of them, not the large extended family that was the norm in Arab households. Growing up, Deya had often felt the sting of loneliness, but it stung the most on Eid celebrations, when she and her sisters would sit at home, knowing there was no one coming to visit them on the most important holiday. Her classmates would boast about the festivities they attended, the family members who gave them gifts and money, while Deya smiled, pretending that she and her sisters did those things, too. That they had uncles and aunts and people who loved them. That they had a family. But they didn't know what it meant to have a family. All they had were grandparents who raised them out of obligation, and each other.

"Nasser would make a fine husband," Fareeda said. "He'll be a doctor someday. He'll be able to give you everything you need.

You'd be a fool to turn him down. Proposals like this don't come around every day."

"But I'm only eighteen, Teta. I'm not ready to get married."

"You act like I'm selling you off to slavery! Every mother I know is preparing her daughter for marriage. Tell me, do you know anyone whose mother isn't doing exactly the same thing?"

Deya sighed. Her grandmother was right. Most of her class-mates sat with a handful of men every month, yet none of them seemed to mind. They slicked on makeup and plucked their brows, as though eagerly waiting for a man to scoop them away. Some were already engaged, wrapping up their final year of high school as if by force. As if they'd found something in the pros-pect of marriage so fulfilling that no amount of education could compare. Deya would often look at them and wonder: *Isn't there more you want to do? There must be more.* But then her thoughts would shift, and uncertainty would kick in. She'd start to think maybe they had it right after all. Maybe marriage was the an-swer.

Fareeda moved closer, shaking her head. "Why are you mak-ing this so difficult? What more do you want?"

Deya met her eyes. "I already told you! I want to go to col-lege!"

"*Ya Allah.*" She drew out her words. "Not this again. How many times do I have to tell you? You're not going to college in this house. If your husband allows you to get an education *after* marriage, that's his decision. But my job is to secure your future by making sure you and your sisters are married off to good men."

"But why can't you secure my future by letting me go to col-lege? Why are you letting some strange man control my fate? What if he turns out like Baba? What if—"

"Not another *word*," Fareeda said, her upper lip twitching. "How many times have I told you not to mention your parents in this house?" From the expression on her face, Deya could tell Fareeda wanted to slap her. But it was true. Deya had seen enough of her mother's life to know it wasn't the life she wanted.

"I'm afraid, Teta," Deya whispered. "I don't want to marry a man I don't know."

"Arranged marriages are what we do," Fareeda said. "Just because we live in America, that doesn't change how things are." She shook her head, reaching inside the cabinet for a teakettle. "If you keep turning down proposals, the next thing you know, you'll be old and no one will want to marry you, and then you'll spend the rest of your life in this house with me." She caught Deya's eyes. "You've seen other girls who've disobeyed their parents, refusing to get married, or worse, getting divorced, and look at them now! Living at home with their parents, their heads hanging in shame! Is that what you want?"

Deya looked away.

"Listen, Deya." Fareeda's voice was softer. "I'm not asking you to marry Nasser tomorrow. Just sit with him again and get to know him."

Deya hated to admit Fareeda was right, but she found herself reconsidering. Maybe it was time to get married. Maybe she should accept Nasser's proposal. It wasn't as if she had a future in Fareeda's house. She could barely go to the grocery store without supervision. Besides, Nasser seemed nice enough. Better than the other men she'd met over the months. If not him, then who? Eventually, she'd have to agree to someone. She could only refuse for so long. Unless she wanted to ruin her reputation and her sisters' reputations as well. She could hear their neighbors in her head. *That girl is bad. She isn't respectable. Something must be wrong with her.*

Deya agreed. There was something wrong with her: she couldn't stop thinking, couldn't make up her mind.

"Fine," she said. "Okay."

Fareeda's eyes sprung wide. "Really?"

"I'll see him again. But only under one condition."

"And what's that?"

"I'm not leaving Brooklyn."

"Don't worry." Fareeda forced a tight smile. "He lives right here in Sunset Park. I know you want to be near your sisters."

"Please," Deya said. "When the time comes, will you make sure they marry in Brooklyn, too?" She spoke softly, hoping to elicit some sympathy. "Can you make sure we stay together? Please."

Fareeda nodded. Deya thought she saw the wetness of tears in her eyes. It was an odd sight. But then Fareeda looked away, twisting her scarf with her fingers.

"Of course," Fareeda said. "That's the least I can do."

Fareeda might have forbidden Deya from speaking of her parents, but she couldn't erase her memories. Deya clearly remembered the day she had learned of Adam's and Isra's deaths. She had been seven years old. It was a bright autumn day, but Deya had watched the sky turn a dull silver through her bedroom window. Fareeda had finished clearing the *sufra* after dinner, washed the dishes, and slipped into her nightgown before creeping downstairs to the basement, where they had lived with their parents. Deya knew something was wrong the minute her grandmother appeared at the doorway. As far back as she could remember, she had never seen Fareeda in the basement.

Fareeda had checked to see if Amal, the youngest of the four, was asleep in her crib, before sitting on the edge of Deya and her sisters' bed.

"Your parents—" Fareeda took a deep breath and pushed the words out. "They're dead. They died in a car accident last night."

After that, it was all a blur. Deya couldn't remember what Fareeda said next, couldn't picture the looks on her sisters' faces. She only remembered disparate bits. Panic. Whimpering. A high-pitched scream. She had dug her fingers into her thighs. She had thought she was going to throw up. She remembered looking out the window and noticing that it had started to rain, as if the universe was grieving with them.

Fareeda had stood up and, weeping, went back upstairs.

That was all Deya knew about her parents' death, even now, more than ten years later. Perhaps that was why she had spent her childhood with a book in front of her face, trying to make sense of her life through stories. Books were her only reliable source of comfort, her only hope. They told the truth in a way the world never seemed to, guided her the way she imagined Isra would've had she still been alive. There were so many things she needed to know, about her family, about the world, about herself.

She often wondered how many people felt this way, spellbound by words, wishing to be tucked inside a book and forgotten there. How many people were hoping to find their story inside, desperate to understand. And yet Deya still felt alone in the end, no matter how many books she read, no matter how many tales she told herself. All her life she'd searched for a story to help her understand who she was and where she belonged. But her story was confined to the walls of her home, to the basement of Seventy-Second Street and Fifth Avenue, and she didn't think she'd ever understand it.

———————

That evening Deya and her sisters ate dinner alone, as they usually did, while Fareeda watched her evening show in the *sala*. They did not spread a *sufra* with a succession of dishes, nor set the table with lemon wedges, green olives, chili peppers, and fresh pita bread, as they did when their grandfather came home. Instead the four sisters huddled around the kitchen table together, deep in conversation. Every now and then they'd lower their voices, listening to the sounds in the hall to make sure Fareeda was still in the *sala* and couldn't overhear them.

Deya's younger sisters were her only companions. All four of them were close in age, only one or two years apart, and complemented one another like school subjects in a class schedule. If Deya was a subject, she thought she would be art—dark, messy, emotional. Nora, the second eldest and her closest companion, would be math—solid, precise, and straightforward. It was Nora who Deya relied on for advice, taking comfort in her clear thinking; Nora who tempered Deya's overspilling emotions, who structured the chaos of Deya's art. Then there was Layla. Deya thought Layla would be science, always curious, always seeking answers, always logical. Then there was Amal, the youngest of the four and, true to her name, the most hopeful. If Amal was a subject, she would be religion, centering every conversation around halal and *haraam*, good and evil. It was Amal who always brought them back to God, rounding them out with a handful of faith.

"So, what did you think of Nasser?" asked Nora as she sipped on her lentil soup. "Was he crazy like the last man?" She blew on her spoon. "You know, the one who insisted you start wearing the hijab at once?"

"I don't think anyone's as crazy as that man," Deya said, laughing.

"Was he nice?" Nora asked.

"He was okay," Deya said, making sure to smile. She didn't want to worry them. "Really, he was."

Layla was studying her. "You don't seem too happy."

Deya could see her sisters watching her intensely, their eyes making her sweat. "I'm just nervous, that's all."

"Are you going to sit with him again?" said Amal, who, Deya realized, was biting her fingertips.

"Yes. Tomorrow, I think."

Nora leaned in, pushing a strand of hair behind her ear. "Does he know about our parents?"

Deya nodded as she stirred her soup. She wasn't surprised Nasser knew what had happened to her parents. News traveled like wind in a community like theirs, where Arabs clung to each other like dough, afraid to get lost among the Irish, Italians, Greeks, and Hasidic Jews. It was as if all the Arabs in Brooklyn stood hand in hand, from Bay Ridge all the way up Atlantic Avenue, and shared everything, from one ear to the next. There were no secrets among them.

"What do you think is going to happen?" Layla asked.

"With what?"

"When you see him again. What will you talk about?"

"The fundamentals, I'm sure," Deya said, one eyebrow cocked. "How many kids I want, where I want to live . . . you know, the basics."

Her sisters laughed.

"But at least you'll know what to expect if you decide to move forward," Nora said. "Better than being taken off guard."

"That's true. He did seem very predictable." Deya looked down into her soup. When she raised her eyes again, the corners crinkled. "You know what he said would make him happy?"

"Money?" said Layla.

"A good job?" added Nora.

Deya laughed. "Exactly. So typical."

"What did you expect him to say?" said Nora. "Love? Romance?"

"No. But I hoped he'd at least *pretend* to have a more interesting answer."

"Not everyone can pretend the way you do," Nora said with a grin.

"Maybe he was nervous," Layla said. "Did he ask what made *you* happy?"

"He did."

"And what did you say?"

"I said nothing made me happy."

"Why did you say that?" said Amal.

"Just to mess with him."

"Sure," Nora said, rolling her eyes. "That's a good question, though. Let's see. What would make me happy?" She stirred her soup. "Freedom," she finally said. "Being able to do anything I wanted."

"Success would make me happy," Layla said. "Being a doctor or doing something great."

"Good luck becoming a doctor in Fareeda's house," Nora said, laughing.

Layla rolled her eyes. "Says the girl who wants freedom."

They all laughed at that.

Deya caught a glimpse of Amal, who was still chewing her fingers. She had yet to touch her soup. "What about you, *habibti*?" Deya asked, reaching out to squeeze her shoulder. "What would make you happy?"

Amal looked out the kitchen window. "Being with you three," she said.

Deya sighed. Even though Amal was far too young to remember them—she'd been barely two years old when the car accident had happened—Deya knew she was thinking of their parents. But it was easier losing something you couldn't quite remember, she thought. At least then there were no memories to look back on, nothing hurtful to relive. Deya envied her sisters that. She remembered too much, too often, though her memories were distorted and spotty, like half-remembered dreams. To make sense of them, she'd weave the scattered fragments together into a full narrative, with a beginning and an end, a purpose and a truth. Sometimes she would find herself mixing up memories, losing track of time, adding pieces here and there until her childhood felt complete, had a logical progression. And then she'd wonder: which pieces could she really remember, and which ones had she made up?

Deya felt cold as she sat at the kitchen table, despite the steam from her soup against her face. She could see Amal staring absently out the kitchen window, and she reached across the table and squeezed her hand.

"I just can't imagine the house without you," Amal whispered.

"Oh, come on," Deya said. "It's not like I'm going to a different country. I'll be right around the corner. You can all come visit anytime."

Nora and Layla smiled, but Amal just sighed. "I'm going to miss you."

"I'm going to miss you, too." Deya's voice cracked as she said it.

Outside the window the light was getting duller, the wind settling. Deya watched a handful of birds gliding across the sky.

"I wish Mama and Baba were here," Nora said.

Layla sighed. "I just wish I remembered them."

"Me too," Amal said.

"I don't remember much either," Nora said. "I was only six when they died."

"But at least you were old enough to remember what they looked like," said Layla. "Amal and I remember nothing."

Nora turned to Deya. "Mama was beautiful, wasn't she?"

Deya forced a smile. She could barely recall their mother's face, just her eyes, how dark they were. Sometimes she wished she could peek inside Nora's brain to see what she remembered about their parents, whether Nora's memories resembled her own. But mostly she wished she would find nothing in Nora's head, not a single memory. It would be easier that way.

"I remember being at the park once." Nora's voice was quieting now. "We were all having a picnic. Do you remember, Deya? Mama and Baba bought us Mister Softee cones. We sat in the shade and watched the ships drift beneath the Verrazano-Narrows Bridge like toy boats. And Mama and Baba stroked my hair and kissed me. I remember they were laughing."

Deya said nothing. That day at the park was her last memory of her parents, but she recalled it differently. She remembered her parents sitting at opposite ends of the blanket, neither saying a word. In Deya's memories, they rarely spoke to each other, and she couldn't remember ever seeing them touch. She used to think they were being modest, that perhaps they loved each other when they were alone. But even when she watched them in secret, she never saw them show affection. Deya couldn't remember why, but that day in the park, staring at her parents at opposite ends of the blanket, she'd felt as though she understood the meaning of the word *sorrow* for the first time.

The sisters spent the rest of their evening chatting about school until it was time for bed. Layla and Amal exchanged goodnight kisses with their older sisters before heading to their room. Nora sat on the bed beside Deya and twisted the blanket with her fingers. "Tell me something," she said.

"Hm?"

"Did you mean what you told Nasser? That nothing can make you happy?"

Deya sat up and leaned against the headboard. "No, I . . . I don't know."

"Why do you think that? It worries me."

When Deya said nothing, Nora leaned in close. "Tell me. What is it?"

"I don't know, it's just . . . Sometimes I think maybe happiness isn't real, at least not for me. I know it sounds dramatic, but . . ." She paused, tried to find the right words. "Maybe if I keep everyone at arm's length, if I don't expect anything from the world, I won't be disappointed."

"But you know it's not healthy, living with that mindset," Nora said.

"Of course I know that, but I can't help how I feel."

"I don't understand. When did you become so negative?"

Deya was silent.

"Is it because of Mama and Baba? Is that it? You always have this look in your eyes when we mention them, like you know something we don't. What is it?"

"It's nothing," Deya said.

"Clearly it's something. It must be. Something happened."

Deya felt Nora's words under her skin. Something had happened, everything had happened, nothing had happened. She remembered the days she'd sat outside Isra's bedroom door, knocking and pounding, calling for her mother over and over. *Mama. Open the door, Mama. Please, Mama. Can you hear me? Are you there? Are you coming, Mama? Please.* But Isra never opened the door. Deya would lie there and wonder what she had done. What was wrong with her that her own mother couldn't love her?

But Deya knew that no matter how clearly she could articulate this memory and countless others, Nora wouldn't be able to understand how she felt, not really.

"Please don't worry," she said. "I'm okay."

"Promise?"

"Promise."

Nora yawned, stretching her arms in the air. "Tell me one of your stories, then," she said. "So I can have good dreams. Tell me about Mama and Baba."

Their bedtime story ritual had started when their parents died and continued throughout the years. Deya didn't mind, but there was only so much she could remember, or wanted to. Telling a story wasn't as simple as recalling memories. It was building on them and deciding which parts were best left unsaid.

Nora didn't need to know about the nights Deya had waited for Adam to come home, pressing her nose against the window so hard it would still hurt by morning. How, on the rare nights he came home before bedtime, he'd scoop her into his arms, all while scanning the halls for Isra, waiting for her to come greet him, too. But Isra never greeted him. She never met his eyes when he entered the house, never even smiled. At best she'd stand in the corner of the hall, the color rushing out of her skin, the muscles in her jaw clenching.

But other times it was worse: nights when Deya would lie in bed and hear Adam yelling on the other side of the wall, her mother weeping, then even more terrible sounds. A bang against the wall. A loud yelp. Adam screaming again. Deya would cover her ears, shut her eyes, curl up in a ball, and tell herself a story in her head until the noises faded in the background, until she could no longer hear her mother pleading, "Adam, please . . . Adam, stop . . ."

"What are you thinking about?" Nora asked, studying her sister's face. "What are you remembering?"

"Nothing," Deya said, though she could feel her face betray her. Sometimes Deya wondered if it was her mother's sadness that made her sad, if perhaps when Isra died, all her sorrows had escaped and settled in Deya instead.

"Come on," Nora said, sitting up. "I can see it on your face. Tell me."

"It's nothing. Besides, it's getting late."

"Pretty please. Soon you'll be married, and then . . ." Her voice dwindled to a whisper. "Your memories are all I have left of them."

"Fine." Deya sighed. "I'll tell you what I remember." She straightened and cleared her throat. But she didn't tell Nora the truth. She told her a story.

Isra

Spring 1990

Isra arrived in New York the day after her wedding ceremony, via a twelve-hour flight from Tel Aviv. Her first glimpse of the city was from the plane as they approached John F. Kennedy Airport. Her eyes widened and she pressed her nose against the window. She thought she had fallen in love. It was the city itself that captivated her first, immaculate buildings stories high— hundreds of them. From above, Manhattan looked so thin, like the buildings could just crack it in half, as though they were too heavy for that small sliver of land. As the plane neared the earth, Isra felt herself swell up. The Manhattan skyline turned from toylike to mountainous, its towers and citadels shooting upward like fireworks bursting into the sky, overwhelming in height and power, making Isra feel small, yet at the same time bewildered by their beauty, as if they were something out of a fairy tale. Even if she had read a thousand books, nothing could compare to the feeling she had now as she inhaled the view.

She could still see the skyline when the plane landed, though now it was a faint outline with a bluish hue on the far horizon.

If Isra squinted, it almost seemed like she was looking at the mountains of Palestine, the buildings like dusty hills in the distance. She wondered what else she would see in the days to come.

"This is Queens," Adam told her as they waited in line for a cab outside the airport. Once inside the minivan, Isra sat near a window in the back row, hoping Adam would sit beside her, but Sarah and Fareeda joined her instead. "It's about a forty-five-minute ride to Brooklyn where we live," Adam continued as he sat beside his brothers in the middle row. "If we're not stuck in traffic, that is."

Isra studied Queens through the taxicab window, eyes wide and watering in the March sunlight. She searched for the immaculate skyline she had seen from the plane, but it was nowhere in sight. All she could see were endless gray roads, curving and looping back in on themselves, with cars—hundreds of cars—zooming along them without stopping. Adam said they were two miles from the exit to Brooklyn, and Isra watched as the cabdriver merged to the left lane, following a sign that read BELT PARKWAY RAMP.

They sailed along a narrow highway so close to the water Isra thought the cab might slip and fall in. She didn't know how to swim. "How are we driving so close to the water?" she managed to ask, eyeing a large ship in the distance, a cluster of birds soaring above it.

"Oh, this is nothing," Adam said. "Wait until you see the bridge."

And then it appeared, right in front of her, long and silver and elegant, like a bird spreading its wings over water. "That's the Verrazano-Narrows Bridge," Adam said, watching Isra's eyes widen. "Isn't it beautiful?"

"It is," she said, panicking. "Are we driving on it?"

"No," Adam said. "That bridge connects Brooklyn to Staten Island."

"Has it ever fallen?" she whispered, eyes glued to the bridge as they neared it.

She could hear his smile in his reply. "Not that I know of."

"But it's so skinny! It looks like it could snap at any minute."

Adam laughed. "Relax," he said. "We're in the greatest city on earth. Everything here is built by the best architects and engineers. Enjoy the view."

Isra tried to relax. She could hear Khaled chuckle in the passenger seat. "Reminds me of the first time Fareeda saw the bridge." He turned back to look at his wife. "I swear she almost cried in fear."

"Sure I did," Fareeda said, though Isra noticed that she still seemed nervous as they drove under the bridge. When they came out the other side, Isra exhaled hard, relieved it hadn't collapsed on them.

It was only after they exited the parkway that Isra had her first glimpse of Brooklyn. It wasn't what she had expected. Magnificent was a word you could put to Manhattan, but Brooklyn seemed plain in comparison, as though it didn't belong alongside. All she saw were dull brick buildings covered in murals and graffiti, many of them dilapidated, and people pushing their way through the crowded streets with solemn looks on their faces. It puzzled her. Growing up, she had often wondered about the world outside Palestine, if it were as beautiful as the places she read about in books. She had been certain it would be, studying the Manhattan skyline, had been excited to call that world home. But now, eyeing Brooklyn through the window, seeing the graffiti scrawled on the walls and across the buildings, she wondered if her books had gotten it wrong, whether Mama had been right all along when she'd said the world would be disappointing regardless of where she stood.

"We live in Bay Ridge," Adam said as the cabdriver stopped

beside a row of old brick houses. Isra, Fareeda, and Sarah stood on the sidewalk while the men unloaded the suitcases. Adam held Isra's suitcase in one hand and gestured around the block with the other. "Many of the Arabs in New York live in this neighborhood," he said. "You'll feel right at home."

Isra surveyed the block. Adam's family lived on a long, tree-lined street with row houses stacked against one another like books on a shelf. Most of the homes were made of red brick and curved in the front. They had two stories and a basement, with a short, narrow staircase leading to the front door on the first floor. Iron gates separated the houses from the sidewalk. It was a well-kept neighborhood—there were no open gutters or garbage littering the street, and the roads were paved, not dirt. But there was hardly any greenery—only a row of London planes lining the walk. No fruit to pick, no balcony, no front yard. She hoped there was at least a backyard.

"This is it," Adam said when they reached the front gate of a house numbered 545.

Adam opened the front door and led her inside. "The houses here are quite cramped," he said as they walked down the hall. Isra silently agreed. She could see the entire first floor from the hall. There was a *sala* to her left, and farther down, a kitchen. To her right was a stairway leading to the second floor, and behind it, almost hidden, a bedroom.

Isra looked around the living room. Though it was much smaller than her parents' *sala* back home, it was decorated as though it were a mansion. The floor was covered with a Turkish rug, crimson with a gold pattern in the center. The same pattern was on the burgundy couches, the red throw pillows, and the long, thick curtains lining the windows. A worn leather sofa sat in the corner of the room, as though forgotten, with a shiny gold vase nestled beside it.

"Do you like it?" Adam asked.

"It's beautiful."

"I know it's not bright and airy like the houses back home." His eyes settled on the windows, which were hidden behind the curtains. "But this is how things are here, what can we do?"

There was something in his voice, and Isra found herself thinking of the day on the balcony, the way his eyes had chased the grapevines, taking in the open scenery. She wondered whether he longed to return to Palestine, whether he wanted to move back home one day.

"Do you miss home?" The sound of her voice startled her, and she dropped her eyes to the floor.

"Yes," Adam said. "I do."

Isra looked up to see that he was still staring at the curtains. "Would you ever move back?" she asked.

"Maybe one day," he said. "If things got better." He turned away and walked down the hall. Isra followed.

"My parents stay here on the first floor," Adam said, pointing to the bedroom. "Sarah and my brothers sleep upstairs."

"Where will we stay?" she asked, hoping her bedroom had a window.

He pointed to a closed door down the hallway. "Downstairs."

Adam opened the door and signaled her to go down. She did, all the while wondering how they could live in a basement. If there was barely enough light upstairs, what would the basement be like? She peered down the shallow steps. At once, she was overwhelmed with darkness. She put both hands in front of her and descended, the light cast from the doorway fading with each step. She reached the bottom of the stairs and fumbled against the wall in search of a light switch. Cold crept through her fingertips until she found it and flicked it on.

A large, gold mirror hung on the wall directly in front of her. It seemed odd that anyone should place a mirror in such a dreary, uninhabited place. What good was a mirror in the middle of the dark with no light to reflect?

She entered the first room of the basement, surveying the dim space. The room was narrow and empty—four gray walls, bare with the exception of a window to her left and, in the center of the wall ahead, a closed door. Isra opened it to find another room, slightly larger than the first and furnished with a queen-size bed, a small dresser, and a large mirror. Beside the mirror was a small closet, and beside that, a doorway that led to a bathroom. This would be their bedroom, Isra knew. It didn't have any windows.

She studied her reflection in the mirror. Her face looked dull and gray in the fluorescent light, and she stared at her small, weak frame. She saw a girl who should've kicked and screamed as her mother tightened her wedding gown, should've begged and hollered as her father secured her in the taxicab to the airport. But she was a coward. She turned away. This is the only familiar face I'll ever see again, Isra thought. And she couldn't stand the sight of it.

Upstairs, the earthy smell of sage filled the kitchen. Fareeda was brewing a kettle of chai. She stood over the stove, back hunched, staring absently at the steam. Watching her, Isra found herself thinking of the *maramiya* plant in her mother's garden, how Mama would cut off a few leaves every morning to brew in their chai because it helped with Yacob's indigestion. Isra wondered if Fareeda grew a *maramiya* plant, too, or if she used dried sage from the market instead.

"Can I help you with something, *hamati*?" Isra asked as she walked over to the stove. It was the first time she had called Fareeda mother-in-law.

"No, no, no," Fareeda said, shaking her head. "Don't call me *hamati*. Call me Fareeda."

Growing up, Isra had never heard a married woman called by her first name. Her mother was always referred to as Umm Waleed, mother of her eldest son Waleed, and never Sawsan. Even her aunt Widad, who had never borne a son, was not called by her first name. People called her Mart Jamal, Jamal's wife.

"I don't like that word," Fareeda said, reading the confusion on her face. "It makes me feel old."

Isra smiled, resting her eyes on the boiling tea.

"Why don't you set the *sufra*?" Fareeda said. "I'm making us something to eat."

"Where's Adam?"

"He left for work."

"Oh." Isra had expected him to stay home today, to take her for a walk around the neighborhood perhaps, introduce her to Brooklyn. Who went to work the day after his wedding?

"He had to run an errand for his father," Fareeda said. "He'll be home soon."

Why couldn't his brothers run the errand instead? Isra wanted to ask, but she was afraid of saying the wrong thing. She cleared her throat and said, "Did Omar and Ali go with him?"

"I have no idea where *they* went," Fareeda said. "Boys are a handful, going and coming as they please. They're not like girls. You can't control them." She handed Isra a stack of plates. "I'm sure you know—you have brothers."

Isra smiled weakly. "I do."

"Sarah!" Fareeda called out.

Sarah was upstairs in her bedroom. "Yes, Mama?" she called back.

"Come down here and help Isra set the *sufra*!" Fareeda said. She turned to Isra. "I don't want her thinking she's excused from her chores now that you're here. That's how trouble starts."

"Does she have a lot of chores?" Isra asked.

"Of course," Fareeda said, looking up to find Sarah at the doorway. "She's eleven years old, practically a woman. Why, when I was her age, my mother didn't even have to lift a finger. I was rolling pots of stuffed grape leaves and kneading dough for the entire family."

"That's because you didn't go to school, Mama," Sarah said. "You had time to do those things. I have homework to catch up on."

"Your homework can wait," Fareeda said, handing her the *ibrik* of chai. "Pour some tea and hurry."

Sarah poured tea into four glass cups. Isra noticed that she didn't hurry like Fareeda had asked.

"Is the chai ready?" A man's voice.

Isra turned to find Khaled in the doorway. She took a good look at him. His hair was thick and silver, his yellow skin wrinkled. He wouldn't meet her eyes, and she wondered if he was uncomfortable because she wasn't wearing her hijab. But she didn't have to wear it in front of him. He was her father-in-law, which, according to Islamic law, made him *mahram*, like her own father.

"How do you like the neighborhood, Isra?" Khaled said, scanning the *sufra*. Despite his faded features and the iron-colored hair across his jaw, it was easy to see he had been handsome as a young man.

"It's beautiful, *ami*," Isra said, wondering if perhaps calling him father-in-law would irritate him the way it had Fareeda.

Fareeda looked at her husband and grinned. "You're '*ami*' now, you old man!"

"You're no young damsel yourself," he said with a smile. "Come on." He signaled them to sit down. "Let's eat."

Isra had never seen so much food on one *sufra*. Hummus topped with ground beef and pine nuts. Fried halloumi cheese. Scrambled eggs. Falafel. Green and black olives. *Labne* and *za'atar*. Fresh pita bread. Even during Ramadan, when Mama made all their favorite meals and Yacob splurged and bought them meat, the food was never this plentiful. The steam of each dish intertwined with the next until the room smelled like home.

Fareeda turned to Khaled, fixing her eyes on his face. "What are your plans today?"

"I don't know." He dipped his bread in olive oil and *za'atar*. "Why?"

"I need you to take me to town."

"What do you need?"

"Meat and groceries."

Isra tried to keep from staring at Fareeda. Even though she was not much older than Mama, they were nothing alike. There were no undertones of fear in Fareeda's voice, nor did she lower her gaze in Khaled's presence. Isra wondered if Khaled beat her.

"Do I have to go too, Baba?" Sarah asked from across the table. "I'm tired."

"You can stay home with Isra," he said without looking up.

Sarah exhaled a sigh of relief. "Thank God. I hate grocery shopping."

Isra watched as Khaled sipped his chai, unfazed by Sarah's boldness. If Isra had spoken to Yacob like that, he would've slapped her. But perhaps parents didn't hit their children in America. She pictured herself raised in America by Khaled and Fareeda, wondered what her life might have been like.

After a moment, Khaled excused himself to get ready. Isra and Sarah got up as well, carrying the empty plates and cups to the sink. Fareeda remained seated, sipping her tea.

"Fareeda!" Khaled called from the hall.

"*Shu*? What do you want?"

"Pour me another cup of chai."

Fareeda popped a ball of falafel into her mouth, clearly in no hurry to obey her husband's command. Isra watched, confused and anxious, as Fareeda sipped her tea. When was she going to pour Khaled another cup of chai? Should Isra offer to do it instead? She looked at Sarah, but the girl seemed unconcerned. Isra forced herself to relax. Maybe this was how wives spoke to their husbands in America. Maybe things were different here after all.

Adam came home at sunset. "Get dressed," he told her. "I'm taking you out."

Isra tried to contain her excitement. She was standing in front of the living room window, where she had been for some time, studying the plane trees outside, wondering if they smelled woody or sweet or a scent she had never smelled before. She kept her eyes on the glass so Adam wouldn't see her blushing.

"Should I tell Fareeda to get ready, too?" she asked.

"No, no." Adam laughed. "She already knows what Brooklyn looks like."

Downstairs, in front of a square mirror propped on her bedroom wall, Isra couldn't decide what to wear. She paced around the room, trying one color of hijab after another. Back home she would've worn the lavender one, with the silver beads stitched across it. But she was in America now. Perhaps she should wear black or brown so she wouldn't stick out. Or maybe not. Maybe a lighter color would work better, would make her seem bright and happy.

She was studying the color of her face against a mossy green headpiece when Adam entered the room. He eyed her hijab nervously, and through the mirror, she could see the straining in his jaw. He moved closer to her, not once looking away from her head, and the whole time he was walking, she felt her heart swelling inside her chest, inching toward her throat. He was looking at her hijab the way he had looked that day on the balcony, and it was only now that Isra understood why: he didn't like it.

"You don't have to wear that thing, you know," Adam finally said. She blinked at him in shock. "It's true." He paused. "You see, people here don't care if your hair is showing. There's no need to cover it up."

Isra didn't know what to say. Growing up, she had been taught that the most important part of being a Muslim girl was wearing the hijab. That modesty was a woman's greatest virtue. "But what about our religion?" she whispered. "What about God?"

Adam gave her a pitying look. "We have to live carefully here, Isra. People flee to America from war-torn countries every day. Some are Arabs. Some are Muslims. Some are both, like us. But we could live here for the rest of our lives and never be Americans. You think you're doing the right thing by wearing this hijab, but that's not what Americans will see when they look at you. They won't see your modesty or your goodness. All they'll see is an outcast, someone who doesn't belong." He sighed, looking up to meet her eyes. "It's hard. But all we can do is try to fit in."

Isra unwrapped her hijab and set it on the bed. She had

never once considered not wearing it in public. But standing in front of the mirror, eyeing the long black strands of hair as they wilted off her shoulders, she found herself feeling hopeful again. Perhaps this would be her first taste of freedom. There was no reason to reject it before she had tried it.

They left the house soon after. Isra fingered a strand of hair nervously as she stepped out of the front door. Adam didn't seem to notice. He told her that the best way to truly experience Brooklyn was not by car or train but by foot. So they walked. The moon shone above them in a starless sky, illuminating the budding trees that lined the street. They strolled down the long, narrow block labeled Seventy-Second Street until they reached the corner, and suddenly Isra felt as if she had been transported to a new world.

"This is Fifth Avenue," Adam said. "The heart of Bay Ridge."

Everywhere Isra looked, lights were flashing. The street was lined with an assortment of shops: bakeries, restaurants, pharmacies, law offices. "Bay Ridge is one of the most diverse neighborhoods in Brooklyn," Adam said as they walked. "Immigrants from all over the world live here. You can see it in the food—meat dumplings, *kofta*, fish stews, challah bread. You see that block?" Adam pointed into the distance. "Every single shop on that block belongs to Arabs. There is a halal butcher shop on the corner, Alsalam, where my father goes every Sunday to get our meats, and then there is the Lebanese pastry shop, where they bake fresh *saj* bread every morning. During Ramadan, they stuff the loaves with melted cheese, syrup, and sesame seeds, just like back home."

Isra scanned the shops, mesmerized. She recognized the smell of meat-stuffed *kibbeh*, lamb shawarma, the thick syrupy musk of baklava, even the faint hint of double-apple hookah. And other familiar smells lingered in the air, too. Fresh basil. Piping grease. Sewers, sweat. The scents merged into one another, became whole, and in an instant Isra felt as if she had fallen through the cracked cement and landed back home.

Around her people strolled down the block, pushing strollers and carrying grocery bags, swirling in and out of shops like marbles. They looked nothing like the Americans she had imagined: women with bright red lipstick, men in polished black suits. Instead, many of the women looked no different than her, plain and modestly dressed, many even wearing a hijab. And the men looked like Adam, with olive skin and rough beards, clothes meant for tough labor.

Isra didn't know what to think, eyeing the familiar faces floating down Fifth Avenue. These people were just like them, living in America and trying to fit in. Yet they still wore their hijabs; they didn't change who they were. So why did Adam insist that she change who she was?

After a long time watching them, Isra was no longer thinking of her hijab. Instead, she thought of all the people drifting under the lamplights, people who lived in America but weren't Americans at all, women who were just like her, displaced from their homes, torn between two cultures and struggling to start anew. She wondered what her new life would be like.

That night, Isra went to bed early. Adam was taking a shower, and she thought it best that he return to find her asleep. It was her first night alone with him, and she knew what would happen if she stayed awake. She knew he would put himself inside her. She knew it would hurt. She also knew—though she wasn't entirely sure she believed it—that she would come to enjoy it.

Mama had told her this. Still, Isra wasn't ready. In bed, she closed her eyes, tried to silence her thoughts. She felt as if she were running frantically, spinning in circles.

In the bathroom she could hear Adam turn off the running water, pulling the shower curtain open, then shut, fumbling for something inside the cabinet. She pulled the blanket over her body like a shield. Lying still beneath the cold sheets, she watched him through half-open eyes as he entered the room. He was wearing nothing but a bath towel, and she had a full view of his lean, golden body, the coarse black hair on his chest. For a moment he stood there, staring at her as though willing her to look at him, but she could not bring herself to open her eyes fully. He took off the bath towel and approached her. She closed her eyes, breathing in and out, trying to relax. But her body only stiffened as he neared.

He climbed onto the bed, pulled back the sheets, and reached out to touch her. She inched away until she thought she would fall off the other side. But he grabbed her, pushing her into the mattress. Then he was on top of her. She could smell his ashy breath as he exhaled in her face. Her hands shook furiously, and she dug her fingers into her ivory nightgown. He pulled her hands away, tugging off her gown and underwear—a bright white set Mama had given her specifically for this night, so Adam would know she was pure. Only Isra didn't feel pure. She felt dirty and afraid.

Adam locked his hands around her hips, pinning down her struggling body. She kept her eyes shut tight as he shoved her legs open, gritted her teeth as he thrust himself inside her. Then she heard a scream. Was it hers? She was afraid to open her eyes. There was something about the darkness that felt safe, familiar. Lying there, eyes closed, memories of her home somehow overwhelmed her. She saw herself running in an open field, picking figs from the trees, saving the best ones for Mama, who waited for her at the top of the hill with an empty basket. She saw herself playing with marbles in the yard, chasing them as they rolled down the hill. She saw herself blowing dandelions in the cemetery, reciting a prayer on every gravestone.

Then she felt a gush down her thighs: she knew it must be blood. She tried to ignore the burning sensation between her legs, as if a fist were punching through her, tried to forget that she was in a strange room with a strange man, her insides being forced open. She wished Mama had warned her about the powerlessness a woman feels when a man puts himself inside her, about the shame that fills her when she is forced to give herself up, forced to be still. But this must be normal, Isra told herself. It must be.

So she lay there as Adam continued to thrust himself in and out of her until, in rapid succession, he let out a deep breath and collapsed on top of her. Then he lifted his body off hers and hobbled out of bed.

Isra rolled over and buried her face in the sheets. The room was dark and cold, and she pulled the blanket over her goosepimpled flesh. Where had he gone? After a moment, she heard him pacing in the bathroom. He flicked the light on, and she heard him open a cabinet. Then he turned the light off and returned to the room.

Isra didn't know why, but in that moment she thought she was going to die. She imagined Adam slicing her neck with a knife, shooting her in the chest, setting her on fire. What made her think these horrible things, she didn't know. But sprawled across the mattress, all she could see was darkness and blood.

She felt him nearing, and her heart began to swell. She couldn't see his face, but she felt him place his hands on her knees, and her legs twitched away instinctively. He leaned closer. Slowly, he spread her legs apart. Then he dabbed a rag against her split flesh.

He cleared his throat. "I'm sorry," he said. "But I have to."

Lying there, trembling, Isra thought of Fareeda. She imagined her creeping down to the bathroom earlier that day, smiling slyly as she placed a bundle of fresh cloth in the cabinet for her son to use. It was clear to Isra what Adam was doing: he was collecting evidence.

Deya

"**We're getting married** this summer," said Naeema as Deya and her classmates ate lunch. As seniors, all twenty-seven girls sat together at a single table in the back of the cafeteria. Deya sat at the very end of the table, curled against the wall in her usual way, head down. Her classmates chatted loudly around her, each engrossed in her own joys and sorrows. She listened to their banter in silence.

"The wedding will be held in Yemen, where Sufyan lives," Naeema continued. "My extended family lives there, too, so it makes sense."

"So you're moving to Yemen?" said Lubna. She was also getting married that summer, to her second cousin who lived in New Jersey.

"Yes," Naeema said with pride. "Sufyan owns a house there."

"But what about your family?" Lubna said. "You'll be alone there."

"I won't be alone. I'll have Sufyan."

For months now, Deya had listened quietly as Naeema explained the comings and goings of her relationship with Sufyan: how her parents had taken her back home to Yemen last summer to find her a suitor, that there she had met Sufyan, a rug maker, and fallen instantly in love. Their families had recited the *fatiha* prayer after the first visit, and by the end of the month, they had summoned a sheikh and signed the marriage contract. When one of her classmates had asked how she knew Sufyan was her *naseeb*, Naeema said that she had prayed *Salat al-Istikhara*, asking God for guidance, and that Sufyan had appeared to her that night in a dream, smiling, which her mother said was a sign to proceed with the marriage. They were in love, Naeema had said over and over, giddy with excitement.

"But you barely know him," Deya said now, the words slipping from her.

Naeema looked at her, startled. "Of course I know him!" she said. "We've been talking on the phone for almost four months now. I swear, I use up at least a hundred dollars a week in phone cards."

"That doesn't mean you know him," Deya said. "It's hard enough knowing someone you see every day, let alone a man who lives in another country." Her classmates stared, but Deya kept her eyes fixed on Naeema. "Aren't you afraid?"

"Afraid of what?"

"Of making the wrong decision. How can you just move to another country with a stranger and think it will all be okay? How can you—" She stopped, feeling her heart begin to race.

"That's how everyone gets married," Naeema said. "And couples move to different places all the time. As long as they love each other, everything is fine."

Deya shook her head. "You can't love someone you don't know."

"How would you know? Have you ever been in love?"

"No."

"So don't talk about something you don't know anything about."

Deya said nothing. It was true. She had never been in love. In fact, besides the nurturing love she had for her sisters, she had never felt love. But she had learned about love through books, knew enough of it to recognize its absence in her life. Everywhere she looked, she was blinded by other forms of love, as if God were taunting her. From her bedroom window, she'd watch mothers pushing strollers, or children hanging from their father's shoulders, or lovers holding hands. At doctors' offices, she'd flip through magazines to find families smiling wildly, couples embracing, even women photographed alone, their bright faces shining with self-love. When she'd watch soap operas with her grandmother, love was the anchor, the glue that seemingly held the whole world together. And when she flipped through American channels when her grandparents weren't looking, again love was the center of every show, while she, Deya, was left dangling on her own, longing for something other than her sisters to hold on to. As much as she loved them, it never felt like enough.

But what did love even mean? Love was Isra staring dully out the window, refusing to look at her; love was Adam barely home; love was Fareeda's endless attempts to marry her off, to rid herself of a burden; love was a family who never visited, not even on holidays. And maybe that was her problem. Maybe that's why she always felt disconnected from her classmates, why she couldn't see the world the way they did, couldn't believe in their version of love. It was because they had mothers and fathers who wanted them, because they were coddled in a blanket of familial love, because they had never celebrated a birthday alone. It was because they had cried in someone's arms after a bad day, had known the comforts of the words "I love you" growing up. It was because they'd been loved in their lives that they believed in love, saw it surely for themselves in their futures, even in places it clearly wasn't.

"I changed my mind," Deya told her grandparents that night as they sat together in the *sala*. It was snowing outside, and Khaled had forgone his nightly ritual of playing cards at the hookah bar because the cold worsened his arthritis. On nights like this, Khaled played cards with them instead, shuffling the deck with a rare smile, his eyes crinkled at the corners.

Deya looked forward to these nights, when Khaled would tell them stories of Palestine, even if many of them were sad. It helped her feel connected to their history, which felt so far away most of the time. Long ago, Khaled's family had owned a beautiful home in Ramla, with red-tile rooftops and bright orange trees. Then one day when he was twelve years old, Israeli soldiers had invaded their land and relocated them to a refugee camp at gunpoint. Khaled told them how his father had been forced to his knees with a rifle dug into his back, how more than 700,000 Palestinian Arabs had been expelled from their homes and forced to flee. It was the *Nakba*, he told them with somber eyes. The day of catastrophe.

They were playing Hand, a Palestinian card game, and Khaled shuffled together two decks of cards before dealing. Deya picked up her hand, scanning all fourteen cards, before saying again, louder, "I changed my mind."

She could feel her sisters exchanging looks. On the sofa beside them, Fareeda turned on the television to Al Jazeera. "Changed your mind about what?"

Deya opened her mouth, but nothing came. Even though she'd been speaking in Arabic her entire life, even though it was her first tongue, sometimes she struggled to find the right words in it. Arabic should've come as naturally to her as English, and it often did, but other times she felt its heaviness on her tongue, needed a split second of thought to check her words before speaking. Her grandparents were the only people she spoke Arabic with after her parents died. She spoke English with her sisters, at school, and all of her books were in English.

She put down her cards, cleared her throat. "I don't want to sit with Nasser again."

"Excuse me?" Fareeda looked up. "And why not?"

She could see Khaled staring at her, and she met his eyes pleadingly. "Please, Seedo. I don't want to marry someone I don't know."

"You'll get to know him soon enough," Khaled said, returning to his cards.

"Maybe if I could just go to college for a few semesters—"

Fareeda slammed the remote down with a thump. "College again? How many times have we talked about this nonsense?"

Khaled gave Deya a sharp glare. She hoped he wouldn't slap her.

"This is all because of those books," Fareeda continued. "Those books putting foolish ideas in your head!" She stood up, waved her hands at Deya. "Tell me, what are you reading for?"

Deya folded her arms across her chest. "To learn."

"Learn what?"

"Everything."

Fareeda shook her head. "There are things you have to learn for yourself, things no book will ever teach you."

"But—"

"*Bikafi!*" Khaled said. "That's enough!" Deya and her sisters exchanged nervous looks. "College can wait until after marriage." Khaled shuffled the cards for a new deck and turned his eyes to Deya again. "*Fahmeh*? Do you understand?"

She sighed. "Yes, Seedo."

"With that said . . ." He returned his eyes to the deck. "I don't see what's wrong with reading."

"You *know* what's wrong with it," Fareeda said, shooting him a wide-eyed look. But Khaled wouldn't look at her. Fareeda's jaw was clenching and unclenching.

"I don't see anything wrong with books," Khaled said, studying his cards. "What I think is wrong is you forbidding them." His eyes shifted to Fareeda. "Don't you think *that* will lead to trouble?"

"The only thing that will lead to trouble is being easy on them."

"Easy on them?" He fixed Fareeda with a glare. "Don't you think we shelter them enough? They come straight home from school every day, help you with all the household chores, never step foot out of the house without us. They don't have cell phones or computers, they don't talk to boys, they barely even have friends. They're good girls, Fareeda, and they'll all be married soon enough. You need to relax."

"Relax?" She placed her hands on her hips. "That's easy for *you* to say. I'm the one who has to keep them out of trouble, who has to make sure they maintain a good reputation until we marry them off. Tell me, who will be blamed if something goes wrong? Huh? Who will you point to when these books start putting ideas in their head?"

The atmosphere shifted. Khaled shook his head. "That's the price of coming to this country," he said. "Abandoning our land and running away. Not a moment goes by when I don't think of what we've done. Maybe we should've stayed and fought for our home. So what if the soldiers had killed us? So what if we

had starved? Better than coming here and losing ourselves, our
culture . . ." His words faded out.

"Hush," Fareeda said. "You know there's no use in that kind
of thinking. The past is the past, and no good will come from
regret. All we can do now is move forward the best we can, and
that means keeping our granddaughters safe."

Khaled did not reply. He sighed and excused himself to
shower.

Deya and her sisters were straightening the *sala* when Fareeda
appeared at the doorway. "Come with me," she said to Deya.

Deya followed her grandmother down the hall into her
bedroom. Inside, Fareeda opened her closet and reached for
something from the very back. She pulled out an old book and
handed it to Deya. A wave of familiarity washed over Deya as
she dusted off the hardcover spine. It was an Arabic edition of
A Thousand and One Nights. She recognized it: it had been her
mother's.

"Open it," Fareeda said.

Deya did as she was told, and an envelope slipped out. Slowly
she lifted the top. Inside was a letter, in Arabic. In the darkness
of the bedroom, she squinted to read:

> *August 12, 1997*
>
> *Dear Mama,*
> *I feel very depressed today. I don't know what's happen-*
> *ing to me. Every morning I wake up with a strange sensation.*
> *I lie beneath the sheets and I don't want to get up. I don't*
> *want to see anyone. All I think of is dying. I know God doesn't*
> *approve of taking a life, be it mine or someone else's, but I*

*can't get the thought out of my mind. My brain is spinning on
its own, out of my control. What's happening to me, Mama?
I'm so scared of what's happening inside me.*

Your daughter,
Isra

Deya read the letter again, then again, then one more time.
She pictured her mother, with her dark, unsmiling face, and felt
a flicker of fear. Was it possible? Could she have killed herself?

"Why didn't you show me this before?" Deya said, springing
from the bed and waving the letter in Fareeda's face. "All these
years you've refused to talk about her, and you've had this all
along?"

"I didn't want you to remember her this way," Fareeda said,
eyeing her granddaughter calmly.

"So why are you showing this to me now?"

"Because I want you to understand." She looked into Deya's
eyes. "I know you're afraid of repeating your mother's life, but
Isra, may Allah have mercy on her soul, was a troubled woman."

"Troubled how?"

"Didn't you just read the letter? Your mother was possessed
by a jinn."

"Possessed?" Deya said in disbelief. But deep down she wondered. "She was probably just depressed. Maybe she needed to
see a doctor." She met Fareeda's eyes. "The jinn aren't real, Teta."

Fareeda frowned and shook her head. "Why do you think
exorcisms have been performed all over the world for thousands of years, hmm?" She moved closer, snatching the letter
from Deya's fingers. "If you don't believe me, go read one of your
books. You'll see."

Deya said nothing. Could her mother have been possessed?

One of the memories she'd tried to forget hurtled to the front of her mind. Deya had come home from school one day to find Isra hurling herself off the basement stairs onto the floor. And not just once, but over and over. She had jumped again and again, both hands curled against her chest, her mouth hanging open, until she had noticed Deya standing there.

"Deya," Isra had said, startled to find her watching. Quickly she had stood, dragged herself across the basement. "Your sister is sick today. Go upstairs and get some medicine from the kitchen."

The feeling that had come over Deya that day, the twist in her stomach, she would never forget. She had wanted to tell Isra that she felt sick, too. Not with a cold or fever but something worse, only she couldn't find the words. Physical symptoms—is that what it meant to be sick? What about what happened on the inside? What about what was happening to her, Deya, what had been happening since she was a child?

Deya cleared her throat. What if Isra had been possessed? It would explain her memories, the letter, why her mother thought about dying. Suddenly she looked up at Fareeda. "The letter," she said. "When was it written?"

Fareeda eyed her nervously. "Why?"

"I need to know when my mother wrote it."

"It doesn't matter," Fareeda said, waving her hand. "No good will come from obsessing over the letter. I just want you to understand that your mother's unhappiness had nothing to do with marriage. You have to move on."

"Tell me when she wrote the letter," Deya demanded. "I won't leave until you do."

Fareeda sighed irritably. "Fine." She took the envelope out of *A Thousand and One Nights* and opened the letter.

Deya squinted at the date: 1997. Her stomach sank. That was

the year her parents had died. How could it be a coincidence? What if her mother hadn't died in a car accident after all?

She looked up at Fareeda. "Tell me the truth."

"About what?"

"Did my mother kill herself?"

Fareeda took a step back. "What?"

"Did she kill herself? Is that why you've refused to talk about her all these years?"

"Of course not!" Fareeda said, her eyes chasing a spot on the floor. "Don't be ridiculous."

But Deya could feel her nervousness—she was certain Fareeda was hiding something. "How do I know you're not lying? You've kept this letter from me all these years!" Deya fixed her eyes on her grandmother, but Fareeda wouldn't look at her.

"Did she?"

Fareeda sighed. "You won't believe me no matter what I say."

Deya blinked at her. "What's that supposed to mean?"

"The truth is, you're very much like your mother. So sensitive to the world." She looked up to meet Deya's eyes. "No matter what I say now, you won't believe me."

Deya looked away. Was it true? Had her fears been warranted? Had her mother planted a seed of sadness inside her from which there was no escape?

"Look at me," said Fareeda. "I might not know many things in life, but of this I am certain. You need to put the past behind you in order to move on. Believe me, this I know."

Isra

Spring 1990

Isra awoke feeling adrift and nauseated. She wondered why she hadn't been awakened at dawn by the distant sound of the *adhan*. Then she remembered: she was in Brooklyn, twelve thousand miles away from home, in her husband's bed. She sprang to her feet. But the bed was empty, and Adam was nowhere to be seen. A wave of shame rose in Isra's chest as she thought of the night before. She swallowed, forcing the feeling down. There was no point in dwelling on what had happened. This was just the way it was.

Isra paced from wall to wall of her new bedroom, running her hands over the wooden bed frame and dresser that filled the narrow space. Why was there not a single window? She thought longingly of all the nights she had spent reading by her open bedroom window back home, looking at the moon glowing over Birzeit, listening to the whisper of the graveyard, the stars so bright against the midnight sky she got goose bumps at the sight. She retreated to the other basement room, the one with the single window. The window was level with the ground, and from it, she could see past the front stoop, where a row of houses stood side by side, and beyond them, only a sliver of sky. America was supposed to be the land of the free, so why did everything feel tight and constricted?

Before long she was tired again and went back to bed. Fareeda had said it would take days for her body to adjust to the time change. When she finally awoke at sunset, Adam still wasn't home, and Isra wondered if he didn't want to be around her. Perhaps she had done something to upset him the night before when he'd put himself inside her. Perhaps she hadn't appeared eager enough. But how was she supposed to know what to do? If anything, Adam should've taken the time to teach her. She knew he must have slept with other women before marriage. Even though the Qur'an forbade the act for both genders, Mama said that men committed *zina* all the time, that they couldn't help themselves.

It was nearly midnight when Adam returned home. Isra was sitting by the window when she heard him descend the stairs, watched him as he switched on the basement light. He flinched when he saw her sitting by the window, both hands wrapped around her knees like a child.

"Why are you sitting here in the dark?"

"I was just looking outside."

"I thought you'd be asleep."

"I've been sleeping all day."

"Oh." He looked away. "Well, in that case, why don't you fix me up something to eat while I shower. I'm starving."

Upstairs, Fareeda had neatly assembled servings of rice and chicken in the fridge, each covered with plastic wrap and marked with one of her sons' names. Isra searched for Adam's plate and heated it in the microwave. Then she set the *sufra* the way Mama had taught her. A cup of water to the right, a spoon to the left.

Two warm loaves of pita. A small bowl of green olives and a few slices of tomatoes. An *ibrik* of mint chai brewed on the stove. Just as the teakettle whistled, Adam appeared in the doorway.

"It smells delicious," he said. "Did you cook?"

"No," Isra said, flushing. "I was asleep for most of the day. Your mother made this for you."

"Ah, I see."

Isra couldn't make out his tone, but his potential disappointment filled her with unease. "I'll be sure to cook for you tomorrow."

"I'm sure you will. Your father mentioned you were a good cook when we came to ask for you."

Was she a good cook? Isra had never stopped to consider this, much less think of it as a skill.

"He also said you were a woman of few words."

If Isra's face had been pink before, she was certain it was now crimson. She opened her mouth to respond, but words wouldn't come.

"I don't mean to embarrass you," Adam said. "There's no shame in being quiet. In fact, I appreciate the quality. There's nothing worse than coming home to a woman whose voice never stops."

Isra nodded, though she didn't know what she was agreeing to. She studied Adam from across the table as he ate, wondering whether he would be capable of giving her the kind of love she yearned for. She looked deep into his face, trying to find warmth in there. But his dark brown eyes were staring absently at something behind her, lost in a faraway place, as though he had forgotten she was there.

It wasn't until they were in bed that Adam looked at her again, and when he did, she smiled at him.

The smile surprised her as much as it surprised him. But Isra was desperate to please him. Last night his body had taken her by surprise, but now she knew what to expect. She told herself perhaps if she smiled and pretended to enjoy it, pleasure would come. Maybe that was all she had to do to make Adam love her: erase all traces of resistance from her face. She had to give him what he wanted and enjoy giving it to him, too. And she would do that. She would give him herself if it meant he'd give her his love.

It didn't take Isra long to learn the shape of her life in America. Despite her hopes that things might be different for women, it was, in most ways, ordinary. And in the ways it wasn't, it was worse. She hardly saw Adam most days. Every morning he left the house at six to catch the train to Manhattan, and he didn't return until midnight. She'd wait for him in the bedroom, listening for the door to open, for the clomp of his feet as he descended the stairs. There was always some reason to explain his absence. "I was working late at the convenience store," he'd say. "I was renovating my father's deli." "I couldn't catch the R train during rush hour." "I met up with friends at the hoo- kah bar." "I lost track of time playing cards." Even when he did manage to come home early, it wouldn't occur to him to take her out somewhere. Instead he spent hours idling in front of the television, a cup of chai in his hand, both feet lifted up on the coffee table, while Isra worked with Fareeda in the kitchen, preparing dinner.

When Isra wasn't helping Fareeda with the daily chores, she spent most of her time peering out the window. Another disap- pointment. Outside all she saw were rectangular houses. Bricks upon bricks, crammed against one another on both sides of the street. Plane trees stood in neat, straight lines along the paved sidewalk, their roots shooting through cracks in the cement. Flocks of pigeons glided across gray, overcast skies. And beyond the row of dull brick houses and worn cement blocks, beyond the line of London plane trees and dark gray pigeons—Fifth Avenue, with its tiny shops and zooming cars.

Fareeda was very much like Mama, Isra soon realized. She cooked and cleaned all day, dressed in loose cotton nightgowns. She sipped on chai and *kahwa* from sunrise until sunset. When Fareeda's sons were around, she doted on them as though they were porcelain dolls instead of grown men. She prepared dinner just the way they liked, baked their favorite sweets, and sent them off to work and school with Tupperware boxes filled with spiced rice and roasted meats. Like Mama, Fareeda had only one daughter, Sarah, who was to Fareeda what Isra had been to her mother—a temporary possession, noticed only when there was cooking or cleaning to be done.

The only difference between Mama and Fareeda was their practice of the five daily prayers, which Isra had never seen Fareeda complete. Fareeda awoke each day at sunrise and headed straight to the kitchen to make chai, muttering a quick prayer as the teakettle whistled: "God, please keep shame and disgrace from my family." Isra would stand quietly at the doorway, listening in awe as Fareeda mumbled at the stove. Once, she had asked Fareeda why she didn't kneel before God to pray, but Fareeda only laughed and said, "What difference does it make how I recite my prayers? This is what's wrong with all these religious folks these days. So hung up on the little things. You would think a prayer is a prayer, no?"

Isra would always agree with Fareeda so as not to upset her. She completed her five prayers downstairs in her bedroom, where Fareeda couldn't see. Sometimes, after Isra was done with her afternoon chores, she snuck to the basement to combine the *zuhr* and *asr* prayers before returning back to the kitchen unnoticed. Fareeda had never forbidden her from praying, but Isra wanted to be safe, wanted to win her love. Mama had never given her much love, only a dash here and there when she'd seasoned the lentil soup properly or scrubbed the floors so hard the cement almost sparkled. But Fareeda was so much stronger than Mama. Perhaps alongside that strength, she had more room for love.

After they had swept the floors, wiped the mirrors, thawed the meat, and soaked the rice, they would sit at the kitchen table, cups of chai to their faces, and talk, or at least Fareeda would, the whole world seeming to swirl between her lips. Fareeda would tell Isra stories about life in America, the things she did to pass time when she wasn't cooking and cleaning, like visiting her friend Umm Ahmed, who lived a few blocks away, or accompanying Khaled to the market on Sundays, or, when she was in a particular mood, attending the mosque on Fridays to catch up on the latest community gossip. Isra leaned forward, wide-eyed, inhaling Fareeda's words. In the few weeks since her arrival to America, she had grown to like Fareeda, admire her even. Fareeda, with her loud, boisterous opinions. Fareeda, with her unusual strength.

Now Isra and Fareeda folded laundry, the last of the day's work. The air between them was damp and smelled of bleach. Fareeda sat with her back against the washing machine, legs crossed under her, arranging black socks in matching pairs. Beside her, Isra sat in her usual way, legs folded tightly together, both arms in her lap as if to make herself smaller. She reached for a bright pair of men's boxers from the pile of unfolded laundry. She didn't recognize them. They must belong to one of Adam's brothers, she thought. She could feel her face flush as her fingers touched the fabric, and she quickly turned from Fareeda.

She didn't want to seem immature, reddening at the sight of men's underpants.

"It's nice to finally have someone to help me," Fareeda said, folding a pair of faded jeans.

Isra smiled wide. "I'm glad I can help."

"That's the life of a woman, you know. Running around taking orders."

Isra pushed aside a pair of mint-green boxers and leaned closer to Fareeda. "Is that what you do all day?"

"Like clockwork," Fareeda said, shaking her head. "Sometimes I wish I could've been born a man, just to see how it feels. It would've spared me a lot of grief in life." She reached for another pair of socks, stopped, and looked at Isra. "Men huff and puff about all the work they do to support their families. But they don't know—" She paused. "They have no idea what it means to be a woman in this world."

"You sound like Mama."

"She's a woman, isn't she? She would know."

There was a pause, and Isra reached for a piece of laundry. She wondered how Mama and Fareeda had come to suffer the same lonely fate, to have both lived a life without love. What had they done wrong?

"I thought things would be different here," Isra confessed.

Fareeda looked up. "Different how?"

"I thought maybe women only had it so tough in Palestine, you know, because of old customs and traditions."

"Ha!" Fareeda said. "You think women have it easier in America because of what you see on television?" Her almond eyes narrowed to slits. "Let me tell you something. A man is the only way up in this world, even though he'll climb a woman's back to get there. Don't let anyone tell you otherwise."

"But Khaled seems like he loves you so much," Isra said.

"Loves me?" Fareeda laughed. "Look at all I do for that man! I spread a full *sufra* for him every day, wash and iron his clothes, scrub every inch of this house so he can be at ease. I raised his children, these men and this girl, all while he was away. And you say he loves me?" Her eyes shifted to Isra. "Learn this now, dear. If you live your life waiting for a man's love, you'll be disappointed."

Isra felt sorry for Fareeda. How tired she must have been raising her children alone in a foreign country, waiting for Khaled to come home and love her. She wondered if that would be her fate as well.

"Do all the men in America work this much?" she asked, folding a white T-shirt.

"I used to wonder the same thing when we first came here," said Fareeda. "Khaled worked so many hours a day, leaving me alone with the children, sometimes until midnight! I was angry with him at first, but I realized it wasn't his fault. Most immigrants in this country work like dogs, especially the men. They have no choice. How else can we survive?"

Isra stared at her. Surely Adam was different, not like the men of Khaled and Yacob's generation. Things were hard right now, yes, but soon that would change. "Will Adam always work this much?"

"Oh, you'll get used to it," Fareeda said. "Soon you'll have children, and there will be other things to worry about." When Isra only looked at her, eyes widening, she added, "Believe me, you'll be thankful he's at work and not at home telling you what to do. I want to rip my hair out when Khaled takes a day off. Do this, do that. It's a nightmare."

But that's not the kind of relationship Isra wanted: she didn't want to be like Mama or Fareeda. She knew things were hard now because they barely knew each other. But surely everything would change when they became parents. Adam would have a reason to come home then. He would want to see his children, hold them, raise them. He would have a reason to love her. She turned to Fareeda. "But Adam will be home more when I bear children, right?"

"Oh, for goodness' *sake*," said Fareeda, her legs unfolding and then folding again. "Don't be a fool. Have you ever seen a man stay home to help raise children? That's your job, dear."

For a moment, Isra could hear Mama's voice in her head, mocking as she hunched over the stove. *Palestine or America. A woman will always be alone.* Had Mama been right all along? No, Isra told herself. That couldn't be true. She just needed to earn Adam's love.

Deya

Winter 2008

The days after reading Isra's letter felt muddled. Deya couldn't stop thinking. Could she have misjudged her mother? Could she have remembered her incorrectly? It was possible. What if her mother *had* been possessed by a jinn? That would explain why she had always been so sad, not because her marriage was unhappy or because she didn't want to be a mother, or worse, because she didn't want her. Still, Deya wasn't convinced. The jinn sounded like something from a fantasy novel—curses and exorcisms didn't happen in real life. Yet her mind raced of its own accord. Could her mother have taken her own life? And if she had, then how had her father died?

At home, Deya hardly spoke to her sisters. In school, she dragged herself from one class to the next, unable to focus even on Sister Buthayna's literature seminar, which she normally enjoyed the most, sitting forward in the very front row, her nose buried in whatever book they were reading. Staring out her classroom window now as Sister Buthayna read a passage from *Lord of the Flies*, Deya wondered if her grandmother was right. Maybe if she hadn't spent her days curled between the pages of a book, her back turned to the world, she'd have a better grasp on her life. Maybe she would know how to let go and move on. Maybe she would have realistic expectations for her future.

After school, she rode the bus home in silence, lifting her eyes from the window only when they reached their stop. She and her sisters walked down Seventy-Ninth street toward home, Deya moving quickly, as if she could outrun her thoughts, and her sisters trailing behind, dragging their feet along the snow-covered sidewalk. It was a cold, overcast day, and the air smelled like wet trees with a faint hint of something. Car fumes. Or stray cats maybe. It was a Brooklyn spice she often smelled on the seven-block walk to and from the bus stop. There was an empty coffee cup on the corner pavement, blue-and-white cardboard, crushed and mud-stained. She caught sight of the gold letters printed on it—WE ARE HAPPY TO SERVE YOU!—and sighed. She couldn't imagine a man coming up with that line. No, it must've been a woman.

Something caught Deya's attention as she turned the corner onto Seventy-Second Street. Farther down the block, a woman was lurking outside their home. Deya stopped to watch her. The woman was tall and thin, dressed in American clothes, with her hair pulled back in a ponytail. Deya couldn't tell exactly how old she was from where she stood—thirty perhaps, or maybe forty. Too young to be one of Fareeda's friends, too old to be one of her sisters'. Deya moved closer, staring.

The woman approached their front stoop in slow, careful movements, looking around as if she didn't want to be seen. Deya scanned her face. She couldn't map her features, but she felt as though she had seen the woman before. Something about her seemed so familiar. But who could she be?

There was something in the woman's hands: Deya couldn't make it out from where she stood. As she watched, the woman placed the thing carefully on their front stoop. Then, all at once, she turned and ran toward a cab waiting at the curb and disappeared inside.

Deya looked behind to find that her sisters had stopped and were talking among themselves. Something about Fareeda marrying them off, one after the other, like dominoes. Good, Deya thought. They hadn't noticed. She walked ahead, scanning the street: the cracked pavement, the dead grass, the green trash cans on the corner block. Everything seemed normal. Everything but the white envelope on the doorstep.

It was likely nothing. Her grandparents received mail all the time. Still, she snatched the envelope off the concrete. As she squinted at it, she realized why the woman had moved with such careful steps. The envelope didn't have her grandparents' names on it. Instead her own name was handwritten across the front in bold ink. A letter. For her. That was unusual. She tucked the envelope away before her sisters could see.

She waited until dark to open it, pretending to read a book until she was certain her sisters had fallen asleep. Then she locked the bedroom door and pulled the envelope out. The letters of her name—DEYA RA'AD—were still there. She hadn't dreamed it. She opened the envelope and looked inside. It wasn't a letter but a business card.

She pulled the card out and held it up under the lamplight. There was nothing unusual about it. Small, rectangular, crisp at the corners. Three bold words—BOOKS AND BEANS—took up most of the white space on the front, leaving room for a few lines at the bottom:

800 Broadway
New York, NY 10003
212-r e a d m o r

She flipped the card over. There was a note handwritten on the back in pen: ASK FOR MANAGER.

She ran her fingers over the card and imagined the strange woman doing the same. Who could she be? Deya closed her eyes and pictured the woman's face, hoping to see something she missed before, but instead, in that instant, all she could see was her mother. Suddenly a thought came to her—absurd, fantastical, but her mind clung to it, bewitched. Could it be? Could the woman be Isra? It was possible. After all, Deya had not seen the car accident, had not been to the funeral, which Fareeda had said was held in Palestine. But what if Fareeda had made the whole thing up? What if Isra was still alive?

Deya sat up in bed. Surely it was impossible. Both of her parents were dead—not just Isra. Fareeda couldn't possibly fake the death of two people. And to what end? Her mother had to be dead. If not in a car accident, then suicide. And even if she were alive, why would she come back after all these years? She wouldn't. She had barely wanted Deya ten years ago. Why would she want her now?

Deya shook her head, tried to will her mother out of her mind. Only she couldn't. The memories rushed to her in the usual, suffocating way: Isra, sitting in the kitchen with her back turned to Deya, rolling grape leaves on the table. Mesmerized, Deya had watched her stuff each leaf with rice and then roll it into a fingerlike shape before placing it in a large metal pot.

"You're really good at this, Mama," she'd whispered.

Isra didn't respond. She just pinched a bit of rice between her fingers and tasted it to make sure it was seasoned well. Then she stuffed another grape leaf.

"Can I try to roll one?" Deya asked. Still no response. "Mama, will you show me how?"

Without looking up, Isra passed her a grape leaf. Deya waited for directions, but Isra said nothing. So Deya imitated her. She cut the stem off a grape leaf, arranged a thin log of rice at the bottom, tucked both sides of the leaf across the top until the rice was completely covered. When she was done, she placed the stuffed leaf in the pot and looked to her mother's face for approval. Isra had said nothing.

Deya was pressing hard against the card now, bending it between her fingers. She hated that memory, hated all her memories. Trembling, she clenched the bookstore card in her fist. Who was this woman, and what did she want? Could she be her mother? Deya breathed in and out, trying to calm herself. She knew what she had to do. She would call the number the next day and find out.

The next day came slowly. In school, Deya walked around in a daze, wondering when she would have the opportunity to call the number. During Islamic studies, the last class before lunch, she waited impatiently for Brother Hakeem to finish his lecture. She stared at him absently as he rotated around the room, watched his mouth as it opened and closed. He had been her Islamic studies teacher ever since she was a child, had taught her everything she knew about Islam.

"The word *Islam* means *tawwakul*," Brother Hakeem said to the class. "Submission to God. Islam is about peace, purity, and kindness. Standing up to injustice and oppression. That's the heart of it."

Deya rolled her eyes. They couldn't possibly be Muslims, if that's what it meant. But then again, what did she know? Religion wasn't something she had learned at home—they weren't a devout Muslim family, not really. Once, Deya had contemplated wearing the hijab permanently, not just for her school uniform, but Fareeda had forbidden it, saying, "No one will marry you with that thing on your head!" Deya had been confused. She had expected Fareeda to be proud of her for trying to be a better Muslim. But after thinking about it more, she had realized that most of the rules Fareeda held highest weren't based on religion at all, only Arab propriety.

Lunch now, and Deya's only chance to call the number. She decided to ask quiet, pale-faced Meriem to use her cell phone. She was one of the few girls in class whose parents let her have a phone. Deya thought it was because Meriem was so innocent. Her parents didn't have to worry about her talking to boys or getting into trouble. In fact, not once in their years of school together had Meriem done anything wrong. Most of the girls in her class had found a way to break the rules at one time or another, even Deya. For her, it had been one Friday afternoon after *jumaa* prayer when she had thrown a metal chair from the fire escape. To this day, Deya didn't know why she had done it. All she could remember was her classmates staring at her with impish smiles, telling her that she didn't have the nerve, and then standing at the edge of the fire escape and plunging the chair down five stories with relish. The principal had called Fareeda to tell her that Deya had been suspended. But when she went home, head bowed, Fareeda had only laughed and said, "It doesn't matter. There are more important things to worry about than school."

It wasn't the only time Deya had broken the rules. She had once asked one of her classmates, Yusra, to buy her an Eminem

CD because she knew Fareeda would never allow it. Yusra's family wasn't as strict as Deya's grandparents, who only allowed her to listen to Arabic music. Yusra smuggled the Eminem CD to her in school, and Deya listened to it obsessively. She identified with the rapper's tension, admired his defiant attitude and courageous voice. If only Deya had that voice. Some nights, whenever she had a bad day at school or Fareeda had upset her, Deya would slip her headphones on and fall asleep listening to Eminem's words, knowing that somewhere out there was another person who felt trapped by the confines of his world—comforted by the fact that you didn't have to be a woman or even an immigrant to understand what it felt like to not belong.

Thinking of it now, that was the only time Deya could remember ever asking anyone to do something for her. It wasn't like her to ask for favors—she never wanted to be an inconvenience, a bother. But it was the only way now. In the lunchroom, she gritted her teeth and approached Meriem. Meriem gave her a small smile as she handed her the phone, and Deya tried not to flush in embarrassment as she rushed to the nearest bathroom. Inside, she turned away from her reflection in the mirrors. The face of a coward. The face of a fool. She entered a bathroom stall, closed the door behind her. She could feel her heart beating against her chest as she dialed the number. After four rings, someone picked up. "Hello," came a woman's voice.

Deya coughed. Her mouth had gone dry. "Umm, hi." She tried to keep her voice from cracking. "Is this Books and Beans?"

"Yes." A brief pause. "Can I help you?"

"Umm . . . can I speak to the manager? My name is Deya."

"Deya?"

"Yes."

Silence. Then, "I can't believe it's you." Deya could hear nervousness in the woman's voice.

She realized her hands were shaking, and she pressed the cell phone against her hijab. "Who is this?"

"This is . . ." The woman trailed off. Adrenaline poured through Deya.

"Who are you?" Deya asked again.

"I don't know where to begin," the woman said. "I know this must seem strange, but I can't tell you who I am over the phone."

"What? Why not?"

"I just can't."

Deya's heart thumped so hard she thought she could hear its echo in the bathroom stall. It all seemed like something out of a mystery novel, not real life.

"Deya," the woman said. "Are you there?"

"Yes."

"Listen—" Her voice was low now, and Deya could hear the dinging of a cash register in the background. "Can we meet in person?"

"In person?"

"Yes. Can you come to the bookstore?"

Deya considered. The only times she ever left the house alone were when Fareeda needed something urgently, like refreshments to serve unexpected visitors. She would hand Deya exact change and tell her to hurry to the deli on the corner of Seventy-Third Street for a box of Lipton tea, or to the Italian bakery on Seventy-Eighth Street for a tray of rainbow cookies. Deya thought of the breeze against her hair as she strolled up the block on those rare occasions. The smell of pizza, the distant jingle of an ice cream truck. It felt good to walk the streets alone, powerful. Usually Khaled and Fareeda accompanied Deya and her sisters everywhere—to their favorite pizzeria, Elegante on Sixty-Ninth Street, to the Bagel Boy on Third Avenue, sometimes even to the mosque on Fridays, crammed in the back of Khaled's '76 Chevy, eyes fastened to the floor whenever they passed a man. But on those rare walks alone, drifting down Fifth Avenue past men and women, Deya didn't have to lower her gaze; no one was watching. Yet she did so instinctively. Her eyes would not stay up even when she willed them to.

"I can't," Deya finally said. "My grandparents don't let me leave the house alone."

There was a long pause. "I know."

"How do you know what my grandparents are like? And how do you know where I live?"

"I can't tell you over the phone. We have to meet." She paused. "Maybe you could skip school. Is it possible?"

"I've never skipped school before," Deya said. "And even if I could, how would I know it's safe? I don't know you."

"I would never hurt you." The woman spoke softly now, and Deya thought her voice sounded familiar. "Believe me, I would never hurt you."

She knew that voice. But was it her mother's? Once again, the thought was absurd, but Deya considered. She remembered clearly the last time she had heard Isra's voice.

"I'm sorry," Isra had whispered, again and again. *I'm sorry.* Ten years later, and Deya still didn't know what her mother had been sorry for.

"Mama?" The words left Deya's lips in a rush.

"What?"

"Is that you, Mama? Is it?" Deya sank inside the bathroom stall. This woman could be her mother. She could. Maybe she was back. Maybe she was different. Maybe she was sorry.

"Oh, Deya! I'm not your mother." The woman's voice was shaking. "I'm so sorry. I'm not trying to upset you."

Deya heard herself sob before she realized she was crying. The next thing she knew, tears were rushing down her cheeks.

How low and desperate she felt, how much she wanted her mother—she'd had no idea until that moment. She swallowed her tears. "I'm sorry," she said. "I know my mother is dead. I know they're both dead." Silence on the line. "Who are you?" Deya finally said.

"Listen, Deya," the woman said. "There's something I need to tell you. Figure out a way to come to the bookstore. It's important." When Deya said nothing, the woman spoke again. "And please," she said. "Please, whatever you do, don't tell your grandparents about this. I'll explain everything when I see you, but don't tell anyone. Okay?"

"Okay."

"Thank you," the woman said. "Have a good day—"

"Wait!" Deya blurted.

"Yes?"

"When am I supposed to meet you?"

"Anytime. I'll be waiting for you."

Isra

Spring 1990

One cool April morning, six weeks after arriving in America, Isra woke to find her face duller than clay. She studied her reflection in the bathroom mirror. There was a deathly smoothness to her skin tone, and she brought her hands to her face, rubbed the dark bags under her eyes, tugged on a dry string of hair. What was happening to her?

Days passed before she felt it: a spool of yarn unraveling deep inside her belly. Then a tightness in her core. Then a warm sensation bubbling in the back of her throat. She rinsed her mouth, hoping to wash away the metallic taste on her tongue, but no amount of water would remove it.

There was a handful of white sticks in the bathroom drawer, pregnancy tests Fareeda had placed there for her to take every month, and Isra trembled as she took off the white wrapping. She could still remember the look on Fareeda's face the month before, when Isra had asked, blushing deeply, if she had any maxi pads. Without a word, Fareeda had sent Khaled to the convenience store, but Isra could tell from the twitch in her right eye, the sudden shift in the room, that she was not happy.

"I'm pregnant," Isra whispered when she met Fareeda in the kitchen, holding up the white stick as if it were fine glass.

Fareeda looked up from a bowl of dough and smiled so widely Isra could see the gold tooth in the back of her mouth. "*Mabrouk*," she said, wetness filling her eyes. "This is wonderful news."

Isra felt a deep happiness at the sight of Fareeda's smile. She had not felt this way in so long she hardly recognized the warm feeling inside her.

"Come, come," Fareeda said. "Sit with me while I bake this bread."

Isra sat. She watched Fareeda as she floured the dough, wrapped it in cloth, and set it in a corner. Fareeda reached for another bundle of dough, stored beneath a thick towel, and pressed her index finger against it. "It's ready," she said, stretching the sticky gob of wheat between her fingers. "Pass me the baking pan."

Fareeda cut the dough into individual knots and arranged each one on the pan. Then she drizzled them with olive oil and popped them in the oven. Isra watched quietly as the bread baked, not knowing what to say or do. Fareeda was humming to herself, plucking the steaming loaves from the oven before they burned. Isra wished she could store her cheeriness in a bottle. The last time Fareeda had smiled widely enough for Isra to see her gold tooth had been when Adam had given her a bundle of bills, five thousand dollars. It was extra money the deli had made that month, and he had told Fareeda he wanted her to have it. Isra could still remember the bulge in Fareeda's eyes at the sight of the money, the way she gripped it close to her chest before disappearing into her bedroom. But now Isra could see, from the approving glimmer in Fareeda's eyes, that her pregnancy was far more important than money. She stared inside the oven, feeling her stomach rise and fall with the swelling and collapsing of every knot of pita. Was this happiness she felt? She thought it must be.

Adam came home early that day. From the kitchen Isra heard him take off his shoes and enter the *sala*, where Fareeda was watching her evening show. "*Salaam*, Mother," he said. Isra listened as Fareeda kissed him on both cheeks and congratulated him.

Was he happy? Isra couldn't tell. She had spent the afternoon worrying about how he would react to the news, wondering whether he wanted a child now, or if he would've preferred to wait a couple of years until they could better afford it. More than once, Fareeda had mentioned that Adam was helping them pay for Ali's college tuition, so how would they have enough money to cover the expense of a newborn? When she'd asked, Fareeda had merely smiled and said, "Don't worry about that. With food stamps and Medicaid, you can have as many children as you want."

Adam hummed a melody from an Abdel Halim song as he walked to the kitchen, grinning when he met Isra's eyes. "I can't believe I'm going to be a father," he said.

Isra exhaled in relief. "*Mabrouk*," she whispered. "Congratulations."

He pulled her to him, wrapping one arm around her waist and placing his hand on her belly. She tried to keep from flinching. She still wasn't used to his touch. Sometimes she thought it was strange to be a girl like her, to go from a man never touching her to the full force of a husband inside her. It was a sudden transition, and she wondered when she would become accustomed

to it, or if she would ever come to crave it like women were supposed to.

"You have to be careful now," Adam said, stroking her flat
stomach. "I don't want anything to happen to our child."

Isra studied him, shocked by the softness of his voice, the
way the lines around his eyes multiplied when he smiled.
Maybe he would spend more time with her now. Maybe all he
needed was a child after all.

"Life will change now, you know," Adam said, looking down
on her. "Having children, a family . . ." He paused, tracing his
finger against her belly as though he were writing across it. "It
changes everything."

Isra met his eyes. "How?"

"Well, for one thing, there will be more work for you to do.
More washing and cooking, more running around. It's tough really." When Isra said nothing, staring at him with wide eyes, he
added, "But children are the pleasure of life, of course. Just like
the Qur'an says."

"Of course," Isra said, remembering that she hadn't yet completed *maghrib* prayer. "But will you help me?"

"What?"

"Will you help me?" she said again, her voice slipping. "With
our child?"

Adam stepped back slightly. "You know I have to work."

"I just thought maybe you'd come home early some days,"
Isra said in a whisper. "Maybe I'd see you more."

He sighed. "You think I want to work day and night? Of
course not. But I have no choice. My parents depend on me to
support the family." He stroked Isra's face with the back of his
hand. "You understand that, right?" She nodded.

"Good." His eyes shifted to the stove, distracted by a cloud of
steam. "Now what's for dinner?"

"Spinach and meat pies," said Isra, feeling slightly embarrassed. It was ludicrous of her to expect Adam to leave work to help her. Had any man she'd ever known helped his wife raise children? Motherhood was her responsibility, her duty.

She moved closer to Adam, hoping he would say something more. But without another word, he walked toward the stove, pulled a spinach pie off the plate, and began to chew.

"No, no, no," Fareeda said one evening after tasting the cup of chai Isra had made her during her soap opera's commercial break. "What is this?"

"What's wrong?" said Isra.

"This chai is bitter."

Isra took a step back. "I brewed it just the way you like, with three springs of *maramiya* and two spoonfuls of sugar."

"Well, it tastes horrible." She handed Isra back the cup. "Just pour it out."

Be grateful, Isra wanted to say. Be grateful that a pregnant woman is making you tea and cooking and cleaning while you sit here watching television. "I'm sorry," she said instead. "Let me make you another cup."

Fareeda gave a burdened smile. "You don't *have* to."

"No, no, I *want* to," Isra said. "I do."

In the kitchen, Isra picked the greenest sprigs of *maramiya* from the sage plant on the windowsill. She placed a tea packet into the kettle only after the water had boiled over twice, making sure the sugar crystals had dissolved. She wanted the chai to be perfect. Yet even as she strove to please, she remembered all the times she'd overspiced her brothers' falafel sandwiches, when they yelled at her for not ironing their school uniforms properly, the time she'd murmured "I hate you" under her breath when

Yacob beat her. But Isra would spend her life with Fareeda. She needed her love, and she would do what was necessary to earn it.

"Where's Sarah?" Fareeda asked when Isra handed her the fresh cup of chai. "Is she in her room?"

"I think so," Isra said.

"*La hawlillah*," Fareeda muttered. "What am I going to do with that girl?"

Isra said nothing. She had learned to recognize when Fareeda was only talking to herself. Sarah was a sensitive subject for Fareeda. On days when Isra was up early enough to pray *fajr*, she would find Fareeda standing in the hall, arms crossed, studying Sarah's outfit to make sure it was appropriate for school. "Behave yourself," Fareeda would say, almost spitting. "And no talking to boys, understood?"

"I *know*, Mama," Sarah would always respond. Later, after school, Fareeda ensured that every second of Sarah's time was spent making up for her time in school. Isra knew how it felt to be the only girl in a house of men, a placemat beneath their feet, but she wondered how Sarah felt about it. From the rebellious look on Sarah's face whenever Fareeda spoke, Isra sensed her resentment.

"Sarah!" Fareeda shouted from the base of the stairs. "Come down here!"

"Coming!" Sarah called back.

"Go see what's taking her so long," Fareeda told Isra when Sarah still hadn't come a minute later. Isra did as she was told. At the top of the staircase, she could see Sarah in her room. She was reading, holding the book to her face like a shield, inhaling the words as if they were fueling her somehow. Isra was mesmerized by the sight.

"What is she doing?" Fareeda yelled from the bottom of the staircase.

"I don't know," Isra lied.

"Sure you don't." Fareeda stomped up the staircase.

"Sarah . . . ," Isra whispered in an attempt to warn her. But it was too late. Fareeda was already at the top of the stairs.

"I knew it!" She stormed into the room and snatched the book from Sarah's hand. "Why didn't you come downstairs like I asked?"

"I wanted to finish the chapter."

"Finish the chapter?" Fareeda placed her hand on her hips. "And what makes you think some book is more important than learning how to cook?"

Sarah let out a sigh, and Isra felt her stomach drop. In her head she could hear Mama's voice saying that books had no use, that all a woman needed to learn was patience, and no book could teach her that.

"Tell me," Fareeda said, moving closer to Sarah. "Will books teach you how to cook and clean? Will they help you find a husband? Will they help you raise children?"

"There's more to life than having a husband and children," Sarah said. "I never hear you telling Ali to stop studying or put down his books. How come he's allowed to go to college? Why don't you ever pressure him about marriage?"

"Because marriage is what's important for girls," Fareeda snapped. "Not college. You're almost a teenager. It's time you grew up and learned this now: A woman is not a man."

"But it's not fair!" Sarah shouted.

"Don't backtalk to me," Fareeda said, lifting her open palm. "Another word, and I'll slap you."

Sarah recoiled from her mother's hand. "But Mama," she said, softer this time, "it really isn't fair."

"Fair or not, that's the way of the world." She turned to leave. "Now go downstairs and help Isra in the kitchen."

Sarah sighed, pulling herself off the bed.

"Let's go!" Fareeda said. "I don't have all day."

In the kitchen, Isra and Sarah stood with their backs to one another, each with a rag in hand. Sarah was a short, slim girl with golden skin and wild, curly hair that dropped past her shoulders. Usually she said very little when they cleaned together, though sometimes she'd catch Isra's eyes and sigh loudly.

In the months that Isra had lived there, she and Sarah had barely spoken to one another. As soon as Sarah came home from school, the first thing she did was sneak into her room to drop off her backpack. Isra realized now she was likely hiding her books. Then Sarah would join her in the kitchen to help set the *sufra*, or wash dishes, or fold any extra laundry Isra had not already finished. Some evenings they sat together in the *sala* with Fareeda and watched her favorite Turkish soap operas. Sarah sipped mint chai and ate tea biscuits, and, when Fareeda wasn't looking, cracked roasted watermelon seeds using only her front teeth, a habit Fareeda usually forbade to stop Sarah from ruining her perfect smile.

Now Isra felt sorry for Sarah as she watched her scurry around the kitchen, wiping counters, washing dishes, and rearranging the cups in the cupboard. Is this what she had looked like back home, in Mama's house, running in circles until all the housework was done?

"So, how are you feeling?" Fareeda asked Isra, squatting in front of the oven to watch a batch of sesame cookies bake. It was her third batch this week.

"*Alhamdulillah*," Isra said, "I feel good."

Fareeda removed the batch of cookies from the oven. "Have you been having morning sickness?"

"No," Isra said, unsure.

"That's a good sign." Isra noticed that Sarah had stopped what she was doing to listen to her mother. "How about cravings?" Fareeda said. "Have you been craving sweets?"

Isra considered the question. "Not more than usual."

Fareeda pinched the edge of a cookie, popped it in her mouth. Her eyes widened as the taste settled on her tongue. "That's also a good sign."

"A good sign of what?" Sarah interrupted. Her face looked almost yellow in the warm evening light cast through the window, and in that instant Isra couldn't help picture Fareeda's open palm against her cheek. She wondered how often Sarah was hit.

"Well," Fareeda said, "according to old wives' tales, a woman who has morning sickness and craves sweets is carrying a girl."

Sarah said nothing but frowned at her mother.

"But you aren't experiencing either," Fareeda told Isra with a grin. "So you must be carrying a boy!"

Isra didn't know what to say. She felt a twist in her core. Maybe she did have morning sickness after all.

"Why the sour face?" said Fareeda, reaching for another cookie. "You don't want a boy?"

"No, I—"

"A boy is better, trust me. They'll care for you when you're older, carry on the family name—"

"Are you saying you weren't happy when you had me?" Sarah asked sharply. "Because I wasn't a precious boy?"

"I'm not saying *that*," Fareeda said. "But everyone wants a boy. You ask anyone, and they'll tell you."

Sarah shook her head. "I don't get it. Girls are the ones that help their mothers. Omar and Ali don't do *anything* for you."

"Nonsense. Your brothers would give me an arm and a leg if I needed."

"Sure they would," Sarah said, rolling her eyes.

Listening to Sarah, Isra wondered if this was what it meant to be an American: having a voice. She wished she knew how to speak her mind, wished she could've said those things to Mama: that girls were just as valuable as boys, that their culture was unfair, and that Mama, as a woman, should've understood that. She wished she could've told Mama that she was sick of always being put second, of being shamed, disrespected, abused, and neglected unless there was cleaning or cooking to be done. That she resented being made to believe she was worthless, just another thing a man could claim at will.

"Don't mind what Mama says," Sarah whispered to Isra when Fareeda left the kitchen.

Isra looked up, startled to hear Sarah speak to her directly. "What do you mean?"

"Your child is a blessing no matter what, even if it's a girl."

Isra tugged on the edges of her nightgown and looked away. She remembered uttering those very same words to Mama when she was pregnant: *It's a blessing no matter what*. She didn't want to be one of those women who didn't want a daughter, didn't want to be like Mama, who told Isra she had cried for days after she was born.

"Of course it's a blessing," Isra said. "Of course."

"I don't understand what's so special about having sons," Sarah said. "Is your mother this way, too?"

"Yes," Isra admitted. "I hoped things would be different here."

Sarah shrugged. "Most of my American friends at school claim their parents don't care. But you should listen to my mom's friends. They're unbelievable. If it was up to them, we'd still live in Arabia and bury our female infants alive."

Sarah made a face at her, and Isra couldn't help but feel as though she was looking at a younger version of herself. She'd never imagined they'd share anything in common: Sarah was raised in America, had attended a co-ed public school, had led a life so different from her own. Isra attempted a small smile and was rewarded when Sarah grinned back.

"So, do you know any English?"

"I can read and write," Isra said proudly.

"Really? I didn't think anyone in Palestine knew English."

"We learn English in school."

"Can you speak it?"

"Not well," Isra said, blushing. "My accent is very heavy."

"I'm sure it's not that bad. My brother said you went to an all-girls school, and that I should be thankful our parents send me to public school."

"I can't imagine what that must be like," Isra said. "You know, going to school with boys. My parents never would've allowed it."

"Well, my parents don't have much choice. They can't afford the all-girls schools around here. Technically, I'm not supposed to talk to the boys in my class, but what am I supposed to do? Walk around with a sign on my head that says 'Please don't talk to me if you're a boy'?" Sarah rolled her eyes.

"But what if your parents find out that you disobey them?" Isra asked. "Fareeda almost slapped you earlier. Won't they beat you?"

"Probably," Sarah said, looking away.

"Do you . . . Do they hit you often?"

"Only if I backtalk or don't listen. Baba beat me with his belt once when he found a note in my bag from my friend at school, but I try to make sure I never get caught doing anything they won't like."

"Is that why you sneak your books home?"

Sarah looked up. "How did you know that?"

Isra gave another small smile. "Because I used to sneak books home, too."

"I didn't know you like to read."

"I do," Isra said. "But I haven't read in a while. I only brought one book here with me."

"Which one is that?"

"*A Thousand and One Nights*. It's my favorite."

"*A Thousand and One Nights*?" Sarah paused to think. "Isn't that the story of a king who vows to marry and kill a different woman every night because his wife cheats on him?"

"Yes!" Isra said, excited that Sarah had read it. "Then he's tricked by Scheherazade, who tells him a new story for a thousand and one nights until he eventually spares her life. I must have read it a million times."

"Really?" Sarah said. "It isn't *that* good."

"But it is. I just love the storytelling, the way so many tales unfold at once, the idea of a woman telling stories for her life. It's beautiful."

Sarah shrugged. "I'm not a big fan of make-believe stories."

Isra's eyes sprung wide. "It's not make-believe!"

"It's about genies and viziers, which don't exist. I prefer stories about real life."

"But it is about real life," Isra said. "It's about the strength and resilience of women. No one asks Scheherazade to marry the king. She volunteers on behalf of all women to save the daughters of Muslims everywhere. For a thousand and one nights, Scheherazade's stories were resistance. Her voice was a weapon—a reminder of the extraordinary power of stories, and even more, the strength of a single woman."

"Someone read the story a little too deeply," Sarah said with a smile. "I didn't see strength or resistance when I read it. All I saw was a made-up story starring a guy murdering a bunch of helpless women."

"Someone's a cynic," Isra said.

"Maybe a little."

"What's your favorite book?"

"*Lord of the Flies*," Sarah said. "Or maybe *To Kill a Mockingbird*. It depends on the day."

"Are those romances?" Isra asked.

Sarah gave a harsh laugh. "No. I prefer more realistic fiction."

"Love is realistic!"

"Not for us."

It was as though Sarah's words had smacked her across the face, and Isra looked down to regain her composure.

"If you want," Sarah said, "I can bring home some books for you tomorrow. Don't worry, I'll make sure they're romances."

Isra smiled, a brief uneasy smile. She thought of Fareeda, catching her one day as she read an English novel, a romance even. No, she didn't want to upset her. She swallowed. "It's okay. I prefer Arabic novels."

"Are you sure? I know a few English novels you'd like."

"Really," Isra said. "I won't have time to read with a newborn, anyway."

"Suit yourself."

Isra meant what she said about not having time to read. In fact, lately she had begun to wonder if she was ready to be a mother. It wasn't just how busy Fareeda kept her, but she worried she had nothing to give to a child. How could she teach a child about the world when she knew nothing of the world herself? Would she be a good mother—and what did a good mother look like? For the first time in her life, Isra wondered if she wanted to be like Mama. She wasn't sure. She hated how easily

Mama had abandoned her to a strange family in a foreign country. But deep down, Isra knew Mama had only done what Yacob
wanted—she'd had no choice. Or had she? Had her mother had
a choice all along? Isra wasn't sure, and later that evening she
found herself sitting by the window thinking about the choices
she might soon have to make as a mother. She hoped she would
make the right ones.

That night, Adam came home from work before the sun had set.
He appeared in the kitchen doorway wearing faded black trou-
sers and a blue collared shirt. Isra didn't notice him standing
there at first, as she stared absently at the orange sky through
the window. But then he cleared his throat and said, "Let's go
out."

Isra tried to hide her excitement. The only time she left the
house was occasionally on Sundays, when Khaled and Fareeda
went grocery shopping and took Sarah with them. When they
didn't take Sarah, Fareeda would ask Isra to stay behind to look
after her, afraid to leave her in the house unsupervised. Adam
hadn't taken Isra out since her first night in Brooklyn.

Outside the air was crisp, the streetlamps already glowing.
They strolled together down Fifth Avenue, past the butcher
shops, supermarkets, bakeries, and dollar stores. The streets
were just as lively as they had been the first time Isra had walked
them. Traffic congested the roads, and crowds of pedestrians
swept in and out of the shops and eateries. The sidewalks were
worn and dirty, and the air smelled faintly of raw fish, which
Adam said came from the Chinese fish market at the corner of
the block. Every now and then, dark green gates framed wide
staircases that descended into the sidewalks.

"These are called subway stations," Adam said, promising to

take her on the train soon. Isra walked closely beside him, one hand over her plump belly, the other dangling freely. She wished he would hold her hand, but he sucked on a cigarette and stared ahead.

They crossed the street to a shop called Elegante's, where Adam bought Isra a slice of pizza. He said it was the best pizzeria in town. Isra had never tasted anything like it. She bit into the warm, thin bread slathered in cheese, sucked the savory sauce from her fingertips. She marveled at the rich combination of flavors, the comfort they brought her even though they were brand-new.

"Did you like it?" Adam asked when she had finished.

"Yes," she said, licking the last bit of sauce from the corners of her mouth.

Adam laughed. "Do you have room for dessert?" She nodded eagerly.

He bought her an ice cream cone from a Mister Softee truck. Vanilla swirl with rainbow sprinkles. Isra devoured it. The ice cream they sold in her village *dukan*—strawberry sorbet or mulberry fruit served plainly on a stick—was nothing like this. This was creamy and so rich.

Adam watched her eat with a proud smile, as though she were a child. "Another?"

She brought both hands to her belly. "*Alhamdullilah.* I'm full."

"Good." He reached into his pocket for a cigarette. "I'm glad." Isra blushed.

They turned to walk home. Isra held her breath as Adam blew cigarette smoke into the air. He was nothing like the men she'd read about in books. No *faris*, or prince charming. He was always restless, even after a long day's work, fidgeting with his dinner or biting his fingertips. He was prone to absentmindedness, a faraway look in his eyes. He clenched his teeth when he was irritated. He always smelled like smoke. Still, she thought, she liked his smile, the way a dozen lines crinkled around his eyes and brought his face to life. She also liked the sound of his voice, slightly melodious, perfect for calling the *adhan*, or so she imagined—she had never seen him pray.

Back outside the house, he turned to look at her. "Did you enjoy our walk?"

"I did."

He took a long drag of his cigarette before crushing it against the sidewalk. "I know I should take you out more often," he said. "But I'm so busy at work. I don't know where the time goes between the deli and my store in the city."

"I understand," Isra said.

"Some days it feels like time is slipping through my fingers like water, as though one day I'll wake up to find it all gone." He stopped, reaching out to touch her belly. "But it will be worth it, you know. Our children won't have to struggle like we did. We'll give them a good life."

Isra looked at him for a moment, feeling, for the first time, grateful for his hard work. She smiled and placed both hands on her belly, her fingers grazing his. "Thank you for everything you do," she said. "Our children will be proud."

Deya

Winter 2008

"**I just got** off the phone with Nasser's mother," Fareeda told Deya when she returned from school that afternoon. Her eyes were full of satisfaction. "He's coming to see you again tomorrow."

Deya poured Fareeda a cup of chai in the *sala*, only half listening. She couldn't stop thinking about the woman from Books and Beans. Should she skip school to go meet her? What if her teacher called Fareeda and said she'd missed school? What if she got lost trying to find the bookstore? What if something happened to her on the train? She'd heard stories about how dangerous the subway was, how women were often mugged, raped, even murdered in its murky corners. There was no way she could afford a cab with the measly vending-machine money Fareeda gave them. But she had to try—she needed to know why the woman had reached out. She couldn't live with not knowing.

"I'm surprised Nasser wants to see you again," Fareeda continued, reaching for the remote. "Seeing as you've managed to scare off every single suitor I've found you this year. Somehow the boy saw through your nonsense."

"I'm sure you're happy," Deya said.

"Well, of course I'm happy." Fareeda flicked through channels. "A good suitor is all a mother wants for her daughter."

"Is this what you wanted for your daughter, too? Even though it meant never seeing her again?" Fareeda had married Sarah to a man from Palestine when Deya was still a small child, and she hadn't seen her since.

"That was different," Fareeda said. Her hands were shaking, and she set the remote down. Mentioning Sarah always hit a nerve. "You're marrying right here in Brooklyn. You're not going anywhere!"

"But still," Deya said. "Don't you miss her?"

"What does it matter? She's gone, and that's the way it is. I've told you a thousand times not to mention my children in this house. Why are you so difficult?"

Deya looked away. She wanted to stomp around the room, kick the door and walls, break the glass of the window. She wanted to scream at Fareeda. *I refuse to listen to you!* she'd tell her. *Not until you tell me the truth about my parents!* But when she drew a breath, the words dissipated. She understood her grandmother well enough to know she would never admit the truth. If Deya wanted answers, she would have to find them herself.

The next morning, at the bus stop, Deya made up her mind. She was going to the bookstore.

"Listen," she told her sisters as they waited for the bus. "I'm not going to school today."

"Where are you going?" Nora asked, eyeing her curiously. Deya could see Layla and Amal staring at her in disbelief.

"There's something I have to do." She felt the tip of the book-store card in her *jilbab* pocket. "Something important."

"Something like what?" Nora asked.

Deya scrambled for a convincing lie. "I'm going to the library to fill out college applications."

"Without Fareeda's permission?"

"What if you get caught?" Layla said. "Fareeda will kill you."

"She's right," Amal added. "I don't think it's a good idea."

Deya looked away, toward the approaching school bus. "Don't worry about me," she said. "I know what I'm doing."

Once the bus had disappeared around the corner, Deya plucked the bookstore card from her pocket and read the address again: 800 Broadway, New York, NY 10003.

She squinted at the tiny print, realizing for the first time that the bookstore wasn't in Brooklyn, it was in Manhattan. A mixture of panic and nausea rose inside her. She'd only been to Manhattan a handful of times, always in the back seat of Khaled's car. How was she supposed to get there on her own? She took a deep breath. She'd have to ask for directions just as she'd planned. Nothing had changed. She walked to the nearest subway station on Bay Ridge Avenue and descended the dark steps, her heart pounding furiously, *beat-beat-beat*. The station was crowded with strange faces, and for a moment Deya wanted to turn around and run home. She froze, watching the people push past her, listening to the beeping sounds their cards made as they swiped them through the metal barricades. There was a glass booth at the back of the platform, with a man slumped behind the counter. Deya approached him.

"Excuse me, sir." She pressed the business card against the glass. "Can you tell me how to get to this address?"

"Broadway?" His eyes shot to the top of his head. "Take the R train. Manhattan bound."

She blinked at him.

"Take the R train," he said again, slower. "Uptown toward Forest Hills–Seventy-First Avenue. Get off at Fourteenth Street–Union Square Station."

R train. Uptown. Union Square Station. She memorized the words.

"Thank you," she said, reaching inside her pocket for a bundle of one-dollar bills. "And how much is a train ticket?"

"Round trip?"

She sounded out the unfamiliar combination of words. "Round trip?"

"Yes."

"I'm not sure what that means."

"Round trip. To get to the city and back."

"Oh." She felt her face burn. He must think she was a fool. But it wasn't her fault. How was she supposed to understand American lingo? Her grandparents had only allowed them to watch Arabic channels growing up.

"Yes," she said. "Round trip, please."

"Four dollars and fifty cents."

Almost half her weekly allowance! She slipped the warm bills through the glass. Luckily, she saved most of her vending-machine money. She only spent it on books, which she bought from yard sales, school catalogs, even off her classmates, who'd become accustomed to selling her their used novels over the years. She knew they felt sorry for her because she didn't have a normal family.

There was a loud rumble in the distance. Startled, she grabbed the mustard-yellow subway card and hurried toward the metal poles. Another rumble, more aggressive this time. From the sudden movement around her, Deya realized the sounds were coming from the trains, and that people were rushing to catch them.

She hurried along with them, mimicking their ease, swiping her card through the metal groove in one smooth motion. When the card didn't register, she swiped it again, more carefully this time. *Beep.* It worked! She pushed through the turnstile.

In the darkness of the platform, Deya bit her fingertips and stared anxiously around her, the racket of passing trains making her jump. A man caught her attention as he walked to the end of the platform. He unzipped his pants and a stream of water began to pour onto the tracks in front of him. It took her a few moments to realize he was urinating. Her breath came in short bursts and she turned away, focusing her attention on a rat scurrying across the tracks. Soon she heard another rattle, then a faint whistling sound. Looking up, she could see a light shining from a tunnel beyond the end of the platform. It was the R train. She took a deep breath as it zoomed past her and shuddered to a halt.

Inside the train was loud, crammed with the onslaught of daily life. Around her people stared absently ahead or into their phones, transfixed. They were Italian, Chinese, Korean, Mexican, Jamaican—every ethnicity Deya could possibly imagine— yet something about them seemed so American. What was it? Deya thought it was the way they spoke—their voices loud, or at least louder than hers. It was the way they stood confidently on the train, not apologizing for taking up the space.

Watching them, she understood yet again what it meant to be an outsider. She kept picturing them looking down at her like a panel of judges. *What are you?* she imagined them thinking. *Why are you dressed this way?* She could see the judgment brewing in their eyes. She could feel them observing how scared she was standing there, how unassuredly she moved, the garb she wore, and deciding instantly that they knew everything about her. Surely she was the victim of an oppressive culture, or the enforcer of a barbaric tradition. She was likely uneducated, un-civilized, a nobody. Perhaps she was even an extremist, a ter-rorist. An entire race of culture and experiences diluted into a single story.

The trouble was, regardless of what they saw, or how little they thought of her, in her own eyes Deya didn't see herself much better. She was a soul torn down the middle, broken in two. Straddled and limited. Here or there, it didn't matter. She didn't belong.

It took her nearly five minutes of squeezing through the train to find an empty seat. A woman had moved her leather suitcase so she could sit. Deya studied her. Bright skin. Honey-colored hair. Perfectly round tortoiseshell glasses. She looked so confident, sitting there in a tiny black dress. Her legs were long and lean, and Deya caught a whiff of her perfume. Flowers. Deya thought she must be someone important. If only she, Deya, could be someone important. There was so much she wanted to do, so many places she wanted to see, yet here she was, a nobody, struggling even to ride the train so many people used every day without a second thought.

The woman was staring back at her now. Deya did her best to smile. These days it was hard enough for people like her to walk around in jeans and a T-shirt, let alone a hijab and *jilbab*. It wasn't fair she had to live this way, always afraid of what peo-ple saw when they looked at her. She finally understood why Fareeda had banned them from wearing the hijab outside of school, finally saw how fear could force you to change who you were.

After a few deep breaths, Deya took a furtive look around the train car. Everywhere she turned, people were staring. There was that feeling again inching up her chest. She swallowed, tried to push it down, but it clung in her throat. She turned to face the

darkened window. Why did she have to be so afraid, so sensitive, so affected by the world? She wished she could be stronger,
wished she could be one of those people who could listen to a
sad song without bursting into tears, who could read something
horrible in the news without feeling sick, who didn't feel so
deeply. But that wasn't her.

The R train seemed to go on forever, stopping at countless
stations. Deya stared out the window, reading the signs three
times at each station to make sure she didn't miss her stop.
Fourteenth Street–Union Square Station. At Court Street, the con-
ductor announced it was the last stop in Brooklyn, and Deya
realized the train was about to pass through a tunnel that ran
under the Hudson River. The thought of being underwater both
frightened and fascinated her. She wondered how it was possible to build a tunnel underwater, how extraordinary its designer
must have been. She tried to picture herself creating something
beautiful, changing the world somehow, but couldn't. Soon she
would get married, and then what? What kind of life would she
lead? A predictable life of duty. She squeezed the card tight. But
maybe Fareeda was right. Maybe her life would turn out differently than Isra's. Maybe Nasser would let her be who she wanted
to be. Maybe once she was married, she could finally be free.

Isra

Fall 1990

One overcast November morning, three weeks before she was due, Isra went into labor. Adam and Fareeda took her to the hospital but refused to come into the delivery room. They said they didn't like the sight of blood. Isra felt a deep terror as they wheeled her into the room alone. She had watched Mama give birth once. The sound of her pain was a permanent fixture in Isra's mind. But this was even worse than she could have imagined. As the contractions came harder and faster, it felt as though crimes were being committed inside her. She wanted to scream out, like Mama had, but for some reason she found herself unable to open her mouth. She didn't want to display her pain, not even in sounds. Instead she sucked on her teeth and wept.

It was a girl. Isra held her baby daughter in her arms for the first time—she stroked the softness of her skin, placed her against her chest. Her heart swelled. I'm a mother now, she thought. I'm a mother.

When, at last, they entered the room, Fareeda and Adam locked their eyes on the ground and murmured a quiet "*Mabrouk.*" Isra wished Adam would say something to comfort her or show excitement.

"Just what we need," Fareeda said, shaking her head. "A girl."

"Not now, Mother," Adam said. He passed Isra an apologetic look.

"What?" Fareeda said. "It's true. As if we need another *balwa*, as if we don't have enough troubles."

Isra felt a jolt at the word. She could almost hear Mama's voice ringing in her ears. Mama had often called Isra a *balwa*—a dilemma, a burden. Any lingering hope that America would be better than Palestine fell away at that moment. A woman would always be a woman. Mama was right. It was as true for her daughter as it had been for Isra. The loneliness of this reality seemed to leach out of the white hospital floor and walls into her.

"Please, Mother," Adam said. "There's nothing we can do about it now."

"Easy for you to say. Do you *know* how hard it is to raise a girl in this country? *Do* you? Soon you'll be pulling your hair out! You need a son to help you. To carry on our name." She was crying now, a deep sucking sound coming from her mouth, and the nurse handed her a box of tissues.

"Congratulations," said the nurse, mistaking Fareeda's tears for happiness. "What a blessing."

Fareeda shook her head. She met Isra's eyes and whispered, "Keep these words close, like a piercing in your ear: If you don't give a man a son, he'll find him a woman who can."

"That's enough, Mother!" Adam said. "Get up, let's go. Isra needs to rest." He turned to leave, shifting his eyes back to Isra on the way out. "Don't worry," he said. "You'll have a son, *inshal-lah*. You're young. We have plenty of time."

Isra passed him a weak smile, holding back tears. How much she wanted to please them. How much she wanted their love. There was music playing in the room, a soft melody the nurse had put on during the labor. Now Isra took it in for the first time, and it soothed her. She asked if the nurse could replay it, asked its name. *Moonlight Sonata*. Isra shut her eyes to the slow, waft-ing melody and told herself everything would be okay.

"*Bint*," Isra heard Fareeda say whenever someone called to con-gratulate them. *A girl*.

Isra pretended not to hear. Her daughter was beautiful. She had coffee-colored hair and fair skin and eyes as deep as midnight. And a good baby, too. Quiet but alert. Isra hummed her awake and lulled her to sleep, skin on skin, hearts touching. In those mo-ments, she felt a newfound warmth spread over her, the way the sun felt on her face when she had gone fruit-picking back home. She named her daughter Deya. *Light*.

Deya's birth had indeed brought light to Isra's life. Within days of coming home from the hospital, Isra's love for Deya had spread over her like a wildfire. Everything seemed brighter. Deya was her *naseeb*, Isra told herself. Motherhood was her pur-pose. This was why she had married Adam, why she had moved to America. Deya was the reason. Isra felt at peace.

She had always imagined love as the kind she read about in books, like the love Rumi and Hafiz described in their poems. Never once had motherly love crossed her mind as her *naseeb*. Perhaps it was because of her relationship with Mama, the sprinkles of love she'd fought so hard for and found so lacking.

Or perhaps it was because Isra had been raised to think that love was something only a man could give her, like everything else.

Shame, she told herself. How selfish she had been to not appreciate Allah's goodness all along. To not trust in His plan. She was lucky. Lucky to be a mother, and lucky—she reminded herself—to have a place to call her own. Many families back home still lived in refugee camps, each shelter barely two feet away from the next. But this basement was her home now. Deya's home. They were lucky.

As Isra placed her daughter in the crib, her heart swelled with hope. She laid down her prayer rug and prayed two *rak'ats* thanking Allah for all he had given her.

Part 2

Part 2

Fareeda

Spring 1991

It was Fareeda's idea to not breastfeed Deya. Breastfeeding prevented pregnancy, and Adam needed a son. Isra obeyed her without resistance, mixing bottles of formula in the kitchen sink, hoping, Fareeda knew, to regain her favor. She studied Isra's swollen breasts, a certain guilt rising beneath her ribs. A certain memory at the familiar sight. Fareeda pushed it away. There's no point in dwelling on the past, she told herself.

And it worked. Four months later, Isra was pregnant again.

On the car ride home from Dr. Jaber's office, Fareeda sat in the passenger seat. Beside her, Khaled tapped his fingers against the steering wheel, humming a melody by the Egyptian singer Umm Kulthum. Fareeda had a full view of Isra in the rearview mirror, holding Deya tightly in the back seat as she stared out the window, watching a flock of pigeons peck crumbs on the sidewalk. Fareeda turned to face her.

"Didn't I tell you?" Fareeda said. "I knew you'd get pregnant soon if you didn't breastfeed."

Isra smiled. "I hope Adam will be happy."

"Of course he will."

"But what if he doesn't want another baby right now?"

"Nonsense. Children are the glue that keep a husband and wife together."

"But what if—" Isra paused, taking a breath. "What if it's another girl?"

"No, no, no," Fareeda said, settling back in her seat. "It'll be a boy this time. I can feel it."

Khaled raised an incredulous eyebrow. "You feel it?"

"Yes, I can! A woman's instinct."

"Sure you can," he said, laughing. "I don't know why you're still obsessing over sons. *Alhamdulillah*, we have plenty."

"Oh, really?" Fareeda turned to him. "And where was this kindness when *I* was getting pregnant, or did you forget the torture you put me through?"

He looked away, red-faced.

"Now you have nothing to say, do you?"

"*Bikafi*." Khaled fixed her with a glare. "Enough."

Fareeda shook her head. How could he be so insensitive after all these years, after everything he had put her through? After everything she had done for him? *Because* of him. She took a breath and pushed the thoughts away. Fareeda understood her place in the world. The wounds of her childhood—poverty, hunger, abuse—had taught her that the traumas of the world were inseparably connected. She was not surprised when her father came home and beat them mercilessly, the tragedy of the *Nakba* bulging in his veins. Nor was she surprised when he married her off to a man who beat her, too. How could he not, when they were so poor that their lives were filled with continuous shame? She knew that the suffering of women started in the suffering of men, that the bondages of one became the bondages of the other. Would the

men in her life have battered her had they not been battered themselves? Fareeda doubted it, and it was this awareness of the hurt
behind the hurt that had enabled her to see past Khaled's violence
over the years and not let it destroy her. There was no point in
moping around. She had decided early on in her marriage to focus
only on the things she could control.

She ripped her eyes away from Khaled and returned her gaze
to the rearview mirror. "Don't listen to him," she told Isra. "*Inshallah*, you'll have a son this time."

But Isra still seemed worried.

Fareeda sighed. "And if it *is* a girl, and it won't be, but if, God
forbid, it *is*, then it won't be the end of the world."

Isra met her eyes in the glass. "It won't?"

"No," Fareeda said. "You'll get pregnant again, that's all." Isra
was lucky. As if anyone had ever been so kind to her.

"Let's go." Fareeda stood in the kitchen doorway and peered
down at Isra, who was on her knees, in a faded pink nightgown,
reaching for a cobweb beneath the fridge. They had just finished
mopping the floors, kneading the dough, and putting a pot of
okra stew on the stove to simmer.

"Where are we going?" Isra asked.

Fareeda straightened the hemline of her navy-blue *thobe*,
pulling it down over her pudgy midsection. "We're going to visit
my friend Umm Ahmed," she said. "Her daughter-in-law just
gave birth to a baby boy. Umm Ahmed's very first grandson."

Isra's hands drifted toward her belly. Forcefully, she pulled
them away. Fareeda knew the subject made her uncomfortable.
Watching Isra tug on the edges of her nightgown, she even felt
sorry for the girl. Perhaps she shouldn't put so much pressure on

her, but how else were they to secure their lineage in this country? How else were they to secure their income in the future?
Besides, it wasn't as if Isra was the only woman in the world
shamed for bearing a girl. It had always been this way, Fareeda
thought. It might not be fair, but she didn't make the rules. It
was just the way it was. And Isra was no exception.

Outside the air was crisp, the tips of their noses stinging from
the leftover winter wind. Fareeda led the way, and Isra followed with Deya in her stroller. It hadn't occurred to Fareeda
until that moment that neither of them had left the house since
the visit to Dr. Jaber. The weather had been too cold. Khaled
had gotten their weekly groceries alone, driving to Fifth Avenue on Sunday mornings to get halal meat from the butcher
shop, and on Fridays, after *jumaa* prayer, to Three Guys from
Brooklyn in search of the zucchini and eggplants Fareeda
liked. She couldn't wait to accompany him again now that the
weather was warming up. Fareeda didn't like to admit it, had
never even said it out loud, but in the fifteen years she had lived
in America, she could easily count the number of times she
had done anything outside their home without Khaled. She
couldn't drive or speak English, so even when she did leave the
house, poking her head uneasily from the door before ventur-
ing out, it was only for a stroll around the corner to visit one
of her Arab neighbors. Even now, walking only a few blocks
to Umm Ahmed's house, Fareeda found herself glancing behind her, wanting to turn back. At home, she knew where her
bed was, how many tugs were needed to start the furnace, how
many steps it took to cross the hall into the kitchen. There, she
knew where the clean rags were, how long it took to preheat

the oven, how many dashes of cumin to sprinkle in the lentil soup. But here, on these streets, she knew nothing. What would happen if she got lost? What if someone assaulted her? What would she do? Fifteen years in this country, and she still didn't feel safe.

But it's better than living in a refugee camp, Fareeda reminded herself as she eyed the passing cars nervously, gathering herself to cross the street. Better than the years she and Khaled had wasted in those shelters. She thought of the broken roads of her childhood, of days spent squatting beside her mother, sleeves rolled up to the elbows, washing clothes in a rusted barrel. Days when she would stand in line for hours at the UN station, waiting to collect bags of rice and flour, or a bundle of blankets to keep them from freezing in the harsh winters, wobbling under their weight as she carried them back to her tent. Days when the open sewers smelled so harshly that she walked around with a laundry pin on her nose. Back then, in the refugee camp, her body carried her worry like an extra limb. At least here, in America, they were warm and had food on their table, their own roof over their heads.

They reached Umm Ahmed's block. All the houses looked the same, and the people strolling the sidewalks looked the same, too. Not in how they dressed, which Fareeda found distasteful, with their ripped jeans and low-cut tops, but how they moved, rushing across the street like insects. She wondered how it felt to be an American, to know exactly where you were heading each time you left your front door, and exactly what you would do when you got there. She had spent her entire life being pushed and pulled, from kitchen to kitchen, child to child. But it was better this way, she thought. Better to be grounded, to know your place, than to live the way these Americans lived, cruising from day to day with no values to anchor them down. It's no wonder they ended up alone—alcoholics, addicts, divorced.

"*Ahlan wasahlan*," Umm Ahmed greeted them as she led Fareeda and Isra into the *sala*. Inside, other women were already seated. Fareeda knew all of them, and they stood to greet her, exchanging kisses on the cheek, smiling as they stole glances at Deya. Fareeda could see Isra flush in embarrassment. Most of these women had come to congratulate them when Deya was born, and made crass remarks about Isra not having a son. More than once, she'd had to pass Isra a look, clearing her throat and signaling her to relax. She wished Isra understood that such comments were normal, that she shouldn't take everything so personally. But Isra was sensitive, Fareeda thought, shaking her head. Too sensitive. She hadn't seen enough of the world to be otherwise.

"Thank you for coming," Umm Ahmed said as she poured Fareeda and Isra cups of chai. Then she served them a purple container of Mackintosh's chocolates, waiting until each woman had plucked a shiny piece from the box before returning to her seat.

"*Alf mabrouk,*" Fareeda said, unwrapping a yellow caramel stick. "A thousand congratulations."

"Thank you." Umm Ahmed turned to Isra, resting her eyes on her swollen belly. "*Inshallah* your turn soon, dear."

Isra nodded, her jaw tightening. Fareeda wished she would say something nice to Umm Ahmed, or to any of the women in the room for that matter. They must all think she was a fool, always so quiet and vacant. Fareeda had wanted a daughter-in-law she could show off to her friends, like a twenty-four-karat gold bangle. Yes, Isra could cook and clean, but the girl knew nothing about entertaining and socializing. She was as dull as dishwater, and there was nothing Fareeda could do about it. She would have to choose more carefully when finding Omar a wife.

"So tell me," Fareeda said to Umm Ahmed, who sat in the middle of the room. "Ahmed must be so excited to give his parents the first grandson."

"Oh yes," Umm Ahmed said, careful not to meet Isra's eyes. "*Alhamdulillah*. We're all very happy."

"There is no better blessing than a healthy baby boy," said one of the women. "Of course, we all love our daughters, but nothing compares to having a son."

"Yes, yes," Fareeda agreed. She could sense Isra's eyes on her, but she didn't want to seem envious by not participating in the conversation. "Adam does everything for us—running the family business, helping with the bills. I don't know what we would've done if he'd been a girl."

The women nodded. "Especially in this country," said one of them. "The boys are twice as needed and the girls are twice as hard to raise."

Fareeda laughed. "Exactly! I only have Sarah, and raising her in this country gives me nightmares. God help any woman who has to raise a daughter in America."

The women nodded in agreement. Glancing at Isra, whose eyes were locked on Deya's face, Fareeda felt sorry she had to hear those words. But it was the truth. It was better she learned now, Fareeda thought. Then maybe she wouldn't think it was just Fareeda who thought this way. It wasn't just her! Every woman in the room knew this to be true, and not just them, but their parents and their parents' parents and all the generations before them. Perhaps if Isra realized how important having a son was, she wouldn't be so sensitive about it.

Umm Ahmed poured the women another round of chai. "Still," she said, her face hidden behind the steam. "What would we have done without our daughters? Fatima and Hannah do everything for me. I wouldn't trade them for a thousand sons."

"Hmm," Fareeda said, snatching a piece of chocolate from the purple Mackintosh's container and shoving it into her mouth. She was glad Sarah wasn't here to hear this.

"So I'm assuming Ahmed named the boy after his father," Fareeda said.

"Yes," Umm Ahmed said, placing the teapot on the coffee table and leaning back in her seat. "Noah."

"So, where is baby Noah?" one of the women asked, looking around the *sala*. "And where is Ahmed's wife?"

"Oh, yes," Fareeda said. "Where *is* your daughter-in-law?"

Umm Ahmed shifted in her seat. "She's upstairs, sleeping."

The women stared at her blankly. Fareeda scoffed. She could see Isra staring at Umm Ahmed, wide-eyed, perhaps wishing that she was her mother-in-law instead.

"Oh, come on," Umm Ahmed said. "Don't you remember how it felt staying up with a baby all night? The girl is exhausted."

"Well, I sure don't remember sleeping," Fareeda said. The women chuckled, and Umm Ahmed dug her hands between her thighs.

"All I remember is cooking, cleaning, and picking up after people," Fareeda said. "And Khaled waiting for me to serve him as soon as he got home."

It was as if Fareeda's words had ignited a fire in the room. The women began crackling with conversation, chatting about how exhausted they were, how there was nothing more to their lives than scurrying around the house like cockroaches.

"Of course I remember," Umm Ahmed said. "But things are different now."

"Are they?" Fareeda asked.

"If my daughter-in-law needs to sleep, then why not? Why can't I help her a little bit?"

"Help her?" Fareeda met Isra's eyes briefly and then turned away, hoping she didn't expect the same from her. "Shouldn't *she* be helping *you*?"

"Fareeda is right," a woman on the opposite sofa added. "What's the point of marrying off our sons if we are going to help their wives? The point is to lessen our burdens, not add to them."

Umm Ahmed laughed quietly, tugging on the rim of her blouse. "Now, ladies," she said. "You all remember how it felt coming to America? We came without a mother or a father. Just a husband and a handful of kids. Do you remember how it felt when our husbands went off to work in the morning, leaving us alone to raise our children, in a place where we didn't even speak the language? Do you remember how awful those years were?"

Fareeda said nothing. The women sipped their chai, peering at Umm Ahmed behind their cups.

"My daughter-in-law is here alone," Umm Ahmed said. "The same way I once was. The least I can do is help her."

Fareeda wished Umm Ahmed hadn't said that. The last thing she wanted was for Isra to start expecting the same treatment from her. That's one thing she always hated about women: how quick they were to compare themselves to others when it suited them. God forbid she remind Isra that at least Umm Ahmed's daughter-in-law had given them a son. Not another girl. As if Fareeda needed another girl. A splotch of memory came to her, but she pushed it away. She hated thinking of it. Hated thinking of them. Trembling, she unwrapped a piece of chocolate, the crisp sound of the foil wrapping like white noise in her ears. She swallowed.

Deya

Winter 2008

One step onto Fourteenth Street, and Deya was shaking. The city was loud—screeching—like all the noise in the world had been let out at once. Yellow cabs slammed on brakes, cars honked, and people swerved by like hundreds of Ping-Pong balls flying jaggedly across a room. It was one thing to look at the city from the back seat of her grandfather's car, another thing entirely to stand dead in the middle of it, to smell every whiff of its garbage and grease. It felt as if someone had let her loose in a giant maze, only she was stuck between thousands of people who knew exactly where to go, shoving past her to get there.

She read the address once, and then again. She had no idea where to go. She could feel the sweat building along the edge of her hijab. What had made her come to Manhattan on her own? It was a stupid idea, and now she was lost. What if she couldn't get back to the bus stop in time? What if her grandparents found out what she had done—that she had skipped school and ridden the subway? That she was in the city? The thought of Khaled's open palm against her face made her knees shake.

A man paused beside her, head bowed, typing into his cell phone. Should she ask him for directions? She looked around for a woman, but they all flew past her. She forced herself to approach him.

"Excuse me, sir," she said, wiping sweat from her hijab.

He didn't look up.

She cleared her throat, said it louder. "Excuse me . . ."

He met her eyes. She felt a conscious effort on his part not to let his eyes wander around her head. "Yes?"

She handed him the card. "Do you know where I can find this bookstore?"

The man read the card and handed it back to her. "I'm not sure," he said. "But eight hundred Broadway should be that way." He pointed to a street in the distance, and she marked the spot where his fingers landed.

"Thank you so much," she said, feeling a heat rise in her cheeks as he walked past her. She was pathetic. She didn't know where she was going, couldn't even look a man in the eye without turning into a bright red crayon. Not only was she not an American, but she could barely even count herself as a person, feeling as small as she did at that moment. But she shoved these thoughts away, saved them for another time when she would sit and think of just how tiny she felt on the city streets. She started down the street in the direction the man had pointed.

Books and Beans stood at the end of an inconspicuous block on Broadway. Except for the black-trimmed door and windows, the entire bookstore was painted a bright, moroccan blue, standing out from the red-brick-faced shops around it. Through the glass, Deya could see a display of books within the dim space, illuminated by amber-shaded lamps. She stared at the windows for what felt like hours before building up the courage to walk in.

Deya stepped into the bookstore and waited for her eyes to adjust to the darkness. Inside was a single room, much longer than it was wide. The walls were lined with black shelves and filled with hundreds of books that towered up to the ceiling. Velvet tufted chairs sat snugly in odd corners of the room, providing a soft contrast to the exposed brick walls, and a cash register stood near the entrance, lit by the dim flicker of a lamp. Beside the register sat a plump white cat.

Slowly, she made her way down the center aisle. A few people floated between the shelves, their faces hidden in shadows. She must be in here somewhere, Deya thought, running her fingers across the spines of old books, inhaling the scent of worn paper. Marveling at the rich selection, she found herself drifting toward a set of chairs near the back of the shop, wanting desperately to curl up against a window and crack open a book. But then she saw a shadow move from beside a pile of unorganized books. A person was staring at her. A woman.

Deya approached her. When she was close enough, the woman's face emerged from the darkness. Now she was certain: it was the same woman who had dropped off the envelope. She was staring at Deya's hijab and school uniform, smiling. Clearly the woman knew who she was.

But Deya still didn't recognize her. She studied her face closely, hoping against hope that it was her mother. It was possible. Like Isra, the woman had deep black hair and fair olive skin. Yet her hair fell wild and wavy over her shoulders, her cheeks were full and bronzed, her lips a crimson red. Isra's hair had been straight and smooth, her features plainer. Deya moved closer. She was startled to see the woman wearing a short skirt, her legs covered only with sheer panty hose, and she wondered how she was able to walk around town without feeling exposed. She must be American, Deya decided.

"Is that you, Deya?"

"Do I know you?"

The woman gave her a sad look. "You don't recognize me?"

Deya moved closer, studying her face again, carefully this time. There was something familiar in the openness of her eyes, the way they held her gaze in the dim light. She froze, a piece clicking into place. Of course! How could she not have recognized her sooner?

"Sarah?"

Isra

Spring 1991

Isra's second pregnancy was a quiet struggle. In the mornings, while Deya slept, she kneaded dough and soaked rice. She diced tomatoes and onions, simmered stews and roasted meat. She swept the floors, washed the dishes, cracked the kitchen window to air the house when she was done. Then she mixed a bottle of formula and returned to the basement, where she crooned her daughter awake. Her growing belly prevented her from holding Deya like she used to, so she propped the bottle against the crib instead, swallowing her growing guilt as she watched her suckle from a distance.

Isra returned downstairs once her afternoon chores were done. She lay in bed and stroked her belly as Deya sucked on her bottle. Upstairs, the sounds followed their usual rhythm. Sarah jerking the front door open when she returned from school, dragging her backpack to her room. Fareeda commanding she join her in the kitchen. Sarah pleading, "I have homework!" More than once, Isra had considered asking Sarah to bring her a book from school, only to change her mind. She couldn't risk upsetting Adam, who'd been working longer hours since Deya's birth. Besides, when would she have the time to read, with another child on the way?

She kept her hands on her belly, tried to picture the baby growing inside her: Was it a boy or a girl? What would happen to her if she bore another girl? The night before, Fareeda had mentioned going back home to find Omar a wife and joked that she would find Adam a new wife, too, if Isra gave them another girl. Isra had forced a laugh, unsure of Fareeda's actual intentions. It was possible. She knew women back home whose husbands had married again because they couldn't bear a son. What if Fareeda was serious? She shook the fear away, feeling foolish at the thought. It shouldn't matter if her baby was a girl. Even the Qur'an said that girls were a blessing, a gift. Lately she had been reciting the verse in her prayers. *Daughters are a means to salvation and a path to Paradise.* She traced her belly and muttered the verse again.

Now she smiled, the prayer filling her with hope. She needed *tawwakul*, submission to God's will. She had to trust in His plan for her. She had to have faith in her *naseeb*. She reminded herself how blessed she had felt when Deya was born. What if Allah had made her pregnant again so soon in order to give her a son? Maybe a son would make Adam love her. She closed her eyes and recited another prayer, asking God to grow love in Adam's heart.

She had failed to earn his love despite her many efforts. She had learned to recognize the patterns of his behavior, to anticipate his shifting temperament, to better please him. Most nights, for instance, Adam's mood was volatile—particularly when Fareeda gave him a new request, like paying another semester of Ali's college tuition, or when Khaled asked him to work longer hours in the deli. To compensate, Isra would be extra accommodating, slipping into her best nightgown, fixing his dinner plate just the way he liked, reminding herself not to complain or provoke him. Then there were nights when he would come home jolly, smiling at her when she greeted him in the kitchen, sometimes even pulling her in for an embrace, rubbing his scratchy beard against her skin. With this small gesture, she would know he was in a good mood, and that, after dinner, he would roll on top of her, pull up her nightgown and, breathing heavily in her ear, press himself into her. In the dark, she would close her eyes and wait for his panting to settle, unsure whether to feel happy or sad about his good mood. Uncertain whether she would have preferred for him to come home angry.

"Why are you so quiet?" Adam said when he came home from work one night, slurping on the *freekeh* soup she had spent the day preparing. "Did I marry a statue?"

Isra looked up from her bowl, which she had placed on the table because Adam said he didn't like eating alone. She could feel her face burn with shock and embarrassment. What did Adam expect her to say? She did nothing besides cook and clean all day, her hand in Fareeda's hand, never a moment's rest. She had nothing interesting to talk about, unlike Adam, who left to work every morning, who spent most of his day in the city. Shouldn't he initiate the conversation? Besides, he had told her he liked quiet women.

"I mean, I knew you were quiet when I married you," Adam said, shoving a spoonful of soup into his mouth. "But a year with my mother should've loosened you up." He looked up from his bowl, and Isra noticed that his eyes were glassy and bloodshot. She wondered if he was sick.

"She is quite the woman, my mother," Adam said. "Nothing like any of the women in your village, I'm sure."

Isra studied his face. Why were his eyes so red? She had never seen him like this before.

"No, not Fareeda," he mumbled to himself. "One of a kind, as her name suggests. But she earned that right, you know, after all she's been through." He propped both elbows on the kitchen table. "Did you know that her family relocated to the refugee camps when she was six years old? Probably not. She doesn't like to talk about it. But she lived a tough life, my mother. She married my father and raised us in those camps, rolled up her sleeves and endured."

Isra met his eyes and then looked quickly away. Even if she tried to act like Fareeda, she couldn't. She wasn't strong enough.

"Speaking of my mother," he said, wiping his mouth with the back of his hand, "what have you two been up to lately?"

"Sometimes we visit the neighbors when the chores are done," Isra said.

"I see, I see."

She watched him shovel food into his mouth. She didn't know what to make of his unusual behavior, but she thought she'd ask if she'd done something wrong. She swallowed dry spit. "Are you angry with me?"

He took a gulp of water and looked at her. "Why would I be angry with you?"

"Because I had a daughter. Or maybe because I'm pregnant again. I don't know." She looked down at her fingers. "It feels like you're avoiding me. You barely come home anymore."

"You think I don't want to come home?" he said, waving his hands. "But who else is going to put food in your mouth? And buy diapers and baby formula and medicine? You think living in this country is cheap?"

"I'm sorry. I didn't mean it like that."

"I'm doing the best I can to support this family! What more do you want from me?"

Isra considered telling him that she wanted his love. That she wanted to see him and get to know him, wanted to feel like she wasn't raising a child on her own. But if he didn't understand that, then how could she explain it? She couldn't. She was a woman, after all. It wasn't her place to be forward in her affections, to ask a man for his time, for his love. Besides, any time she tried, he scorned her attempts.

Instead Isra willed herself to make a request she had been brewing in her mind but had been too scared to ask: "I was hoping maybe you could teach me how to navigate Fifth Avenue. Sometimes I want to take Deya for a walk in the stroller, but I'm afraid I'll get lost."

Adam put his fork down and looked up at her. "Go out to Fifth Avenue on your own? Surely that's out of the question."

Isra stared at him.

"You want to take a stroll down the block? Sure. But there's no reason for you to be out on Fifth Avenue alone. A young girl like you on the streets? Someone would take advantage of you. So many corrupt people in this country. Besides, we have a reputation here. What will Arabs say if they see my young wife wandering the streets alone? You need anything, my parents will get it for you." He pushed himself up from the table. "*Fahmeh*? Do you understand?"

She couldn't stop looking at his eyes. How red they were. For a moment she thought perhaps he had been drinking, but she quickly dismissed it. Drinking *sharaab* was forbidden in Islam, and Adam would never commit such a sin. No, no. He worked too hard, that was all. He must be getting sick.

"Do you understand?" he said again, more slowly.

"Yes," she whispered.

"Good."

Isra stared at her plate. She thought back to her silly hopes, before coming to America, that she might have more freedom here. She had the familiar urge to break one of the plates on the *sufra*, but instead she dug her fingers into her thighs, squeezed tight. She breathed and breathed until the familiar throb of rebellion dissipated. She was only nineteen, she reasoned. Adam must be afraid for her safety. Surely he would give her more freedom when she got older. And then a new hope occurred to her: perhaps his overprotectiveness was out of love. Isra wasn't sure if that was one of the things love made you do, possess someone. But the possibility made a warm feeling rise up inside her. She put her hands on her stomach and allowed herself a small smile, a rare moment of peace.

Deya

Winter 2008

Deya was convinced she was dreaming. She stood in the center of the bookstore, staring at Sarah, stunned. There was so much to say, and she opened her mouth, searching for the right words, but none came to her.

"Let's sit," Sarah said with a wave of her hand. Her voice was strong, declamatory.

Deya followed her down the bookstore, mesmerized. She glanced at all the books, hundreds of them, covering most of the exposed brick walls. There was a café bar at the end of the room, with coffee tables arranged around it, and a few people sat with books and cups of coffee in hand. She followed Sarah to the corner of the café, where they settled opposite each other on a pair of chairs by a window. The smell of coffee and the overcast winter sun through the window created a warm glow between them.

"I'm sorry I couldn't tell you who I was over the phone," Sarah began. "I was afraid you'd tell my parents I called."

"I'm confused," Deya said, sitting up. "I thought you were in

Palestine. How long have you been back? Why don't Teta and Seedo know you're here?"

"That's a long story," Sarah said in a soft voice. "It's part of the reason I reached out."

Deya blinked at her. "What's the rest?"

"I know they want you to marry soon. I wanted you to know you have choices."

"Choices?" Deya could feel herself start to laugh. "Is that a joke?"

Sarah smiled a small smile. "No, Deya. Quite the opposite, actually."

Deya opened her mouth, but nothing came out at first. Then she said, "But why would you come all the way back to New York for that? And why now? I don't get it."

"I've wanted to see you for years, but I had to wait until you were old enough to understand. When I heard you've been sitting with suitors, I was afraid you'd get married before I had a chance to talk to you. But now that you're here, I don't know where to begin."

"Is it about my parents?"

There was a pause, and Sarah looked out the window. "Yes, them. And a lot of other things too."

Deya studied Sarah's expression. She could see from the look in her eyes, the way she stared at the glass, there was something safeguarded. "Why should I trust you?"

"I have no reason to lie to you," Sarah said. "You don't have to believe me, though. All I ask is that you listen to me before you decide for yourself."

"Well, I don't trust anyone."

Sarah smiled and leaned back into her chair. "Not so long ago, I was just like you," she said. "I remember what it was like being raised in that house. How could I forget? I understand what you're going through, and I want to help you make the right decisions, or at least let you know you have options."

"You mean about getting married?"

Sarah nodded.

"Do you think I have a choice? I don't! You, of all people, should understand that."

"I do understand. That's why I had to see you."

"I don't see how you can help me," Deya said. "If you could, you would have helped yourself."

"But I *did* help myself."

"How?"

Sarah spoke slowly, a half smile on her lips. "I haven't been in Palestine this entire time, or at all, in fact. I never got married."

Fareeda

Summer 1991

That summer, Fareeda and Khaled decided to take Omar back home in search of a bride. There was no shortage of Muslim Palestinian girls in Brooklyn, but Fareeda refused to marry her son to one of them. No, no, no. Everyone knew that girls raised in America blatantly disregarded their Arab upbringings. Some of them walked around town in tight clothes and a face full of makeup. Some dated behind their parents' back. Some weren't even virgins! The thought alone made Fareeda shudder. Not that Omar was a virgin, necessarily. But it was different for a man, of course. You couldn't prove whether or not he was a virgin. No one's reputation was on the line. She could hear her mother's voice now: "A man leaves the house a man and comes back a man. No one can take that away from him." *But* a woman was a fragile thing. This was precisely why Fareeda couldn't bear the thought of raising more girls in this country. Wasn't it enough she had Sarah to worry about? And now Deya, too? She prayed Isra wasn't pregnant with another girl.

Fareeda held on to this hope as she boarded the plane, walk-

ing uneasily behind Omar and Khaled. She couldn't believe it
had been fifteen years since they first came to America. When
they first landed in New York, Khaled had promised it was only
a temporary situation, that once they made enough money they
would gather their children and return home to die on holy land.
But as the years passed, Fareeda knew that day would never
come. She did what she could to ease this truth. She made sure
her children knew Arabic, that Sarah was raised conservatively,
and that her sons, as Americanized as they were becoming, still
ended up doing what was expected of Palestinian men: marrying Palestinian girls and passing down the traditions to their
own children. If she didn't preserve their culture, their identity,
then she would lose them. She knew this in her core.

That had been her biggest fear lately, especially watching
Omar and Ali come and go as they pleased. But that's just the
way things were, Fareeda thought, studying the Manhattan
skyline as the plane climbed into the air, her hand clutching
Khaled's. There was nothing she could do but marry Omar off
before it was too late.

Two months later they returned to New York with Nadine.

"Congratulations," Isra murmured when she greeted them at
the front door, looking first to Nadine's face and then to the floor.

Fareeda could tell Nadine's dazzling smile and bright blue
eyes intimidated Isra. She had expected this. In fact, she had
planned it. Not to hurt Isra, no, but to show her what womanhood *should* look like. As soon as Fareeda reached Palestine, she
had made it clear to all the mothers that she was not looking
for another Isra. The last time she had searched for a bride, she
had asked for a shy, modest woman who knew how to cook and
clean, wanting the opposite of all the disrespectful women she

had become used to in America. But this time, she had asked for a lively girl. They needed some good spirits around the house, Fareeda thought, glancing at Isra's meek smile. Perhaps Nadine's presence would even force Isra to grow up and start acting like a woman.

"Be sure to put your foot down," Fareeda warned Omar that evening while Nadine was upstairs, settling in. She had whispered those very same words the day the couple signed the marriage contract in Nadine's *sala*, and again on the night of the wedding ceremony, but it didn't hurt to remind him. Omar was practically an American, staring at her with his large, dopey eyes, oblivious to the workings of the world. So typical of men these days. Why, when she had first married Khaled, he would slap her if she even raised her eyes off the ground—pop after pop, until she was as quiet as a mouse. She remembered the early days of her marriage, years before they came to America, when she had lived in fear of his hostile moods, his slaps and kicks if she dared to talk back. She remembered how he would enter their shelter every night after plowing the fields, enraged at the quality of their life—the hardness of the mattress they slept on, the sparseness of food, the aching of his bones—only to take his anger out on her and the children. Some days he'd beat them for even the slightest confrontation, while other days he'd say nothing, grinding his teeth, fury bubbling in his eyes.

"Forget all this American nonsense about love and respect," Fareeda said to Omar now, turning to make sure Isra was setting the table. "You need to make sure our culture survives, and that means teaching a woman her place."

They ate dinner all together for the first time in months. The men sat at one end of the table, the women at the other. Fareeda couldn't remember the last time she'd had all her sons on one *su-fra*. She watched Isra filling Adam's bowl with rice, Nadine passing Omar a glass of water. As it should be! Now all she had left was to marry off Ali and Sarah. She looked over at her daughter, who sat slouched with teenage gracelessness. It shouldn't be too long now before that burden was off Fareeda's shoulders. She was tired and—though she would never admit it—eagerly awaiting the day she could stop worrying about her family.

The men were lost in conversation—something about opening a new convenience store for Omar, who needed a steady income. Fareeda eyed them. "Maybe Adam could open the store," she said. "Help his brother out."

She could see Adam's face redden. "I'd love to help," he said, putting down his spoon. "But I barely have enough time to run Father's store. Between paying the bills and taking care of the family . . ." He stopped, looked over to Isra. "I never see my own family. I'm always working."

"I know, son," Khaled said, reaching out to pat Adam's shoulder. "You do so much for us."

"Still," Fareeda said, reaching for another piece of pita, "your father is getting old. It's your duty to help."

"I am helping," Adam said, his voice suddenly cold. "But where will I find the time to open up another store? And what about Omar? Why can't he take on some responsibility?"

"Where's all this animosity coming from?" Fareeda smacked her lips, waving her greasy fingers around the kitchen table. "What's wrong with helping the family out? You're the eldest son. It's your responsibility." She bit into a stuffed squash. "Your *duty*."

"I understand that, Mother," Adam said. "But what about Omar and Ali? Why am I the one doing everything?"

"That's not true," Fareeda said. "Your brothers do what they can."

"Omar barely puts in any hours at the deli, and Ali spends all day 'studying,' according to him, while I run the store on my own. You need to give my brothers some responsibilities too. You're spoiling them."

"He's right," Khaled said, reaching for a drumstick. "You *are* spoiling them."

Fareeda straightened. "So now it's my fault? Of course, blame it on the woman!" Her eyes shifted to Khaled. "Let's not forget who the real backbone of this family is."

Khaled shot her a hard look. "What are you saying, woman?"

She could see Nadine eyeing her from across the table, so she refrained from saying what she would have usually said, reminding Khaled of all she had done for their family.

Though more than thirty years had passed since Khaled and Fareeda married, she still remembered those early days with resentment: the many ways he had hurt and disappointed her, his sudden and immense anger, the violence. She had been so young, less than half his age, and in the first days of their marriage she had always reminded herself of her subordinate role, submitting to his temperament for fear of being beaten. But no matter how quiet she was, how hard she tried to please, many nights ended with a beating. Of course her father had beaten her growing up, but it was nothing like this: beatings that left her face black and blue, her ribs so sore they ached when she breathed, an arm so badly sprained she couldn't carry water for weeks.

Then one night a neighbor told her that Khaled was an alcoholic, that he purchased a liter of whiskey most mornings from the corner *dukan*, and that he sipped on the bottle until he got home. Each liter cost fifteen shekels, almost half of Khaled's daily earnings. Something inside Fareeda had snapped. A liter of whiskey a day! Fifteen shekels! And after everything she had done for him, scraping to feed their children in the refugee camp, slaving in the fields, bearing him sons, even . . . She stopped, trembling at the memory. No. Enough was enough.

"I won't allow you to spend our hard-earned money on *sharaab*," Fareeda had told Khaled that night, her eyes so wide she knew she must have looked possessed. He wouldn't look at her, but she stared him down. "I've endured many things for your sake"—her voice quivered—"but I won't endure this. From now on, I want to know what you do with our money."

The next thing she knew, Khaled had slapped her. "Who do you think you are talking to me like that?"

Fareeda stared at him. "I'm the reason this family has food to eat." Her voice was surprisingly clear. She didn't recognize it as her own.

Another slap. "Shut your mouth, woman!"

"I won't shut my mouth unless you stop drinking," she said, unwavering. "If you don't, I'll tell your children the truth! I'll tell them that we barely have enough food because their father is an alcoholic. I'll tell everyone! Your reputation will be ruined, and your children will never respect you."

Khaled had shifted back, his head heavy with whiskey, his knees unable to hold him. He lifted his head and let out a shuddering exhale. When he opened his mouth to speak, nothing came. If it wasn't for his pride, Fareeda was certain he would have cried. From that day on, Khaled had brought home his wages to her. Something essential between them had shifted.

"Oh, for goodness sake!" Fareeda said now, not meeting Khaled's eyes. "Let's not get into this mess in front of our new daughter-in-law." She bit into a chicken thigh and turned to face Adam. "Listen, son, you've been handling everything for years. Your brothers know nothing about business. It'll only take you a few months to get the store up and running, and then Omar can take over."

Adam sighed. He looked over to Omar, who sat quietly at the opposite end of the table, eyes fixed on his plate. After a moment had passed, Omar lifted his head to find Adam still watching him and, flushing deeply, said, "Thank you, brother."

Fareeda refilled Omar's plate. "We're family," she said. "There's no need to thank your brother. Why, if everyone went around saying thank you for every little thing they were supposed to do, we wouldn't get anything done, would we?" She scooped a spoonful of rice onto Ali's plate. "Eat up, son. Look at how thin you're getting." Then she turned to Nadine, who sat with her hands in her lap. "You too, dear. Come on." Nadine smiled and reached for her spoon.

Fareeda could feel Isra staring at her. "You need to eat, too, Isra. You haven't gained much weight this pregnancy."

Isra nodded and refilled her plate. Though Fareeda hadn't mentioned it, she was worried about the gender. Why hadn't Isra asked the doctor for an ultrasound while she was gone? Because she was an idiot, Fareeda thought, scooping another serving of rice onto her plate. But she should stop worrying and enjoy this moment with her sons. Yes, she should savor it. It was a reminder of how far she had come since that day. How long had it been— thirty years? Longer? She'd tried so hard to forget. For a long time Fareeda had believed she was cursed, haunted by the jinn. But then Adam had been born, and then Omar and Ali, and her memory of what happened began to fade, bit by bit, until it was almost gone. Like a bad dream. But then Sarah was born—a daughter—and the memories Fareeda thought she had put to rest burned a hole inside her anew. How much she hated looking at Sarah, how much she hated to remember. She had hoped her memories would fade when Sarah got older. Only they hadn't. And now it was Deya who reminded her.

Please, God, Fareeda thought, staring at Isra's belly. Don't let this one be another girl.

Isra

Winter 1991

It was a girl.

The delivery room was quiet, and Isra lay beneath the thin hospital sheet, cold and bare, staring at the midnight December sky through the window. She longed for company, but Adam had said he needed to return to work. She had hoped that children would bring them closer, but they had not. In fact, it seemed as if each pregnancy pushed him farther away, as if the more her belly grew, the wider the space between them became.

She began to cry. What was it that moved her to tears? She wasn't sure. Was it that she had disappointed Adam once again? Or was it because she couldn't be happy as she looked at her newborn daughter?

She was still crying when Adam returned to visit her the next morning. "What's wrong?" he asked, startling her.

"Nothing," Isra said. She sat up and wiped her face.

"Then why are you crying? Did my mother say something to upset you?"

"No."

"Then what is it?"

He took a brief look at the baby basket before walking toward the window. Was Isra imagining, or had Adam's eyes reddened over the years? The thought that he was drinking *sharaab* crossed her mind again but she dismissed it. Not Adam, the man who had once wanted to be a priest, who had memorized the entire Qur'an. He would never commit *haraam*. He must be tired or sick, or perhaps it was something she had done.

"I'm afraid that you're upset with me," Isra said in a soft voice. "For having another daughter."

He sighed irritably. "I'm not upset."

"But you don't seem happy."

"Happy?" He met her eyes. "What's there to be happy about?" Isra stiffened. "All I do is work day and night like a donkey! 'Do this, Adam! Do that, Adam! More money! We need a grandson!' I'm doing everything I can to please my parents, but no matter what I do, I fall short. And now I've given them another thing to complain about."

"I'm sorry," Isra said, her eyes brimming with tears. "It's not your fault. You're a good son . . . a good father."

He didn't smile when she said this. Instead, he turned to leave, saying, "Some days I envy you for leaving your family behind. At least you had the chance to start a new life. Do you know what I would've done for an opportunity like that?"

Isra wanted to be angry at him for not seeing how much she had given up, but instead she found herself pitying him. He was only doing what was expected of him. How could she be mad at him for wanting the same things she wanted: love, acceptance, approval? If anything, this side of him only made her want to please him more. To show him that the place he could find love was with her.

Isra searched for the basket at the end of her bed, pulled her newborn daughter to her chest. She decided she would name her Nora, "light" once again, desperate for a flicker at the end of the tunnel ahead to push her forward.

When Isra returned home, all she heard from Fareeda's lips was the word *balwa* over and over again—in conversations on the phone, to her best friend Umm Ahmed, to Nadine, to the neighbors, to Khaled, and worst of all, to Adam.

Isra hoped Mama wouldn't call her daughter a *balwa*. She had mailed a letter back home informing Mama of Nora's birth. The letter was brief. Isra had not seen her mother in two years. Mama was a stranger now. Isra called her on occasion, like after the month of Ramadan, to wish her *Eid Mubarak*, their conversations stilted and formal, but Fareeda said phone calls to Ramallah were expensive and encouraged Isra to send letters instead. But she couldn't bring herself to write to Mama. It was anger at first that stifled her—anger at Mama for abandoning her—but now she simply didn't have much to say.

After Nora's birth, Isra again busied herself with routine chores. In the mornings she awoke with the sun, sending Adam off to work with a light breakfast, Tupperwares of rice and meat for lunch, and a steaming cup of mint chai. Then her daughters would wake, Deya first, followed by Nora's newborn whimpers, and Isra fed them breakfast. Deya was one year old, Nora only two weeks, both bottle-feeding. A tide of guilt rose in Isra's chest whenever she mixed their formula, ashamed she wasn't breast-feeding them. But Adam needs a son, Fareeda insisted, and Isra obeyed, hoping a son would make him happy.

But deep down was a hidden fear: Isra didn't know if she could handle a third child. With two children now, she was beginning to discover that she was not particularly motherly.

She had been too overwhelmed by the newness to realize this
when she was first mothering Deya, too optimistic about what
motherhood might hold. But as soon as Nora was born, Isra had
found her spirit changed. She couldn't remember the last time
she'd cradled her children with joy, not merely out of a sense
of obligation. Her emotions seesawed constantly: anger, resentment, shame, despair. She tried to justify her frustrations by
telling herself that childbearing was wearisome. That had she
known how constricting a second child would feel, she wouldn't
have rushed into another pregnancy (as if she'd had a choice, she
thought in the back of her head, then pushed the thought away).
In the evenings as she hummed Deya and Nora to sleep, a dark,
desperate feeling overwhelmed her. She wanted to scream.

What were her options now? What could she do to change
her fate? Nothing. All she could do was try to make the best
of her situation. It wasn't like there was any turning back. She
couldn't return to Palestine, couldn't flip back a few chapters
in the story of her life and change things. And what a foolish
thought that was—even if she could go back, she had nothing
to go back to. She was in America now. She was married. She
was a mother. She just had to do better. She'd done everything
the way her parents had wanted, so surely things would turn
out for the best. After all, they'd known what life would be like.
She just needed to trust them. As the Qur'an said, she needed to
have more faith.

Maybe she would become a better mother with time. Maybe
motherhood was something that grew on you, an acquired taste.
Still, Isra wondered if her daughters could sense her failure, staring up at her with their coffee-colored eyes. She wondered if she
had betrayed them.

Deya

Winter 2008

Deya straightened in her seat and stared at her aunt. "You've never been married?"

"No."

"And you haven't been in Palestine?"

Sarah shook her head.

"But why would Teta lie about that?"

Sarah looked away for the first time since they'd sat down together. "I think she was trying to cover up the shame of what I'd done," she said.

"What did you do?"

"I ran away from home before my mother could marry me off. That's why I never visited all these years. That's why I had to reach out to you in secret."

Deya stared at her in disbelief. "You ran away from Teta's house? How?"

"I waited until the last day of senior year, and then I left. I got on the school bus and never came back. I've been living on my own ever since."

"But you were so young! I could barely come to the city today without a panic attack. How did you make it?"

"It wasn't easy," Sarah said. "But I managed. I stayed with a friend for the first year until I could afford to live on my own. Then I rented a small apartment in Staten Island. I worked two jobs to pay for community college and changed my last name so no one could find me."

"But what if they had found you?" Deya said. "Weren't you afraid of what they would've done?"

"I was," Sarah said. "But I was afraid of other things, too. Fear has a way of putting things in perspective."

Deya shifted in her seat, trying to absorb the image of her aunt running away from Fareeda's house at eighteen, her own age. It was unthinkable. She could never run away from home. No matter how much she was afraid of life in Fareeda's house, the real world scared her much more.

"I don't understand," Deya said. "Is that why you reached out? To help me run away?"

"No! That's the last thing I want for you."

"Why?"

"Because running away was so hard," Sarah said. "I lost everyone I loved."

"Then why am I here?" Deya asked.

There was a moment of silence, and Sarah glanced over to the coffee bar. She stood. "Let me get us something to drink." She returned with two vanilla lattes minutes later and handed one to Deya. "Careful," she said as she settled back in her seat. "It's hot."

Deya set the mug on the table. "Tell me why I'm here."

Sarah pursed her lips and blew on her coffee. "I already told you," she said before taking a sip. "I want to help you make the right decision."

"You mean about marriage?"

"That, and other things, too. I want to help you stand up for what you want."

Deya sighed and brought her hands to her temples, pressing her fingers against her hijab. "I've already tried standing up to Teta. I told her I don't want to get married right now. That I want to go to college. But she doesn't listen. You know that."

"So that's it? You're going to give up?"

"What else can I do?"

"Stand up to her," Sarah said. "Apply to college anyway. Turn down the suitors she finds you. Keep trying to change her mind."

Deya shook her head. "I can't possibly do that."

"Why not? What are you afraid of?"

"Nothing . . . I don't know . . ."

"I don't think that's true," Sarah said, placing her mug on the table. "I think you know exactly what you're afraid of. Tell me, what is it?"

Deya started to protest but stopped herself. "It's nothing."

"I know you're trying to protect yourself, but you can trust me."

The way Sarah saw her so clearly was unnerving. She shook her head. "There's nothing wrong with protecting myself."

"Maybe not. But pretending nothing's wrong is not protecting yourself. If anything, it's much more dangerous to live pretending to be someone you're not."

Deya shrugged.

"Believe me, I know how you feel. I've been exactly where you are now. You don't have to pretend with me."

"Well, I've been pretending my whole life," Deya said. "It's not something I can just turn off. You see, I'm a storyteller."

"A storyteller?"

Deya nodded.

"But don't you think stories should be used to tell the truth?"

"No, I think we need stories to protect us from the truth."

"Is that how you plan to live your life? Pretending?"

"What else am I supposed to do?" Deya could feel her hands begin to sweat. "What's the point of saying what I think, or asking for what I want, if it will only lead to trouble? It's not like speaking up will get me anywhere. It's better to just pretend everything is fine and do what I'm supposed to do."

"Oh, Deya, that's not true," Sarah said. "Please give me a chance to help. To be your friend. I grew up in the same house as you did, with the same people. If anyone is going to understand you, it's me. All I'm asking is that you give me a chance. What you choose to do in the end is up to you. I just want you to know all your options."

Deya considered. "Are you going to be honest with me?"

"Yes," she said with conviction.

"What about my parents? Will you tell me the truth about the car accident?"

Sarah paused. "What are you talking about?"

"The car accident that killed them. I know there's more to it."

Another pause. For the first time, Deya could see nervousness on Sarah's face.

"How much do you know about your parents? About Isra?"

"Not much," Deya said. "Teta refuses to talk about them most of the time, but last week she showed me a letter my mother wrote before she died."

"What letter?"

"It was to her mother. Teta found it in one of her books after she died."

"What did it say?"

Deya unpinned her hijab, feeling herself getting hot. "She wrote about how sad she was. That she wished she would die. She sounded depressed, maybe even . . ." Her voice trailed.

"Maybe what?"

"Suicidal. She sounded like she wanted to kill herself."

"Kill herself?" There was a pause, and Deya could see that Sarah appeared to consider the possibility. "Are you sure?"

"That's how it sounded. But Teta denied it."

Sarah stared at her. "But why would my mother show you that letter now after all these years?"

"She said it would help me let go of the past and move on."

"That doesn't make any sense. How would reading that help you move on?"

Deya bit her lip. What was the point in holding back? She had already defied her grandparents to be here. She had nothing left to lose. Perhaps Sarah could even help her. "It's because my memories are so bad," she finally said.

"Your memories? What do you mean?"

"Teta knows I'm afraid to get married because I remember how bad things were with my parents. She thought showing me the letter would help me understand that there was something wrong with my mother. She said Mama was possessed."

Sarah stared at her. "But there was nothing wrong with Isra."

"Yes, there was. I remember, okay? And how would you know, anyway? You ran away. You weren't even there."

"I knew your mother well. I can promise you, Isra wasn't possessed."

"How would you know? Were you there when she died?"

Sarah dropped her gaze to the floor. "No."

"Then you don't know for certain." Deya wiped sweat off her forehead.

"I don't understand," Sarah said. "Why do you think she was possessed?"

"It doesn't matter what I think," Deya said. "Shouldn't you be telling me what you think? Isn't that why I'm here?"

Sarah leaned back into her seat. "What do you want to know?"

"Everything. Tell me everything."

"Do you know how Isra and I became friends?" Deya shook her head. "It was because of you."

"Me?"

Sarah smiled. "It happened when she was pregnant with you. My mother wanted a boy, of course. One day she said so to Isra, and we started talking for the first time."

"What did my mother say?"

"She disagreed, of course. She said she'd never belittle a daughter."

"She said that?"

"Yes. She loved you and your sisters so much."

Deya turned to look out the window. There were tears in her eyes, and she tried to keep them from falling.

"You know she loved you," Sarah said. "Don't you?"

Deya kept her eyes on the glass. "She didn't seem like she loved anyone. She was so sad all the time."

"That doesn't mean she didn't love you."

Deya met her eyes again. "What about my father?"

A pause, then, "What about him?"

"What was he like?"

"He was . . ." Sarah cleared her throat. "He was a hard worker."

"Most men I know are hard workers. Tell me something else."

"I honestly didn't see him much," Sarah said. "He was always working. He was the eldest son, and there was a lot of pressure on him."

"Pressure from who?"

"My parents. They expected so much. Sometimes I think they pushed him . . ." Sarah paused. "He was under a lot of pressure."

Deya was certain she was hiding something. "What about

his relationship with my mother? Did he treat her well?"

Sarah shifted in her seat, tucking her long black curls behind her ears. "I didn't see them together very often."

"But you said you were friends with my mom. Wouldn't you know how she felt? She didn't talk about it?"

"Isra was a very private person. And she was raised in Palestine—she was old-fashioned in certain ways. She never would have talked to me about her relationship with him."

"So you didn't know that he hit her?"

Sarah froze, and from the look in her eyes, Deya was sure she had known. "You didn't think I knew, did you?" Sarah opened her mouth to speak, but Deya cut her off. "I used to hear him screaming at her in the middle of the night. I'd hear him hitting her and her crying and trying to muffle the sound. Growing up, I used to wonder if I'd imagined it. I thought maybe I was just feeding my own sadness. That's a disease, you know. I read about it. There are people who like to be sad, and I used to worry I was one of them. I thought maybe I was making up a story to try to make sense of my life." She met Sarah's eyes. "But I know that's not true. I know he used to hit her."

"I'm so sorry, Deya," Sarah said. "I didn't realize you knew."

"You said you'd tell me the truth."

"I want to tell you everything, but it makes sense for us to get to know each other better first. I wanted to earn your trust."

"You can't earn my trust by lying to me."

"I know," Sarah said. "I'm sorry. This is hard for me to navigate as well. I haven't talked about my family in years."

Deya shook her head, struggling to keep her voice down. "I have enough people lying to me. I don't need your lies, too."

There was a clock on the opposite wall: it was nearly 2:00 p.m. Deya stood. "I have to go. My sisters will be waiting for me at the bus stop soon."

"Wait!" Sarah stood and followed Deya out the door. "Will you come back?"

Deya didn't answer. Outside, clouds were gathering, cool air slipping through her hijab. It seemed as though it was about to rain, and she secured her *jilbab* for warmth.

"You have to come back," Sarah said.

"Why?"

"Because there's more I need to tell you."

"So you can lie to me again?"

"No!"

Deya met her eyes. "How do I know you'll tell me the truth?"

"I promise, I will." Sarah kept her face blank as she said this, but there was hesitation in her voice. Sarah *wanted* to tell her the truth—Deya did not doubt that. Surely Sarah had decided to be honest when she reached out to her. Only Deya didn't believe Sarah would give up the truth so easily. Not yet. She would have to wait until Sarah was ready. What choice did she have? In her head she likened it to reading. You had to finish a story to know all the answers, and life was no different. Nothing was ever handed to you from the start.

Isra

Fall 1992

Seasons passed in a blur. Isra was pregnant with her third child. She peered into the oven, flipping over a batch of *za'atar* pies she had baked for lunch, while Fareeda and Nadine sipped chai at the kitchen table.

"Brew another *ibrik*," Fareeda told Isra when she set the *za'atar* pies on a rack to cool. As Isra did, she watched Nadine place Fareeda's hand on her swollen belly.

"Do you feel it kicking?" Nadine said.

"Yes!"

Isra could see Nadine smirking, and she hid her face inside the cabinet. In the beginning, when Nadine first arrived, Isra had thought she would finally have a friend, a sister even. But they barely spoke, despite the small efforts Isra made to befriend her.

"Come, come," Fareeda said when Isra had set the kettle on the stove. "Sit with us."

Isra sat. She could feel Fareeda studying her belly, trying to make out the child inside. The look in her eyes sent a prick of fear down Isra's spine. Not a day had passed when Fareeda had not mentioned the child's gender, how they needed a grandson, how Isra had disgraced them in the community. Some days Fareeda would dangle a necklace over the globe of Isra's belly, trying to discern the baby's gender. Other days she would read the grounds of Isra's Turkish coffee.

"It's a boy this time," Fareeda said, studying a spot on Isra's stomach, calculating whether the baby sat high or low, wide or narrow. "I can feel it."

"*Inshallah*," Isra whispered.

"No, no, no," Fareeda said. "It's a boy for sure. Look how high your belly sits."

Isra looked. It didn't seem high to her, but she hoped Fareeda was right. Dr. Jaber had offered to tell Isra on her last visit, but Isra had refused. She didn't see any reason to suffer prematurely. At least now, not knowing the gender, she had a bit of hope to move her forward. She wouldn't be able to push the baby out if she knew it was a girl.

"We'll name him Khaled," Fareeda said, standing up. "After your father-in-law."

Isra wished she wouldn't do that, bring her hopes up for a boy. What if it was another girl—what would Fareeda do? Isra could still remember the look on Fareeda's face the night Nora was born, one hand swept across her forehead, a pained sigh escaping her. And here Isra was again, with another child on the way. Soon she would have three children when she still felt like a child herself. But what choice did she have? Fareeda had insisted she get pregnant before Nadine. "It's your duty to bear the first grandson," she'd said. Only now Nadine was pregnant, too, and might still bear a son before Isra.

"Please, Allah," Isra whispered, a prayer she'd been muttering for weeks. "Please give me a son this time."

Nadine squinted her bright blue eyes and laughed. "Don't worry, Fareeda," she said, tracing her fingers across her slim belly. "*Inshallah* you'll have a little Khaled sooner or later."

Fareeda beamed. "Oh, *inshallah*."

Later that evening, Fareeda asked Isra to teach Sarah how to make *kofta*. A single ray of light fell through the kitchen window as they gathered the ingredients on the counter: minced lamb, tomatoes, garlic, parsley.

Sarah sighed. Her eyes were round and her lips sat in a quiet sneer, as though she had sensed something foul. She sighed again, reaching for the minced lamb. "How do you *do* this all day?"

Isra looked up. "Do what?"

"*This*." She motioned to the *kofta* balls. "It would drive me crazy!"

"I'm used to it. And you might as well get used to it too. It will be your life soon enough."

Sarah shot her a sidelong glance. "Maybe."

Isra shrugged. Sarah had matured so much in the past two years. She was thirteen years old, creeping up on womanhood. Isra wished she could save her from it.

"Whatever happened to your romantic streak?" Sarah said.

"Nothing happened," Isra said. "I grew up, that's all."

"Not everyone ends up in the kitchen, you know. There is such a thing as a happy ending."

"Now who sounds like a romantic?" Isra asked with a smile. She thought back to how naive she had been when she'd first arrived in America, walking around dreaming of love. But she wasn't naive anymore. She had finally figured it out. Life was nothing more than a bad joke for women. One she didn't find funny.

"You know what your problem is?" Sarah said.

"What's that?"

"You stopped reading."

"I don't have time to read."

"Well, you should make time. It would make you feel better."
When Isra said nothing, she added, "Don't you miss it?"

"Of course I do."

"Then what's stopping you?"

Isra lowered her voice to a whisper. "Adam and Fareeda are
already disappointed in me for having two girls. They wouldn't
like me reading, and I don't want to make things worse."

"Then read in secret like me. Isn't that what you used to do
back home?"

"Yes." Isra entertained the idea for a moment and then
pushed it away, amazed at how little defiance she had left. How
could she tell Sarah that she was afraid of adding tension to her
marital life? That she couldn't handle any more blame for the
family's unhappiness? Sarah wouldn't even understand if she
did tell her. Sarah, with her bold, bright eyes and thick school-
books. Sarah, who still had hope. Isra couldn't bear to tell her
the truth.

"No, no." Isra shook her head. "I don't want to risk it."

"Whatever you say."

They stood by the oven, dropping balls of minced lamb into
a sizzling pan of oil, one after another, waiting until each piece
turned a crisp brown before setting it on old newspaper to cool.
The heat stung their fingers, and Sarah laughed every time Isra
dropped a ball of *kofta* on the floor.

"Better pick it up before Lord Fareeda sees you!" Sarah said,
mimicking the look her mother always gave at the sight of sloppy
cooking. "Or I might never see you again."

"Shhh!"

"Oh, come on. She won't hear us. She's completely engrossed in her soap opera."

Isra looked over her shoulder. It bothered her that she couldn't even laugh without worrying about Fareeda. She knew she was only getting duller as the years passed, but she couldn't help it. She wanted to be happy. But she felt as though she wore a stain she couldn't wash off.

Deya

Winter 2008

"**Nasser is waiting** for you," Fareeda told Deya when she returned home from school. "Go change out of your uniform! Quickly!"

It took a tremendous amount of effort for Deya not to confront Fareeda right then. All these years lying about Sarah! What else was she hiding? But Deya knew better than to challenge Fareeda. It would only jeopardize her future visits with Sarah and her chance to learn the truth, so she bit her tongue and said nothing, stomping down the stairs. When she came back up, Nasser and his mother were sipping chai and eating from a platter of *ma'amool* cookies in the *sala*. Deya refilled their cups before heading to the kitchen, Nasser closely behind. She settled across from him at the table, bringing the warm cup to her face for comfort.

"Sorry to make you wait," she said.

"It's okay," Nasser said. "How was school?"

"Fine."

"Learn anything interesting?"

She sipped on her chai. "Not really."

There was an awkward pause, and he fidgeted with his tea-cup. "You didn't think you'd see me again, did you? You thought you'd scared me away."

"It's worked so far," she said without looking at him.

He let out a small chuckle. "Well, not on me." Another pause. "So, should we talk about the next step?"

She met his eyes. "Next step?"

"I mean, marriage."

"Marriage?"

He nodded.

"What about it?"

"What do you think about marrying me?"

Deya opened her mouth to object, but thought better of it. She needed to prolong her sittings with him until she knew what to do. "I'm not sure what I think," she said. "This is only the second time I've ever met you."

"I know," Nasser said, blushing. "But they say people usually know if something feels right instantly."

"Maybe when deciding on a pair of shoes," Deya said. "But picking a life partner is a bit more serious, don't you think?"

Nasser laughed, but she could tell she had embarrassed him. "To be honest," he said, "this is my first time agreeing to sit with the same girl twice. I mean, I've sat with a lot of girls—it's exhausting, really, how many my mother has found at weddings. But nothing serious ever happened with any of them."

"Why not?"

"There was no *naseeb*, I guess. You know the Arabic proverb, 'What's meant for you will reach you even if it's beneath two mountains, and what's not meant for you won't reach you even if it's between your two lips'?"

Deya's contempt must have been written across her face. "What?" he asked. "You don't believe in *naseeb*?"

"It's not that I don't believe in it, but sitting around waiting for destiny to hit feels so passive. I hate the idea that I have no control over my life."

"But that's what *naseeb* means," Nasser said. "Your life is already written for you, already *maktub*."

"Then why do you wake up in the morning? Why do you bother going to work or school or even leaving your room, if the outcome of your life is out of your hands?"

Nasser shook his head. "Just because my fate has already been decided, that doesn't mean I should stay in bed all day. It just means that God already knows what I'll do."

"But don't you think this mentality stops you from giving things your all? Like, if it's already written, then what's the point?"

"Maybe," Nasser said. "But it also reminds me of my place in the world, helps me cope when things don't go my way."

Deya didn't know whether she found weakness or courage in his answer. "I'd like to think I have more control over my life," she said. "I want to believe I actually have a choice."

"We always have a choice. I never said we don't." Deya blinked at him. "It's true. Like this marriage arrangement, for instance."

"Maybe *you* can go around proposing to any girl you want," she said. "But I don't see any choice here for me."

"But there is! You can choose to say no until you meet the right person."

She rolled her eyes. "That's not a choice."

"That depends on how you look at it."

"No matter how I look at it, I'm still being forced to get married. Just because I'm offered options, that doesn't mean I have a choice. Don't you see?" She shook her head. "A real choice doesn't have conditions. A real choice is free."

"Maybe," Nasser said. "But sometimes you have to make the best of things. Take life as it comes, accept things as they are."

Deya exhaled, a wave of self-doubt washing over her. She didn't want to accept things as they were. She wanted to be in control of her own life, decide her own future for a change.

"So, should I tell them yes?" Fareeda asked Deya after Nasser left. She was standing in the kitchen doorway, a cup of *kahwa* to her lips.

"I need more time," Deya said.

"Shouldn't you at least know if you like him by now?"

"I barely know him, Teta."

Fareeda sighed. "Have I ever told you the story of how I met your grandfather?" Deya shook her head. "Come, come. Let me tell you."

Fareeda proceeded to tell her the story of her wedding night, nearly fifty years before, in the al-Am'ari refugee camp. She had just turned fourteen.

"My sister Huda and I were both getting married that day," Fareeda said. "To brothers. I remember sitting inside our shelter, our palms henna-stained, our eyes smeared with kohl, while Mama wrapped our hair with hairpins she had borrowed from a neighbor. It was only after we'd signed the marriage contracts that we saw our husbands for the first time! Huda and I were so nervous as Mama led us to them. The first brother was tall and thin, with small eyes and a freckled face; the second was tan, with broad shoulders and cinnamon hair. The second brother smiled. He had a beautiful row of white teeth, and I remember secretly hoping *he* was my husband. But Mama led me by the elbow to the first man and whispered: 'This man is your home now.'"

"But that was a million years ago," Deya said. "Just because it happened to you doesn't mean it should happen to me."

"It's not happening to you!" Fareeda said. "You've already said no to several men, and you've sat with Nasser twice! No one is telling you to marry him tomorrow. Sit with him a few more times and get to know him."

"So, sitting with him five times will make me know him?"

"No one really knows anyone, daughter. Even after a life-time."

"Which is why this is so ridiculous."

"Well, this ridiculousness is how it's been done for centuries."

"Maybe that's why everyone is so miserable."

"Miserable?" Fareeda waved her hands in the air. "You think your life is miserable? Unbelievable." Deya took a step back, knowing what was coming. "You've never seen misera-ble. I was only six years old when my family relocated to the refugee camp, settling in a corner tent with a single room, as far as we could get from the open sewage, the rotting corpses on the dirt road. You wouldn't believe how dirty I always was—hair uncombed, clothes soiled, feet as black as coal. I used to see young boys kicking a ball around the sewage or riding bikes on the dirt roads and wish I could run along with them. But even as a child, I knew my place. I knew my mother needed help, squatting in front of a bucket, washing clothes in whatever water we could find. Even though I was only a child, I knew I was a woman first."

"But that was a long time ago in Palestine," Deya said. "We live in America now. Isn't that why you came here? For a better life? Well, why can't that mean a better life for us, too?"

"We didn't come here so our daughters could become Americans," Fareeda said. "Besides, American women get married, too, you know. If not at your age, then soon enough. Marriage is what women do."

"But it's not fair!"

Fareeda sighed. "I never said it was, daughter." Her voice was soft, and she reached out to touch Deya's shoulder. "But this country is not safe for girls like you. I only want your protection. If you're afraid to rush into marriage, that's fine. I understand. You can sit with Nasser as often as you'd like if it makes you feel better. Would that help?"

As if sitting with a stranger a few more times could help alleviate the uncertainty she felt about everything in the wake of her grandparents' lies. But at least she'd bought herself more time to figure out what to do. "I guess."

"Good," Fareeda said. "But promise me one thing."

"What's that?"

"You need to let the past go, daughter. Let your mother go."

Deya refused to meet Fareeda's eyes as she went back downstairs to change.

Later that night, after Deya and her sisters ate dinner and retreated to their rooms, Deya told Nora about her visit with Sarah. She had planned to keep the story to herself at first, but she knew Nora would suspect something was going on when she skipped school again. Nora said nothing the whole time she spoke, listening with the same calm interest as when Deya told her a story, turning to the doorway every now and then to make sure Fareeda wasn't there.

"She must have something important to tell you," Nora said when Deya finished speaking. "Or else she wouldn't have risked reaching out."

"I don't know. She says she wants to help me, but I feel like she's hiding something."

"Even if she is, there must be a reason she reached out. She'll have to tell you eventually."

"I'll make sure to find out tomorrow."

"What? You're skipping school again? What if you get caught?"

"I won't get caught. Besides, don't you want to know what she has to say? Teta has been lying to us all these years. If she lied about Sarah, what else is she lying about? We deserve the truth."

Nora gave her a long, hard stare. "Just be careful," she said. "You don't know this woman. You can't trust her."

"Don't worry. I know."

"Oh, right," Nora said with a crooked smile. "I forgot who I was talking to."

Isra

Summer–Fall 1993

Summer again. Isra's fourth in America. In August she'd given birth to her third daughter. When the doctor declared the baby a girl, a darkness had washed over her that even the morning light through the window could not relieve. She'd named her Layla. *Night.*

Adam made no effort to conceal his disappointment this time around. He'd barely spoken to her since. In the evenings, when he'd returned from work, she would sit and watch him eat the dinner she had prepared him, eager to meet his faraway gaze. But his eyes never met hers, and the clinking of his spoon against his plate was the only sound between them.

After Layla's birth, Isra had not prayed two *rak'ats* thanking Allah for his blessings. In fact, she hardly completed her five daily prayers in time. She was tired. Every morning she woke up to the sound of three children wailing. After sending Adam off to work, she made the beds, swept the basement floor, folded a load of laundry. Then she entered the kitchen, sleeves rolled up

to the elbows, to find Fareeda hovering over the stove, the teakettle whistling as she announced the day's chores.

Sunset, and Isra had yet to pray *maghrib*. Downstairs, she
opened her dresser and took out a prayer rug. Normally she
laid the rug facing the *kiblah*, the eastern wall where the sun
rose. But today she tossed the prayer rug on the mattress and
threw herself on the bed. She took in the four bare walls, the
thick wooden bedposts, the matching dresser. There was a
black sock jamming the bottom drawer—Adam's drawer. The
one she only opened to put clean socks and underwear inside.
But that was enough to know he kept a layer of personal things
at the bottom. She rolled off the bed and leaped toward the
dresser in a single step. She crouched down and froze, fingers
inches from it. Did she dare open it? Would Adam want her
rummaging through his things? But how would he find out?
And besides, what good had obedience done her? She had been
so good for so long, and where was she now? More miserable
than ever. She reached for the drawer and pulled it open. One
by one, she placed Adam's socks and underwear on the floor beside her. Underneath was a folded blanket, which she removed
as well, and beneath it lay several stacks of hundred-dollar
bills, two packs of Marlboro cigarettes, a half-empty black-
and-white composition notebook, three pens, and five pocket
lighters. Isra sighed in disgust—what had she expected? Gold
and rubies? Love letters to another woman? She placed everything back where it was, shoved the drawer shut, and returned
to the bed.

Sprawled across her prayer rug, she couldn't stop thinking.
Why hadn't Allah given her a son? Why was her *naseeb* so terrible? Surely she had done something wrong. That must be why

Adam couldn't love her. She could tell from the way he touched her at night, huffing and puffing, looking at anything but her. She knew she could never please him. His appetite was fierce, aggressive, and she could never seem to quench it. And worse, not only had she deprived him of a son, but she had given him three daughters instead. She didn't deserve his love. She wasn't worthy.

She reached under the mattress, grazed her fingers against *A Thousand and One Nights*. It had been years since she had looked at its beautiful pages. She pulled it out and opened it wide. It was full of pictures: glimmering lights, flying carpets, grand architecture, jewels, magic lamps. She felt sick. How foolish she had been to believe that such a life was real. How foolish she had been to think she would find love. She slammed the book shut and threw it across the room. Then she folded up her prayer rug and put it away. She knew she should pray, but she had nothing to say to God.

That night, after putting her daughters to bed, Isra retreated to the basement window. She cracked it open, cold air slapping her in the face for a few moments, before she slammed it shut again. She wrapped her arms around her knees and began to weep.

The next thing she knew, she was on her feet, darting to the bedroom. She pulled open Adam's drawer, grabbed the composition notebook and pen, and returned to the windowsill, where she ripped out a few empty pages from the back and began to write.

> *Dear Mama,*
> *Life here isn't so different from life back home, with all the cooking, cleaning, folding, and ironing. And the*

women here—they live no better. They still scrub floors
and raise children and wait on men to order them around.
A part of me hoped that women would be liberated in this
country. But you were right, Mama. A woman will always
be a woman.

She was gritting her teeth in anger and despair. She crumpled the letter, started again, then crumpled the next as well, then the next and the one after it, until she had rewritten her letter a dozen times, and all of them lay balled at her feet. She could picture Mama's disapproval now, could hear her voice: *But aren't you fed, clothed, and sheltered? Tell me, don't you have a home? Be grateful, Isra! At least you have a home. No one will ever come and take it from you. Living in Brooklyn is a hundred times better than living in Palestine.*

"But it's not better, Mama," Isra wrote on a new sheet of paper.

Do you think about me? Do you wonder if I'm treated
well? Do I ever cross your mind? Or am I not even part of
your family anymore? Isn't that what you always said to me,
that a girl belongs to her husband after marriage? I can see
you now, coddling my brothers, your pride and joy, the men
who will carry on the family name, who will always belong
to you.

I know what you'd say to me: once a woman becomes
a mother, her children come first. That she belongs to them
now. Isn't that right? But I'm a terrible mother. It's true.
Every time I look at my daughters, I'm filled with sorrow.
Sometimes they are so needy, I think they'll drive me mad.
And then I'm ashamed I can't give them more. I thought having daughters in this country would be a blessing. I thought

they'd have a better life. But I was wrong, Mama, and I'm reminded of how much I failed them every time I look in their eyes.

I am alone here, Mama. I wake up every morning in this foreign country, where I don't have a mother or a sister or a brother. Did you know this would happen to me? Did you? No. You couldn't have known. You wouldn't have let this happen to me if you had. Or did you know and let it happen anyway? But that can't be. No, it can't.

Two weeks later, on a cool September day, Nadine went into labor. Khaled and Omar drove her to the hospital, leaving Fareeda to pace from room to room, a phone in hand, waiting for the news. Fareeda had wanted to accompany them, but Omar had refused. He hadn't wanted to put pressure on Nadine, he'd said, without meeting Isra's eyes, especially if she had a girl. Fareeda had said nothing, storming into the kitchen to brew a kettle of chai. Now she paced around the *sala*, muttering to herself, while Adam sat on the sofa, looking at Isra in his absent way, eyes half hidden behind a cloud of hookah smoke. When she couldn't take it any longer, she stood to go brew some coffee.

In the kitchen, Isra let out a silent prayer that Nadine would have a girl. No sooner had she thought it than she felt disgusted with herself. What ugliness inside her had made her think such a wicked prayer? It was just that she didn't want to be the only woman in the house who couldn't bear a son. If Nadine had a son, Isra might as well flatten herself on the floor like a kitchen mat, because that's all she'd be.

The phone rang, and Isra clenched her teeth. She heard Fareeda squeal, then Adam choking on the hookah smoke.

"Oh, Omar!" Fareeda said into the phone. "A baby boy? *Alf mabrouk.*"

The next thing Isra knew, she was standing in front of Fareeda and Adam, though she couldn't remember walking down the hall and into the *sala*. Trembling, she set a tray of Turkish coffee on the table.

"*Alf mabrouk*," Isra said, remembering to smile. "Congratulations." The voice she heard was not her own. It belonged to a stronger woman.

Fareeda's gold tooth sparkled as she held the receiver to her ear. Beside her, Adam sat perfectly still. He inhaled a long puff of smoke and released it into the air. Isra moved closer to him, hoping he would say something to her, but he just sucked in the smoke and exhaled. She had become accustomed to the silence between them, had learned to shrink herself in his presence so as not to upset him the same way she had with Yacob growing up. It was better that way. But Isra worried no amount of shrinking would prevent Adam's anger now. He was the eldest; *he* was expected to have the first grandson. But now he hadn't, and it was all her fault.

He turned to Fareeda. "*Alf mabrouk*, Mother."

"Thank you, son. *Inshallah* your turn soon."

Adam smiled but said nothing. He leaned into the sofa, closed his eyes, inhaled another puff of smoke. Isra fixated on the long, sleek hookah rope in his hands, the shiny silver tip clutched between his lips. Every time he let out a rush of smoke, the room fogged, and she disappeared from sight. Standing there, she wished she could disappear like that forever.

That night, Adam entered their bedroom without saying a word. He shook his head, mumbling something under his breath, and all Isra could think was how slender he looked standing there, thinner than she had ever seen him. His fingers appeared longer, pointier than usual, and it seemed as though the veins on his hands had either multiplied or become engorged. He moved closer to her, lifting his eyes to meet hers. It gave her a strange feeling.

"Is there anything I can do?" she asked in a low voice. Her compliance eased her on days like this, when she felt as though she was useless. If she couldn't give him a son, the least she could do was be a good wife and please him.

He stared at her. She looked away. She knew that if he looked at her too closely, the thoughts—fear, anger, defiance, loneliness, confusion, helplessness—would burst from her and the tears would rush out of her eyes and she'd collapse right there in front of him. And Isra couldn't have that. It was one thing to think, another thing entirely to speak your mind.

"I'm sorry," Isra whispered. Adam continued to stare. The look in his eyes was unsteady, like he was under a spell and trying hard to focus. He took a few steps closer, and she took a few steps back into the corner of the room, trying not to flinch. He hated when she flinched. She wondered if Nadine flinched when Omar touched her. But Nadine was different, she thought. She must have been loved in her life that she knew how to love and be loved in return.

Adam reached out to touch her. He traced the outline of her face, almost as if daring her to move. But she kept still. She closed her eyes, waited for him to stop, to step away and go to bed. But then, all at once, it came.

He slapped her.

What terrified Isra most was not the force of his palm against her face. It was the voice inside her head telling her to be still— not the stillness itself, but the ease of it, how naturally it came to her.

Deya

Winter 2008

"I still can't believe you ran away," Deya told Sarah the next day at the bookstore. Upon emerging from the subway at Union Square, she had taken off her hijab and tucked it in her backpack, felt the cool breeze run through her hair, the winter sun on her skin. "You left everything you knew. I wish I was brave like you."

"I'm not as brave as you think," Sarah said.

Deya studied her aunt from across the small table. Sarah wore a flowered miniskirt with thin stockings, long black boots, and a fitted cream blouse. Her hair was wrapped in a loose bun. "Yes, you are," Deya said. "I could never run away. I'd be terrified out here alone." She met Sarah's eyes. "How did you leave? Weren't you afraid?"

"Of course I was afraid. But I was more afraid of staying."

"Why?"

"I was afraid of what my parents would do if they found out . . ." Her words faded.

"Found out what?"

Sarah looked down at her fingers. "I don't know how to say this. I'm worried you'll think less of me."

"It's okay. You can tell me." Deya could see hesitation in her aunt's face as she turned toward the window.

"I had a boyfriend," Sarah finally said.

"A boyfriend? Is that why you ran away?"

"No, not exactly."

"Then why?"

Sarah stared out the window.

"Come on, tell me."

She drew a breath and started again. "The truth is, I wasn't a virgin."

Deya stared at her with wide eyes. "In Teta's house? How . . . how could you?" Sarah's face grew red, and she looked away. "I'm sorry—I'm not trying to judge you or anything. It's just, all I can think of is Teta's face. Seedo beating you. Maybe even a knife at your throat. Our reputation would've been ruined if people found out."

"I know," Sarah said quietly. "That's why I ran. I was terrified what would happen when everyone found out. I was scared of what my parents would do."

Deya said nothing. She couldn't picture herself in Sarah's shoes, couldn't imagine losing her virginity. She would never have the nerve to go that far with a man, to disobey her grandparents so severely, but it wasn't just that. The act itself seemed far too intimate. She couldn't imagine letting anyone close enough to touch her skin, much less peel her clothes back, touch her deep inside. She flushed.

"Is that why you don't think you're brave?" Deya asked. "Because you didn't have the courage to face your family after what you'd done? Because you chose to run away instead?"

"Yes." Sarah looked up to meet Deya's eyes. "Even though

I was afraid for my life, I shouldn't have run. I should've confronted my mother about what I'd done. It's not that I wasn't strong enough to face my parents—I was. Books were my armor. Everything I'd ever learned growing up, all my thoughts, dreams, goals, experiences, it all came from the books I read. It was like I went around collecting knowledge, plucking it from pages and storing it up, waiting for a chance to use it. I could've stood up to my parents, but I let fear control my decisions, and instead of facing them, I ran. I was a coward."

Deya didn't quite agree with her aunt. She would've run away too had she been in Sarah's shoes. Staying after she'd committed such a sin would have been unthinkable, unwise even—she would have risked getting killed. Deya passed her aunt a comforting smile. In an attempt to lighten the conversation, she said, "I never knew you loved to read so much. But I guess it should've been obvious, seeing where you work and all."

"You caught me," Sarah said with a grin.

"Fareeda didn't mind your books?"

"Oh, she did!" Sarah laughed. "But I hid them from her. Did you know Isra loved to read, too? We used to read together."

"Really? I remember she used to read to us all the time."

Sarah smiled. "You remember that?"

"It's one of the only good memories I have of her. Sometimes I think that's why I love to read so much."

"You like to read, too?"

"There's nothing else in the world I'd rather do."

"Well, in that case, you're more than welcome to any of these." Sarah gestured at the shelves piled high with books.

"Really?"

"Of course."

"Thank you," Deya said, feeling her cheeks burn. "You're so lucky."

"For what?"

"To have all these books. All these stories all around."

"I am lucky," Sarah said. "Books have always kept me company when I felt most alone."

"You sound like me."

Sarah laughed. "Well, guess what?"

"What?"

"You're not alone anymore."

Deya curled into her seat, unsure of what to say. She knew she should feel excited, connected even. But all she felt was fear, the need to retreat inside herself. Why couldn't she let her guard down? Why couldn't she believe that someone could actually care about her? She wasn't sure of the precise reason, but if her own family was willing to throw her away to the first man who asked, then why should she expect more from anyone else? She shouldn't. She was only being safe, she reasoned. She was only protecting herself.

"You know what's strange?" Deya said after a moment.

"What's that?"

"What are the odds that me, you, and my mother would all love to read?"

"It's not strange at all," Sarah said. "It's the loneliest people who love books the most."

"Is that why you loved reading? Because you were lonely?"

"Something like that." Sarah looked toward the window. "Growing up in that family was hard, being treated differently than my brothers because I was a girl, waking up every morning knowing my future was limited. Knowing I was so different from most of the other kids at school. It was more than loneliness. Sometimes I think it was the opposite of loneliness, too, like there were too many people around me, forced connections, that I needed a little isolation to think on my own, to be my own person. Does that make sense?"

Deya nodded, hearing herself in Sarah's words. "And now?"

"What do you mean?"

"Are you happy?"

Sarah paused for a moment then said, "I don't care about being happy." Deya's surprise must have been written across her face because Sarah continued, "Too often being happy means being passive or playing it safe. There's no skill required in happiness, no strength of character, nothing extraordinary. Its discontent that drives creation the most—passion, desire, defiance. Revolutions don't come from a place of happiness. If anything, I think it's sadness, or discontent at least, that's at the root of everything beautiful."

Deya listened, captivated. "Are you sad, then?"

"I was sad for a long time," Sarah said without meeting her eyes. "But I'm not anymore. I'm grateful to have accomplished something with my life. I spend my days doing something I love." She gestured to the books.

"Do you think you would've had this life if you'd stayed? If you'd gotten married?"

Sarah hesitated before replying. "I'm not sure. I think a lot about the kind of life I would've had if I'd stayed. Would I have been able to go to college? Would I have managed a bookstore in the city? Probably not, at least not ten years ago . . . But it seems like things have changed." She paused to think. "But then again, maybe they haven't changed that much. I don't know. It just depends . . ."

"On what?"

"On the family you're from. I know many Arab families who firmly believe in educating their women, and I've met some who graduated from college and have good jobs. But I think in my case, if I'd married a man my parents chose for me, who thinks the way my parents think, then he probably wouldn't have let me go to college or work. He would've wanted me to stay at home and raise children instead."

"You know, this isn't making me feel better," Deya said, thinking of the pitiful possibilities of her life. "If I'm going to be forced to stay at home and have children, then why shouldn't I run away?"

"Because it's the cowardly thing to do."

"But what's the point of being courageous? Where will that get me?"

"Courage will get you everywhere, so long as you believe in yourself and what you stand for," said Sarah. "You don't know what your life will be like, and neither do I. The only thing I know for sure is that you alone are in control of your destiny. No one else. You have the power to make your life whatever you want it to be, and in order to do that, you have to find the courage to stand up for yourself, even if you're standing alone."

Deya stared at Sarah's pale olive complexion, the way her eyes glittered in the dim room. She was starting to sound like a self-help book, and though Deya frequently read those sorts of things, it was beginning to annoy her. It was one thing to read theoretical advice and another thing entirely to listen to the words come out of someone's mouth.

"That all sounds great in theory," Deya said. "But this isn't a Dr. Phil show. What am I supposed to do? Ignore my grandparents and do whatever I want? It's not that simple. I have to listen to them. I don't have a choice."

"Yes, you do," Sarah said. "You always have a choice. You're always in control. Have you ever heard of a self-fulfilling prophecy?"

Deya sighed irritably. "I've read about it."

"It says we attract what we think. Whatever belief a person

has about the future comes true because the person believes it."

"You mean, like Voldemort in *Harry Potter*?"

Sarah laughed. "That's one example. Everything we draw into our life is a mirror of our thought patterns and beliefs. In a way, we can control the outcome of our future just by thinking more positively and visualizing only the things we want for ourselves. Of course, Voldemort did the exact opposite. He made his own worst-case scenario come true by believing in it too hard."

Deya only looked at her.

"What I'm trying to say is that if you believe you have power over your life, then you ultimately will. And if you believe you don't, then you won't."

"Now you're really starting to sound like Dr. Phil," Deya said, rolling her eyes.

Sarah clucked her tongue. "I'm serious, Deya. You know what you have right now? The entire world at your fingertips. You can go home and tell my mother, 'I'm not getting married right now. No matter how many suitors you find me, I refuse to marry any of them. I'm going to college first!'"

"I can't say that."

"Why not?"

"Because there's no way Fareeda will let me go to college."

"What is she going to do if you apply to college and get accepted? Stand at the door every morning and stop you from going to class?"

"I don't know what she'll do, but I don't want to find out."

"Why not? What do you have to lose?"

"I don't know . . . I don't know. But I don't want to upset her. I can't just defy her. I'm scared . . ."

"Scared of what? What could she possibly do? Hit you? Don't you think standing up for your future is worth a beating or two?"

"I don't know!" Deya said, feeling herself bubble with anger. "Please, just stop. You're making light of the situation. You're making it sound like I have more power over my life than I actually do, and it's not fair. If things were really that simple, then why didn't you do that yourself? You could've said the same thing to Teta, you could've never run away. But it's not that simple, is it?"

"It is simple," Sarah said softly. "No matter how you may feel now, this is a fact: your life is in your hands. If I had known that when I was your age, I would've done many things differently. I would've been less afraid of the future. I would've had more faith in myself. Believe me, not a day goes by that I don't regret not standing up to my family. I haven't seen them in over ten years, and I miss them. But most of all I wish I could've stayed and watched you and your sisters grow up, maybe even raised you myself." She paused. "I don't want you to end up like me, thinking your life isn't in your hands. Making decisions out of weakness and fear. I ran away to escape the shame of what I'd done, but that came at a cost."

"What cost? Your life seems pretty great to me."

"Belonging," Sarah said.

"Belonging?"

"It's hard to explain. . . . I still struggle to accept myself and it would have been better if I'd started sooner, much sooner. It's hard to belong anywhere, truly belong, if we don't belong to ourselves first."

Deya stared at her. "Are you saying you never made any friends? You never dated?"

"No, I've made friends and I've dated."

"Are you with someone now?"

"No."

"Why not? You live by yourself. You can do whatever you want."

"I think that's what I mean by truly belonging," Sarah said. "I've met a lot of guys over the years, but it was hard for me to really connect with anyone. I wasted a lot of years pretending to be someone that I wasn't." She met Deya's eyes. "Maybe if I'd had someone to trust back then, to help me find courage and believe in myself, I wouldn't have had to lose my family to find freedom. That's why I reached out, Deya. I want to help you find another way."

Deya looked at her aunt for a long time. If Sarah, this Americanized woman, who had gone to college and managed a bookstore and lived freely—if she had regretted her choices, was there any hope for her? She felt herself sink into her chair. Would she always be afraid? Would she ever learn courage? Listening to Sarah now, she didn't think so.

"What's wrong?" Sarah asked, trying to meet her eyes. "Why the sad face?"

"I just don't understand what I'm supposed to do. I thought I was confused about my life before—but now I'm even more confused. You're telling me I need to accept myself for who I am, that I need to stand up for what I truly believe in instead of running away, but that only sounds good in theory. It doesn't work like that in the real world. Self-acceptance won't solve my problems, and courage won't get me anywhere. These things sound great in some inspirational speech, or in a book, but the real world is much more complicated."

"Tell me," Sarah said, sitting up in her chair. "Why can't you stand up to my parents?"

Deya fixed her eyes on the window.

"You can tell me," Sarah said. "Be honest with me, with yourself. What are you so afraid of?"

"Everything!" Deya heard the sound of her voice before she knew she was speaking. "I'm afraid of everything! I'm afraid of letting down my family and culture, only to find out that they were right in the end. I'm afraid of what people will think of me if I don't do what I'm supposed to do. But I'm also afraid of listening to them and coming to regret it. I'm afraid of getting married, but I'm even more afraid of being alone. There's a thousand voices in my head, and I don't know which one to listen to! The rest of my life is staring me in the face, and I don't know what to do!" She willed herself to stop talking, but the words spilled out. "Sometimes I think I'm so scared because of my parents, but then I wonder if it's my memories of them that make me sad, or if I've been sad all along, before my brain could even make memories. And then there are days when I'm certain I've remembered everything wrong, and there's this horrible feeling inside me, and I think maybe if I remember something good, I'll be cured. But it never works."

Sarah reached out and squeezed Deya's knee. "Why do your memories of your parents make you so sad? What could you possibly remember to make you feel like that?"

"I don't know. . . . I don't even know if my memories are real. All I know is that my mother was sad all the time. She hated marriage, and she hated being a mother."

"But you're wrong," Sarah said. "Isra didn't hate being a mother."

"That's how it seemed to me."

"Just because she was sad, that doesn't mean she hated being a mother."

"Then why—"

But Sarah cut her off. "You have to understand, Isra was only seventeen when she married Adam, and she had no one here besides him. She was exhausted—cooking, cleaning, raising children, trying to please Adam and my mom. She struggled more than any woman I've ever met, but she loved you dearly. It hurts me that you don't remember that."

"I'm sure she struggled," Deya said, "but it was her choice to have all those children. She never stood up for herself, much less for us."

A small smile returned to Sarah's face. "Interesting you should say that. For a minute there, I thought you didn't believe women like us had a choice at all."

"Well, yes, but—"

Sarah shook her head. "You can't take it back now. You've just admitted you have choices. You've done worse than that, really."

Deya frowned.

"If you believe Isra—a Palestinian immigrant, with no job or education and four children to look after, and who didn't even speak English well—if you believe *she* had a choice, then that speaks volumes about the amount of choice a bright, educated Arab American girl like yourself has." Sarah shot Deya a playful smile. "Don't you think?"

Deya started to protest but found nothing to say. Sarah was right. She did have choices. What she didn't have was enough courage to make them.

"I should get going," Deya said, looking at the clock on the wall. "I don't want to be late to meet my sisters." She stood and gathered her backpack. "Time seems to fly in here," she said as Sarah walked her out.

"Does that mean you like my company?"

"Maybe a little."

"Well, come back soon then. I want to tell you a story."

"A story?"

Sarah nodded. "About why Isra started reading."

"Tomorrow?"

"Tomorrow."

Isra

Winter 1993

The **leaves turned** brown. The trees were bare. Snow came. Isra watched it all from the basement window. People on the side-walks rushed by, cars blinked and honked, traffic lights flashed in the distance. But all she saw was a dull painting, flat behind the glass. She had days of overwhelming sadness, followed by days of helplessness. It had been like this ever since the birth of Nadine and Omar's son. Whenever Adam came home to find her staring dully out the basement window, she did not protest when he neared her. In some perverse way she even looked for-ward to it. It felt like her way of apologizing for all she had done.

"What is this?" Fareeda asked one December morning when Isra came up to help with breakfast, squinting at the blue and purple mark on Isra's cheek. "You think anyone wants to see this?"

Isra opened her mouth, but nothing came out. What was there to say? A husband hitting his wife was normal. How many times had Yacob hit Mama? She wondered if Khaled had ever hit Fareeda. She had never seen it, but that meant nothing.

"There are things in this life no one should see," Fareeda said. "When I was your age, I never let anyone see my shame."

Watching Fareeda, Isra thought she was the strongest woman she'd ever known, much stronger than her own mother. Mama had always wept violently when Yacob beat her, unashamed to display her weakness. Isra wondered what in Fareeda's life had made her so bold. She must have suffered something worse than being beaten, Isra thought. The world had made a warrior out of her.

Fareeda led Isra upstairs to her bedroom. She opened her nightstand drawer, pulled out a small blue pouch, and fumbled for something within. First she pulled out a stick of red lipstick, a deep maroon, then shoved it back in. Isra pictured Fareeda's lips covered in the color. She had worn red lipstick at Isra's wedding, a bright and upbeat shade. But the dark shade of maroon, the deepness of it, suited her much more.

"Here," Fareeda said, her fingers finally producing what she had been searching for. She pumped a few drops of liquid foundation onto the back of her hand. Isra winced when Fareeda touched her skin, but she didn't seem to notice. She continued smearing the makeup on Isra's face, coat after coat over the bruises, until satisfied. "There," she said. Isra risked a peek at herself in the mirror: every inch of shame, every shade of blue and purple and red, had disappeared.

As she turned to leave, Fareeda grabbed her elbow and pulled her close, thrusting the bottle of foundation into her hands. "What happens between a husband and wife must stay between them. Always. No matter what."

The next time Adam left bruises, Isra covered them herself. She had hoped Fareeda might notice her efforts, that it might bring them closer somehow, maybe even back to the way things were in the beginning, before Deya was born. But if Fareeda did notice, she didn't let on. In fact, she pretended as if nothing had happened, as though Adam had never hit Isra, as though Fareeda had never covered her bruises. It bothered Isra, but she willed herself to remain calm. Fareeda was right. What happened between a husband and wife must stay between them, not from fear or respect, as Isra had initially thought, but shame. She couldn't have Sarah or Nadine suspecting anything. How foolish would she look if they knew Adam beat her? If she were back home, where a husband beating his wife was as ordinary as a father beating his child, Isra might have had someone to talk to. But Sarah was practically an American, and Nadine had Omar wrapped around her finger. Isra had to pretend nothing was wrong.

But pretending only worked on the outside. Inside, Isra was filled with a paralyzing shame. She knew there must be something dark stemming from within her to make the men in her life do these terrible things—first her father and now her husband. Everywhere she looked, the view was dreary and dismal, as gray as the black-and-white Egyptian movies she and Mama had loved to watch. Isra remembered clearly the colors of her childhood—the pink *sabra* fruit, the olive trees, the pale blue skies, even the wide, grassy cemetery—and she understood with dread that color was only seen by worthy eyes.

That winter, Isra did little but sit by the window, retreating to the basement as soon as her chores were done. She hardly spoke unless spoken to, and even then her responses were muted. She avoided her daughters' eyes, even when she held them, mothering them in a rush, desperate to return to the window, where she stared in a daze through the glass until it was time for bed. Only she barely slept, and when she did, she wept in her dreams, sometimes even waking in a scream. On those nights, she'd look over to Adam, afraid to have woken him, only to find him in a rough sleep, his mouth hanging wide.

Isra sometimes wondered if she was possessed. It was possible. She'd heard countless stories growing up about a jinn entering a person's body, making her do unseemly things—commit violence or murder, or, most often, go mad. Isra had seen it with her own eyes as a child. Their neighbor, Umm Hassan, had collapsed to the floor one afternoon after learning that her son had been killed by an Israeli soldier on his way home from school. Her eyes had rolled back in her head, her hands pounded her own face wildly, her body shook. Later that night, news had reached Isra that Umm Hassan had been found dead in her home, that she had swallowed her tongue and died. But Mama had told Isra the truth: a jinn had entered Umm Hassan's body and sucked the life from her, killing her. She wondered if the same thing was happening to her now, only more slowly. If it was, she deserved it.

Morning, and Isra stared out the window. Her daughters wanted to build a castle with their blocks, but she was too tired to play. She didn't like the way they looked at her with their dark eyes and sunken cheeks, as though they were judging her. In the glass reflection she could see three-year-old Deya watching her from the corner, her tiny fingers curled around a worn Barbie doll. It was her eyes that haunted Isra the most. Deya was a solemn child. She did not smile easily, let alone laugh the way other children did. Her mouth sat in a tight line, closely guarded, a dark worry behind her eyes. The sight was intolerable, but Isra didn't know how to make it go away.

She turned her gaze away from the window, signaling to Deya to come sit in her lap. When she did, Isra clutched her close and whispered, "I don't mean to be this way."

Deya squinted at her, holding the Barbie doll tight. "When I was a little girl," Isra continued, "my mother never spoke to me much. She was always so busy." Deya was quiet, but Isra could tell she was listening. She pulled her closer. "Sometimes I felt forgotten. Sometimes I even thought she didn't love me. But she did love me. Of course she loved me. She's my mother. And I love you, *habibti*. Always remember that." Deya smiled, and Isra held her tight.

In the kitchen that evening, Isra and Sarah seasoned a chunk of ground lamb for dinner. The men were craving *malfouf*, cabbage leaves stuffed with rice and meat, and the women only had a few hours to prepare it before they returned from work. They would've had more time if Nadine had been helping, but she was upstairs breastfeeding her son, whom, to Fareeda's fury, she had named Ameer, and not Khaled. More than once Fareeda had called on her, shouting from the end of the staircase that she should stop breastfeeding so she could get pregnant again, only for Nadine to call back, "But I already gave Omar a son, didn't I?"

Sarah passed Isra a smirk, but Isra looked away. Deep down she wondered why she couldn't be like Nadine. Why was speaking up so hard for her? In the four years she had lived in this house, she could not name a single time she had spoken up to Adam or Fareeda, and it felt as though someone had struck her when she realized this. Her pathetic weakness. When Adam came home and asked for dinner, she nodded, eager to please, and when he reached across the bed to touch her, she let him, and when he chose to beat her instead, she said nothing, sucking down her words. And again she said nothing to Fareeda's constant demands, even when her body ached from all the housework. What did the rest of it matter then—what she thought or felt, whether she was obedient or defiant—if she could not do something as basic as speaking her mind?

Tears came, rushing to her eyes. She shook them away. She thought about Mama. Had she felt as Isra felt now, a fool? Holding her tongue in an attempt to earn love, teaching her daughter to do the same? Did Mama live as she lived now—full of shame and guilt for not speaking up? Had she known this would happen to her daughter?

"She must have done *something* wrong," Fareeda said into the phone, both feet propped up on the kitchen table, a small smile on her face. Umm Ahmed's eldest daughter, Fatima, was getting divorced.

Isra looked out the window. She wondered what she had done wrong to provoke Adam's beatings. She wondered if he would divorce her.

"Poor, poor Umm Ahmed," Fareeda said into the phone. "Having to look people in the eye after her daughter's divorce." But she was smirking so broadly that her gold tooth glowed like the moon. Isra didn't understand—Umm Ahmed was Fareeda's closest friend. There was no reason to be happy. Only hadn't she prayed Nadine would have a girl just to ease her own suffering? She felt her heart squeeze tight.

"This will be good for you, daughter," Fareeda told Sarah when she hung up the phone. "If Fatima gets divorced, no one will marry her sister, Hannah."

"What does that have to do with me?" Sarah said.

"It has everything to do with you! Think of how much easier

it will be for you to find a suitor with Hannah out of the way." She stood up, tasting a pinch of the rice stuffing to make sure it was seasoned properly. "There are hardly enough Palestinian men in Brooklyn as it is. The less competition, the better." She met Isra's eyes. "Aren't I right?"

Isra nodded, placing a mixture of rice and meat in the center of a cabbage leaf. She could see Fareeda eyeing her, so she made sure to roll the leaf into a perfect fingerlike roll.

"Not that there's much competition between you girls, anyway," Fareeda said, licking her fingers. "Have you seen Hannah's dark skin and course hair? And the girl is barely five feet tall. You're much prettier."

Sarah stood and carried a stack of dirty plates to the sink, her face noticeably redder. Isra wondered what she was thinking. She thought back to when Mama used to compare her to other girls, saying she was nothing but sticks and bones, that no man would want to marry her. She'd tell Isra to eat more, and when she gained weight, she'd tell her to eat less, and when she went outside, she'd tell her to stay out of the sun so her skin wouldn't get dark. Mama had looked at her so often then, scanning her from head to toe to ensure she was in good condition. To ensure that a man would find her worthy. Isra wondered if Sarah felt now as she'd felt then, like she was the most worthless thing on earth. She wondered if her daughters would feel the same way.

"Maybe now is your chance," Fareeda said, following Sarah to the sink.

Sarah did not reply. She grabbed a sponge and turned on the faucet, her tiny frame lost beneath a blue turtleneck sweater and loose corduroy pants. She had worn those clothes to school, and Isra wondered if her classmates dressed in the same way, or if they wore tight-fitted, revealing clothes like the girls on television. More than once, she had overheard Sarah beg her mother for trendier outfits, but Fareeda would always shout, "You're not an American!" as if Sarah had somehow forgotten.

"Well, don't be *so* excited," said Fareeda. Sarah shrugged. "You're fifteen now. Marriage is around the corner. You need to start preparing."

"And what if I don't want to get married?" Sarah's angry voice was like a gunshot in the room.

Fareeda glared at her. "Excuse me?"

Sarah turned off the faucet and met her mother's eyes. "Why are you so eager to marry me off?"

"I'm not asking you to get married tomorrow. We can wait until after high school."

"No."

"What?"

"I don't want to get married after high school."

"What do you mean, you don't want to get married? What else are you going to do, you foolish girl?"

"I'm going to go to college."

"College? Do you think your father and I will let you leave the house alone so you can turn into an American?"

"It isn't like that. Everyone goes to college here!"

"Oh, yeah? And what do you suppose everyone back home will think when they find out our daughter is roaming the streets of New York alone? Think of our reputation."

"Reputation? Why don't my brothers have to worry about our reputation? No one prevents Omar and Ali from roaming the streets alone, doing as they please. Baba had to practically beg Ali to go to college!"

"You can't compare yourself to your brothers," Fareeda said. "You're not a man."

"That's what you always say, but it's not fair!"

"Fair or not, no girl of mine is going to college. *Fahmeh*?" She moved closer, her open palm twitching. "Do you understand me?"

Sarah took a step back. "Yes, Mama."

"Instead of worrying about college, why don't you learn a thing or two about being a woman. You have your sisters-in-law here. Did any of them go to college?"

Sarah mumbled something under her breath, but Fareeda didn't seem to notice. "As a matter of fact," she said, turning to leave, "from now on you can cook dinner with Isra every night." She met Isra's eyes. "You'll make sure she knows how to make every dish properly."

"Of course," Isra said.

"This woman is ridiculous," Sarah said when Fareeda had left to watch her evening show. "She treats me as if I'm some unworn hijab in her closet that she's desperate to give away."

"She just wants what's best for you," Isra said, only half convinced by her own words.

"What's best for me?" Sarah said, laughing. "You really believe that?"

Isra said nothing. It was moments like this when she was reminded of how different they were. Unlike Isra, Sarah wasn't easily defined. She was split between two very different cultures, and this divide was written all over her: the girl who shrank whenever Fareeda lifted her open palm, who barely spoke when her father and brothers entered the house, who rotated around the kitchen table until they had been served, and the girl who read American novels voraciously, who wanted to go to college, whose eyes, she saw now, sparked rebellion. Isra wished she could regain the defiance she once had, but that young girl was long gone.

"If she really wanted what's best for me," Sarah said, "she wouldn't want me to have a life like yours."

Isra looked up. "What do you mean?"

"I'm sorry, Isra, but it's obvious, you know."

"What is?"

"Your bruises. I can see them through the makeup."

"I . . ." Isra brought her hands to her face. "I tripped on Deya's Barbie doll."

"I'm not stupid. I know Adam hits you."

Isra said nothing. How did Sarah know? Did she hear Adam shouting at night? Or had she overheard Fareeda talking about it on the phone? Did Nadine know, too? She looked down, burying her face in the stuffed cabbage.

"You shouldn't let him touch you," Sarah said. Though her voice was low, Isra could hear her anger. "You have to stand up for yourself."

"He didn't mean to. He was just having a bad day."

"A bad day? Are you kidding me? You know domestic abuse is illegal here, right? If a man ever put his hands on me, I'd call the cops right away. It's one thing for our parents to hit us, but after marriage, as a grown woman?"

Isra kept her gaze averted. "Husbands beat their wives all the time back home. If a woman called the cops every time her husband beat her, all our men would be in jail."

"Maybe that's the way it should be," Sarah said. "Maybe if our women stood up for themselves and called the cops, their husbands wouldn't beat them."

"It doesn't work like that, Sarah," Isra whispered. "There is no government in Palestine. It's an occupied country. There's no one to call. And even if there was a police, they'd drag you back to your husband and he'd beat you some more for leaving."

"So men can just beat on their wives whenever they want?" Isra shrugged. "Well, that's not how it works in America."

A flurry of shame ran across Isra's body as Sarah stared at

her, wide-eyed. She looked away. How could she make Sarah
understand what it was like back home, where no woman
would think to call the cops if her husband beat her? And even
if she somehow found the strength to stand up for herself, what
good would it do when she had no money, no education, no job
to fall back on? That was the real reason abuse was so common, Isra thought for the first time. Not only because there was
no government protection, but because women were raised to
believe they were worthless, shameful creatures who deserved
to get beaten, who were made to depend on the men who beat
them. Isra wanted to cry at the thought. She was ashamed to be
a woman, ashamed for herself and for her daughters.

She looked back up to find Sarah staring at her. "You know
Adam drinks *sharaab*, right?"

"What?"

"Seriously, Isra? You haven't noticed that he comes home drunk
most nights?"

"I don't know. I thought he was sick."

"He's not sick. He's an alcoholic. Sometimes I even smell
hashish on his clothes when we do the laundry. You've never noticed the smell?"

"I don't know what hashish smells like," Isra said, feeling stupid. "I thought it was just the smell of the city on him."

Sarah stared at her, dumbfounded. "How can you be so naive?"

Isra straightened at the kitchen table. "Of course I'm naive!"
she said, a sliver of defiance rising up, surprising her. "I've been
stuck in the kitchen my entire life, first in Palestine and now
here. How am I supposed to know anything about the world?
The only places I've ever traveled are in the pages of my books,
and I don't even have that anymore."

"I'm sorry," Sarah said. "I'm not trying to hurt your feelings.

But sometimes you have to take things for yourself. I told you I'd bring you some books. Why didn't you let me? What are you so afraid of?"

Isra stared out the kitchen window. Sarah was right. She had abandoned reading for fear of upsetting Fareeda and Adam, thinking that servitude would earn their love. But she had been wrong. "Would you still do it?" she asked.

"Do what?"

"Would you still bring me some books?"

"Yes," Sarah said, smiling. "Of course. I'll bring some home for you tomorrow."

Deya

Winter 2008

In the coming days, Deya visited Sarah as often as she could without raising her grandmother's suspicions. Luckily Fareeda was occupied lining up another suitor, in case Nasser withdrew his proposal, and it seemed that school hadn't called home to report her absences, which were common in senior year as girls began sitting with suitors. At the bookstore, Deya and Sarah sat in the same velvet chairs by the window. Deya listened eagerly as her aunt told her stories of Isra, each tale unspooling like a chapter in a book, often in unexpected ways. The more Deya learned about her mother, the more she began to feel that she hadn't known her after all. All the stories she had told herself growing up, the memories she had pieced together, they had failed to paint a full picture of Isra. Now, gradually, one began to emerge. Still, Deya wondered if Sarah was telling her the entire truth—if she, too, was filtering her stories, the way Deya had to her sisters for so many years. Yet despite her suspicions, for once in her life she wasn't impatient for the whole truth. She had found a friend in Sarah, and she didn't feel so alone.

———————

"Tell me something," Deya asked her grandparents one cold Thursday night while they drank chai in the *sala*.

Fareeda looked up from the television. "What?"

"Why hasn't Aunt Sarah ever visited us?"

Fareeda's face became pink. Across from her, Khaled sank deeper into the sofa. Though he kept his eyes on the television screen, Deya could see that his hands were shaking. He set his teacup on the coffee table.

"Really," Deya continued. "I don't think either of you have ever explained it. Doesn't she have enough money to travel? Is she married to one of those controlling men who doesn't let his wife leave the house? Or maybe . . ." She kept her eyes on Fareeda as she said this. "Maybe she's never visited because she's angry with you for sending her away? That seems entirely possible."

"I don't see any reason for her to be upset," Fareeda said, bringing the cup to her face. "It's marriage, not murder."

"I guess, but then why hasn't she visited?" Deya turned to Khaled, waited for him to say something. But his eyes remained fixed on the television. She turned again to Fareeda. "Have you ever tried to reach out? You know, to ask if she was upset, or maybe even to apologize? I'm sure she'd forgive you after all these years. You are her mother, after all."

Fareeda's face grew pinker. "Apologize?" She set her teacup down with a thud. "What do I have to apologize for? *She's* the one who should apologize for never calling or visiting after everything we did for her."

"Maybe she feels like you've abandoned her," Deya said, keeping her voice innocent and light.

"*Khalas!*" Khaled stood up, glaring at her. "Not another word. I don't want to hear her name in this house. Never again.

Do you understand me?" He stormed out of the room before Deya could respond.

"You know, it's obvious," Deya said.

Fareeda turned to her. "What's obvious?"

"That Seedo feels guilty."

"Seedo doesn't feel guilty! What does he have to feel guilty for?"

Deya kept her words vague. "For forcing Sarah into marriage. For sending her to Palestine. He must feel guilty. Why else would he be so angry?"

Fareeda didn't reply.

"That must be it," Deya said, leaning closer. "Is that why you're always on the verge of tears whenever I mention Sarah? Because you didn't want her to go? It's all right. You can tell me."

"Enough of this!" Fareeda said. "You heard your grandfather."

"No, it's not enough!" Deya's voice was sharp. "Why can't you just tell me the truth?"

Fareeda sat up and grabbed the remote. "Is that what you really want?"

"*Please.*"

"Well, then," Fareeda said, gritting her teeth. "The truth is, I had no trouble sending my daughter away, and I certainly won't have trouble doing the same to you." She turned her attention back to the television. "Now get out of my face. *Go!*"

Fareeda

Spring 1994

One crisp Friday afternoon, while Isra and Nadine fried a skillet of shakshuka and Sarah brewed a kettle of chai, Fareeda paced the kitchen. The men were stopping by for lunch after *jumaa* prayer, and Fareeda didn't have enough food for them. There was no meat to roast, no vegetables to sauté, not even a single can of chickpeas to make hummus, and she rotated around the kitchen with her fingertips in her mouth, trying to calm herself.

"I don't understand," Sarah said to Fareeda, who had stopped to open the pantry yet again. "Why do you wait for Baba to bring groceries every Sunday?"

Fareeda stuffed her head into the pantry. How many times had she answered that question? Usually she would brush it off, saying that she couldn't possibly do everything in the house, that Khaled had to help somehow. But today was one of those days when she felt an unexpected pulse of anger pumping through her. This was all her life had amounted to, all she was good for: sitting around taking criticism and orders.

"But really, Mama," Sarah said, leaning forward in her seat.

"The supermarket is only a few blocks away. Why not go your-self?"

Fareeda didn't even look up. She reached inside the pantry for a box of cookies before taking a seat at the table. "Because," she said, pulling one out and taking a bite. She could see the three young women staring at her blankly, waiting for her to fin-ish chewing. But she just reached for another cookie and stuffed it into her mouth.

"Because what?" Sarah said.

"Because I don't feel like it," Fareeda said between mouthfuls.

"You know, Mama," Sarah said, reaching for a cookie, "I could go to the grocery store for you."

Fareeda looked around the table. Nadine nibbled on the edge of a cookie, while Isra stared straight ahead. She didn't know which of them she disliked more: Nadine, who had refused to name her son after Khaled and constantly did as she pleased, or Isra, who followed commands like a zombie and still had not borne a son. "Don't be ridiculous."

"Really," Sarah said. "I could go right after school. That way you don't have to wait until Sunday each week."

At once, Fareeda stopped chewing. She swallowed. "Are you crazy?"

Sarah looked confused. "What do you mean?"

"What would I look like, sending my unmarried daughter to the market by herself? Do you want the neighbors to start talking? Saying my daughter is out and about alone, that I don't know how to raise her?"

"I didn't think of it like that," Sarah said.

"Of course you didn't! You're too busy stuffing your head in those books of yours to notice what really goes on in the world."

Fareeda wanted to shake Sarah. It seemed like everything she tried to teach her about their culture rolled off her shoulders. Her only daughter was turning into an American, despite everything she had done to stop it. She had even asked Isra to teach Sarah how to cook, hoping her complacency would rub off on her daughter, but it hadn't worked. Sarah was still as rebellious as ever.

"That's what I get for coming to this damn country," Fareeda said, snatching a handful of cookies. "We should've let those soldiers kill us. Do you even know what it means to be a Palestinian girl? Huh? Or did I raise a damn American?"

Sarah said nothing, her eyes glistening with something Fareeda couldn't quite place. Fareeda scoffed and turned to Nadine. "Tell me, Nadine," she said. "Did *you* ever dare ask your mother to go to the supermarket alone back home?"

"Of course not," Nadine said with a smirk.

"And you—" Fareeda turned to Isra. "Did you ever step foot in Ramallah without your mother?"

Isra shook her head.

"You see," Fareeda said. "That's how it's done. You ask any woman, and she'll tell you."

Sarah stared out the window in silence. Fareeda wished her daughter would understand that she didn't make the world the way it was. She was just trying to help her survive in it. Besides, Sarah should be thankful for the life she had, living in a country where she had food to eat and a roof over her head—enough of everything.

Later, Fareeda gathered the men around the kitchen table, crossing her plump ankles as she admired the view around her. Khaled sat to her right, Omar and Ali to her left. All of them strong and healthy, even if Khaled wasn't as young as he used to be. She wished Adam was with them, but he was working. He had so much to do, maybe too much. In the mornings, he helped Khaled in the deli, staying up front near the cash register to fill orders. Then he stopped by Omar's shop to count inventory and deposit checks before heading to his own store. Fareeda was grateful for Adam's help, though she didn't tell him as often as she should. She told herself she would thank him tonight.

"How's business?" she asked Omar, reaching for a warm pita from the plate Nadine had just set on the table.

"*Alhamdulillah*, bringing in a steady income," he said, smiling gently as he caught Nadine's eyes.

Fareeda raised her eyebrows at the sight. She reached for the shakshuka, her favorite dish, scooping a bite full of poached eggs and tomatoes into her mouth. Still chewing, she said, "Maybe now you can focus on having another child." She stole a glance at Nadine, who was blushing, as she said this. Fareeda knew her words were pointless, that Omar and Nadine would have another child when they wanted to, but she spoke anyway. The satisfaction of making Nadine uncomfortable was enough. Omar was a fool. Instead of putting his foot down, as she'd told him, he let his wife run the show. At least Adam had listened to her, and look at Isra now. As quiet as a graveyard. Not mouthy and insolent like Nadine. Let's see where that will get Omar, Fareeda thought. She turned to Ali. "What about you, son? How is college going?"

"It's going," Ali mumbled.

Khaled looked up. "What did you say?"

Ali slumped into his chair. "I said it's going."

"What's that supposed to mean?"

Here he goes again, Fareeda thought, regretting that she had asked. Lately, most of her fights with Khaled had been about Ali. He thought she was too lenient with him; she thought he was too tough. That he expected too much.

"I'm trying," Ali said. "I'm really trying. I just"—Khaled's eyes were wide now, and Fareeda realized she was holding her breath—"I just don't see the point of college."

"You don't see the point of college?" Khaled was shouting now. "You're the first person in this family to go! Adam couldn't because he was working to help us pay the bills, Omar couldn't even get in, and now you're saying you don't see the point of it? *Walek*, do you know what I would've done for an education?" The room was silent. All Fareeda could hear was the sound of her own chewing. "I would've given an arm and a leg. But instead I worked like an animal to bring you here, so that *you* could go to college! So that *you* could live the life your mother and I couldn't have! And *this* is how you repay me?"

Ali looked at him with panic. Fareeda knew her children couldn't understand what she and Khaled had endured. They weren't even born when the Israeli soldiers had come, sweeping them out of their homes like dust. They knew nothing about life, about how easily everything could be taken from you.

She reached for another scoop of shakshuka. But what did she know about life then, either? She was only six years old when the occupation began. Fareeda could still remember the look on her father's face as he surrendered, both hands in the air, when they were forced to evacuate. But it wasn't only her family. Tanks had rolled into Ramla to drive out its inhabitants. Some villagers had been killed as Israeli militia burned their olive groves. Others had died in the makeshift trenches, trying to protect their homes. She had always wondered why her family had fled, why they hadn't stayed and fought for their land. But her father would always say, "We had to leave. We never stood a chance."

"The boy doesn't like school," Fareeda said. "We can't force him."

"What about all the money we've already spent on his tuition?" said Khaled.

"Didn't you want sons *so* badly?" Fareeda shot him a sidelong glance. "Well, this is what having sons means, paying for things. It's an investment in the future of our family. You should've known it would be expensive. Besides, you have Adam to help you out. I'm sure he'll understand."

She hoped Adam would understand. Lately he hardly spoke to anyone, including her. Especially her. At first, she thought he blamed her for Isra, who was only getting worse, retreating to the basement as soon as her chores were completed, barely a word to anyone. But now Fareeda was beginning to wonder if he was mad at her, at them, for all the responsibility they put on him. She thought back to when he was sixteen, how he would spend his days after school reading the Holy Qur'an. He'd wanted to be an imam, he'd told her. But he was forced to leave that dream behind when they went to America. What was she supposed to do? He was the eldest son, and they needed him. They'd all left things behind.

She turned to Ali. "So what do you want to do now?"

He shrugged. "Work, I guess."

"Why don't you work in the deli?" She turned to Khaled. "Can't you hire him?"

Khaled shook his head, looking at her like she was an idiot. "The deli barely brings in enough money to pay the bills. Don't you see all the work Adam does just to keep it running? Why do you think I want Ali to go to college?" He waved his hands. "So he isn't stuck behind a cash register like we are. Don't you understand a thing, woman?"

"I don't know," Fareeda mocked. "Do I? The last time I checked, I'm the reason we made it to America in the first place."

Khaled said nothing. It was true. If it hadn't been for Fareeda, if *she* hadn't forced Khaled to give her his daily earnings, they never would've made it to America in 1976, or likely ever. It was Fareeda who had saved enough money for them to purchase their plane tickets to New York, and later, she who had saved Khaled's earnings at his first job, an electronics store on Flatbush Avenue, in a navy-blue shoe box under her bed. She who had become ever more resourceful, limiting the amount of money she spent on food and household items, washing her children's clothes daily so they didn't need more than two outfits each, even baking *ma'amool* cookies for Khaled to sell his customers, who were enthralled by the foreign combination of figs and butterbread. Soon she had saved ten thousand dollars in the navy-blue shoe box stuffed beneath their bed, which Khaled had used to open his deli.

Fareeda took a sip of her chai, looking away from Khaled. "The boy wants to work, so let him work," she said. "Maybe I'll ask Adam to give him a job in his store."

Ali jumped in. "What about Omar's store?"

"What about it?"

"Maybe I can work there instead?"

"No, no, no," Fareeda said, reaching for another loaf of pita. "Omar is still getting on his feet. He can't afford to hire anyone right now. Adam has a steady business going. He'll hire you."

Khaled stood up. "So that's your solution? Instead of encouraging him to stay in school, to do something on his own, you turn to Adam, again, as though he is the only man among them? When will you stop spoiling them? When will you start treating them like men?" He turned to his younger sons, his index finger shaking. "You two don't know a thing about this world. Not one damn thing."

Oh, for goodness sake, Fareeda thought, though she said nothing. Instead, she pulled the skillet of shakshuka closer, taking two, three bites in a row, chugging her chai to keep the food moving. Food, it was the only thing left that gave her comfort. She was considerably thicker now than she'd once been. But that didn't bother her. In fact, she would spend all day eating if it didn't cost so much. Of course she knew that burying her feelings in food was unhealthy—that it could kill her. But there were other things that could kill her, too, things like failure and loneliness. Like growing old one day and looking around to find a husband who resented you, kids who no longer needed you, who despised you despite all you'd done for them. At least eating felt good.

Isra

Spring 1994

The books kept Isra company. All it took to soothe her worries was to slip inside their pages. In an instant, her world would cease to exist, and another would rush to life. She felt herself come alive, felt something inside her crack open. What was it? Isra didn't know. But the longing to connect to something filled her. She went to bed bewildered that she had felt herself so vividly in another place, that she could almost swear she'd come to life by night and the fictional world was the place she actually existed.

But there were also days when the books didn't seem quite as soothing. Days when reading would turn her mind and force her to question the patterns of her life, which only made her more upset. On these days, Isra dreaded getting up in the morning. She was aware in a fresh way of how powerless she was, and this realization flipped her upside down. Listening to the characters in her books, it was clear to Isra how weak she was, and the enormous effort it would take to transform herself into one of the worthy heroines of these tales, each managing to find her voice by her story's end.

Isra didn't know what to do with her conflicting thoughts, didn't know how to fix her life. If she were a character in one of her books, what would she be expected to do? Stand up to Adam? How, when she had a handful of children depending on her in a foreign place, with nowhere to go? Isra resented her books in these moments when she thought about the limits of her life and how easy courage seemed when you boiled it down to a few words on paper.

You can't compare your life to fiction, a voice inside her head whispered. *In the real world, a woman belongs at home. Mama was right all along.*

But Isra wasn't entirely convinced. As much as she tried to console herself with these thoughts, inside her a flicker of hope had been reignited. The hope that perhaps, she, Isra, deserved a better life than the one she had, as far-fetched as that hope seemed.

Some days she believed she could actually achieve this life if she tried. Hadn't the characters in her books struggled, too? Hadn't they stood up for themselves? Hadn't they been weak and powerless, too? Wasn't it true that she had as much control over her life as they had? Perhaps she too had a chance to be happy. But just as quickly as these thoughts came, they went, leaving Isra overwhelmed with hopelessness. She couldn't possibly take control of her life. And it wasn't Adam's fault but her own. It was her fault for asking Sarah to bring her books, for reading them obsessively in this way. She was to blame for raising her expectations of the world, for not focusing on Adam and her daughters instead, for dreaming and wanting too much. Or maybe it was her books' fault for turning her mind the way they had. For tempting her to disobey Mama as a young girl, to believe in love and happiness, and now, for taunting her over her greatest weakness: that she had no control over her own life.

But despite the war inside her mind, Isra couldn't part with her books. Each night she read by the window. She decided she would rather go on living conflicted with books by her side than be tormented all alone.

"I have some books for you," Sarah whispered to Isra one evening as they cooked dinner together. As the sun set, the windows darkened, and Fareeda retreated to the *sala* to watch her favorite Turkish soap opera, Isra and Sarah roasted vegetables, simmered stews, and prepared assortments of hummus, baba ghanoush, and tabbouleh. Sometimes Nadine would enter the kitchen to find them whispering together, and to their relief, she would join Fareeda in the *sala*. In these private moments, as they lingered near the stove, wrapped in a blanket of steam, the savory smell of allspice thickening the air, Isra would feel her heart swell.

Lately, Sarah had been sneaking into the basement a few times a week after dinner with a handful of books she had brought home for Isra. In the past, on nights like this one, Isra would have put her daughters to sleep and spent the evening gazing out the basement window until Adam came home. But now she waited up for Sarah, eager to see which books she'd brought. Some nights they would even read together. Last week they'd rushed through *Pride and Prejudice* in four nights so Sarah could write an essay on it for her English class. They'd sat together on Isra's bed, knees grazing, the book like a warm fire between them.

"You're going to love these," Sarah told Isra that night. She placed a pile of books on the bed, and Isra scanned them, noticing that a few were picture books. She picked up *Oh, the Places You'll Go!* by Dr. Seuss.

"I know you wanted more books for the girls," Sarah said. "I think it's really great that you're reading to them. It will help with their English. You don't want them to struggle with it when they start school like I did."

"Thank you," Isra said with a smile. Ever since Sarah had started bringing her picture books for the girls, she had begun gathering her daughters around her before she put them to bed, a picture book spread across her lap. She thought they liked the softness of her voice in English, the sound of her tongue as she pronounced unfamiliar words. A gust of happiness would fill her in those moments as she watched her daughters, smiling wide, looking up at her as though she was the best mother in the world, as though she hadn't failed them every day of their lives.

"Is there anything specific you want to read tonight?" Sarah asked. "There's lots of good books here." She pointed to a black-and-white cover. "*A Tree Grows in Brooklyn* is one of my favorites, but I don't know if you'll love it as much as I do."

Isra looked up. "Why not?"

"Because it's not a romance."

"Good. I'm glad."

"Glad of what?"

"That it's not a romance."

Sarah met her eyes. "Since when?"

"I just don't have a taste for romances anymore," Isra said. "I'd rather read a book that teaches me something." She paused. "A story that is more realistic."

"Are you saying you don't think love stories are realistic?"

Isra shrugged.

"What's this? Isra, a cynic?" Sarah laughed. "I can't believe my ears. What have I done to you?"

Isra only smiled. "What are you reading in class?"

"We just started one of my favorites, a novel about a world

where books are outlawed and burned. Can you imagine life without books?"

If Sarah had asked this question four years before or even one year before, back when Isra had abandoned her books, she would've said yes. But now, reading with the same dedication with which she had once performed her five daily prayers, Isra couldn't imagine it.

"I hope that never happens," she said. "I don't know what I'd do."

Sarah looked at her curiously.

"What?" Isra asked.

"I don't think I've ever seen you like this."

"What do you mean?"

"You just seem different."

"Different how?"

"I don't know. I can't explain it."

Isra smiled at her. "I'm just happy, that's all."

"Really?"

"Yes. Thanks to you."

"Me?"

Isra nodded. "Ever since I started reading again, I feel like I'm in a trance, or maybe like I've come out of one. Something has come over me—I don't know how to describe it—it might sound dramatic, but I feel hopeful for the first time in years. I don't know why exactly, but I have you to thank for it."

"You don't have to thank me," Sarah said, blushing. "It's nothing."

Isra met her eyes. "It's not nothing, and it's not just the books. It's your friendship, too. You've given me something to look forward to for the first time in years."

"I hope you always feel happy," Sarah whispered.

Isra smiled. "Me too."

———————

In her bedroom closet, Isra was careful to keep her books hidden beneath a pile of clothes. She didn't know how Adam would react if she told him she had been reading while he was at work. She assumed he would hit her, or worse, prevent Sarah from bringing her books. After all, if Mama had forbidden Isra from reading Middle Eastern books for fear of any nontraditional influence, she could only imagine what Adam would do if he knew she was reading Western novels. But to her relief, he was barely home.

Still, Isra was surprised Fareeda hadn't noticed a change in her. Lately, she performed all her responsibilities—soaking the rice, roasting the meats, bathing her daughters, brewing Fareeda her *maramiya* chai twice daily—in a rush, desperate for a moment alone. Most days, she read by the window in the girls' room, the sun bright and warm against her face. She pulled the curtains open and leaned against the windowpane. The touch of each hardcover book sent shivers down her spine.

She couldn't remember the precise moment she had stopped reading. Perhaps it had been when she first arrived in America, glancing over her copy of *A Thousand and One Nights* when she couldn't sleep and finding it insufficient comfort. Or maybe it was during her pregnancy with Nora, when Fareeda had dangled a necklace over Isra's belly and predicted a girl, and Isra had read a *sura* from the Holy Qur'an every night, asking God to change the gender. She had almost forgotten the weight of a book between her hands, the smell of old paper as she turned each page, the way it soothed her someplace deep within. Is this what Adam felt, she wondered, when he drank *sharaab* and smoked hashish? A surge of happiness. An elation. If this was how he felt—floating as she was now, with a book in her hands—then she couldn't blame him for drinking and smoking. She understood the need to escape from the ordinary world.

"What makes you happy?" Isra asked Adam one night as she watched him eat his dinner. She didn't know where the question came from, but by the time it had left her lips, she found herself leaning forward in her seat, both eyes glued on Adam for his answer.

He looked up from his plate, swaying a bit in his seat. She knew he was drunk—Sarah had taught her how to recognize the state. "What makes me happy?" he said. "What kind of question is that?"

Why did she care what made him happy? The man who beat her mercilessly, who had sucked the hope from her? She wasn't sure, but in that moment it felt important, intensely so. She poured him a cup of water. "I just want to know what makes my husband happy. Surely something must."

Adam took a gulp of water and wiped his mouth with the back of his hand. "You know, not once in my entire life has anyone ever asked me that question. What makes Adam happy? No one cares what makes Adam happy. All they care about is what Adam can do for them. Yes, yes," he said, slurring a little. "How much money can Adam bring home? How many businesses can he run? How much can he help his brothers? How many male heirs can he produce?" He paused, looking at Isra. "But happiness? There's no such thing as happiness for people like us. Family duty comes first."

"But I care what makes you happy," Isra said.

He shook his head. "Why should you care? I haven't been good to you."

"Still," she said, her voice low and soft. "I know what you're going through. I know you're under a lot of pressure, too. I can understand how that can make you act—" She stopped, looked away.

"Walking the Brooklyn Bridge at dawn," Adam said. Isra turned back to him to find his face had softened. "Some early mornings on my way to work, I don't take the train straight into the city. Instead I stop to walk the bridge in time for sunrise." His words slipped out as though he had forgotten Isra was in the room. "There's something magical about watching the sunrise when I'm so high up there. In that moment, when the first light hits my face, I feel like the sun has swallowed me up. Everything goes quiet. The cars rush beneath my feet, but I don't hear a thing. I can see the whole city, and I think about the millions of people living here, the struggles they face, and then I think about the men back home and their struggles, too, and in an instant my worries vanish. I stare at the sky and remind myself that at least I am here, in this beautiful country, at least I have this view."

"You never told me that before," Isra whispered. He nodded but averted his gaze, as though he had said too much. "It sounds lovely," she said, smiling at him. "It reminds me of when I used to watch the sunset back home, how the sun would sink into the mountains and disappear. It always made me feel better, too, knowing I wasn't the only person staring up at the mountains, that in those moments I was connected to everyone watching the sunset, all of us held together by this magnificent view." She tried to catch his eyes, but he stared at his plate and resumed eating. "Maybe we can watch the sunrise together one day," Isra said.

"*Inshallah*," he said between mouthfuls of food, but from the look on his face, Isra knew they never would. There had been a time when this would have hurt her, and she was surprised to find that she was no longer upset. For so many years she had believed that if a woman was good enough, obedient enough, she might be worthy of a man's love. But now, reading her books, she was beginning to find a different kind of love. A love that came from inside her, one she felt when she was all alone, reading by the window. And through this love, she was beginning to believe, for the first time in her life, that maybe she was worthy after all.

"I don't understand why you're wasting time," Fareeda said to Isra one Sunday afternoon in March. They were all gathered together at Fort Hamilton Park to celebrate Eid al-Fitr, which Isra found strange, considering that most of them hadn't observed the Ramadan fast that year. Fareeda couldn't fast because of her diabetes, Nadine was pregnant, and Sarah only pretended to fast so as not to upset Khaled, who, besides Isra, was the only one who fasted every year. She wondered if Adam only pretended to fast, too, but had never dared ask him.

She didn't know why she herself still observed Ramadan. Some days she thought she fasted out of guilt—for often failing to perform her five daily prayers, for failing to trust in Allah and her *naseeb*. Other days fasting reminded her of her childhood, of evenings seated with her family around a *sufra* of lentil soup and fresh dates, counting down the minutes until sunset so they could eat and drink again. But most days Isra suspected she fasted purely from habit, a soothing familiarity in performing ritual for ritual's sake alone.

"Really," Fareeda said now, "why aren't you pregnant again? What are you waiting for? You still need a son, you know."

Isra sat at the edge of the picnic blanket, as far away from Fareeda as possible, and watched the rest of the family. Sarah and Deya fed pigeons by the pier. Khaled carried Ameer over his shoulders. Omar and Nadine held hands and looked out onto the Hudson River. Adam lit a cigarette. Behind them, the Verrazano Bridge stood high and wide, like a mountain on the horizon. "I already have three children," Isra said. "I'm tired."

"Tired?" Fareeda said. "When I was your age, I'd already given birth to—" She stopped. "Never mind the number. My point is that Adam needs a son, and you need to get pregnant soon to give him one."

"I'm only twenty-one," Isra said, startled by the defiance in her tone. "And I already have three children. Why can't I wait a little?"

"Why wait? Why not just get them out of the way?"

"Because I wouldn't be able to raise another kid right now."

Fareeda scoffed. "Three or four, what difference does it make?"

"It makes a difference to me. I'm the one who has to raise them."

Fareeda glared, and Isra looked away. Not from shame, but rather to conceal her pleasure. She couldn't believe she had spoken her mind and defied Fareeda for the first time in years.

"Still eating?" Adam asked when he approached them.

Isra passed him a small smile, but Fareeda wasted no time. She cleared her throat and began. "Tell your wife," she said. "Tell her it's time to get pregnant again."

Adam sighed. "She'll get pregnant soon, Mother. Don't worry."

"You've been saying that for months! You're not getting any younger, you know. And neither is Isra. What do you think will happen if you get a fourth girl? You think you're going to just stop trying for a son? Of course not! That's why it's important to hurry."

Adam fumbled inside his pocket for a pack of Marlboro Red. "You think I don't want a son? I'm trying my best."

"Well, keep trying."

"I will, Mother."

"Good."

Adam looked away, squeezing the pack of cigarettes tight. Even though he was looking out toward the river, Isra could see it in his eyes: he would beat her tonight. She stared at him, hoping she was wrong, that he wouldn't take out his anger on her. But the signs were all too familiar now. First, he'd beat her loud and hard, shaking with rage. Then he'd reach out to touch her again, only slightly softer this time, pushing himself inside her. She'd shut her eyes tight, clench her fists, and keep still in hopes she might just disappear.

Deya

Winter 2008

"Something doesn't make sense," Deya told Sarah one Friday afternoon, after her aunt had finished telling her yet another story about Isra. They sat huddled by the window, sipping on vanilla lattes Sarah had brewed for them.

"What?" Sarah asked.

Deya set her cup down. "If my mother loved books so much, why didn't she want a better life for us?"

"She did," Sarah said. "But there was only so much she could do."

"Then why did she stop us from going to school?"

Sarah looked at her, startled. "What are you talking about?"

"She said we had to stop going to school," Deya said, feeling her stomach twist at the memory. "She even called me a *sharmouta*."

"Isra would've never said that word, especially to you."

"But she did say it. I remember."

"The Isra I knew never would've uttered that word," Sarah said. "Was this after I left?"

"I think so," Deya said, suddenly uncertain. She had been so young. Her memories were so fragmented.

"Do you remember why she said it?"

"Not really."

"Do you remember when?"

"It must've been right before the car accident . . . I don't know . . . I mean, the memory is clear, but I'm not certain of the exact—"

"Tell me then," Sarah interrupted. "Tell me everything you remember."

Outside the sky was dark gray, as Deya and Nora rode the school bus home. When they reached their stop, Mama was waiting for them, as she always did. Her belly was slightly bigger than usual, and Deya wondered if Mama was pregnant again. She imagined a fifth child in their narrow bedroom. She wondered where the baby would sleep, if Baba would buy another crib, or if it would sleep in Amal's crib, and if Amal would share the bed with her and Nora. The baby's face was in her head, already big and swelling bigger, suffocating her. She took a deep breath and loosened the backpack from her shoulders.

She touched Mama's arm when she reached her, earning a quick smile before Isra looked away. It was the same smile Isra always gave her, just the slightest curve of the lips.

Behind her, she could hear her classmates calling from the bus. "Bye, Deya! See you tomorrow!"

Deya turned to wave goodbye. When she turned back, Mama's eyes were intently fixed on her face.

"Why are those boys speaking to you?" Mama said. It was strange to hear words leave her mouth with such force.

"They're in my class, Mama."

"Why are you talking to boys in your class?"

"They're my friends."

"Friends?"

Deya nodded and lowered her eyes to the ground.

"You can't be friends with boys! Did I raise a *sharmouta*?"

Deya stumbled back, struck by the word. "No, Mama, I didn't do anything—"

"*Uskuti!* You know you're not allowed to speak to boys! What were you thinking? You're an Arab girl. Do you understand? An *Arab* girl." But Deya didn't understand. "Listen to me, Deya. Open your ears and listen." Her voice lowered to a tight whisper. "Just because you were born here, that doesn't make you an American. As long as you live in this family, you will never be an American."

Deya couldn't remember the walk home, couldn't recall how she felt as she tiptoed across the pavement, crept down the basement steps, and settled into her bed. All she remembered was sinking between the sheets with a book in hand—*Matilda*—willing herself to escape between its pages. She dug her fingers into the spine, flipping page after page until she could no longer hear the ringing between her ears.

The next thing she knew Mama was downstairs with her. The room was quiet, and Mama settled on the edge of her bed, hugging her knees. How long before Deya had inched up to her? She didn't know. All she remembered was blinking up at Mama, desperate to meet her eyes, to catch even the hint of a smile. But she could barely see her face, couldn't see her eyes at all. She reached out to touch her hand. Mama flinched.

She waited for Mama to say something. Maybe she was thinking of a way to punish her. And why shouldn't she be punished? She deserved it. There she was, making Mama sad, as if she needed any more reasons.

Deya wondered how she would be punished. She looked around the room. There was nothing worth taking. Just a handful of toys scattered across the floor. She thought maybe her mother would take the television. Or the cassette player. She wasn't sure. She had nothing.

But then she saw it, the book resting beneath her fingers, and she realized she did have something to be taken away. She started to think of the words Mama would use when she told her to hand over her books, that she was forbidden from the school library, that she was no longer allowed to—

"Deya," Mama began. "Your father . . ."

Please don't say it. Please don't take my books.

"Listen . . ." Mama was shaking now. "I know you love school . . ."

I'll do anything, please. Not my books.

"But . . ." She breathed in. "You can't go to PS 170 anymore."

Deya's heart stopped. For a moment, she had an overwhelming feeling of breathlessness. She felt the way a book must feel, the unseen weight beneath its cover. She swallowed. "What?"

"Not just you. Nora, too."

"No, Mama—please—"

"I'm sorry, daughter," Isra said in a choked voice. "I'm so sorry. I don't have a choice."

"Is that when you started going to Islamic school?" Sarah asked when Deya had finished. "After they took you out of PS 170?"

"I think so," Deya said. "Do you know why they took us out?"

Sarah shook her head, shifting in her seat.

"Wait a minute," Deya said. "What year did you run away?"

"Why?"

"I want to know."

"Nineteen ninety-seven."

"You were still there," Deya said. "Surely you must remember something."

Sarah stared at her knees. "I think it was because I ran away. They must've been afraid that you and your sisters would follow in my footsteps one day."

"That makes sense."

There was a pause, and Sarah met Deya's eyes. "Do you remember how things were after I left?"

"Not exactly. Why?"

"What's the last thing you remember?" Sarah asked.

"What?"

"Do you remember the last time you saw your parents?"

Deya considered. "I think so. I'm not sure."

"What do you remember?"

She felt the enormity of the memory on her tongue, words she had never said aloud. "They took us to the park. That's the last thing I remember."

"Tell me what happened," Sarah said.

Deya had replayed this memory so many times before she could picture it vividly: Mama waiting for her and Nora at the bus stop, with Layla and Amal asleep in the stroller. "We're going to the park," Mama had said, smiling wider than Deya had ever seen. Deya felt a rainbow bloom inside her. They walked down Fifth Avenue, teeth chattering, cold air forming goose bumps on their skin. Cars honked. People rushed by. When they reached a subway station, Deya realized Mama meant to take them inside and her stomach clenched in fear: she had never ridden a train before. She breathed and breathed as they descended the dirty staircase. Below, the dimness hurt her eyes. The platform was a dingy gray, smeared with garbage and wads of chewing gum, then dropped steeply to the subway rails. Rats ran across the tracks, and Deya inched back from the edge. At the end of the tunnel, she could see a bright light, fast approaching. It was the train. She gripped Mama's leg as it swept by. When the train stopped in front of them, the doors opened, and there stood Adam. He rushed over to them, wrapping her in his arms. Then they went to the park, all six of them, a family.

"So Adam met you all in the subway and took you to the park?" Sarah asked.

"Yes."

Sarah eyed her in silence.

"What?"

"It's nothing," she said, shaking her head. "So, what happened after that?"

"I don't know." Deya slumped in the chair. "I've tried to remember so many times, but I can't. For all I know, I could've made it up. Maybe I've even made everything up. That would explain why nothing makes sense."

"I'm sorry," Sarah said after a moment.

"I don't get it. You said you would help me understand the past, but you can't even explain why my mother wrote that letter. What if something happened to her after you left? How would you know? You weren't with her."

"I'm sorry," Sarah said again, looking down at the floor. "I think about it every day. I wish I'd never left her."

Now that Deya had started to unleash the words she'd held at bay these weeks, she couldn't stop them. "Did you even try to help her? If you knew Baba beat her, why didn't you do something? I thought she was your friend."

"She was my friend, my sister."

"Then why didn't you take her with you? Why did you leave her? Why did you leave all of us?"

"She wouldn't come with me." Sarah's eyes were filled with

tears. "I begged her to come, but she wouldn't leave. Maybe I should've tried harder. It's something I have to live with. But I'm here to help you now." She wiped tears from her face. "Please, Deya. For her sake. She'd want me to help you."

"Then help me! Tell me what to do."

"I can't tell you what to do. If you don't decide for yourself, then what's the point? It won't matter what you do if it's not your own choice. It has to come from inside you. That's the only way I can help. What do you want to do?"

"I don't know. It's not that simple."

"But it is. You're letting fear cloud your thoughts. Dig deep inside yourself. What do you want?"

"I want to make my own decisions. I want to have a choice."

"Then do it! Starting now."

Deya shook her head. "You make it sound so easy, but it's not. That's what you don't understand."

"There are many things you can say to me, but you can't say I don't understand. I never said it was easy. But it's what you have to do."

Deya sighed and rubbed her temples. Her body ached, her head hurt. She had no idea what to do, or where to begin. She stood to leave. "I have to go."

Isra

A year passed and Isra was pregnant again. Her fourth pregnancy. After completing her chores, she spent her days curled againt the basement window, a book in her hands, hoping to silence the gnawing fear of giving birth to another girl. But no amount of reading had alleviated her angst. In fact, it seemed as if the more she read, the more her worries grew, and her belly along with it, so that she got bigger and bigger and the walls around her narrower and narrower, hemming her in.

"Are you okay?" Sarah asked Isra one night as they stood over the stove, sleeves rolled up to the elbows. They were cooking *mujaddara*, and the air smelled of lentils and rice, sautéed onions and cumin. Sarah put down the stirring spoon and met her eyes. "You haven't been yourself lately."

"I'm just tired," Isra said, stooping slightly, one hand under her belly. "This baby is wearing me out."

"No," Sarah said. "I can tell something else is wrong. Is it Adam? Is he hitting you?"

"No . . ." Isra looked away.

"Then what is it?"

"I really don't know what's wrong . . . ," Isra said, averting her gaze. "I'm just a little worried."

"About what?"

"You'll think it's stupid."

"No, I won't. I promise. What is it?"

"I'm worried about the baby," Isra whispered. "What if it's another girl? What will your family do? What will Adam do?"

"They can't do anything," Sarah said. "Having a girl isn't in your control." She moved closer and touched Isra's shoulder. "And you never know, you might be carrying a boy this time."

Isra sighed. "Even if I have a boy, I don't know how I'll raise four children. Where will I find the time? What if I can't read anymore?"

"You can always find time to read," Sarah said. "Soon Deya will be in school, and it won't be so bad. And I'll be here to help you."

"You don't understand." Isra sighed again, pressing her fingers against her temples. "I know it sounds selfish, but I was finally starting to feel like a person, like I had a purpose, like there was something else in my life besides raising children all day and waiting for Adam to come home." She stopped, startled by her words. "Not that I don't like being a mother. I love my children, of course I do. But for so long I haven't had anything to call my own. All I have is a husband who barely comes home and beats me when he does, and children who depend on me for everything. And the worst part is, I have nothing to give them! I never thought it would be like this." The feeling she had now, that this was all her life would ever be, caught her by surprise. She began to cry.

"Please don't cry," Sarah said, wrapping her arms around Isra and squeezing tight. "You're a good mother. You're doing your best for your daughters, and they're going to see that one day. I know this is hard, but you're not alone. I'm right here. You have me. I promise."

"I have something to cheer you up," Sarah told her when they retreated to the basement after dinner. She spread a pile of books across the floor. "There are so many good books in here. I don't even know where to start. There's *Anna Karenina, Lolita, The Stranger* . . . Oh, and Kafka, I think you'd love his—"

"No," Isra interrupted.

Sarah met her eyes. "No?"

"What I mean is . . ." She paused. "I want to read something else."

"Like what?"

"I want to read something written by a woman."

"Sure. We've already read lots of books written by women," Sarah said. "Do you have a specific author in mind?"

"Not really."

"A specific book, then?"

Isra shook her head. "I was hoping you'd help. I want to read a book about someone like me."

Sarah blinked at her. "Like you how?"

"I don't know. But I want to read a book about what it really means to be a woman."

Fareeda

Ever since Sarah turned sixteen, Fareeda had taken to parading her up and down Fifth Avenue as though she were a shank of lamb for sale. Her usual fears of leaving the house alone now paled in comparison to her fear of Sarah not finding a suitor. Earlier that day, after the *mansaf* stew simmered, they had gone to the pharmacy on Seventy-Fifth Street to pick up Fareeda's diabetes medicine. Khaled normally picked up her medicine, but Fareeda wanted people to see Sarah. She had realized one evening, after hearing the engagement news of Umm Ramy's daughter, Nadia, that perhaps she had been doing something wrong. Nadia, for goodness sake, who was always roaming Fifth Avenue alone, whose parents let her ride the subway to school. It didn't make sense! But maybe it was because no one ever saw Sarah, who took the bus to school and never left the house alone. Perhaps people didn't even know what Sarah looked like. So Fareeda began taking her places nearby, despite her fears of going out alone. The Alsalam meat market at Seventy-Second Street, the Bay Ridge Bakery at Seventy-Eighth, sometimes even all the

way down Fifth Avenue. But most days they visited their neighbors. Sarah still needed to learn some culture, and there was no
better place to learn culture, Fareeda knew, than in the company
of women.

Now she squatted in front of the oven and pulled out a pan
of baked *knafa*. The smell of rose syrup filled the house, and she
remembered her father bringing her slices as a child, before they
were forced into the camps. She had always loved the red-colored
dough, the sweet and savory cheese melted inside. She took a
deep breath, warmed by memory.

"Brew a kettle of chai," Fareeda told Sarah when she entered
the kitchen. "Umm Ahmed will be here any minute."

Sarah groaned. The summer sun had darkened her olive
complexion, and her black curls held a tint of red in them. Fareeda thought she looked beautiful, a spitting image of what she
herself had once looked like. But Fareeda herself was withering
away now, as much as she hated to admit it. Her hair, which had
once been full and bouncy, lay flat behind her ears after years
of dyeing it. All that henna had done her scalp no good, but she
couldn't bear the sight of gray hair. It reminded her of how fast
life slipped by.

"Where's Isra?" Sarah asked.

"Downstairs," said Fareeda. She knew Sarah and Isra had
grown close lately, and she wasn't sure how she felt about it. It
had been her idea, after all, to teach Sarah some compliance,
but more than once Fareeda had found them huddled at the
kitchen table, whispering to each other, sometimes even reading
together—reading, of all things! She had to listen with half an
ear as she watched her evening show to make sure they weren't
up to no good. Once she had overheard Sarah translating a
novel about a man attracted to his twelve-year-old stepdaugh-
ter, pausing to explain that she had borrowed the book from a

friend because the school library had banned it. Fareeda had snatched the book from her at once! The last thing she needed was for either of them to read that sort of Americanized smut. Who knew what ideas it was giving them? But otherwise, their friendship seemed harmless enough. She just needed to make sure Isra rubbed off on Sarah and not the other way around. She smiled to herself—as if anyone could shake some backbone into Isra. No, she didn't have to worry too much about that.

Fareeda sliced the *knafa* into small rectangles and sprinkled them with crushed pistachios. She glanced at Sarah. "What are you wearing?"

"Clothes."

Fareeda moved closer. "Are you smartmouthing me?"

"It's jeans and a T-shirt, Mama. What's the big deal?"

"Go upstairs and change," Fareeda said. "Put your cream-colored dress on. It flatters your skin. Hurry." As Sarah turned to leave, she couldn't help but add, "And fix your hair, too."

"But it's just Umm Ahmed. She's seen me a thousand times."

"Well, you're older now, and Umm Ahmed is looking for a wife for her son. It doesn't hurt to take some care with your appearance."

"I'm only sixteen, Mama."

Fareeda sighed. "I'm not saying you need to get married right this second. There's nothing wrong with a one- or two-year engagement."

"But Hannah is my age." Sarah's voice was louder now. "And I don't see Umm Ahmed trying to get her engaged."

Fareeda laughed, reaching for a serving tray from the cabinet. "What do you know about Umm Ahmed? As a matter of fact, Hannah accepted a marriage proposal last night."

"But—"

"Go change and let me worry about these things."

Fareeda could hear Sarah mutter under her breath as she left the room. Something about being advertised. Or showcased. Poor girl, Fareeda thought, if she was just now realizing this. That this was a woman's worth. Sometimes she wished she could sit her daughter down, explain life to her—God knew she had tried. But there were some things you couldn't explain. Words could do extraordinary things, but sometimes they were not enough.

Deya

Winter 2008

By Sunday, Fareeda had arranged another meeting with Nasser. It was a cold winter day, and Deya circled the *sala* with a serving tray. She served Nasser's mother Turkish coffee and roasted watermelon seeds, while Fareeda chatted on, her gold tooth flashing between her lips. Deya wanted to fling the serving tray across the room. How could she trust her grandmother, after all she had learned from Sarah? How could she pretend nothing was wrong? She couldn't. She needed to stop stalling, needed to speak up for herself before it was too late.

"My grandmother thinks I should marry you," she said as she settled across from Nasser at the kitchen table. "She says I'd be a fool to turn down your proposal. But I can't marry you. I'm sorry."

Nasser straightened. "Why not?"

She had the sudden urge to take her words back, but she made herself go on. She could hear Sarah's voice in her ear: *Be brave. Speak up for what you want.* She turned to meet Nasser's eyes. "What I mean is, I'm not ready to get married. I want to go to college first."

"Oh," Nasser said. "Well, you can do both. Many girls go to college after marriage."

"Are you saying you would let me go to college?"

"I don't see why not."

She blinked at him. "What about after college? Would you let me work?"

Nasser stared at her. "Why would you need to work? You'll be well provided for."

"But what if I want to work with my degree?"

"If both of us were working, then who would raise the children?"

"See? That's my point."

"What point?"

"Why do I have to stay at home and raise the children? Why do I have to give up my dreams?"

"Because one of us has to do it," Nasser said, seeming confused. "And of course that should be the mother. It's only natural."

"Excuse me?"

"What? It's true. I'm not trying to offend you, but everyone knows it's a woman's job to raise children."

Deya pushed herself up from the table. "See? That's exactly what I mean. You're just like the rest of them."

Nasser stared at her, his face contorted with shock and anger—and something else. Deya wasn't sure what it was. "I'm not trying to upset you," he said. "I'm only telling the truth."

"What's next? You're going to beat me and say that's natural, too?"

"What are you talking about?" Nasser said. "I would never put my hands on a woman. Maybe that's how it used to be, but I know better."

Deya observed him. He sat up straight, breathing heavily, a spot on his forehead flushed pink. She cleared her throat. "What about your father?"

"What about him?"

"Does he beat your mother?"

"What kind of question is that?"

"He does, doesn't he?"

"Of course not!" Nasser said. "My father would never beat my mother. He treats her like a queen."

"Sure he does."

"You're being really rude, you know that? I know you've been through a lot, but that doesn't give you the right to talk to people like that."

"What do you know about what I've been through?"

"Are you kidding me, Deya? Everyone knows *everything* in this town. But just because your father beat your mother, that doesn't mean every man beats his wife." Deya stared at him, and he scoffed. "I mean, for God's sake, it's not like he didn't have a reason!"

It was as though he'd smashed a brick into her face. "What are you talking about?"

"Nothing." Nasser stood. "It was nothing. I shouldn't have said that. I'm sorry." He walked toward the doorway without meeting her eyes. "I have to go. I'm sorry."

"Wait," Deya said, following him across the kitchen. "Don't go. Tell me what you meant."

But Nasser rushed down the hall and out the door in a blink, his startled mother following suit, before Deya could say another word.

Fareeda

Fall 1995

Fareeda had suspected all along that Umm Ahmed would not be interested in Sarah for her son. It was because Umm Ahmed didn't share Fareeda's view of the world. She thought Fareeda wasn't religious enough, that she shamed girls too much. But at least Fareeda understood the way the world worked, unlike Umm Ahmed, whose daughter Fatima had gotten divorced. She was sure Hannah would get divorced, too. That's what happens, Fareeda thought, when you live life as though you're in a TV commercial, everyone running around laughing, falling in and out of love.

"The phone never rings when you wait for it," Fareeda said now, chomping on a stick of gum and staring at Nadine, who had joined her in the *sala*. It was the beginning of the school year, and Isra was waiting for Deya at the bus stop. It was her first day of preschool.

"Who are you expecting to call?" Nadine asked, smoothing her hair.

"Just a potential marriage suitor."

"Oh."

Fareeda knew what she must be thinking. Somehow the summer had passed, and not one suitor had asked for Sarah's hand in marriage. Perhaps the other Arab mothers thought Sarah wasn't good enough, Arab enough. Perhaps, like her, they preferred a girl from back home. All of this was possible, but deep down Fareeda couldn't help but fear it was the jinn, still haunting their family after all those years, as if Isra's girls were a payback for what she had done.

Nadine cleared her throat and Fareeda straightened. She hoped the girl couldn't sense her fear.

"You'll miss her, you know," Nadine said, looking at her with her stupid blue eyes. "She'll be married soon, and you'll miss her."

"Miss her?" Fareeda tucked her yellow nightgown over her knees. "What does that have to do with anything?"

"I just mean you shouldn't worry about marrying her off so quickly. You should enjoy the time you have left."

Fareeda didn't like the look on Nadine's face. There was a time when she had enjoyed Nadine's company, a break from Isra's dullness and Sarah's rebellions. But now it was Nadine who irritated her the most, with her constant sense of entitlement. The girl did whatever she pleased, regardless of what Fareeda asked of her. As annoying as Isra was, at least she did what she was told. At least she knew her place. But one damn child, and Nadine walked around as though the world owed her something. As though she wasn't a woman like the rest of them. You have to earn the right to bend the rules, Fareeda thought, and Nadine hadn't earned a thing.

"But I guess you're lucky," Nadine said. "She'll get married right here, and you'll see her all the time."

"See her all the time? Do you think you'd see your mother all the time if you were living back home?"

"Of course."

Fareeda laughed, her eyes squinting into tiny slits. "When a girl gets married, she puts a big X on her parents' door." Fareeda drew the letter with her index finger as large as she could in front of her. "A very big X." Nadine stared at her, fingering the tips of her hair. "No man wants a wife still stuck up her family's back end when she should be home cooking and cleaning." Fareeda spit out her gum, squashed it into a tissue. "Believe me, I'll kick Sarah right back into her husband's lap if she starts coming around here after she's married."

Deya

Winter 2008

"**What are you** hiding from me?" Deya asked Sarah the next day, as soon as she walked into the bookstore. There were customers, but Deya didn't bother to keep her voice low. "Nasser—*Nasser*, of all people—said there was a reason Baba beat Mama. What was he talking about?"

"I don't know—"

"Stop! I thought we said we wouldn't lie to each other." Deya lowered her voice, trying not to cry. "Please. Just tell me the truth already. What happened to my parents?"

Sarah took a step back. She rubbed both hands over her face. "I'm so sorry," she whispered. She walked to her desk, opened the bottom drawer, and reached inside. When she returned, she was holding a piece of paper. She handed it to Deya.

"I'm so sorry," she said again. "When I left the note for you, I had no idea you didn't know. And then when I found out, I was afraid to tell you. I thought if I told you too soon, you'd run away and I'd never see you again. I'm so sorry, Deya."

Deya said nothing, inspecting the paper in her hand. It was a newspaper clipping. She brought it close to her face until she could make out the ant-size print, and then, all at once, the room went dark. Her tears came in a rush. What a terrible daughter she must have been to not have known it all along.

"Please," Sarah said, reaching out to hold her. "Let me explain."

But Deya took one step back, and then another, and the next she knew she was running.

Fareeda

1970

One of the memories that came unbidden when Fareeda was alone: she was at a gathering while she and Khaled still lived in the camps, a few years before they moved to America. The women sat on the veranda of Fareeda's cement shelter, sipping on mint chai and eating from a fresh platter of *za'atar* rolls Fareeda had baked over the *soba* oven. Their kids were riding bikes on the unpaved road. A soccer ball flew from one end of the street to the other. They were surrounded by noise, laughter.

"Did you hear about Ramsy's wife?" Hala, Fareeda's next-door neighbor, asked between mouthfuls of bread. "The girl who lives on the other side of the camp? What's her name? Suhayla, isn't it?"

"Yes," said Awatif, who lived eight doors down, in a shelter by the open sewers. "The one who went crazy after her newborn daughter died."

"But did you hear the rumor"—Hala leaned in, her voice a whisper—"about what really happened to her daughter?

They're saying she drowned her in the bathtub. Ramsy and his family tried to pass it off as an accident, said she's still a young bride and didn't know how to bathe the girl properly. But I heard she did it on purpose. She didn't want a daughter."

Fareeda felt nauseous, her tongue dry. She swallowed, then took another sip of her chai.

"I mean, it makes sense," Hala went on. "The girl was raped as a child, then married off at once. Poor girl was barely thirteen. And we all know Ramsy. A drunk. Day and night with *sharaab* in his hands. He probably beats the poor girl every night. You can imagine the rest. She likely thought she was saving her daughter. It's sad, really."

Fareeda kept her eyes on her legs. Her fingers trembled against her teacup, and she placed it on the old barrel they used for a coffee table. The barrel was rusted and moldy but had been standing strong for over ten years, ever since Khaled and Fareeda first married in the camps. It had served many uses then. She remembered using it as a bucket to shower.

"Nonsense," Awatif said, pulling Fareeda back into the conversation. "No mother in her right mind would kill her child. She must have been possessed. I guarantee it." She turned to Fareeda, who sat silently beside her. "Tell them, Fareeda. You would know. Your twin daughters died right in your arms. Would a mother ever do such a thing unless she wasn't in her right mind? It was a jinn. Tell them."

A flush spread across Fareeda's face. She made an excuse to grab something from the kitchen, knees buckling as she rose from the plastic chair. She tried to keep from falling as she walked across the dirt garden, past the *marimaya* plant and the mint bush, and into the kitchen. It was three feet by three across, equipped only with a sink, *soba* oven, and small cabinet. Fareeda could hear Nadia on the veranda whispering,

"Why would you bring up such a thing? The woman lost her firstborns. Why would you remind her?"

"It was over ten years ago," Awatif said. "I didn't mean anything by it. Besides, look at her life now. She has three sons. Her *naseeb* turned out pretty good, if you ask me. No reason to fuss."

In the kitchen, Fareeda trembled violently. She remembered her daughters' death in bits and pieces only. Their bodies turning blue in her arms. The sharp scent of death in the tent. The way she kept them wrapped in blankets so Khaled wouldn't notice, kept flipping and turning their limp bodies, hoping the color would return to their faces. Then the scrambling prayers. The small hole Khaled dug in the back of the tent, tears in his eyes. And somewhere, in the tight confines of their tent, that thing which had never left her since, the jinn. Watching her. She closed her eyes, muttered a quick prayer under her breath.

Forgive me, daughters. Forgive me.

Part 3

Deya

Deya ran out of the bookstore, the newspaper clipping crushed in her fist. At the subway station, she paced up and down the platform as she waited for the R train. Once on board she paced in circles by the metal door. She shoved past people down the center aisle, her fear and deference forgotten. At the back of the train, she opened the exit door—ignoring the EMERGENCY ONLY sign—and crossed into the next train car, even as the tracks rattled under her feet in the dark tunnel. In the next car she did the same—pacing, shoving, escaping from one car to the next as though the next car might hold a different story, any other story, so long as it was one in which her mother had not been murdered by her father.

When she finally paused, all she could do was stare again at the newspaper clipping in her hands:

MOTHER OF FOUR MURDERED IN BROOKLYN BASEMENT

Brooklyn, NY. October 17, 1997—Isra Ra'ad, twenty-five-year-old mother of four, was found beaten

to death in Bay Ridge late Wednesday night. The victim appeared to have been beaten by her husband,
thirty-eight-year-old Adam Ra'ad, who fled the scene
of the crime. Police found his body in the East River
Thursday morning after witnesses saw him jump off
the Brooklyn Bridge.

How many times did Deya read the words and burst into
tears? How many times did she scream in the middle of the
train, stopping only when she realized that people around her
were staring? What did they see when they looked at her? Did
they see what she saw, staring at her darkened reflection in the
glass window, the face of a fool? For now Deya saw how foolish
she'd been. How could she have lived with her grandparents all
these years and not known that her mother had been murdered
by her own father? Beaten to death in their home, in the very
rooms where she and her sisters spent their days? Why hadn't
she acted on her suspicions after reading Isra's letter? Why
hadn't she questioned Fareeda until she'd admitted the truth?
How had she believed her so easily? After all the lies she knew
Fareeda to be capable of. Did she not have a mind of her own?
Could she not think for herself? How had she lived her entire
life letting Fareeda make her choices for her? Because she was
a fool.

Deya clenched the newspaper clipping tight. Then she was
screaming again, banging her fists against the train window.
Her father had killed her mother. He had killed her, taken her
life, stolen her away from them. Then the coward had taken his
own life! How could he? Deya closed her eyes, tried to picture
Baba's face. The most clearly she could remember him was the
day of her seventh birthday. He had come home with a Carvel

ice cream cake, smiling as he sang her a birthday melody in Arabic. The way he had looked at her, the way he had smiled—the memory had always comforted Deya on a bad day.

Now she wanted to rip the memory out of her head. How could that same man have killed her mother? And how could her grandparents have covered for him? How could they have hidden the truth from his daughters all these years? And, as if that wasn't enough, how could they have urged her to get married young and quickly, as her parents had done? How could they risk something like this happening again? Happening to *her*? She shuddered at the thought.

"No," Deya said aloud when the train stopped at Bay Ridge Avenue. As soon as the metal doors slid open, she ran. "No!" she screamed. It would not happen again. Not to her. Not to her sisters. Isra's story would not become theirs. She ran until she reached the bus stop, telling herself again and again: *I will not repeat my mother's life.* As the bus turned the corner and she watched her sisters climb down its steps, Deya realized that Sarah was right: her life was her own, and only she controlled it.

Isra

Fall 1996

Isra could no longer remember her life before America. There had been a time when she knew precisely when the mulberries back home would ripen, which trees would grow the sweetest figs, how many walnuts would fall to the ground by autumn. She had known which olives made the best oil, the sound a ripe watermelon made when you thumped it, the smell of the ceme- tery after it rained. But none of this came to her anymore. Many days, Isra felt as though she had never had a life before marriage, before motherhood. What had her own childhood been like? She couldn't remember being a child.

And yet motherhood still did not come naturally to her. Sometimes she had to remind herself that she was a mother, that she had four daughters who were hers to raise. In the mornings, after she woke and made the bed and sent Adam off to work with a cup of *kahwa* and a *labne* sandwich, she'd wake her daughters and make them breakfast—scrambled eggs, *za'atar* and olive oil rolls, cereal—running around the kitchen to make sure all four of them were fed. Then she'd take them downstairs and run a bath. She'd soap their hair, digging her fingers into their scalps, rubbing their bodies until they reddened, rinsing them off only to start over again. She'd dry their shivering bodies and comb their wild hair, untangling it strand by strand, willing herself to be gentle though her fingers moved frantically, aggressively. Sometimes one of them would scream or let out a whimper. On days when she was feeling patient, Isra would tell herself to take a breath and slow down. But most days she'd snap at them to keep their mouths shut. Then she'd drop Deya and Nora off at the bus stop and set Layla and Amal in front of the television, eager to complete the day's chores and return to her books.

Now Isra leaned against the window, reading. Outside the trees were bare, their stark branches covered with frost. Isra thought they looked like tiny arms, thin and bleak, reaching for her, like her daughters. Lately it seemed as though she saw mothers everywhere, smiling wildly as they pushed strollers, a glow emanating from their faces. She wondered how they found it so easy to smile. The happiness she had felt at being a mother when Deya was born was so far away she couldn't even grasp it. A dismal feeling loomed over Isra now, a feeling that had only intensified since Amal was born. She had thought that the meaning of her daughter's name, *hope*, might grow a seed of hope in her heart, but it had not. She woke up every morning feeling very young, yet at the same time terribly old. Some days she felt as though she were still a child, other days as though she had felt far too much of the world for one life. That she had been burdened with duty ever since she was a child. That she had never really lived. She felt empty; she felt full. She needed people; she needed to be alone. She couldn't get the equation right. Who was to blame? She thought it was herself. She thought it was her mother, and her mother's mother, and the mothers of all their mothers, all the way back in time.

When Isra first arrived in America, when she first became a wife, she hadn't understood why she felt so empty. She had thought it was temporary, that she would adjust in time. She knew there were many girls who left their families to come to America, having children when they were still children themselves. Yet they had managed. But lately Isra had finally understood why she couldn't manage, why she constantly felt as though she were drifting far out to sea. She understood that life was nothing but a dark melody, playing over and over again. A track stuck on repeat. That was all she would ever amount to. Worse was that her daughters would repeat it, and she was to blame.

"Let's watch a movie," Deya said in Arabic, her high six-year-old voice drawing Isra out of her book.

"Not now."

"But I want to," Deya said. She walked over to Isra and pulled on her bleach-spotted nightgown. "Please."

"Not now, Deya."

"Please, Mama."

Isra sighed. Once she'd realized that *Aladdin* was adapted from *A Thousand and One Nights*, she'd gathered her daughters in front of the television, a bowl of popcorn between them, and watched all the Disney movies they owned, longing to find more moments of connection that brought her back to her childhood. Maybe she would find the story of Ali Baba and the Forty Thieves, or the Seven Voyages of Sinbad the Sailor, or even, if she was particularly lucky, the Lovers of Bassorah. She had popped each movie in the cassette player, giddy with excitement, only to be disappointed. Snow White, Cinderella, Sleeping Beauty, Ariel—none of those characters were in the stories she'd read growing up. Disappointed, she had turned off the television and ignored it ever since.

"But I want to see the princesses," Deya said.

"We've seen enough princesses."

The princesses irritated her now. Those Disney movies, with their love stories and fairy-tale endings—how could they be a good influence on her daughters? What would her daughters think, Isra wondered, watching these women fall in love? Would they grow up believing these fairy tales were reality, that love and romance existed for girls like them? That one day men would come and save them? Isra could feel her chest tighten. She wanted to go into the *sala* and shred the cassettes, ripping the film from each piece of plastic casing until they no longer played. But she feared what Adam would say if he found out, the violent look in his eyes, the questions, a slap awaiting, and her without an answer. What could she say? That her books had finally taught her the truth: love was not something a man could give you, and she didn't want her daughters thinking it was? That she couldn't let her daughters grow up hoping a man would save them? She knew she had to teach them how to love themselves, that this was the only way they had a chance at happiness. Only she didn't see how she could when the world pressed shame into women like pillows into their faces. She wanted to save her daughters from her fate, but she couldn't seem to find a way out.

"Will you read to me?" Deya asked, looking at her with soft, wide eyes, her fingers clenched around her nightgown.

"Sure," Isra said.

"Now?"

"I have to make dinner first."

"But then you're coming?"

"Then I'm coming."

"Promise?"

"I promise."

"Okay." She let go of Isra's nightgown, turned to leave.

"Wait," Isra said.

"What, Mama?"

"You know I love you, right?"

Deya smiled.

"I love you very much."

Deya

Deya met Nora in their bedroom. She shut the door, locked it, and asked Nora to sit down. She handed her the newspaper clipping. Then she told her everything. For a long time after, they wept in each other's arms.

"I just can't believe it," Nora said, staring down at the newspaper clipping. "Should we tell Layla and Amal?"

"Not yet," Deya said. "First I have to confront Teta."

"What are you going to say?"

"I'm going to make her tell me everything."

"Then what?"

"Then we come up with a plan."

"What kind of plan?" asked Nora.

"A plan to run away."

Isra

Winter 1996

One Saturday morning, after Isra and Sarah had washed the morning dishes and retreated to the kitchen table with a steaming *ibrik* of chai, Fareeda entered the kitchen. "Pour me a cup," she said.

At once, Isra grabbed a teacup from the cabinet. She had become so accustomed to following Fareeda's demands that her body obeyed unthinkingly. As Isra presented the chai to her, Fareeda turned to Sarah. "Today is your lucky day," she said.

"And why's that?" Sarah asked.

"Because"—Fareeda paused, running her finger around the rim of her teacup—"I've found you a suitor."

Isra felt something drain from her. She tried to keep from dropping her tea. How could she carry on without Sarah's friendship? Without her books?

"Are you serious?" Sarah said, sinking into her chair.

"Of course I'm serious! He'll be here this afternoon."

"Who is he?"

"Umm Ali's youngest son, Nader." Fareeda's smile was triumphant. "He was at the pharmacy last month. I pointed him out to you, remember?"

"No," Sarah said. "Not that it makes a difference. I don't know him."

"Oh, don't be so negative. You'll get to know him soon enough."

"Whatever."

"Roll your eyes all you want," Fareeda said. "But marriage is the single most important part of a woman's life, and there's nothing you can do about it."

"Can you believe the woman?" Sarah asked Isra when Fareeda had left the kitchen. She stared out the window, her brown eyes watering against the light.

"I'm so sorry," Isra managed to say.

"I don't understand why she insists on marrying me off so soon. For God's sake, I haven't even finished high school!"

Isra passed her a warm look. She understood why: Sarah had become increasingly rebellious over the years. She could imagine how worried Fareeda was, watching Sarah refuse to take part in any of the traditions, barely speaking Arabic anymore. Sometimes Isra watched Sarah from the window as she walked home from school, rushing to wipe her makeup off before she entered the house. Last month, when Sarah had handed her a copy of *The Bell Jar* by Sylvia Plath, Isra had noticed a sleeveless top in her bag. She hadn't mentioned it, and Sarah hadn't either, stuffing the blouse deep beneath her books, but Isra wondered what else Sarah was hiding. She considered how she would feel if she was in Fareeda's shoes. She didn't know what lengths she would go to in order to keep her own daughters safe.

"I don't want to get married. She can't force me!"

"Lower your voice. She'll hear you."

"I don't care if she hears me. This is America. She can't force me to get married!"

"Yes, she can," Isra whispered. "She'll punish you if you defy her."

"What could she possibly do? Beat me? I'll take a beating daily if it means avoiding marriage."

Isra shook her head. "Sarah, I don't think you understand. It won't be a single beating by Fareeda. Soon your father and brothers will start beating you, too. Then how long will you stand it?"

Sarah crossed her arms. "For as long as it takes."

Isra examined her bright face and catlike eyes. She wished she could've had her strength as a girl. How different her life could have been had she only had courage. Sarah's eyes narrowed further. "I refuse to have a life like yours."

"And what kind of life is that?" Isra asked, though she already knew the answer.

"I'm not going to let anyone control me."

"No one will control you," Isra said, but her tone betrayed her.

"Maybe you can lie to yourself, but you don't fool me."

Though her books had shown her otherwise, the old words spilled out. "This is the life of a woman, you know."

"You don't actually believe that, do you?"

"I don't see any other way," Isra whispered.

"How can you say that? There's more to life than marriage. I thought you believed that. I know you do."

"I do, but that doesn't mean we have the power to change our circumstances."

Sarah blinked at her. "So you want me to just accept my life for what they tell me it should be? What kind of life is that?"

"I never said it was right, but I don't see anything we can do about it."

"I'll stand up for myself! I'll refuse!"

"It won't matter. Fareeda won't listen."

"Then I'll tell the man myself! I'll look him straight in the eyes and say, 'I don't want to marry you. I'll make your life a living hell.'"

Isra shook her head. "She'll marry you off eventually. If not to this man, then the next."

"No," Sarah said, standing up. "I won't let that happen. Even if I have to scare every last man away."

"But don't you see, Sarah?"

"See what?"

"You don't have a choice."

"Is that what you think? That I don't have a choice?" Despite the defiance in Sarah's voice, Isra sensed her anxiety. "We'll see about that."

Later, Sarah appeared in the kitchen wearing an ivory kaftan. Outside, the trees moved slowly, their branches still bare, a residue of ice visible from the kitchen window. "You look beautiful," Isra told her.

"Whatever," Sarah said, walking past her. She grabbed a serving bowl from the cabinet and began filling it with fruit. "Let's just get this over with."

"What are you doing?" Isra asked.

"What does it look like I'm doing? I'm trying to serve our guests."

Isra took the bowl from her. "You're not supposed to serve the fruit first."

"Then I'll make coffee," Sarah said, grabbing a small beaker from the drawer.

"Coffee?"

"Yeah."

"Sarah, you never serve coffee first."

She shrugged. "I've never paid attention to these stupid things."

Isra wondered if Sarah was serving the Turkish coffee first on purpose, the way she had done years ago, or if she really didn't know better. "Just arrange the teacups on a serving tray," Isra said. "I'll brew the chai."

Sarah leaned against the counter, arranging glass cups on a serving tray. Isra counted them in her head: Fareeda. Khaled. The suitor. His mother. His father. Five in total.

"Here," she said, handing Sarah a tray of sesame cookies. "Go serve these while I pour the tea."

Sarah stood frozen in the kitchen doorway. Isra wished she could do something to help her. But this was the way of life, she told herself. There was nothing she could do about it. Her powerlessness even comforted her somehow. Knowing that she couldn't change things—that she didn't have a choice—made living it more bearable. She realized she was a coward, but she also knew a person could only do so much. She couldn't change centuries of culture on her own, and neither could Sarah. "Come on," she whispered, nudging Sarah down the hall. "They're waiting for you."

That night, Isra couldn't sleep. She couldn't stop thinking about the fact that Sarah would be gone soon. She wondered if they would still be friends after she left, if Sarah would be able to visit still, if she would miss her. She wondered if she would ever read again. Isra had grown enough now to know that the world hurt less when you weren't hoping. She had even started to think that perhaps her books had done more harm than good, waking her up to the reality of her life and its imperfections. Maybe she would have been better without them. All they had done was stir up false hope. Still, the possibility of a life without books was far worse.

In the *sala* the next day, Fareeda waited for the suitor's mother to call and announce her son's decision. Isra flinched every time the phone rang—at least half a dozen times in the course of the afternoon. She studied Fareeda's expression as she answered each call, a rush of panic rising in her. Sarah alone seemed undisturbed. She sat cross-legged on the sofa, her face in a book, as if she hadn't a care in the world.

The phone rang again, and Fareeda rushed to answer it. Isra watched as she muttered a lively *salaam* into the phone, noticed how quickly she fell quiet. Her eyes grew wide and her mouth hung open as she listened, but she didn't say a word. Isra bit her fingers.

"They said no," Fareeda said when she'd hung up the phone. "No. Just like that."

Sarah looked up from a copy of *The Handmaid's Tale.* "Oh," she said, before flipping the page. Isra felt her heart thumping wildly against her nightgown.

"But why would she say no?" Fareeda looked hard into Sarah's eyes. "You said your conversation with the boy went well."

"I don't know, Mama. Maybe he didn't like me. Just because you have a decent conversation with someone, that doesn't mean you should necessarily marry them."

"There you go again with your smart remarks." Fareeda's eyes were bulging. She snatched the book from Sarah's fingers, flung it across the room. "Just wait!" she said, turning to leave. "Just wait until I find a man to take you off my shoulders. *Wallahi*, I don't care if he's old and fat. I'm giving you away to the first man who agrees to take you!"

Isra turned to Sarah, expecting to find her caved into the sofa, but her friend had sprung gracefully to her feet and was scanning the floor for her book. Catching Isra's eyes, she said, "There is nothing in the world I hate more than that woman."

"Shhh," Isra said. "She'll hear you."

"Let her."

When she'd finished brewing a kettle of chai to calm Freeda's nerves, Isra retreated downstairs to read. Beside her, Deya scribbled in a coloring book. Nora and Layla played with Legos. Amal slept in her crib. Watching them as they scattered across the room, glancing over to her every now and then, Isra felt a jolt of helplessness deep within her. She had to do something, anything, to help her daughters.

"Mama," Deya said. Isra smiled. Inside she wanted to scream. "My teacher said we have to read this for homework." Deya handed Isra a Dr. Seuss book. Isra took the book from her hands and signaled for her to sit. As she read, she could see Deya's eyes widen in curiosity and excitement. She reached out and stroked her daughter's face. Nora and Layla listened with half an ear each, building a bridge of Legos around her. Amal slept peacefully.

"I love when you read to me," Deya said when Isra had finished.

"You do?"

Deya nodded slowly. "Can you always be this way?"

"What way?" Isra asked.

Deya stared at her feet. "Happy."

"I am happy," Isra said.

"You always look sad."

Isra swallowed hard, tried to steady her voice. "I'm not sad."

"You're not?"

"I promise I'm not."

Deya frowned, and Isra knew she was unconvinced. Isra felt a sense of failure rising in her. She had tried her best to shelter her daughters from her sadness, the way she wished Mama had sheltered her. She had made sure they were asleep when Adam came home, made sure they never saw him hit her. Sadness was like a cancer, she thought, a presence that staked its claim so quietly you might not even notice it until it was too late. She hoped her other daughters didn't see. Maybe Deya could even forget. She was still young, after all. She wouldn't remember these days. Isra could still learn to be a good mother. Maybe she could still save them. Maybe it wasn't too late.

"I'm not sad," Isra said again, with a smile this time. "I have you." She pulled her daughter in for a hug. "I love you, *habibti*."

"I love you, too, Mama."

Fareeda

Winter 2008

The sun faded beyond the bare trees, a sliver of it visible from the kitchen window as Fareeda washed the last of the day's dishes. One of the girls should be washing these, she thought, carefully arranging the wet plates in the dish rack. But they had hurried to the basement after dinner, feigning sickness, leaving Fareeda no choice but to do the dishes herself. "I'm the one who's sick," she mumbled to herself. An old woman washing dishes—it was disgraceful! With four teenage girls in the house, she should have been giving orders like a queen. But she still had to cook and clean, still had to pick up after them. She shook her head. Fareeda couldn't understand how her granddaughters had turned out so unlike her, so unlike their mother. Surely it was America. One quick wipe of the kitchen table, and these girls thought they were done. As if things could be washed so easily. They didn't understand you needed to scrub hard, crouched on hands and knees, until the house was spotless. These spoiled American children knew nothing about real work.

When she was done, Fareeda retired to her bedroom. Brushing her hair, she wondered when she had last fallen asleep beside Khaled. It had been so many years she couldn't remember. She didn't even know where he was tonight—likely at the hookah bar, playing cards. Not that it mattered. He rarely looked at her most nights, staring absently ahead as he ate his dinner in silence, not even thanking her for the food she had labored over all day. The younger Khaled would've had some remark to fault her cooking, saying the rice was overcooked, or the vegetables oversalted, or that there was not enough green pepper in the *ful*. But now he hardly spoke at all. She wanted to shake him. What had happened to the man who used to break belts across her skin? Who never went a day without insulting her? But that man had faded over the years. When had it begun? When had he first started to lose the spark in his eyes, the iron grip he had around his life? She thought it was the day they came to America. She hadn't noticed it then, the transformation had been too gradual. But she saw it now, looking back. She remembered the day they'd left Palestine. How Khaled had shook as he locked the door of their shelter, weeping while he waved goodbye to his family and friends as their cab drove away. How, at the Tel Aviv airport, he had stopped several times to catch himself, his knees buckling beneath him. How he had worked day and night in a foreign country where he didn't even speak the language, just to ensure they were fed. The loss of his home had broken his spirit. She hadn't seen it then, hadn't recognized that his world was slowly unraveling. But maybe that's the way of life, Fareeda thought. To understand things only after they had passed, only once it was too late.

She slipped out of her evening gown and into something warmer. The heating unit in her bedroom didn't work as well as it once had. Either that, or her bones were getting frail, but she didn't like to think that way. She sighed. She couldn't believe

how quickly time had passed, that she had gotten old. *Old*—
she shook the thought away. It was not the thought of being
old that bothered her rather the realization of what her life had
amounted to. What a shame, she thought now as she waited for
sleep to come, shuffling through her bank of memories. She
didn't have even a single good memory to look back on. They
had all been tainted.

There was a sound at the door. Startled, Fareeda pulled the
blanket over her body. But it was only Deya, breathing heavily
in the doorway. Fareeda could sense unease in her presence, perhaps even defiance. It reminded her of Sarah, and suddenly she
was afraid. "What do you want?" Fareeda said. "Why aren't you
in bed?"

Deya took several steps into the room. "I know my parents
didn't die in a car accident!" She was shouting even though she
only stood a few feet away. "Why did you lie?"

For goodness sake, Fareeda thought, holding her breath. Not
this again. How many times had she been over this? *Your parents died in a car accident, your parents died in a car accident.* She
had said those words so many times that sometimes even she believed them. She wished she could believe them entirely. Unlike
Sarah's disappearance, Isra's murder was not something she had
been able to hide from the community. By morning, the news had
traveled all over Bay Ridge, had even made it to Palestine. Khaled
and Fareeda's son had murdered his wife. Khaled and Fareeda's
son had committed suicide. Their shame was terrible.

The one thing she had done right was to manage to keep it
from the girls. She couldn't tell them the truth—why, of course
she couldn't! How could she explain what had happened—that
their father had killed their mother, that their father had killed
himself—without ruining them, too? Sometimes it was best
to keep quiet. Sometimes the truth hurt the most. She couldn't

have them walking around like they were damaged goods. Sheltering them was the only way they had a chance at normal lives. She had hoped people would forget in time, wouldn't ostracize them, would even ask for their hands in marriage one day. She had wanted to save their reputations, save them the shame.

"Not this again," Fareeda said, keeping her face steady. "Is that why you woke me up? To talk about this?"

"I know my father killed my mother! I know he killed himself, too!"

Fareeda swallowed hard. She felt as though a rock was stuck in her throat. Where was all this coming from? Had she heard something at school? It was possible, though unlikely. For years Fareeda had asked her friends never to mention the subject in front of her granddaughters, asking them to tell their children to do the same. And in a community as tightly knit as theirs, it had worked. Over a decade, and not one slipup. Sometimes she wondered if the girls at her granddaughters' school even knew what had happened. Perhaps their parents hadn't told them, afraid it would give them the wrong idea about marriage. Sometimes Fareeda wondered the same thing herself. She knew she shouldn't have told Sarah what had happened to Hannah. Perhaps that's why she'd run away, Fareeda often told herself. But she brushed these thoughts aside. She couldn't be sure what Deya knew, so she decided to feign ignorance. "I don't know what you're talking about. Your parents died in a car accident."

"Did you hear me? I know what he did!"

Fareeda remained silent. What would she look like, admitting the truth after all these years? A complete fool. She couldn't do it. Why dwell on the past? People should always move on, no matter what. They should never look back.

"Fine." Deya reached into her pocket and pulled out a crumpled newspaper clipping. She held it up so Fareeda could see it.

"It doesn't matter if you say nothing. Sarah already told me everything."

Fareeda began to shiver as though all the heating units in the house had let out at once. She pulled her nightgown over her knees, tugging on the fabric forcefully, as if by doing so she could will the words away. She stared at the window for a moment, then leaped out of bed and wrapped herself in a thick robe. She turned on her bedroom lamps, the sconces in the hall, all the lights in the kitchen. There she retrieved a tea packet from the pantry, set a kettle on the stove. She felt strange, as though she was there and not there at the same time. What was happening? It took her a moment to find her mental footing. Finally she said, "Sarah?"

Deya stood in the kitchen doorway, still holding up the newspaper clipping. "I saw her. She told me everything."

"It must be a mistake," Fareeda said, refusing to look at the clipping. "Sarah is in Palestine. Someone must be playing a trick on you."

"Why do you keep lying? The truth is right here!" Deya waved the clipping in front of her. "You can't hide it anymore."

Fareeda knew Deya was right. Nothing she said could cover up the truth this time. Yet still, she found herself searching for a way to dispel it. She reached out and took the newspaper clipping, her fingers trembling as she scanned it. It seemed like only yesterday that Sarah had run away, leaving Fareeda in a panic. If anyone found out that Sarah had left, disappeared into the streets of America, their family's honor would have been ruined. And so Fareeda had done what she'd always done: she'd fixed it. It hadn't taken her long to convince her friends that Sarah had married a man in Palestine. She'd been so pleased with herself. But murder, suicide—these public shames had been impossible to hide. And for that, her granddaughters would forever pay a price.

"Why did you lie to us all these years?" Deya said. "Why didn't you tell us the truth about our parents?"

Fareeda began to sweat. There was no escape. As with everything else she had done in her life, she didn't have much choice.

She drew a slow, long breath, feeling a weight about to come undone. Then she told Deya everything—that Adam had been drunk, that he hadn't realized how hard he was hitting Isra, that he hadn't meant to kill her. This last part she said again and again. *He didn't mean to kill her.*

"I was only trying to protect you," Fareeda said. "I had to tell you something that wouldn't traumatize you for the rest of your life."

"But why did you make up the car accident? Why didn't you tell us—at least later?"

"Should I have gone around advertising it? Tell me, what good would it have done? The news had already disgraced our family name, but I tried to shelter you! I didn't stand by and do nothing. I tried to stop it from ruining your lives! Don't you understand?"

"No, I don't!" Deya shouted. "How can you expect me to understand something like this? None of it makes any sense. Why would he kill her—*murder* the mother of his children, his wife?"

"He just—he just . . . he lost control."

"Oh, so you thought it was okay that he beat her? Why didn't you do something?"

"What was I supposed to do? It's not like I could've stopped him!"

"You could've stopped him if you wanted to!" Fareeda opened her mouth, but Deya cut her off. "Why did he kill her? Tell me what happened!"

"Nothing happened," Fareeda lied. "He was drunk, completely out of his mind. That night, I heard him screaming from upstairs. I found him on the floor, shaking beside your mother's body. I was terrified. I begged him to leave before the police came. I told him to pack his bags and run, that I would take care of you all. But he just looked at me. I don't even know that he could hear me. And the next thing I knew, the police were at my door, saying they'd found my son's body in the river."

"You tried to cover for him?" Deya said in disbelief. "How could you cover for him? What's wrong with you?"

Fareeda chided herself—she had said too much. Deya was staring at her in horror. She could see pain in her granddaughter's eyes.

"How could you cover for him after he killed our mother?" Deya said. "How could you take his side?"

"I did what any mother would've done."

Deya shook her head in disgust.

"Your father was possessed," Fareeda said. "He had to be. No man in his right mind would kill the mother of his children and then kill himself."

Adam was out of his mind. She had no doubt about this. After the police had come and told her what Adam had done, Fareeda had sat on the porch, dumbfounded, staring out into the sky, feeling as though it had collapsed on her. She thought back on all her years with Adam, from his birth one hot summer day as she squatted in the back of their shelter to years later, when they'd made it to America and Adam had helped them run the deli, working day and night without end. Not once would she have suspected this from her son. Not Adam, who had never missed a prayer growing up, who had wanted to be an imam. Adam, who did everything for them, who always bent over backward to please, who never denied them. Adam, a murderer? Perhaps Fareeda should have known from the way he came home every night, reeking with *sharaab*. But she had just shrugged her fears aside, told herself everything was okay. After all, how many times had Khaled gotten drunk in their youth? How many times had he beaten her senseless? It was only normal. And she was stronger for it. But murder and suicide—that wasn't normal. She was sure Adam had been possessed.

"So Mama and Baba were both possessed? Really? That's your explanation for everything?"

Fareeda bit the inside of her lip. "Believe it or not, it's the truth."

"No, it's not! Sarah said there was nothing wrong with Mama."

Fareeda sighed. If only that were true, if only she had invented all of Isra's trouble. But she and Deya both knew there had been something wrong with her. Quietly, she said, "You don't remember how she was?"

Deya flushed. "It doesn't mean she was possessed."

"But she was." Fareeda met Deya's eyes. "And Adam was possessed, too. He wasn't in his right mind. Only a *majnoon*, a crazy person, would kill his wife like that."

"That still doesn't mean he was possessed! He could've been—" Deya searched for the right translation in Arabic. "He could've had a mental illness. He could have been depressed, or suicidal, or just a bad person!"

Fareeda shook her head. It was typical of her granddaughter to revert to Western concepts to understand everything. Why couldn't she accept that Western medicine had no understanding of these things, much less a cure?

The teakettle whistled, puncturing the silence between them. Fareeda turned off the stove. In moments like this, when the smell of *maramiya* filled the kitchen, she had to admit how much she missed Isra, who used to brew chai just the way she liked it, who, even when she was upset, never disrespected her. Isra would never have yelled at her the way Nadine had screamed the morning before she and Omar packed their bags and moved, just like that, leaving Fareeda alone. And what had she done to deserve it? Fareeda wondered, pouring herself some tea. She remembered Omar saying how controlling she was, how he couldn't even be nice to Nadine in her presence, how he had to pretend to be tough, manly. How much he hated the word *manly*, he had said, almost spitting as he did. Well, that's because he wasn't a man, Fareeda told herself now, adding two spoonfuls of sugar to her tea. Neither was Ali, who had taken off to live in the city with some girl, leaving her to raise her granddaughters on her own. Leaving her to clean up the family mess once again.

"You know," Fareeda said after a moment, "Arabs use the term *majnoon* to mean madness, but if you break the word apart, what do you see?" Deya only looked at her. "The word *jinn*," Fareeda said, settling back in her seat. "Madness is derived from the jinn, an evil spirit inside you. Therapy and medicine can't fix that."

"Are you serious? That's your explanation for everything? You think you can just blame this on the jinn? That's not good enough. This isn't some story, where you can tie up everything as you please at the end. This isn't make-believe."

"If only it were make-believe," Fareeda said.

"That still doesn't explain why you tried to cover for him," Deya said. "How could you? You won't even forgive your own daughter when all she ever did was run away! You're such a hypocrite!"

Fareeda tightened her grip around the teacup. Outside, the sky was dark, only the glow of a few lampposts visible through the window. She stared absently at the darkness as she considered Deya's words. Why had she never really blamed Adam— had forgiven him, even? Sarah hadn't killed anyone, hadn't left

her with four girls to look after. And yet it was true, she had
never been able to forgive her. She and Khaled had erased Sarah
from their lives completely, as if they had never had a daughter,
as if she had committed the grossest of crimes. She was so afraid
of the shame the family would face that she had never even questioned it. Deya was right: she was a hypocrite. An ocean of sadness rushed through her, and she began to weep.

For a long time Fareeda wept. Though she had buried her
face in her hands, she could feel Deya's eyes on her, waiting for
an explanation, an answer. If only life were so simple.

Isra

Winter 1996

Isra couldn't sleep. She couldn't stop thinking. Every time she closed her eyes, she heard Deya whispering, *You always look sad.* She wept silently in her bed. How would her daughters remember their childhood? What would they think of her? These questions had occupied most of her thinking lately. Some days she thought she should apologize for all the kisses she'd never given them, all the times she'd looked over their shoulders while they spoke, for slapping them when she was angry, for not saying "I love you" often enough. Other days—days that were becoming increasingly rare—she would comfort herself with the hope that everything could still be okay, or—rarer still—that everything had been okay all along, that there was nothing wrong with her mothering, that she was only doing what was best for her daughters. What would she do with them when they got older? Would she force them down her same path?

"I need to talk to you," Isra told Adam when he returned from work that night. From the edge of the bed, she watched him slip out of his work clothes, waiting for him to respond. But he said nothing. "Won't you say something?" she asked. "You've barely said a word to me since Amal was born."

"What do you want me to say?"

She could smell the beer on him every night now. Perhaps that's why he beat her more regularly. But sometimes it was her fault. Sometimes she provoked him. Isra thought back to the previous night, when she had put an extra spoonful of coriander in the *mulukhiya* to irritate him. "What's wrong?" she had asked innocently as he spat out his food. When he shook his head angrily, pushing the bowl away, she kept a straight face, but inside she had been ecstatic at her small revenge. If overseasoning his food was the only thing within her power, then she would do that for as long as she could.

"I want to talk to you," Isra said. "About our daughters."

"What about them?"

"Deya said something today, something that worries me."

His eyes shifted to her. "What did she say?"

"She said . . ." Her voice trailed off. "She said I always look sad."

"Well, she's right. You mope around the house like you're dying."

Isra blinked at him.

"It's true. What does this have to do with me?"

"I don't know," Isra said. "But ever since Amal was born, you've been—"

"Are you blaming me? After everything I've done for you?"

"No! That's not what I'm saying."

"Then what are you saying?"

"Nothing, I'm sorry. It's just lately I've been afraid . . ."

He shook his head, walking over to open his drawer. "Afraid of what, exactly?"

Isra opened her mouth to respond, but the fear overwhelmed

her, and no words would come out. What exactly *was* she afraid
of? Being a bad mother? Scarring her daughters the way her parents had scarred her? Being too lenient, not teaching them the
truth about the world? She was afraid of so many things. How
could she explain it?

Adam sighed. "Well, are you going to say something?"

"I'm just worried about the kind of lives our daughters will
have. If they'll have any choices."

He stared at her. "What kind of choices?"

"I just wonder if they'll be expected to be married at a young
age."

"Well, of course," he said sharply. "What else would they do?"

She looked away, but she could feel his eyes on her skin. "I
was hoping maybe we wouldn't rush them into marriage. That
maybe we could, you know, give them a choice."

"A choice? What for?"

"I don't know. I'm just afraid they won't be happy."

"What kind of nonsense is this? Have you forgotten where
you came from? Do you think we're American?"

"No! That's not what I meant."

But Adam wasn't listening. "Is that the sort of woman you've
become, after everything I've done for you? It's not enough that
you've birthed four daughters for me to take care of, but now I
have to worry about how you want to raise them—"

"No! You don't have to worry."

"Is that so?" Adam stepped toward her, and she shrunk back
against the headboard, feeling the room close in on her.

"Please, Adam, I swear, I didn't mean—"

"Shut up!"

She turned from him, but he smashed her head into the headboard. Then he grabbed her by the hair and dragged her into
their daughters' bedroom.

"Stop, please! The girls—"

"What's the matter? You don't want them to see? Maybe it's time they see what it means to be a woman."

"Please, Adam, they shouldn't see this."

"Why not? Don't you walk around sad all the time, anyway? Are you trying to scare them off marriage? Is that your plan?"

He grabbed her by the sides of her face and twisted her head so she had a full view of her daughters in bed. His hands moved to her neck, holding her still. "Do you see these girls? Do you?" She struggled to catch her breath. "Do you?"

"Yes," she managed to choke out.

"Listen closely, because I won't say this again. My daughters are Arabs. Are we clear? *Arabs.* If I ever hear any talk of choices again, I'll make sure they wake up to your screams. I'll make sure they see what happens when a woman disobeys her husband. *Fahmeh?* Do you understand me?"

Isra nodded, gasping for air, until Adam released his grip. He left to shower without another word.

Isra cupped her hand to the side of her head and felt blood.

Later she would think it was her books that had made her do it. All the feelings that had silenced her for so long—denial, shame, fear, unworthiness—were no longer enough. As soon as she heard the water running, she went back into the girls' bedroom. She opened the window. The cool air was harsh against her skin. She climbed out. As soon as her feet hit the cement, she ran.

Where was she heading? She didn't know. She ran down Seventy-Second Street and onto Fifth Avenue, pausing only to catch her breath. It was midnight, and all the shops were closed with the exception of a deli on the corner of Seventy-

Third Street, a pool hall on Seventy-Ninth, a Rite Aid on Eighty-First. Where was she going? What would she do when she got there? A gust of wind blew into her face, and she slowed as her body began to shake, but she pushed herself forward nonetheless, forced her legs to keep moving. The cold air burned against her open wound, but she kept running. This is what her life had come down to, she thought. This is what all her patience had amounted to. Where had she gone wrong? And what was she supposed to do now? What were her options? Palestine or America—wherever she looked, she was only reminded of how powerless she was. All she'd wanted in this life was to find happiness, and now it was clear that she never would, and just thinking of that fact made her want to stand dead in the middle of the road until someone ran her over.

She stopped again to catch her breath on Eighty-Sixth Street, in front of Century 21, a department store that covered half the block. She had been inside with Khaled and Fareeda once, but she couldn't remember why they'd gone. Perhaps Fareeda had needed shoes. She walked down the street, searching for something, anything, to soothe her, but her body only shook with more force the farther she walked from home. The sky was charcoal, without a single star in sight. Around her people rushed by, even at this late hour. Teenagers laughed, men in tattered clothes lay on the pavement. They stared at her, and she looked away. She had the sensation that she was looking down at herself from the sky, as though she were a tiny infant in the middle of the massive street. She pressed her feet into the concrete and tried to ground herself.

She paced in circles and began to weep. She crossed the street and paced in circles again. What should she do? Where could she go? She had no money, no job, no education, no friends, no family. And what would happen to her daughters without her?

They couldn't be raised without a mother. She couldn't leave them alone with Adam and Fareeda. She had to go back.

But she couldn't go back, not to him, not now. She could picture Adam now, his eyes bulging, his jaw clenching and un-clenching. She could feel his fingers around her arms, squeezing tight. Feel him shoving her against the wall, pulling her hair, slapping her across the face. Feel his fingers around her throat, her skin starting to numb, could see the room going white. No. She couldn't face him.

She walked down Eighty-Sixth Street, stopping in front of a pharmacy. It was open, to her relief, and she sat on the front stoop. The stinging along the side of her head was easing. She pressed her fingers against her temples. She was cold, and she wept. She wept tears of all sorts—anger, fear, sorrow, but mostly regret. How could she have been so naive to think she could ever be happy? She should've listened to Mama. Happiness was something people made up in books, and she had been foolish to believe she could ever find it in the real world.

Isra looked up to see a man approaching her.

"Excuse me, are you okay?" he said. "You're bleeding."

Isra wrapped her arms around herself and looked at the ground. The man moved closer. "What happened to your head?"

"N—nothing," she stammered, the English strange on her tongue.

"Did someone do this to you? Did someone hurt you?" She shook her head. "You need to call the police. Hurting someone like this is illegal. Whoever did this to you will go to jail." Isra started to cry again. She didn't want to send the father of her daughters to jail. She just wanted to go home. "You need to go to an emergency room," the man said. "You need stitches. Do you have anyone to call?" He pointed to a phone booth at the end of the block. "Come with me," he said, gesturing toward the booth.

Isra followed. The man placed two quarters into the shiny box and handed Isra the receiver. "You need to call someone."

It was the first time Isra had held a public telephone. The metal felt crisp against her fingertips and sent a chill through her. Once she started shaking again, she couldn't stop. She held the phone to her ear. There was a beeping noise on the other end.

"You have to dial a number," the man said.

She didn't know who to call. In those seconds, holding the phone to her ear, Isra's loneliness was the clearest it had ever been. She knew she couldn't call Palestine without a phone card, and besides, what would Mama say except to go home at once, to stop parading her shame for the whole world to see? She couldn't call Adam's beeper, not after what she'd done. She had only one person to call, and she wept as she dialed the number.

"Get in," Fareeda said from the passenger window as Khaled parallel-parked. Isra climbed into the car. "What were you thinking leaving the house alone this late at night?"

"Who is that man over there?" Khaled snapped, shooting her a sidelong look

"I don't know," Isra said. "He was trying to help me, and—"

"Tell me," Khaled cut her off. "What kind of decent woman leaves her house in the middle of the night?"

"Calm down," Fareeda said sharply. She was eyeing Isra's head by the light of the streetlamp. "Can't you see the girl is shaken up?"

"*You* be quiet." He turned around to see Isra fully. "Tell me, where were you going? Who is that man?"

"I—I don't know. He was just trying to help," Isra said. "I was scared. My head wouldn't stop bleeding. . . . It won't stop."

"That's no reason to leave the house," Khaled said. "How do we know you weren't out with some man?"

"Man? What man?" Isra curled up in the back seat. "I wasn't with anyone. I swear."

"And how do we know that? How do we know you didn't sneak out with some man and now you're calling us to come get you?"

"I'm telling the truth!" Isra cried. "I wasn't with anyone. Adam hit me!"

"Of course he did," Fareeda said, flashing Khaled a look.

"We don't know anything," Khaled said. "Only a *sharmouta* leaves her house in the middle of the night."

Isra was too tired to fight anymore. She leaned her head back, nauseated by her own helplessness.

"That's enough!" Fareeda snapped. "Look at the girl's head."

"She could've hit her head on the sidewalk," Khaled said. "She could've just been with another man, and *he* could've done this to her. How do we know she's telling the truth?"

"You cruel, disgusting men! Always quick to point a finger. Always quick to put the blame on a woman. Your son is a drunk—of course he is, why wouldn't he be? Just like his father!"

"*Uskuti!* Shut up!"

"What? You don't like hearing the truth? Look at the girl!" Fareeda turned around and pointed at Isra in the back seat. "Look at her head! It will need a dozen stitches to close it. And you're sitting here talking about another man. *Ttfu.*" She made a spitting sound. "The cruelest thing on this earth is a man's heart."

Khaled raised his hand. "I said *uskuti*! Shut your mouth!"

"Or what? You're going to start beating me again? Do it! Put your hands on an old lady, you filthy man! Instead of screaming at this girl, why don't you go punish your damn son for beating her senseless? What are we going to tell her parents, huh? That our son beat her so hard she needed stitches? And what if someone at the doctor calls the cops? What if your son goes to jail? Tell me, have you thought about that? Have you?" She turned to look out the window. "Of course you haven't. I'm the one who has to do all the thinking around here."

Khaled sighed. "She shouldn't have left the house like that." He met Isra's eyes in the rearview mirror. "A woman's place is her home. Do you understand?" Isra didn't reply. "Do you understand?" he said more loudly.

Isra nodded and looked away. She feared what she might say if she spoke. It was the first time Khaled had ever reminded her of Yacob—loud, overpowering, furious with her—and she felt herself involuntarily shrinking away whenever she glanced up to find him still studying her in the rearview mirror. She looked away again, panicking. If Khaled was this angry, what would Adam do to her when he saw her?

Isra faced the window the rest of the ride home. Every now and then, she looked up to find Fareeda staring absently out the passenger window. Isra wondered what she was thinking. Fareeda had never once in the past seven years defended her. What did it mean? Did Fareeda understand her after all? Did she love her, even? Her own mother had never stood up for her despite the many times Yacob had beaten Isra in her presence.

Isra felt a tide of helplessness spread through her as she thought of her life. She hadn't asked for much. Why couldn't she get it? She must have done something to deserve her miserable fate, only she didn't know what, so she didn't know how to fix it. She wished God would tell her what to do. But in the silence of the car she asked God, and He said nothing.

Fareeda

Winter 2008

"I'll stand here all night if I have to," Deya told Fareeda in the kitchen. "I won't leave until you tell me what happened." She moved closer. "If you refuse, I'll never speak to you again. I'll take my sisters and leave, and you'll never see us again."

"No." Fareeda reached out to touch her, but Deya stepped away. "Please."

"Then tell me the truth. All of it."

"It's the jinn," she croaked. "It's the jinn from my daughters."

Whatever answer Deya had been expecting, it was clearly not this. She stared at Fareeda with confusion in her eyes. "What are you talking about?"

"That's what possessed Adam and Isra. That's what's been haunting this family all these years. The jinn from my daughters."

"What daughters?"

She told Deya all of it: how her belly had swelled soon after her marriage to Khaled, how hopeful he had been at the gift of new life, the possibility of a new beginning in such a desperate time. Only Fareeda hadn't given him the son he had dreamed of, the young man who would help him find food and water, who would help him cope with the burden of their family's loss, who would carry on the family's name. She had given him *balwas* instead—not one but two. She had known, even before seeing the mournful look on his face, that he would be disappointed. She hadn't blamed him. The shame of her gender was engraved on her bones.

Deya sat down. "What happened to them?"

"They died." The words felt heavy on Fareeda's tongue. They had remained unspoken for so long.

"How?" It was clear she was still angry, but her tone had softened slightly.

"Khaled's mother made me feed them formula. She said breastfeeding would stop me from getting pregnant, and we needed a son. But there were shortages of food and medicine. One day I ran out of formula, so I stole a cup of goat's milk from our neighbor's tent and fed them and . . ."

"I don't see how this has anything to do with my parents being possessed," Deya said.

How could she make her see? Fareeda sucked back tears. It had everything to do with Adam and Isra. Her daughters had been punishing her all these years for what she had done. When Isra gave birth to daughter after daughter, when Adam came home, eyes glazed, Fareeda could feel her firstborn daughters in the air, could almost hear their cries.

"Say something!" Deya said. "What do your daughters have to do with my parents?"

"Because I killed them. I didn't know! I promise you, I didn't know! I was so young—I had no idea—but it doesn't matter. It was my fault. I killed them, and they've been haunting me ever since."

Deya stared at her, her face twisted, unreadable. Fareeda knew her granddaughter could never understand how shame could grow and morph and swallow someone until she had no choice but to pass it along so that she wasn't forced to bear it alone. She searched for the right words now, but there were none that could explain it. Deep down she knew what she had done—that she had pushed everyone away, that all she could do now was wait for the day when God would snatch her off this earth. She hoped it would be quick. What was the point of living, really, when you were like her—a fist of loneliness clenched around an empty heart?

Fareeda closed her eyes and breathed. Something inside her shifted, as if her whole life she had been looking in the wrong direction, not seeing the precise moment that turned everything upside down. She saw the chain of shame passed from one woman to the next so clearly now, saw her place in the cycle so vividly. She sighed. It was cruel, this life. But a woman could only do so much.

Deya

Winter 2008

The next morning Deya left her sisters at the corner of Seventy-Second Street and walked past them to the subway station, head bowed to avoid meeting their eyes. Her hands were sweating, and she wiped them on her *jilbab*. She pictured fleetingly how composed she had been the night before, when she'd told her sisters that they should run away, that she had a plan. She had smiled as she painted the future for them, a forced hope in her eyes.

But then they had done the unexpected. They had refused to leave. Nora said running away was a bad idea, that it wouldn't bring back their parents, that it would only isolate them more. Layla had agreed, adding that they'd been sheltered their entire lives, and would never be able to survive on their own. They had no money. They had nowhere to go. Amal only nodded as the other two spoke, her eyes large and teary. They were sorry, they told her. But they were too afraid. Deya had said she was afraid, too. The difference was, she was also afraid of staying.

"I need to leave home," Deya told Sarah when they'd settled in their usual spot. "Could I stay with you?"

"What about everything we've talked about? I don't think running away is the answer."

"But you ran away. And look at you now. Besides, I thought you said you wanted me to make my own choices. Well, this is my choice."

Sarah sighed. "I lost my virginity and was afraid for my life. The circumstances were completely different. But you—you've done nothing wrong." Deya could tell she was holding back tears. "If you go, you'll lose your sisters. Maybe if I had stayed, Isra would still be here."

"Don't say that! Mama's death had nothing to do with you. It was only his fault. His and Teta's. Besides, what would've happened to you if you'd stayed? You would've been married off, probably have five or six kids by now. And that's what'll happen to me if I don't leave. I have to go."

"No! You have to try harder to fight for what you want."

"Teta will never let me—"

"Listen to me." Sarah cut her off. "You want to go to college, make your own choices, fine. Do that. You don't want to get married? Then don't. Put your foot down—*refuse*. Have the courage to speak up for yourself. Leaving your family is not the answer. Running away is cowardly, and you'd regret it for the rest of your life. What if you never see your sisters again? Never see their children? Is that what you want? Living your life as an outcast? You can do this the right way, Deya. You don't have to lose your family."

Sarah didn't understand, thought Deya. She had forgotten what it was like. Deya couldn't fight for anything in Fareeda's house. She had a better chance of sawing off her own leg. "Then I'll just get married," she said. "Leave the house and start over."

"That's not a reason to get married. You know that."

"Tell me then, what am I supposed to do? Tell me! I came here thinking you would help me leave them. But all you've done is scare me more." She turned to go. "I thought you wanted to help me."

"I do!" Sarah grabbed her hand. "I'm only telling you what I wish someone had told me—that running away is not the answer."

"Then what is?"

"Only you know that. You have to shove your fears and worries aside and listen to that clear voice in your head."

"But there are conflicting voices in my head. How am I supposed to know which one to listen to?"

"You'll know," Sarah said. "Find something you love, something that calms you, and do that for a while. Your answer will come. You will just know. As for Fareeda, at least try. What have you got to lose?"

Deya gave her a hard look and then stood, turned, and walked out the door. Couldn't Sarah see by now that Deya knew nothing? Even after learning the truth about her parents, she still knew nothing. She couldn't be trusted to figure things out on her own. All the thinking she had ever done was for nothing, or she would've realized that her mother hadn't just died, that she had been murdered. She felt a jolt of shame inside. A violent stab of foolishness. All these years she had thought Isra abandoned them. She had been so sure, and she had been wrong, terribly wrong. How could she trust herself now?

Fareeda

Spring 1997

By March of 1997, the London planes lining Seventy-Second Street were starting to bud, yellow dandelions scattered along the sidewalk beside them. In a couple of months Sarah would graduate from high school. The passing of time brought a panic to Fareeda that no amount of food was able to bury. She spent her mornings propped on the kitchen table, phone in hand, mumbling to Umm Ahmed about her daughter's misfortune, that no suitors had proposed to marry her. But at least the idea that Sarah was cursed no longer gripped her. Over the winter she had taken Sarah to visit a jinn sheikh on Eighty-Sixth Street. Fareeda, who had once been afraid to walk to Umm Ahmed's house, crossing entire blocks for her daughter's sake. This is what motherhood is all about, she thought. Not sitting around smiling, but doing everything you can for your child. Inside a darkened room, the jinn sheikh had recited an incantation over Sarah to see if she was cursed. He had turned to Fareeda and pronounced that there were no traces of evil spirits on the girl.

In the kitchen, Fareeda sat across from Isra and Nadine, who were stuffing grape leaves. "I just don't understand it," she said into the receiver as she cracked the shell of a pistachio nut open with one hand. "Sarah is slim, with fair skin and soft hair. She knows how to cook, clean, iron, sew. I mean, for goodness sake, she's the only girl in a family of men. She's practically been trained for wifedom her entire life!"

She shook her head, stuffing the pistachio into her mouth. She wished Isra and Nadine would stop staring at her. She couldn't stand to be around either of them. Isra, who had made a fool of them by running out in the middle of the night, and Nadine, who was only now pregnant with her second child. It was about damn time. Ameer needed a brother. She wondered when Isra would get pregnant again, but quickly dismissed the thought. Fareeda couldn't bear the heartache of another girl right now, staying up all night wondering if God was punishing her through Isra.

In fact, Fareeda was doubly glad Isra wasn't pregnant; she could barely handle the four children she had. Fareeda noticed how Isra looked at her girls, a flatness in her eyes, as though they were sucking the life from her. The last thing Fareeda needed was to worry about her running away again, as though she hadn't heard anything Fareeda had said about covering her shame.

Something came to Fareeda then, a puzzle piece snapping into place. Her eyes shot to the door. She cut off Umm Ahmed, slammed the phone down, and rushed outside. She lowered herself onto the front stoop, pulling her nightgown over her knees as she did so. A hint of sunlight flickered on her legs, making them yellower than usual. She fingered the edge of her nightgown, pulling it lower still. Behind her Isra and Nadine called her name, softly at first but then with more force, but she refused to look at them. No. She would sit there until Sarah came home from school, until she figured out what was wrong. If her daughter wasn't cursed, then why hadn't any of the suitors proposed marriage? What had her daughter done?

The sky darkened and rain started to fall, beating against Fareeda's face. She didn't get up, didn't move. All she could think of was Sarah. Her daughter must have done something to have ruined her reputation. But what? And how? She came home straight from school every day, she had never once left the house alone. So what could she have possibly done? She heard Isra and Nadine approaching again.

"I'm staying right here," she said when Nadine touched her shoulder. "Right here until Sarah comes home." She turned to stare them down. Nadine squinted at her, but Isra's eyes skirted to one side. Fareeda couldn't tell whether it was one of her stupid expressions or if she knew something Fareeda didn't. It was possible. With all the time they spent together, Isra could've picked up on something. Sarah could've even told her. Right there under her nose all this time.

"Isra," she said, lifting herself up. "Has Sarah told you something? Something that might explain why none of her suitors have proposed?"

Isra stared back at her with round eyes. "No. She hasn't told me anything." She said each word as though they pained her on the way out. Fareeda studied Isra's face, the trembling lip, the meek expression. The face of a child. Clearly she knew nothing. She wondered how Adam must feel, coming home to that face every night. It was no wonder he came in reeking of *sharaab*. Despite her disapproval, she couldn't blame him, had even covered up for him once when Khaled had found a can of Budweiser in the trash outside. She sighed and sat back down to wait for her daughter.

———————

By the time the school bus finally let Sarah off at the corner, the sky had mostly cleared. Fareeda rose to meet her.

"What are you up to?" Fareeda began as Sarah approached the house.

Sarah dropped her backpack to the ground, took another step toward her. "What are you talking about?"

"All the girls in your class have had marriage proposals," Fareeda said, waving her hands. "All but you!" Sarah took a step back, stealing a glance at Isra. "It doesn't make sense. Umm Fadi is turning down suitors for her daughter left and right. Umm Ali's daughter is already engaged, and she's hideous. Even Hannah is married!"

Sarah opened her mouth but said nothing. Fareeda moved closer. "You must be up to something," she said, her index finger almost touching Sarah's forehead. "All these suitors, and not one has come back. Tell me! What have you done?"

"Nothing, Mama!" Sarah said. "I haven't done anything."

"You expect me to believe that? *Walek*, look at you! Men should be lined up at my door. Mothers should be calling me day and night begging for you! But they take one look at you and never return. What are you doing behind my back?" Sarah gave no answer but there was defiance in her eyes. "I asked you a question. Answer me!"

"I already told you. I haven't done anything wrong."

"You have the nerve to give me an attitude? Unbelievable!" Fareeda reached out and struck Sarah full in the face with the flat of her palm. The force of her blow caused the girl to step back, cupping her cheek in her hand.

"Come here!" Fareeda reached out, grabbed Sarah's hair, and pulled it hard. "This is what I get for not beating you more often! I must have raised a *sharmouta*! That's why no one will come near us! That's why I still have an eighteen-year-old girl sitting in my face!" She pulled on her hair again, harder this time, jerked her head toward the ground.

"Fareeda!" Isra cried out, grabbing her arm. Nadine started to do the same, but Fareeda pushed them off.

"Don't you dare interfere! Get away!" She tightened her fist around Sarah's hair and dragged her through the front door. Inside she shoved the girl onto the hallway floor. "I'll show you what you get for disobeying me!"

Sarah said nothing, her cheeks flushed red, her eyes two wells of fury. Her silence infuriated Fareeda most of all. How dare her daughter disobey her like this, how dare she defy her, after all Fareeda had done for her, for all of them? All she had given up, day after day until there was nothing left of her but a sack of bones. And they still blamed her in the end.

She took off her slipper and slammed it against Sarah's body, over and over, her jaw clenching each time the slipper struck her daughter's skin. It wasn't fair! Sarah tried to crawl away, but Fareeda stooped down and seized her, pushing her into the ground with all her might. The next thing she knew, her hands were clutched around Sarah's throat, all ten fingers digging in as if kneading a chunk of dough.

"STOP!" Isra's voice cut through Fareeda's rage. What was she doing? She let go. The feeling she had now, like the jinn had entered her, would not shake. She stared at her hands for what seemed like an eternity. Finally she spoke in a quiet voice. "I'm doing all this for you." Sarah was shaking her head, rubbing tears from her eyes. "You think I'm a monster, but I know things about this life you can't imagine. I could sit around and play house with you, making jokes and spinning fairy tales, but it would all be lies. I'm choosing to teach you about the world instead. To want what you can't have in this life is the greatest pain of all."

Sarah stared at the floor. A moaning sound came from her lips, but she said nothing. Fareeda swallowed, studying the runner beneath her feet. Her eyes followed the fabric, its embroidered lines spinning in and out of each other, again and again. She felt as though her life was bound by the same pattern. She couldn't breathe.

"Just go," Fareeda muttered, closing her eyes. "I don't want to look at you right now. Go."

Isra

Spring 1997

On a humid Saturday afternoon, Isra and Sarah stuffed eggplants on the kitchen table. Fareeda sat across from them, phone
pressed to her ear. Isra wondered if this was one of her renewed
attempts to find Sarah a suitor. If it was, Sarah seemed unconcerned. Her full attention was on the eggplant before her as she
carefully stuffed it with rice and minced meat. It occurred to
Isra that despite the many threats Fareeda had made to Sarah
since her beating, nothing she'd said had elicited even the slightest appearance of fear from her daughter.

Fareeda hung up and turned to face them. Isra froze when
she saw her face—it was as if she had seen death in her cup of
Turkish coffee.

"It's Hannah," she began. "It's Hannah . . . Umm Ahmed . . .
Hannah has been killed."

"*Killed?* What are you talking about?" Sarah jumped from
her seat, her eggplant rolling off the table.

Isra felt her heart thumping beneath her nightgown. She
didn't know much about Sarah's classmate Hannah, Umm

Ahmed's youngest daughter. Fareeda had considered her for Ali at one point, but had decided against the idea when she'd sensed that Umm Ahmed hadn't wanted Sarah for her son. Isra remembered thinking how lucky Hannah was that this family hadn't been her *naseeb*—surely Hannah's life would've turned out like hers. But now, listening to the news, a panicky feeling moved through her. Sadness was an inescapable part of a woman's life.

"What do you mean, killed?" Sarah asked again, louder this time, beating her thighs with the edges of her palms. "What are you talking about?"

Fareeda straightened in her seat, her eyes glistening. "Her husband . . . he . . . he . . ."

"Her *husband*?"

"Hannah told him she wanted a divorce," Fareeda said, her voice cracking. "He says he doesn't know what happened. They found him standing over her body with a knife."

Sarah let out a wail. "And you want to do this to me? 'Get married! Get married!' That's all you can say to me. You don't care what happens to me!"

"Not now," Fareeda said, staring at a spot outside the window. "This has nothing to do with you."

"It has everything to do with me! What if some man kills me? Would you even care? Or would you just be glad that I was no longer your *balwa*?"

"Don't be ridiculous," Fareeda said, though Isra could see her upper lip trembling.

"Hannah was only eighteen!" Sarah shouted. "That could've been me."

Fareeda's eyes were locked on the window. A fly buzzed against the glass. She squashed it with the edge of her nightgown. She had told Isra once, years ago when Adam first beat her, that a woman was put on this earth to please her husband.

Even if he was wrong, she had said, a woman must be patient. A woman must endure. And Isra had understood why Fareeda said it. Just like Mama, she believed silence was the only way. That it was safer to submit than speak up. But watching the tears gather in her eyes, Isra wondered what Fareeda thought about her words now.

Deya

Winter 2008

"Assalamu alaikum," **Khaled** said when Deya returned home that afternoon.

"Walikum assalam." Why was he home so early? Surely Fareeda had told him that Deya knew the truth. Did he want to know where Sarah was? Fareeda had been so consumed with hiding the truth that she had barely asked anything about her daughter.

She placed her hijab on the kitchen table. "Why did you lie to us?"

Khaled stepped away from the open pantry and looked down at her. "I'm sorry, Deya," he said in a low voice. "We didn't want to hurt you."

"How did you think we'd feel when we found out you lied to us all these years? You didn't think that would hurt us?" Her grandfather didn't reply, only looked away from her again. "Why did Baba do it? Why did he kill her?"

"He was drunk, Deya. He wasn't in his right mind."

"That doesn't make sense. There must be a reason!"

"There was no reason."

"Why did he kill himself?"

"I don't know, daughter." Khaled reached inside the pantry for a jar of sesame seeds. "I don't know what your father was thinking that night. It's haunted me for years. I wish I knew what made him do those terrible things. I wish I could've stopped him somehow. There are so many things about that night I don't understand. All I know is that we're sorry. Your grandmother and I only wanted to protect you."

"You weren't protecting us. You were only protecting yourselves."

He still didn't meet her gaze. "I'm sorry, daughter."

"Sorry? That's all you have to say?"

"We only want what's best for you."

"Best for us?" The loudness of her voice startled her, but she kept going. "If you wanted what's best for us, you would let me go to college. You wouldn't force me to get married to a stranger. You wouldn't risk putting me in a situation where that man might kill me, and everyone would look the other way! How could you want that life for me?"

"We would never let anyone hurt you."

"That's not true! You let my father hurt my mother. Here. In this very house! You and Teta knew he beat her, and you did *nothing!*"

"I'm sorry, Deya." Those meaningless words again. His expression when he looked at her was one of deep sorrow. "I was wrong not to protect your mother," he said after a moment. "I wish I could go back in time. Where we're from, this is how it was between a husband and wife. I never for a moment thought Adam would . . . I didn't know . . ." He stopped, his wrinkled face on the verge of crumpling into tears. Deya had never seen him cry before. "Did you know Isra used to help me make *za'atar?*"

Deya swallowed. "No."

"Every Friday after *jumaa* prayer. She even taught me her mother's secret recipe." He reached inside the pantry and pulled out a few spice jars. "Do you want me to show you?"

Deya was filled with anger, but this was the first time he'd mentioned her mother in years. She needed his memories of her. She moved closer.

"The most important part of making *za'atar* is roasting the sesame seeds perfectly."

Deya watched him pour the sesame seeds into an iron skillet, curious to see him the way her mother had. She wondered how Isra had felt standing beside Khaled, only a few inches between them as they roasted the sesame seeds. She pictured her smiling shyly, saying no more than a few words, perhaps afraid that Fareeda would overhear them. "Did you and my mother ever talk?" Deya asked.

"She was never much of a talker," he said, opening a jar of marjoram leaves. "But she opened up sometimes."

"What did she talk about?"

"Different things." He scooped a spoonful of leaves into the mortar and began to grind them. "How much she missed Palestine." He poured the ground marjoram on top of the sesame seeds. "How impressed she was by your curiosity."

"She said that?"

He nodded. "She used to read to you and your sisters daily. Do you remember? Sometimes I used to hear her on the front stoop, making funny noises as she read. You all used to laugh so hard. I rarely heard Isra laugh throughout the years, but in those moments she sounded like a child."

Deya felt her mouth go dry. "What else?"

Khaled opened a jar of sumac. The burnt-red powder had always reminded Deya of her parents. Isra had liked to sauté onions in sumac and olive oil until they turned a light purple. Then she'd place the sautéed mixture on top of warm pita bread. *Msakhan*. It was her father's favorite dish. She felt sick at the thought.

Khaled sprinkled a pinch of salt into the mixture. "What exactly do you want to know?"

What did she want to know? Even the question felt like a vast oversimplification of everything she was feeling. "I've been lied to all these years. I don't know what to believe anymore, what to think, what to do."

"I knew we should've told you the truth right away," Khaled said, "but Fareeda was afraid . . . We were afraid . . . We didn't want you to get hurt, that's all. We only wanted to protect you."

"There's so much I don't know."

He met her eyes. "There's so much none of us know. I still don't understand why my daughter ran away, why my son killed his wife, killed himself. My own children, and I don't understand them."

"But at least Sarah is alive," Deya said. "You can ask her why she ran away. You can get answers, you just choose not to." Khaled looked away. From his expression Deya knew he was still angry with his daughter. "Will you ever forgive her?" He didn't look up. "She misses you, and she's sorry—she's sorry she ran away."

"It's not that easy."

"Why not? Because she's a girl? Is that it? Because she was only a girl and she dared to shame you? Would you have forgiven my father if he were still alive? Tell me, would you have forgiven him for killing my mother?"

"It's not that simple."

Deya shook her head. "What does that even mean?"

"It isn't Sarah's fault I can't forgive her, it's mine. My pride won't let me forgive her. In this her crime is less than mine, much less. In this I have failed her. I have failed all of you."

"You talk as though it's too late, Seedo, but it's not. You can still forgive her. There's still time."

"Time?" Khaled said. "No amount of time can bring back our family's reputation."

Isra

Spring 1997

"Are you okay?" Isra asked Sarah that evening, after Fareeda and Nadine had settled in the *sala* to watch their favorite show. She and Sarah would sometimes join them, but tonight they stuffed cabbage leaves in the kitchen.

"I'm fine," Sarah said.

Isra was careful with her words. "I know you're worried about marriage, especially now that . . ." She brought her voice to a whisper. "After Hannah died."

"She didn't die," Sarah corrected her, not bothering to lower her voice. "She was murdered by her husband. And yet my mother still insists on marrying me off like nothing happened."

Isra didn't know what to say. She didn't see what Hannah's death had to do with Sarah. If every woman refused to get married after a woman died at the hands of her husband, then no one would ever get married. Secretly Isra had begun to suspect that Hannah had done something to get herself killed. Not that she deserved to get killed, no. But there was no way a man would kill his wife for no reason, Isra told herself.

"I'm sorry," she said. "I'm here if you want to talk about it."

Sarah shrugged. "There's no point in talking."

"Are you afraid? Is that it? Because I understand if you are, I—"

"I'm not afraid."

"Then what is it?"

"I can't do this anymore."

"What do you mean?"

"This." Sarah pointed to the pot of stuffed cabbage leaves between them. "This isn't life. I don't want to live like this."

Isra stared at her. "But there is no other life, Sarah. You know that."

"For you, maybe. But there is for me."

Isra could feel her face burn. She looked away.

"You know I snuck out of school the other day."

"What?"

"It's true. Me and my friends went out to celebrate the last week of school. We watched this movie in the theaters. *Anna Karenina*. You must have seen the commercials, no? It was the most romantic love story I've ever seen, and you know me—I don't even like love stories. But you know what I was thinking the whole time we were watching the movie?"

Isra shook her head.

"All I kept thinking was that I would never have a love like that. I will never fall in love, Isra. Not if I stay in this house."

"Of course you will," Isra lied. "Of course."

"Yeah, sure."

Isra knew her voice had betrayed her. "Don't be foolish, Sarah. Books and movies, that's not how the real world works."

Sarah crossed her arms. "Then why do you spend all day reading?"

Isra felt a lump in her throat she could not swallow. Why was it so hard for her to admit the truth, not only to Sarah, but to herself? She knew she had to stop pretending things were okay. She was seized to confess, at last, the fear that circled her brain in endless loops: that she would do the same thing to her daughters that Mama had done to her. That she would force them to repeat her life.

"I'm sorry for what's happening to you," she said.

Sarah gave a harsh laugh. "No, you're not. If you were really sorry, then you'd admit that this isn't a life."

"I know that."

"Do you? Then why do you think it's okay, living the way you do? Is this the life you want for yourself? For your daughters?"

"Of course not, but I'm afraid."

"Of what?"

"So many things." Isra's eyes watered. "Adam, Fareeda . . . myself."

"Yourself? Why?"

"I can't pinpoint it exactly. Maybe I've been reading too much. But sometimes I think there's something wrong with me."

"In what way?" Sarah stared, concern etched on her face.

Isra had to look away, or she knew she wouldn't be able to continue. "It's hard to put in words without sounding crazy," she said. "I lie in bed every morning, and I feel so desperate. I don't want to wake up, I don't want to see anyone, I don't want to look at my daughters, and I don't want them looking at me. Then I think, if I just push the sluggish thoughts away, if I just get up and make the bed and pour some cereal and brew an *ibrik* of chai, then everything will be okay. But it's never okay, and sometimes I—" She stopped.

"Sometimes what?"

"Nothing," Isra lied. She looked away, gathering her thoughts. "It's just that . . . I don't know . . . I worry. That's the heart of it. I worry that my daughters will hate me when they grow up, the way you hate Fareeda. I worry that I will end up doing the same thing to them that she's done to you."

"But you don't have to do that to them," Sarah said. "You can give them a better life."

Isra shook her head. She wished she could tell Sarah the truth: that even though she willed herself not to, she secretly resented her daughters for being girls, couldn't even look at them without stirring up shame. She wanted to say that it was a shame that had been passed down to her and cultivated in her since she was in the womb, that she couldn't shake it off even if she tried. But all she said was, "It's not that simple."

"You're starting to sound like my mother." Sarah shook her head. "It seems pretty simple to me. All you have to do is let your daughters make their own choices. Tell me—shouldn't a mother want her daughter to be happy? So why does mine only hurt me?"

Isra could feel the tears coming, but she held them back. "I don't think Fareeda wants to hurt you. Of course she wants you to be happy. But she doesn't know better. She's never seen better."

"That's not an excuse. Why are you defending her?"

Isra didn't know how to explain it. She had her own resentments toward Fareeda. The woman was tough. But Isra also knew the world had made her that way. That it was a hard world, and it was hardest on its women, and there was no escaping that.

"I'm not defending her," she said. "I just want you to be safe, that's all."

"Safe from what?"

"I don't know. . . . You've been scaring away your suitors. Now you're sneaking out of school, going to the movies. I just worry your family will find out, and . . . I don't want you to get hurt."

Sarah laughed. "What do you suppose will happen to me if I accept one of the proposals my mother wants? Do you think I'll ever be loved? Respected? Accomplished? Tell me, do you?"

"No."

"How is that not hurting me? That's why I refuse to listen to my family anymore."

Isra stared at her in horror. "What are you saying?"

Sarah looked briefly at the door before whispering, "I'm running away."

There was a moment of silence as Isra registered the words. She opened her mouth to speak, stopped, felt herself choke. Then she swallowed. "What, are you crazy?"

"I don't have a choice, Isra. I have to leave."

"Why?"

"I . . . I have to. I can't live like this anymore."

"What are you saying? You can't just leave!" She reached for Sarah's arm, clutched it. "Please, I'm begging you, don't do this!"

"I'm sorry," Sarah said, shaking her arm free. "But nothing you say will change my mind. I'm leaving." Isra opened her mouth to speak, but Sarah cut her off. "And you should come with me."

"Have you lost your mind?"

"Says the girl who ran out the basement window in the middle of the night."

"That was different! I was upset. I didn't plan to run away . . . and I came back! Even if I wanted to, I couldn't. I have daughters to think of."

"Exactly. If I had a daughter, I would do anything to save her from this."

Deep down, Isra knew her daughters would live out this same life. That one day she would become like Fareeda and push them into marriages, no matter how much they hated her for it. But that wasn't a reason to run away. She was a foreigner here, with no money or skills, nothing to live on, nowhere to go. She turned to Sarah. "What will you do? How will you live?"

"I'll go to college, get a job."

"It's not that easy," Isra said. "You've never even spent a night away from home, let alone lived on your own. You need someone to take care of you."

"I can take care of myself," Sarah said. Then, in a softer voice, she added, "You can take care of yourself, too. We can take care of each other." Their eyes met. "If you're not strong enough to do it for yourself, then do it for your daughters."

Isra looked away. "I can't . . . I can't raise them on my own."

"Why not? You already do, practically. America is full of single mothers."

"No! I don't want to put my daughters through that. I don't want to uproot them—snatch them from home and force them to grow up alone, without a family, in shame."

Sarah sneered at her. "You have to have a home first to be uprooted from it. You have to know what love is to feel alone."

"Aren't you scared?"

"Of course I am." Sarah studied an invisible spot on the floor. "But whatever happens . . . It can't be worse than what's happening now."

Isra knew Sarah was right, but awareness and action, she also knew, were very different things. "I don't know where you've found this courage," she whispered. "And I envy you for it. But I can't go with you. I'm sorry."

Sarah looked at her with sad eyes. "You'll regret this, you know. Your daughters will grow up, and they'll hate you for your weakness." She walked away, pausing at the doorway. "And don't think they'll understand, because they won't. They'll never see you as a victim. You're supposed to be the one who protects them."

Deya

A **new year** began, and nothing changed. In class, Deya found it
hard to pay attention. She felt adrift and nauseous. When school
let out and she got home, she retreated quietly to her room,
where she ate alone, emerging only to wash the dishes after dinner. A thousand thoughts flicked through her mind like cars on
a subway train: she should visit Sarah again, she should leave,
she should stay and marry Nasser if he would still have her.
But nothing felt right. Every time she tried to talk to her sisters,
she'd clench up, racked with nerves and anger. To them, nothing
had really changed. Nora had even said as much one night while
trying to comfort Deya. Their parents might as well have died in
a car accident, she'd said; they needed to move on. Deya hadn't
been that kind of person before; she definitely wasn't now.

Most of all she thought about Isra, trying to understand
the woman she thought she'd known all these years, yet had so
grossly misjudged. When Sarah had first started telling her stories of Isra, they had felt like precisely that: fiction. But now Deya
clutched at the stories desperately, each one a clue to the woman

her mother really was. She tried to stitch together the scattered pieces of Isra's life, to weave them into a full narrative, a complete story, a truth. But she couldn't—something was missing. There was more to Isra. After everything she had learned over the past weeks, she knew there had to be.

She sat in Islamic studies class, staring blankly ahead as Brother Hakeem paced in front of the chalkboard. He was discussing the role of women in Islam. Once or twice she could feel him looking at her, waiting for her to question something in her usual way, but she kept her eyes trained on the window. He recited a verse, in Arabic: "Heaven lies under a mother's feet." The words meant nothing to her. She didn't have a mother.

"But why is heaven under the mother's feet?" a girl asked. "Why not under the father's feet? He's the head of the household."

"Good question," Brother Hakeem said, clearing his throat. "The father might be the head of the household, but the mother serves an important role. Can anyone tell me what that is?"

The class said nothing, looking at him with wide eyes. Deya was tempted to say that a woman's role was to sit tight and wait until a man beat her to death, but she stayed quiet.

"None of you know the role your mother plays in the family?" Brother Hakeem asked.

"Well, she bears the children," said one girl.

"And she takes care of the family," said another.

They were all so dumb, sitting there, smiling with their stupid answers. Deya wondered what lies they'd been told, what secrets their parents kept from them, the things they didn't know. The things they'd only find out too late.

"Very good," Brother Hakeem said. "Mothers carry the entire family—arguably the entire world—on their shoulders. That's why heaven lies under their feet."

Deya listened to his words, unconvinced. Nothing she learned in Islamic studies class ever made sense. If heaven lay under a mother's feet, then why had her father hit her mother? Why had he killed her? They were Muslims, weren't they?

"But I still don't understand what it means," said a girl in the back.

"It's a metaphor," Brother Hakeem said, "to remind us of the importance of our women. When we accept that heaven lies underneath the feet of a woman, we are more respectful of women everywhere. That is how we are told to treat women in the Qur'an. It's a powerful verse."

Deya wanted to scream. No one she'd ever met actually lived according to the doctrines of Islam. They were all hypocrites and liars! But she was tired of fighting. Instead she closed her eyes and thought of her parents, replaying memories, trying to think of anything she might have forgotten, anything that could make better sense of things.

On the bus ride home, Deya wondered if she would ever learn the full story of Isra's life and death. She knew that no matter how many times she replayed her memories, how many stories she told herself, she would never know the full truth on her own. But she hoped against hope that she'd remember something new. A repressed memory. A piece that would change everything. She thought back to the last thing she remembered her mother saying.

"I'm sorry," Isra had whispered. "I'm sorry."

Looking out the window, waiting for the traffic light to change, Deya wished she knew what her mother had been thinking in her final days. But she didn't know, and she didn't think she ever would.

Fareeda

Summer 1997

It was Adam who first pointed his finger at Fareeda.

"It's all your fault," he said. Sarah had been gone for seven days, and the entire family was gathered around the *sufra*.

Fareeda looked up from her dinner plate. She could feel everyone staring. "What are you talking about?"

"You're the reason she ran away."

Fareeda raised both eyebrows, opened her mouth to protest—but Adam waved a hand, dismissing her words before she'd had a chance to say them.

"This was all your doing!" He slurred his words. "I told you sending her to a public school was a bad idea, that you should homeschool her, but you didn't listen. And for what? So she could learn English and help you with doctor appointments?" He snorted and shook his head. "But that's what you get for being easy on her, on all of them. Everyone except me."

It wasn't as though Fareeda hadn't considered this—that perhaps she was to blame. But she kept her face calm and stony. "Is that what you're upset about? All the pressure we've put on you because you're the eldest?" She pushed herself up from the table. "In that case, why don't you grab a drink and sulk over it? You're good at that."

Adam rose from the table and stormed downstairs.

It wasn't long before Omar and Ali pointed their fingers at Fareeda, too. She made a spitting sound at them. Why, of course it was her fault! Blame it on the woman! But she had only done what was best, raised her children the best she knew how in this foreign place.

Khaled would've blamed her, too, only he was too busy blaming himself. Nightly, he hid his pain behind a cloud of hookah smoke, but it was clear the loss of his daughter had awakened a new feeling within him: regret. Fareeda could see it in his eyes. She knew what he was thinking—he had spent his entire life fighting to stay strong, trying not to collapse like his father had when the soldiers snatched their home, trying to preserve their family honor. And for what? Now he had no honor left.

What had made them leave their country and come to America, where something like this could happen? *Something like this.* Fareeda's mouth dried up as she asked herself this. Would their daughter have disobeyed them, disgraced them, had they raised her back home? So what if they might have starved? So what if they could've been shot in the back crossing a checkpoint, or blown up with tear gas on the way to school or the mosque? Maybe they should've stayed and let the soldiers kill them. Should've stayed and fought for their land, should've stayed and died. Any pain other than the pain of guilt and regret.

In her bedroom, Fareeda couldn't sleep. Her mind raced the moment her head hit the pillow, thinking about her past, her children. About Sarah. Had she failed as a mother? Some nights, she managed to convince herself she hadn't. After all, hadn't she raised her children the same way her parents had raised her? Hadn't she taught them what it meant to be tough, resilient? Hadn't she taught them what it meant to be Arab, to always put family first? Not to run away, for goodness sake. She couldn't be blamed for their weaknesses. For this country and its low morals.

Fareeda knew it did no good to worry about things she couldn't change. Her mind turned to Umm Ahmed, who had become a shell of her old self, blaming herself for Hannah's death, thinking she could've stopped it somehow and saved her daughter. Privately Fareeda disagreed. If Sarah had come to Fareeda as a married woman and said, "Mama, my husband beats me and I'm unhappy," would Fareeda have told her to leave him, to get a divorce? Fareeda knew she wouldn't have. What had Umm Ahmed been thinking?

Fareeda knew that no matter what any woman said, culture could not be escaped. Even if it meant tragedy. Even if it meant death. At least she was able to recognize her role in their culture, own up to it, instead of sitting around saying "If only I had done things differently." It took more than one woman to do things differently. It took a world of them. She had comforted herself with these thoughts so many times before, but tonight they only filled her with shame.

Isra

Summer 1997

Isra sat by the window, nose pressed up against the glass, feeling a turbulence rise within her. It will be okay, she told herself. But she was not okay. At first when Sarah had left she had wept so violently that it seemed as though the tears were rising from a deep spring inside her and would never stop. But now she sat in a heavy silence. She was furious. How could Sarah run away? Leave her alone like this? Give up on everything they knew, on the life they'd shared together? Growing up, Isra had never once considered running away, not even when her parents sent her to America. What was Sarah thinking?

But worse than her anger was the other thought that kept returning to her: What if Sarah had been right? Isra thought about Khaled and Fareeda, how they had carried their children out of the refugee camp, leaving their country behind and coming to America. Did they see what Isra saw now? They had run away to survive, and now their daughter had done the same. Maybe that's the only way, she thought. The only way to survive.

A day passed, then another, then another. Every morning Isra would wake up to the sound of her daughters calling her name, jumping into bed, and a sickness would fill her. She wondered if it was the jinn. *Just leave me alone!* she wanted to scream. *Just let me breathe!* Eventually she would force herself to get up, gather her daughters, dress them, comb their hair—all that hair, how they moaned as she untangled it!—sucking on her teeth as she yanked a brush through their curls. Then she'd walk Deya and Nora to the corner, waiting for the yellow school bus to take them away, and she'd think, filled with shame and disgust at her weakness, If only the bus would take the rest of her daughters, too.

In the kitchen now, Isra could hear Fareeda's voice in the *sala*. Lately Fareeda spent her days weaving a story of Sarah's marriage to tell the world, only to cry silently into her hands when she was done. Sometimes, like now, Isra felt a duty to comfort her. She brewed a kettle of chai, adding an extra twig of *maramiya*, hoping the smell would soothe her. But Fareeda would never drink it. All she did was pound her palms against her face, like Isra's mama had often done after Yacob hit her. The sight made Isra sick with guilt. She had known that Sarah was leaving and had done nothing to stop her. She should've told Fareeda, should've told Khaled. Only she hadn't, and now Sarah was gone, and it felt as though she had slipped into a pocket of sadness and would never emerge from it.

When she'd finished preparing dinner that night, Isra crept downstairs. Deya, Nora, and Layla were watching cartoons; Amal slept in her crib. Isra tiptoed across the basement quietly so as not to wake her. From the back of their closet, she pulled out *A Thousand and One Nights*, her heart quickening at the touch of the brown spine. Then she turned to the last page, where she kept a stash of paper. She grabbed a blank sheet and began to write another letter she would never send.

"Dear Mama," Isra wrote,

I don't understand what's happening to me. I don't know why I feel this way. Do you know, Mama? What have I done to deserve this? I must have done something. Haven't you always said that God gives everyone what they deserve in life? That we must endure our naseeb because it's written in the stars just for us? But I don't understand, Mama. Is this punishment for the days I rebelled as a young girl? The days I read those books behind your back? The days I questioned your judgment? Is that why God is taunting me now, giving me a life that is the opposite of everything I wanted? A life without love, a life of loneliness. I've stopped praying, Mama. I know it's kofr, sacrilege, to say this, but I'm so angry. And the worst part is, I don't know who I am angry with—God, or Adam, or the woman I've become.

No. Not God. Not Adam. I am to blame. I am the one who can't pull myself together, who can't smile at my children, who can't be happy. It's me. There's something wrong with me, Mama. Something dark lurking in me. I feel it from the moment I wake up until the moment I sleep, something sluggish dragging me under, suffocating me. Why do I feel this way? Do you think I am possessed? A jinn inside me. It must be.

Tell me, Mama. Did you know this would happen to me? Did you know? Is this why you never looked at me as a child? Is this why I always felt like you were drifting far, far away? Is this what I saw when you finally met my eyes? Anger? Resentment? Shame? Am I becoming like you, Mama?

I'm so scared, and nobody understands me. Do you even
understand me? I don't think so.
   Why am I even writing this now? Even if I mailed this off
to you, what good would it do? Would you help me, Mama?
Tell me, what would you do? Only I know what you would do.
You'd tell me, Be patient, endure. You'd tell me that women
everywhere are suffering, and that no pain is worse than be-
ing divorced, a world of shame on my shoulders. You'd tell me
to make it work for my kids. My girls. To be patient so I don't
bring them shame. So I don't ruin their lives. But don't you
see, Mama? Don't you see? I'm ruining their lives anyway.
I'm ruining them.

Isra paused after finishing the letter. She folded it twice before tucking it between the pages of *A Thousand and One Nights*.
Then she returned the book to the back of the closet, where she
knew no one would find it.

I'm crazy, she thought. If anyone finds this, they'll think
I've gone mad. They'll know there's something dark inside me.
But writing was the only thing that helped. With Sarah gone,
she didn't have anyone to talk to anymore. And the loss of this
thing, this connection she hadn't even realized she needed until
she'd had it, made her want to cry all the time. She knew she
would always be alone now.

Bedtime, and her daughters wanted a story.

"But we don't have any books," Isra said. With Sarah gone,
they were limited to the books Deya brought home from school,
and now they were on summer break. Thinking of Sarah's absence, of all the books she would no longer read, Isra felt a wave

of darkness wash over her. Sharing her favorite thing with her daughters had once been the best part of her day.

"But I want a story," Deya cried. Isra looked away. How much she hated the sight of Deya's troubled eyes. How much they reminded her of her failure.

"I'll read to you tomorrow," she said. "It's time for bed."

She sat by the window and watched them fall asleep, telling herself everything was okay. That it was normal for her to feel frustrated, that her daughters wouldn't even remember her sadness. She told herself she would feel better tomorrow. But she knew she was lying to herself—tomorrow her anger would only multiply. Because it wasn't okay. Because she knew she was getting worse, that this deep, dark thing inside her was not going anywhere. Was it a jinn, or was it herself? How was she to know? All she knew was that she was afraid of what would become of her, of how much her daughters would come to resent her, of how, even though she knew she was wrong, she couldn't stop hurting them. Is this what Adam felt, Isra wondered, when he came into the room at night, ripping off his belt and whipping her? Did he feel powerless, too? Like he needed to stop but couldn't, like he was the worst person on earth? Only he wasn't the worst person on earth. She was, and she deserved to get beaten for all of it.

Deya

Winter 2009

As the weeks passed, Deya realized a change had come over Fareeda. She did not arrange for any marriage suitors to visit. She said nothing when she saw Deya reading. She even smiled timidly whenever their eyes met in the kitchen. But Deya looked away.

"I'm sorry," Fareeda said one night as Deya cleared the *sufra* after dinner. Fareeda stood slumped against the kitchen doorway. "I know you're still angry with me. But I hope you know I was only trying to protect you."

Deya said nothing, busying herself with a stack of dirty plates in the sink. What good were apologies now, after everything Fareeda had done?

"Please, Deya," she whispered. "How long are you going to stay angry? You have to know I didn't mean to hurt you. I'm your grandmother. I would never hurt you on purpose. You have to know that. You have to forgive me. Please, I'm sorry."

"What good is your apology if nothing has changed?"

For a long time Fareeda stared at her with wet eyes from the doorway. Then she sighed heavily. "I have something for you."

Deya followed Fareeda to her bedroom, where she reached for something inside her closet. It was a stack of paper. She handed it to Deya. "I never thought I'd give this to you."

"What is it?" Deya asked, even as she caught sight of the familiar Arabic handwriting.

"Letters your mother wrote. These are the rest of them. They are all I found."

Deya held the letters tight. "Why are you giving them to me now?"

"Because I want you to know I understand. Because I should've never kept her from you. I'm sorry, daughter. I'm so sorry."

Downstairs, in the darkness of her room, Deya held her mother's words up to the window, where a faint light came in from the streetlamps outside. There were at least a hundred letters in her hands, each stacked behind the other in no particular order, all addressed to Mama—Isra's mother. Deya didn't know which to read first. Trembling, she sifted through them until her eyes settled on one. She began to read.

Isra

Summer 1997

Summer passed slowly. During the days, nothing could be heard in the house except the whistle of a teakettle. Fareeda hardly spoke, the phone no longer rang, and Isra completed her chores in silence. Sometimes Khaled joined her in the kitchen on Fridays to make *za'atar*. It was a new ritual. Isra thought the *za'atar* brought him comfort. She would stand quietly by his side, the way she had done years ago with Mama, handing him skillets and spatulas, washing dishes he no longer needed. Neither of them ever looked at each other. Neither said a word.

Nadine hardly spoke to her, either. Isra remembered how much she had minded this at first, feeling a bubble of rage burst in her chest whenever Nadine ignored her. But now their distance was a relief. At least she knew where she stood with Nadine. They were not friends, they never would be. She never had to worry about pleasing her, never had to pretend to like her. Their relationship was so much easier than hers with Adam and Fareeda. And yet in this silence, Sarah's absence seemed to reverberate within Isra all the more. But Isra blamed herself for this hurt—she should've learned many years ago not to hope.

"Why do you always sit by the window?" Deya asked one day after lunch, walking toward Isra, who was indeed in her favorite spot.

Isra wrapped her arms around her knees. She hesitated, her eyes fixed on a spot outside the window, before replying, "I like the view."

"Do you want to play a game?" Deya asked, touching her arm. Isra tried not to flinch. She looked at her daughter and noticed that she had gotten a little taller, a little thinner over the summer. She felt a pinch of guilt for not being more mentally present during their days together.

"Not today," Isra said, looking back out the window.

"Why not?"

"I don't feel like playing. Maybe another time."

"But you always say that," Deya said, touching her arm again. Isra shrank back. "You always say tomorrow, and we never play."

"I don't have time to play!" Isra snapped, moving Deya's arm away. "Go play with your sisters." She returned her gaze to the window.

The view outside was gray, the sun hidden behind a broken cloud. Every now and then, she turned to look back at Deya. Why had she spoken to her daughter like that? Would it have been so hard to play one little game? When had she become so harsh? She didn't want to be harsh. She wanted to be a good mother.

The next day Isra watched Nadine tossing a ball with Ameer in the driveway. Nadine's smiling face made Isra sick. Nadine stood straight and tall, her belly round as a basketball in front of her. Her third son was on his way. What had she done in her life to deserve three boys? All while Isra had none. But this failure paled in comparison to Isra's biggest shame: what she had done to her daughters. What she continued to do to them.

Later that afternoon, while Isra soaked lentils to prepare *adas* for dinner, Khaled entered the kitchen to make *za'atar*. But instead of heading straight to the pantry to collect the spices, he stopped in front of Isra and spoke. "I'm sorry, daughter," he said, "for what I said the night Adam hit you."

Isra stepped away from the kitchen sink. Khaled had barely spoken a word to anyone since Sarah had left.

"I've been thinking of that night for some time now." His voice was almost a whisper. "I've been thinking maybe God took Sarah from us as punishment for what we've done to you."

"No. That's not true," Isra managed to say.

"But it is."

"Don't say that," Isra said, trying to meet his gaze. She noticed that his eyes were wet.

"Something like this—it makes you reconsider things." Khaled walked past Isra to the pantry and returned to the kitchen, spices in hand. He poured the sesame seeds into an iron skillet. "It makes you wonder if any of this would've happened if we'd never left home."

Isra had wondered this, too, only she hadn't dared admit it. "Do you want to go back?" she asked, remembering what Adam had once said about wishing he could return. "I mean, would you if you could?"

"I don't know." He stood, slightly stooped, by the stove, stirring the sesame seeds occasionally and opening spice jars he had gathered from the pantry: sumac, thyme, marjoram, oregano. "Whenever we go home to visit my brothers and sisters, I see how they live. I don't know how they do it." He turned off the stove.

Isra watched him pour the roasted sesame seeds into an empty jar. "Why did you come to America?" she asked.

"I was twelve when we relocated to the al-Am'ari camp. My parents had ten children—I was the eldest. We lived in tents for the first few years, thick nylon shelters that kept us dry from the rain, though just barely." He stopped, reaching for the spice jars. Next he would mix a tablespoon or two of each into the roasted seeds. She handed him a measuring spoon.

"We were very poor," Khaled continued. "There wasn't water or electricity. Our toilet was a bucket at the back of our tents, and my father would bury our waste in the woods. The winters were cold, and we chopped wood from the mountains to make a fire. It was hard. We lived that way for a few years before our tents were replaced with cement shelters."

Isra felt the ache of his words inside her. She had grown up poor, yes, but she could not imagine the kind of poverty Khaled described. As far back as she could remember, her family had always had water, electricity, a toilet. She swallowed a lump in her throat. "How did you survive?"

"It was hard. My father worked as a builder, but his salary wasn't enough to support our family. The UNRWA gave out food parcels and financial support. We would stand in line every month for thick blankets and bags of rice and sugar. But the tents were overcrowded, and the food was never enough. My brothers and I would go to the mountains to pick our own food." He stopped to taste the *za'atar* and then reached for the saltshaker, giving Isra a nod. She returned the remaining spices to the cabinet. "People were different back then, you know," Khaled said, placing the dirty skillet in the sink. "If you ran out of milk or sugar, then you walked next door and asked your neighbor. We were all a family back home. We had a community. Nothing like here."

Isra felt a deep and sudden pity, looking at Khaled. "How did you leave?" she asked.

"Ahhh," he said, turning to face her. "For years I worked in a small *dukan* outside the camp. I worked until I had saved five thousand shekels, enough to buy plane tickets for us to America. When we arrived, I had nothing but two hundred dollars in my pocket and a family relying on me to feed them. We settled in Brooklyn because it was where the most Palestinians lived, but still, the community here isn't what it is there. It never could be."

"And you would never go back?"

"Oh, Isra," he said, turning away to wash his hands. "Do you think we can go back to how things were after all these years?"

Isra stared at him blankly. In all her years in America, she had never stopped to consider whether she would return home if given the chance. Would she be able to eat the small meals of her childhood, sleep on that old lumpy mattress, boil a barrel of water every time she needed to bathe? Surely those were only luxuries, creature comforts that paled in comparison to community, to belonging.

When she didn't respond, Khaled gathered his *za'atar* and turned to leave. For a moment his gaze drifted toward the window. Outside the sky had gone gray. Isra felt a shudder of sadness at the sight of his face. As he walked away, she wished she knew how to answer his question, how to find the right words. But saying the right thing was a skill it seemed she would never learn.

"Maybe someday," Khaled said, pausing in the doorway. "Maybe someday we'll have the courage to return."

Deya

For the remainder of the winter, Deya did little but read Isra's letters over and over, desperate to understand her mother. She read on the school bus every morning, her eyes buried in her lap. In class she hid the letters inside her open textbook pages, unable to focus on the lesson at hand. During lunch she read in the library, hidden between bookshelves. Some days she even read Isra's Arabic edition of *A Thousand and One Nights*, flipping page after page, searching for herself and her mother in its stories.

What was Deya looking for exactly? She wasn't sure. A part of her hoped Isra had left her a clue to finding her path, even though she knew such thinking was fruitless—clearly her mother had never even found her own. Most days she could hear Isra's words echoing in her head: *I'm afraid of what will happen to my daughters.* She could hear the voice of Isra's mama, too: *A woman will always be a woman.* Every time Deya closed her eyes, she pictured Isra's face, afraid and confused, wishing she had the courage to stand up for what she wanted, wishing she had defied Mama and Yacob, had defied Adam and Fareeda, had done what she wanted for herself rather than what she was expected to do.

Then one day in early spring, as Deya reread one of Isra's letters, something came to her. It was so obvious she couldn't understand how she hadn't realized it before, but reading her mother's words, Deya finally saw how much she resembled Isra. She, too, had spent her life trying to please her family, desperate for their validation and approval. She, too, had let fear of disappointing them stand in her way. But seeking approval had not worked for Isra, and Deya could see now that it would not work for her either.

Alongside this realization, an old voice that had lived in the back of her head for as long as she could remember—so long she had never before seen it for the fear that it was, only as the absolute truth—rose up inside of her. The voice cautioned her to surrender, be quiet, endure. It told her that standing up for herself would only lead to disappointment when she lost the battle. That the things she wanted for herself were a fight she could never win. That it was safer to surrender and do what she was supposed to do.

What would happen if she disobeyed her family? the old voice asked. Would she be able to shake off her culture that easily? What if her community turned out to be right after all? What if she would never truly belong anywhere? What if she ended up all alone? Deya hesitated. She had finally come to understand the depths of Isra's love, which she had terribly misjudged, had finally learned that there was more to people below the surface, that despite everything her family had done, they loved her in their own way. What would she do without them? Without her sisters? Even without Fareeda and Khaled? As angry as she might be, she didn't want to lose them.

And yet even as she heard this old voice in her head, she could still feel the shift that had just occurred inside her. The old voice was no longer strong enough to hold her back—Deya knew this now. She knew this voice that she had always taken as the absolute truth was actually the very thing preventing her from achieving everything she wanted. The voice was the lie, and all the things she wanted for herself were the truth, perhaps the most important truth in the world. And because of this she had to stand up for herself. She had to fight. She had to. The fight was worth everything if it meant finally having a voice.

Did she want to put her life in the hands of other people? Could she ever achieve her dreams if she remained dependent on pleasing her family? Perhaps her life would be more than it was now if she hadn't tried so hard to live up to her grandparents' opinion of her. It was more important to honor her own values in life, to live her own dreams and her own vision, than to allow others to choose that path for her, even if standing up for herself was terrifying. That was what she must do. What did it matter if her grandparents were mad? What did it matter if she defied her community? What did it matter if people thought negatively of her? What did all these people's opinions of her life matter? She needed to follow her own path in life. She needed to apply to college.

Deya spent the night thinking things over and devising a plan. The next morning, she decided to visit Sarah. She'd visited her aunt less frequently in the weeks since Sarah had given her the newspaper clipping. They were still working to repair the damage Sarah had done by concealing the truth about her parents. But now Deya needed her aunt the most. She told Sarah her decision as soon as she walked into the bookstore.

"Really?" Sarah said. "I'm so proud of you! Has my mother agreed?"

"I haven't told her yet. But I'm going to. I promise."

Sarah smiled. "What about your marriage suitors?"

"I'm going to tell Teta that marriage can wait," Deya said. "And if she doesn't listen, then I'll just scare them away."

Sarah laughed, but Deya saw fear in her eyes. "Promise me you'll go to college. No matter what Fareeda says."

"I promise."

Sarah's smile widened.

"I wanted to thank you," Deya said.

"There's no need to thank me."

"There is," Deya said. "I know I've been angry at you a lot over the past few months, but that doesn't mean I'm not grateful for everything you've done. I should say it more. You reached out to me when I was all alone. You told me the truth when no one else would. Even when I was mad, you stood by me. You've been an incredible friend. If my mother was here, she'd thank you, too."

Sarah met her eyes, on the verge of tears. "I hope so."

Deya stood and hugged her aunt tight. As Sarah walked her out, Deya said, "By the way, I've been thinking about what you told me, about courage. Do you think maybe you'll feel better if you have courage, too?"

"Courage to do what?"

"To come back home."

Sarah blinked at her.

"I know you want to. All you have to do is come knock on the door."

"I . . . I don't know,"

"You can do it," Deya said, turning to leave. "I'll be waiting for you."

Isra

Fall 1997

By the time the school year started again, so many weeks had passed since Sarah had left that Isra was surprised when Adam told her: he was taking the girls out of public school.

"These American schools will corrupt our daughters," Adam said, swaying in the bedroom doorway.

Isra was in bed. She pulled the blanket closer, feeling a sudden chill. "But the school year just started," she whispered. "Where will they go?"

"An Islamic school has just opened on Fourth Avenue. Madrast al-Noor. School of Light. They start next month."

Isra opened her mouth to respond, but thought better of it. Instead she sank into bed and disappeared beneath the sheets.

Over the next few weeks, Isra considered Adam's plan. As much as she hated admitting it, he was right. She had also come to fear the public schools, afraid that one day her daughters might follow in Sarah's footsteps. Just the other day she had witnessed

Deya waving goodbye to the boys on her school bus! It had made her rigid with terror, and she had yelled at Deya, called her a *sharmouta*. Deya's face had crumpled, and Isra had been overcome with shame ever since. How could she call her daughter—a seven-year-old child—such a dirty word? What had she been thinking? Her head ached, and she tapped her forehead against the window to relieve the pain.

It was shame that made her do it, Isra thought now, shame at being a woman. Shame that made her abort her most recent pregnancy. She hadn't told anyone that she had gotten pregnant last month, not even Fareeda, who, in the midst of grieving Sarah, still found energy to remind her that Adam needed a son. But there had been no need to tell: Isra had not planned to keep the baby. As soon as the white strip turned red, she had stood at the top of the staircase and jumped off, over and over again, pounding on her belly with clenched fists. Fareeda hadn't known what Isra was doing, only that she was jumping off the stairs. It had clearly scared her. Fareeda had demanded she stop, had called her a *majnoona*, screaming that she was crazy, possessed, going so far as to call Adam to come home and control his wife. But Isra hadn't stopped. She'd needed to bleed. So she'd kept jumping until the blood gushed down her thighs.

Who had she intended to save, Isra wondered now, herself or the child? She wasn't sure. All she knew was that she had failed as a mother. She could still see the horrible look in Deya's eyes when she'd found her jumping. The pain of that moment had been so great that for a second Isra had considered killing herself, too, sticking her head in the oven like her favorite author had done. But Isra was too much of a coward even for that.

On the nights since, she had lain awake in bed and tried to push the thoughts away, telling herself stories, like the ones from *A Thousand and One Nights*. Sometimes she pulled out a sheet of paper from the stack she stashed in the back of their closet and wrote letters to Mama, pages and pages she would never send.

"I'm afraid for our daughters," Isra told Adam late one night when he returned from the deli. She had practiced the words in front of the mirror, making sure her eyebrows didn't flinch when she spoke, that she kept her gaze direct. "I'm afraid for our daughters," she repeated when Adam said nothing. She could tell that he was startled to hear her speak so boldly. She was startled, too—even with all her practice—but enough was enough. How long was she going to let him silence her? No matter what, he was going to beat her—whether she defied him or submitted, whether she spoke up or said nothing. The least she could do was stand up for her daughters. She owed them that.

She stood up, moving closer to him. "I know Sarah running away has been terrible, but I don't want our daughters to suffer because of it."

"What are you saying, woman?"

"I know you don't want to hear this," Isra said, trying to keep her voice steady. "But I'm worried about our daughters. I'm afraid of what kind of life we're going to give them. I'm scared of losing them, too. But I don't think it's wise to take them out of public school."

Adam stared at her. Isra wasn't sure what he was thinking, but from the bulge in his eyes, she was sure he was drunk. He crossed the room in three long strides and grabbed her.

"Adam, stop! Please. I'm only thinking of our daughters."

But he didn't stop. In one smooth movement, he shoved her against the wall and slammed his fists against her body over and over, her stomach, sides, arms, head. Isra shut her eyes, and then, when she thought it was over, Adam grabbed her by the hair and slapped her, the force of his palm knocking her to the floor.

"How dare you question me?" Adam said, his jaw quivering. "Never speak of this again." Then he left, disappearing into the bathroom.

On her knees on the floor, she could barely breathe. Blood leaked from her nose and down her chin. But she wiped her face and told herself she would take a beating every night if it meant standing up for her girls.

Deya

Fall 2009

Deya stands on the corner of Seventy-Third Street, in front of the Brooklyn Public Library. Her hair dances in the fall breeze, and she scans the stash of syllabi in her hands. Required reading: *The Yellow Wallpaper. The Bell Jar. Beloved.* She thinks of Fareeda, the look on her face when Deya received her acceptance letter and scholarship from New York University. She had put off telling her in case she hadn't gotten in, despite Sarah's insistence. There was no point in bringing up the matter if she didn't even get an offer. But then she'd had no more excuses. She'd found Fareeda seated at the kitchen table, a cup of chai in hand.

"I got accepted into a college in Manhattan," Deya had told her, keeping her voice steady. "I'm going."

"Manhattan?" She could see fear in Fareeda's eyes.

"I know you're worried about me out there, but I've navigated the city on my own every time I've visited Sarah. I promise to come home straight after class. You can trust me. You need to trust me."

Fareeda eyed her. "What about marriage?"

"Marriage can wait. After everything I know now, do you think I'm just going to sit here and let you marry me off? Nothing you say will change my mind." Fareeda started to object, but Deya cut her off. "If you don't let me go, then I'll leave. I'll take my sisters and go."

"No!"

"Then don't stand in my way," Deya said. "Let me go." When Fareeda said nothing, she added, "Do you know what Sarah told me the last time I saw her?"

"What?" Fareeda whispered. She still had not seen her grown daughter.

"She told me to learn. She said this was the only way to make my own *naseeb*."

"But, daughter, we don't control our *naseeb*. Our destiny comes for us. That's what *naseeb* means."

"That's not true. My destiny is in my hands. Men make these sorts of choices all the time. Now I'm going to as well."

Fareeda shook her head, blinking back tears. Deya had expected her to protest, to wail and argue and beg and refuse. But to her surprise, Fareeda did nothing of the sort.

"She wants to see you, you know," Deya whispered. "She's sorry, and she wants to come back home. But she's afraid . . . she's afraid you haven't changed."

Fareeda looked away, wiping tears from her eyes. "Tell her I've changed, daughter. Tell her I'm sorry."

Deya walks between the library bookshelves now. They are thick and tall, each one twice as wide as her. She thinks about the stories stacked across the shelves, leaning against one another like burdened bodies, supporting the worlds within each other.

There must be hundreds of them, thousands even. Maybe her story is in here somewhere. Maybe she will finally find it. She runs her fingers along the hardcover spines, inhales the smell of old paper, searching. But then it hits her, like falling into water.

I can tell my own story now, she thinks. And then she does.

Isra

Fall 1997

Isra didn't know the precise moment the fear overcame her so completely, but once it did it had hit her with a force so strong she couldn't eat or sleep for days. Since Adam had beaten her to a pulp over the girls' schooling, she had become increasingly afraid for her daughters and their futures. She wished she had listened to Sarah and found the courage to go with her. But she had no time to waste on such thinking now. She had to save her daughters. They had to leave.

Isra looked at her silver wristwatch—3:29 p.m. She didn't have much time. Fareeda was visiting Umm Ahmed, and Nadine was in the shower. They had to hurry. She gathered her daughters' birth documents, as well as all the money from Adam's drawer, and then went upstairs to take the money and gold hidden beneath Fareeda's mattress. She had practiced these motions in her head for days, and they went more smoothly than she had anticipated. I should've left with Sarah, she thought for the hundredth time as she secured Layla and Amal in the stroller. She took a deep breath and opened the front door.

Isra arrived at the bus stop early. She had grown accustomed to her daily walk to meet Deya and Nora after school, had even come to look forward to it. But today the blocks felt longer than usual, the pavement wide and foreign under her feet. She told herself to be brave for her daughters. She saw the long yellow bus from a distance and eyed it anxiously until it halted to a complete stop in front of her. Her watch read 3:43 p.m. Two minutes early. Maybe God is helping me, she thought as the bus opened its double doors and her daughters emerged.

Step by step, they walked away from the bus stop. When they made it around the corner, Isra's legs started to go numb, but she didn't stop. Be strong, she told herself. This isn't for you, it's for them.

They reached the subway on Bay Ridge Avenue at 4:15 p.m. As they descended the steps, Deya and Nora helping with the stroller, Isra exhaled a deep breath. At the bottom, the station was dark and hot and claustrophobic. She looked around, trying to figure out where to go next. There was a line of metal poles blocking the entrance, and Isra didn't know how to get through them. She watched men and women slide through the pole, dropping coins into metal slots, and she realized they would need tokens to pass.

There was a glass booth to her right, with a woman standing inside it. Isra pushed the stroller toward her. "Where can I get coins?" she asked, feeling the English words heavy on her tongue.

"Here," the woman said, not meeting Isra's gaze. "How much do you want?" Isra was confused. "How many tokens do you want?" the woman said again, more slowly, shooting her an irritated look.

Isra pointed to the metal poles. "I need to go on the train."

The woman explained the cost of each single ride. Overwhelmed by all the information, Isra pulled out a ten-dollar bill and pushed it through the glass.

"Th—thank you," she stuttered when the woman handed her a fist of tokens in return.

Isra's hands were shaking. Inside the subway were two short staircases leading farther down. Isra didn't know which to take. She looked around, but people rushed past her as though they were competing in a race. She decided to take the staircase on the left.

"Are we lost, Mama?" Deya asked when they had reached the bottom of the stairs.

"No, *habibti*. Not at all."

Isra scanned the space around them. They stood in the middle of a dim platform crowded with people. On both sides of the platform the concrete floor dropped off like the edge of a cliff to the track. Isra traced the rail lines with her eyes, curious to see where they led, but they disappeared into the darkness beyond the platform's end.

A black rectangular sign hung above the track, the letter R stamped in a yellow circle on it. Isra didn't know what the letter R stood for or where the train would take her. But it didn't matter. The best thing was to get on a train, any train, and stay on it until the very last stop, until they were as far from Bay Ridge as possible. There was no turning back now. If Adam knew she was running away, if he found her now, he would beat her to death. She was sure of it. But it didn't matter. She had made her choice.

Isra stood on the platform, surrounded by her daughters, and waited for the train. The world seemed to slip away from her bit by bit, and she felt as though she were floating in a mist high above their bodies. Then there was a light shining at her, and a dull whistling. Slowly, very slowly, the light moved closer and the whistle blew louder until Isra could see the train emerging from the darkness, sweeping her hair as it neared. When it stopped in front of them and its metal doors opened wide, a pulse of victory swooned through her chest. They would finally be free.

Acknowledgments

To **Julia Kardon,** the agent who believed in me even when I didn't believe in myself. Thank you for your patience, your friendship, and the many hours you've spent working with me on this novel. You've stood by me not only as an agent, but as a sister too. Finding you was one of the best moments of my life, and I will be forever grateful for everything you've done for me.

To Erin Wicks, my wise and passionate editor. Thank you for your brilliant insight, your innate understanding of everything I've wanted to accomplish, the many hours we spent on the phone, and the connection I've found in you. You've taken this story where no one could and helped me grow as both a writer and a person. I'm immensely grateful to call you my friend.

I would like to thank my HarperCollins family—Mary Gaule, Christine Choe, Jane Beirn, and countless others—for being advocates of this story and making this a wonderful experience for me. I'd like to thank my former colleagues and students at Nash Community College, who supported me while I wrote the early pages of this book. I also want to thank my very first reader, Jennifer Azantian, for believing in this story from the start. Finally, I would like to thank my family and friends—

especially my beautiful sisters, particularly Saja—for encouraging me while I wrote this story and for talking with me about it for hours upon hours, whenever I needed it.

This book was inspired by my two children, Reyann and Isah, and by the women of Palestine.

About the Author

ETAF RUM was born and raised in Brooklyn, New York, by Palestinian immigrants. She has taught English literature in North Carolina, where she lives with her two children. Etaf also runs the Instagram account @booksandbeans and is a Book of the Month Club Ambassador.